I0537232

Acknowledgments

I would like to thank god for giving me the strength to compose this novel. Human Farm has been a tough journey with many obstacles over the course of two years. However, my only aim, was to make sure that every page of this book was gripping and exciting for you, the reader. My only goal, was to prepare a novel with the most breathtaking and meaningful story. I would like to dedicate this book to humanity... To every person that has ever come on our earth, and every person who will. I'd like to thank every person who has made a positive impact in my life, and every person who is going to. I would also like to thank you, the reader, without whom my work would not be appreciated.

I would also like to thank the religious institutions for their contribution in my book, this includes the Jain Temple, the Jewish Synagogue, the Christian Church, the Islamic Mosque, the Buddhist Temple, the Sikh Gurudwara and the Hindu Temple. Certain elements have had a vast impact on my life, and given me the strength of character to be able to compose my work, this includes: The Mahabharat, and Ramayan scriptures and TV series, from there immortal actors such as Nitish Bharadwaj, and the director B.R Chopra. The Swadhyay parivar, and the Hare Krishna Movement. I'd also like to pay my respects to Mother Teresa, Princess Diana, Mahatma Gandhi and Martin Luther King.

I would like to request the blessings of my ancestors. This includes my late grandparents, Kuntalaxmi Thakkar & Kantilal Thakkar. Also to my uncle and aunty who passed away at a young age: Harshad Thakkar and Jayshree Thakkar, also my maternal grandfather Narandas Thakkar. To all the people who may have lost somebody near and dear to them, please don't worry, they are safe, and god is looking after them. I would like to thank my parents, for allowing me to become educated & knowledgeable enough to compose this book. I'd like to pray for the peace of every person, family, friend or otherwise, to attain peace and salvation in their journey. I would like to thank each and every person, whose good wishes have come from their heart, for me, and for Human Farm.

I would additionally like to thank the following people for helping me like true family & friends: Richard Pebardy, Alysha Shetye, Anish Thakkar, Sanjay Chauhan, Pradeep Nathwani, Krshna Chauhan, Nand Patel, Bhavesh Thakkar, Shehz & John Bell.

Finally, I would like to thank all my human and animal brothers and sisters.

Love Religion Laughter REVENGE

Dedicated to Humanity

Rupesh Thakkar

HUMAN FARM

Love Religion Laughter REVENGE

To all those that have come,
and to all those guests who will go...
Your existence in human form is
merely an illusion.

Be kind to the powerless,
And the powerful will be kind to you.
Stand against injustice, because the time is now,
the place is here, and you are the chosen one.

Enjoy my gift to you

Because this book is not based on the past,
And it's not based on the present,
But it is based on...

It's time.
Brace yourself.

Rupesh Thakkar

Chapter One

The Farm

All the humans were rounded up, completely naked, and sorted into types. Fat Males in one section, and thin ones in another. Beautiful girls in this area, and ugly girls in the other area, a separate cordon for pregnant women. All the humans were stuffed into cages with up to thirty others. They could hardly move. The dirty drinking water was stored in buckets just outside the cage, enough for the humans to stick their heads out and drink from. Food was a precious commodity, provided just once a day. Which type food would be provided however, was always a mystery. The water sprinklers were started, allowing the caged beings to wash themselves. It seemed like a rare moment of humane cleanliness.

The news headlines all around the world showed that a mysterious psychopath had abducted 347 people in the biggest kidnapping spree of its kind in recent history. The motive was unknown. The whereabouts of these people was unknown, and most importantly, the identity of the kidnapper, was also unknown.

Although this barbaric act had taken place in America, people across America and also the world were conducting candle-light vigils out of respect for the victims. Peaceful rallies were organised in many cities in the United Kingdom, across Europe, Australia, China, India, Russia, Africa and even as far out as the Middle East. This event had gripped the entire world, and almost transformed it into a close-knit community. The people marching in protests were holding banners with statements such as; *Find the victims. When will they get justice? Find him, kill him.* Every person who had heard about this news story was shocked as to how one person could repeatedly conduct such atrocities.

Two of the victims in captivity, belonged to the same mother. She was giving an interview on TV. The Reporter asked "Can you tell us when and where your daughters went missing?"

The grieving mother replied "My daughters both went to a charity dinner two weeks ago, and that evening they never returned home."

"Could you tell us more about the background of your missing daughters?"

"My first daughter is twenty-five years old, and she was working in a small restaurant. My second daughter is only twenty-one, she worked as a Hotel manager and she is expecting her first child," the mother became emotional, unable to hold in her tears.

The journalist finally asked "Is there a message that you would like to give to the kidnapper if he's watching?"

The mother replied "Yes." She looked straight at the camera, as if talking directly to the kidnapper. "Why have you destroyed the lives of so many people? Why have you enslaved my children? What wrong did they do to you? Every Human being is equal, no human deserves to go through this. God will never forgive you, there is justice in this world, and however many of you killers there are, justice will be served. God will never forgive you," she burst into tears.

In an unknown location, in a small room, a television was showing the mother's plight for her daughters. Watching the TV, was a man who was sat in his armchair rocking back and forth, back and forth. He stopped rocking the chair, and slowly stood up, he nodded at the mother's plea for her daughters. He walked out of the room wearing nothing but a pair of ripped denim jeans & long Wellington boots. He looked like a tall, tough structure, with big, strong muscles and a well-built body. He walked over to the Storage room, and took out fifty loaves of bread. He then escorted the loaves of bread in a trolley, and ripped the loaves into pieces. He distributed the shredded bread into feeding containers for the enslaved humans. He took the hosepipe, and filled the water buckets with water so that they could drink. He washed his face with the hosepipe, and he walked towards the house situated next to the farm. He had a sense of revenge on his face. A look of determination and purpose. He was the one. He was, the kidnapper.

Meanwhile detectives had gathered from all across the USA at the FBI headquarters to try and figure out where this mad man could be. Special Head of the FBI Mr. Williams was in charge of the meeting. He started by briefing the officers. "Gentlemen, we have all gathered here today to track down a maniac who is solely responsible for the kidnapping of 347 innocent civilians. His motive is unknown. He could be a terrorist, rapist, he could be a total and utter mad psychopath, we don't know. But let me tell you what we do know. All the kidnappings have taken place between October 2nd and December 21st. He always covers his face with something, a balaclava or face mask of some sort. The way he carries out the kidnapping is assumed to be one of two ways. He either covers his victims' faces with some sort of chemical to knock them out. Or he threatens them with a weapon, driving off in the victim's car itself. He texts a family member from the victim's phone contacts list to say that the victim will be late. He then destroys and disposes of the victim's phone, meaning we can't trace his location. By the time that family members find out that something doesn't seem right, it's too late, and the kidnapper reaches his destination."

An FBI agent in the front row raised his hand to ask a question. The special head of the FBI, Mr. Williams said "Go ahead Mike."

"Sir, what if we contacted the Federal Highways Administration obtaining CCTV footage allowing us to trace where the victim's car was taken?" asked Mike.

"We already have," explained Mr. Williams. "And the fact of the matter is that yes, the Highways have a lot of cameras, but they don't have cameras everywhere. However, from all the intelligence gathered over the past 11 and a half weeks, I can confirm to you that there is an area where the victims have all been taken. They've all been taken to the same place." Williams drew a circle in the eastern part of the state of Massachusetts, "this is where he is."

An officer in the middle row asked "So we should get started searching the area sir."

Williams replied "This is an area spanning 4,700 square kilometers. He could be anywhere in this circle, and to search this whole area will take up to three months, even with the help of hundreds of officers. So, until then we can hope for only one thing…"

"That he doesn't kidnap anyone else?" asked an officer.

"No, that he does," responded Williams. All the officers looked confused as to why Mr. Williams wanted yet another victim to become enslaved. "If we want to catch him, then that's the only way we can."

"But sir, he used an explosive in his very first kidnapping. What if he causes another explosion? What if civilians die this time?" asked another officer.

"He won't make that mistake again," said Williams. "The kidnapper knows he made a mistake by using an explosive, and that's why he stopped after the very first kidnapping. There are too many clues that could be left behind."

"And he doesn't need to risk using explosives and leaving behind clues if the peaceful method is working, right?"

"Right. And for the past week, the FBI has been working with the Federal Highways Administration to install cameras on almost every part of every highway contained in this circle. One more kidnapping and we'll be able to track him down to the nearest twenty kilometer radius. Mr. Kidnapper, you're dead meat…" said Mr. Williams with a vengeful look on his face.

Meanwhile, the kidnapper was in the human farm. After feeding the captives, he was preparing to leave and drove off in a car. He drove along the highway and seemed to be in an introspective mood. While driving he stared at a passing fast food restaurant like a hungry monster! Then, he saw something else which immediately grabbed his attention. He spotted a crew of workers installing a camera on the highway. He smiled to himself as he knew exactly what was going on. He turned his car back at the next junction and returned to the farm. He went to the cages where the humans were enslaved. One man in the fat man's cage spoke out. "You will never get away with this, you will get justice. I will take you to court, I will put you in jail."

The kidnapper picked up his gun and walked towards the fat men's cage absolutely fuming. He pointed the gun at the man and he Roared like a lion in his face. The fat man finally lowered his head and shut up.

A woman from the beautiful women's cage cried "Kill me! I don't want to live any more. We have no dignity, no respect, and what will you do in the end, you'll kill us anyway. Just kill me now." The Kidnapper walked towards her, and opened the cage, all the women screamed. He grabbed the protesting woman by the hair, and dragged her along the floor to the conveyor belt. He clipped her legs to the clamp above so that she was hanging upside down. He pressed the Green button to get the conveyor belt moving. She began travelling towards the chopper. All the captives were shouting and screaming to stop the machine. The kidnapper didn't listen, but anticipated what was about to happen. The humans were in anarchy, there was chaos. The woman about to be killed finally broke her silence and shouted "*NO, stop the machine, stop the machine.*" The kidnapper stopped the conveyor belt just before her throat was about to be chopped off. He grabbed her hair, gritted his teeth and with every muscle in his face clenched, he asked "You wanna live, or you wanna die?"

She replied while crying "I want to live, please I want to live." He un-clipped her from the clamp, and dragged her along the floor by her hair, threw her back into the cage, and said to her "then shut up."

Just then the kidnapper saw that a woman from the pregnant woman's cage was about to give birth, she was screaming from labor pain. He asked the captives, "Now listen up, are any of you humans a doctor or nurse?"

One lady from the fat lady's cage responded "I am." He opened the cage for her and escorted her to the pregnant women's cage.

The nurse reassured the pregnant woman, "Don't worry, everything will be okay." The kidnapper gave the nurse a pair of scissors to cut the umbilical cord of the newborn baby. He then walked back into his room. A few tantalizing moments later, the woman gave birth. "Congratulations on giving birth to the most adorable baby boy!" said the nurse enthusiastically. The mother kissed the baby on the forehead many times.

The kidnapper heard the crying baby and came out of his room to view the outcome. He walked over to the cage and asked the mother "What is it?"

"A boy," she replied with a hesitant smile on her face.

"Oh. Then keep it with you."

"He is not an *it*. He has a name," she said protectively.

"What?" he asked.

"My husband and I had thought of a name beforehand, if it would be a boy then Joseph and if it would be a girl then Josephine."

The kidnapper confirmed, "Joseph?"

"Yes" the mother replied, this time with a more relaxed smile.

"No! None of you have names. For me, you are all just numbers in a cage. That's it, nothing more nothing less. You are all animals for me, you understand?"

"But have a heart," said the new mother. "Look at my baby's face. Can you not see that this is an innocent sweet child who should be in a hospital receiving medical care, and not trapped in some make shift barn? At least let us go, do you think this is right?"

The kidnapper came close and looked at the baby. He smiled. Looking at him smile, the mother also smiled. "Hi Joseph," said the kidnapper, taking the baby from her hand. He then locked the cage and took the baby a few steps away. "This world is too painful for you Joseph, you don't want to live here."

The mother and nurse looked cautiously without any idea about what was about to happen.

The kidnapper slapped the baby's head against the ground with extreme force. The baby died instantly.

"*No, no, no...*" cried the grieving mother. The kidnapper ignored her and went on to chop the baby into pieces with a sharp knife. He then tore the baby's leg off and ate it like a barbaric monster. The mother was crying in agony. She didn't know what to do, she was helpless, trapped in the cage. The shouting captives had no effect on the kidnapper, as he continued to eat baby Joseph, as if he was a piece of meat. This was perhaps the lowest level the kidnapper had dropped to so far.

The entire mood of the captives changed, there was extreme fear amongst them. No human revolted from then on. Nobody argued a single word.

Three days later, at the FBI headquarters, the officers were investigating traces of DNA found at some of the kidnapping sites. Officer mike was speaking to Mr. Williams said "Sir, the forensic department have concluded that there's a common DNA group in multiple kidnapping locations." Mr. Williams said "I need a search done on the database to see if we have any wanted criminals matching that DNA group."

"Yes sir, I'll have the results back to you within three hours," responded officer Mike.

Williams told another officer "I think the kidnapper may have figured out that we've installed cameras on the highway. And maybe that's why he's hiding like a snake in his underground hideout."

Meanwhile the kidnapper was in his little room, speaking on the phone. Once he finished his conversation, he stood up to enter the farm again. He walked over to the beautiful women's cage. He said "I need milk." The women all looked at each other without knowing what to say. The kidnapper shouted " I need milk! Who will give me milk?" The women were shivering with fear. Then he opened the women's cage, grabbed one of the women by the hair, and squeezed her nipple to find out if she had any milk in her breast. She didn't have any milk, so he threw her back into the cage. He grabbed another woman by the hair and squeezed her nipple. This time milk came out, so he sucked her breasts and drank all the milk he could, and said "thanks." He threw her back in the cage once he was finished. Then he suddenly started to do what none of the captives expected. He started grabbing women one by one and clipping them onto the conveyor belt upside down. After clipping thirty naked women upside down on the conveyor belt, he walked towards the green switch. The whole human farm was in anarchy. There were cries of *"NO," "STOP,"* from each and every one of the 347 human captives, but he didn't listen. He walked towards the operating board, and pushed the green button. The conveyor belt began to move. By this time, the entire farm had burst into complete chaos, the captive humans were all shouting and screaming in vain to stop what was about to happen. But everyone was helpless, either trapped by a cage, or trapped by the shackles holding them upside down.

Just then, the police entered the farm. A swarm of police officers ran towards the kidnapper and circled him. They pointed guns to his head and shouted "Stop the conveyor belt, *now*." The kidnapper didn't do anything at first. The police officer asked again at the top of his voice, "*stop the conveyor belt now or I will shoot you.*" The kidnapper reluctantly walked towards the conveyor belt and just as the first woman was about to be killed, he pushed the red switch. The conveyor belt stopped.

All the women were released from the clamps that held them upside down. The kidnapper was arrested immediately. All the human captives were released from their cages. The women were crying, the men were relieved and the entire farm was full of a quiet sense of relief, emotion and freedom. The officers handcuffed the kidnapper and escorted him to the police car. As he was about to enter the car, the kidnapper gave a long vengeful stare to one of the captives, Mr. Brown. The long fleet of police cars then proceeded to take the kidnaper to a maximum-security police Station for questioning.

The kidnapper waited in the interview room with three other officers and numerous cameras recording his every move. Everybody was silent. Mr. Williams entered the room. One officer whispered in his ears, "he's not saying anything sir." Mr. Williams ordered the other officers to leave.

He walked right up to the kidnapper, staring at him directly in his face "You see these eyes? See how red they are? For the past eighty-nine days, I haven't slept properly because of you. Day and night, I put everything together to catch you. For the eighty-nine days… all I could see, is you."

"I love you too," responded the kidnapper.

Mr. Williams paused, then continued "You have made my life a living nightmare. Do you know how many people are depressed because of you? The families, the loved ones, the captives themselves, do you realize how many years it's going to take for these guys to forget the past months of hell and de-humanization you have put them through?" The kidnapper didn't say anything. Williams asked purposefully "Why did you do this? What have you gained by doing this?" The kidnapper looked at the floor. Williams asked again "Tell me why you did this, or I will have to lock you up in jail and you'll just have to explain yourself in court in three days time."

The kidnapper was un-phased, he responded in agreement, "Lock me up, that's the least I deserve for doing this."

Williams looked at the kidnapper like a little child who was upset. Then he cried out "Now I won't be able to sleep for another three days, just tell me… *Who are you?*" Mr. Williams looked as though he was about to break down.

The kidnapper asked "Are you okay?"

"I'm not talking to you any more," answered Williams like an upset child.

The kidnapper watched Mr. Williams suffer for a while and then put him out of his misery, "Okay Mr. Williams, just so that you can sleep at night, I'll tell you what happened."

Mr. Williams looked back up at the kidnapper as though he had found a ray of hope in life again.

The kidnapper started to explain, "My name is Rion. I am twenty-eight years old."

"Were you always like this?" asked Mr. Williams.

"Like this?" said Rion.

"Yes like this. It's not normal for somebody to kidnap 347 innocent people. Were you always like this?!"

Rion went on to explain what happened in his childhood, and here began the most fascinating story you're likely to hear.

It was the first day of nursery. A sweet, innocent child called Rion entered the classroom with his mother. Hillary was a lovely, grandmother like teacher. She was narrating a story to the children about the importance of a balanced diet and different types of food including vegetables, egg, fish, meat and fruit.

Rion's mother was emotionally attached to him, but Hillary's smile was reassuring. Rion sat on the floor next to another toddler, Jenny. That was it, the beginning of love. Rion saw Jenny and felt instantly attracted to her, If only the same could be said about Jenny. who was too busy to notice him. Jenny had silky blonde hair, tied into two ponytails. When she smiled, there were two dimples that would appear on her cheeks. She had an angelic charm about her.

Burbage Nursery & primary School, London, this is where Rion was to receive his most important education, love. Although he was only three years old, he had an eye for beauty. He adapted to the new environment like a fish in water.

Rion was in awe of Jenny, and would always come up with ingenious ways to impress her.

One day there was a class trip to the zoo. The teacher said to the children, "These are the lions. Don't put your hands in the cage." but as soon as Rion had a chance, he put his fingers through a small opening in the cage to show Jenny how brave he was. "Look Jenny, I can fight with lions."

Jenny said "You're so childish," and walked away. Rion was left dumbfounded.

Rion was the tallest in his class. One day the school gathered for assembly as they did every morning. All the pupils entered the assembly hall line by line, class by class and were sat on the floor with their legs crossed. The teacher stood at the front, was Mr. McClymont, he was an idol of Rion's.

Mr. McClymont started speaking, "In life, whenever you do something wrong, or you have an argument, it is always important to say *sorry*. When you are all playing football in the playground, if one of your team mates falls over or hurts themselves, it's important that you all stop and see if your friend is okay. Even if you were all professional footballers, you should still stop and see if your teammate is okay. This is called *sportsmanship*. And, stopping and asking *are you okay?* is one of the most important gestures of sportsmanship and mankind. Saying "Sorry" is a very easy thing, but sometimes, it could be the most important thing that you could ever say. It might save your relationship." Mr. McClymont had a tear in his eye. All the pupils gave him a round of applause.

Then, another teacher, Miss Edelle came to the front. She said "Thank you Mr. McClymont for that very important lesson, see children, saying sorry is very important. Miss Edelle's sight fell on Rion, whose head was the highest, above all other students.

"Rion, sit down!" said Miss Edelle authoritatively.

Rion was perplexed, he said, "I am sat down!"

"No, sit on your bottom Rion Rai."

"I am sat on my bottom miss!" he said, not knowing what he did wrong.

"Rion, you must say sorry for your behaviour," said Miss Edelle.

Rion said "Why miss, I am sat down!"

Miss Edelle had enough, she exclaimed "Stand up! Stand up!" Rion stood up. "Go and stand in the corner!" Rion went and stood in the corner of the assembly hall in front of the whole school, everybody was laughing at him.

A few years passed by and Rion's heart was still filled with just one name, Jenny. One day he saw that another boy, Charlie was sitting next to Jenny building a castle from building blocks. Rion's protectiveness of Jenny didn't allow him to be a bystander. So he sat next to Jenny and said, "Building a castle like that is easy, I can do it!"

"No you can't," said Jenny. "Charlie is very good at building castles."

"I can do it in one second," said Rion confidently.

Jenny instantly counted "One. There, you haven't made it yet." Rion was left feeling like an abandoned sailor in the middle of the ocean.

Although Rion was not achieving much luck in the department of love, his academic skills were to be envied. He was a hard-working student, and from a young age his work was always appreciated by his teachers. As he grew older, by the age of twelve, his hard work allowed him to reach the final of the annual speech competition. The speech competition was a prestigious event in which the best students from every class would give a five-minute speech on their desired topic. The winner would be crowned the best speaker in the school.

Rion's opportunity to perform would soon come. But right now, it was his best friend who was about to give his speech...

Chapter Two

Nutmeg Rush

Sebastian was on the stage. The whole school was watching. Rion's turn was next, he would be the third speaker in the annual Burbage school speech competition.

Sebastian looked up to compose himself one last time, and then he began to speak:

"Money makes the world go around. Everybody needs money to survive. Therefore, it is important to have an education, where we can earn money to thrive in this dog eat dog world. We need to reach the top, a place where only the privileged few can go. If we climb to the top, we can make others work for us, instead of us working for them. We can provide jobs for people. Not only will the workers be under our control, the economy and the world can benefit too. We can invent machines, which will power the future, and we can train humans to power those machines. Our path to success cannot be obstructed. It is destiny that awaits those who understand the importance of money. I have started to save money in the bank," Sebastian showed everybody a bank statement which he took out from his pocket.

He continued speaking, "my bank balance is £6,700, and I think by the time I am eighteen, I will have saved more than £23,000. I can put this money towards my University education. I want to do a master of business administration degree. Once I do this, I want to start a business and then the world will be my oyster. Thank you."

Everybody gave Sebastian a rapturous round of applause. Michael said to Rion "He was good."

But Rion was listening carefully to Sebastian's speech, and didn't quite agree, he said "Some things are more important than money Michael."

"Like what?" he asked.

Just as Rion was going to reply, the head teacher, Mr. Hill announced "And the next speaker in this year's speech competition is Rion Rai." Michael wished him good luck as Rion stood up and walked to the front of the Assembly Hall, and up onto the stage. Everybody gave him an initial round of applause. He faced the audience and looked at everybody. Rion saw Jenny in the audience. He felt as though he was skating on ice, he felt like was cool as a cucumber, he felt as though... he was ready. Rion began to speak.

"Love is the most important thing in the world. It makes the world go around. Without love, we cannot survive. Love is in the trees, love is in the rivers, love is in the oceans, love is in the Earth, love is everywhere. Love is in the eyes, love is in the heart, love is in our soul, love is in each breath we take. However, love should not just be for those who are near us, love should be for everybody. I love the world we live in, and I love all living beings in the world. My love does not discriminate, my love is fair for all. Money is finite, it will run out, if you have to share it with the world, then you can only share a limited amount. But love is infinite. No matter how much love you give, you will always have more love to give, because love is not limited by numbers. Love is like this candle," Rion showed everybody a candle he had in his pocket. "With just one candle, I can light every candle in the world. I love people in England, but I also love all the people in Africa. I love all the living beings in America, but I also love all the living beings in Russia. I love India, and I also love China. I love every country, I love every living being. Because everybody has a heart, everybody has a soul. Everybody has blood which is the same colour. Everybody feels pain when they are hurt, everybody feels sad when they face difficulty. Everybody deserves to live, everybody deserves food, everybody deserves water, everybody deserves safety, and everybody deserves love. I love the whole world. I want to give you all a gift today, and that gift is love. I just hope that you all pass that gift on to others. And one day it will reach everybody in the world and come back to you, thank you."

The whole assembly hall erupted into applause for Rion, and although reluctantly, even Sebastian applauded his speech. While Rion walked back to sit down at his chair, he smiled and nodded at Jenny who also acknowledged his speech. Rion went back to his place with a feeling of immense relief. He had finally shared his feelings with what felt like the whole world. At the end of all the speeches, Mr. Hill stood up to announce the results of the speech competition. "Thank you all for listening so patiently to all the speakers. One more time for all the participants, a huge round of applause."

After another round of applause, the entire assembly hall was eager to find out who had won the speech competition. Mr. Hill continued, "So, the judges have discussed the performance of all the competitors, and they have given me the names of the top three speakers. In third place, is Bethan Ward." Everybody gave a round of applause to Bethan from Mr. Wilson's class. She came up to collect her third prize trophy from the head teacher.

After awarding the trophy, Mr. Hill continued "In a speech competition which has really impressed me in terms of content and expression, I would like to say that the judges have never experienced such a difficult time in selecting the winner. I want to congratulate all the participants and say that you have all done a fantastic job. However, a winner must be selected, and we must therefore declare Rion as our second prize winner. Rion was a little surprised, but nevertheless he stood up, and went to collect his second prize, as the whole assembly applauded him. After Rion sat back down, Mr. Hill announced the winner of the competition, "And finally what remains is for me to announce the winner of this competition. In first place, the winner of the Burbage school speech competition for this year is... Sebastian Davies." Sebastian stood up, and claimed his prize, he looked at Rion with vengeance as if he had extreme pride in beating him.

After the assembly, all his classmates were gathered around Rion. They congratulated him on his performance. Just then, Sebastian arrived. Rion and all his friends were looking at him, Sebastian said "Unlucky Rion, nice little speech."

"Thanks," replied Rion.

"But it seems that love has lost to money. Money is much more powerful than love Rion, and the sooner you realise this, the better."

Rion didn't want to say anything back to Sebastian, because he was actually his best friend. He knew that Sebastian was short tempered. Sebastian walked away with a sense of immense pride and over confidence.

The next morning was the day that Rion's class went to swimming. Rion always enjoyed swimming, he felt as though he could get away from his troubles and be more peaceful. This time, the instructor was Lilly.

Lilly was a very beautiful swimming instructor, she was kind and caring towards all the students. Rion secretly admired her, and would always dream about if she could be his girlfriend. Sebastian, also in Rion's class, occasionally passed remarks about her, and Rion would not like it. Sebastian said to Rion "She looks fit today."

Rion was frustrated inside, but he kept a calm exterior and reluctantly replied "She's okay I suppose." Lilly instructed the class as usual for the first fifty minutes. In the last ten minutes of class, Lilly organised a race from one end of the swimming pool to the other and back again, for the boys. Rion thought to himself, *this is my chance to impress both Jenny, and Lilly! I have to win this race.*

All the boys lined up at the starting point. Jenny was standing at the side of the pool with all the other girls. Rion was looking at Jenny, Jenny looked towards Rion. It was as if time stood still, and at one thousand frames per second, Lilly said "On your marks, get set, go!" Rion wanted to get off to the best start possible and was swimming as fast as all the other boys. The arms were powering and the legs were propelling as water was splashing everywhere with thunderous echoes. After crossing half the swimming pool, he could see the other end in front of him, it was all happening so quickly. He could see Sebastian and Charlie both alongside him, he tried his best to swim faster and faster, but they were all neck and neck. Rion reached the other end just split seconds behind Sebastian and Charlie as they all turned around to go back to the other end. He was giving his best, he overtook Charlie, who was running out of steam. Now, he was level with Sebastian. Rion took in every breath of oxygen to fill his lungs to power him forward. He pushed harder with every muscle in his body. Sebastian looked behind, and could see Rion was catching up with him. The finishing line was getting closer and closer, Rion and Sebastian were the only two contenders in this race now, as the rest of the class were too far behind to make a comeback. The race was tantalizing, nobody could tell who would win. In the last split seconds of the Race, Sebastian managed to push himself that much harder to beat Rion and let him finish second again. Rion looked towards Jenny. She seemed unimpressed. The instructor Lilly however was impressed with everybody. Sebastian was on the receiving end of much respect and admiration from his friends. They all congratulated him. Rion however, was deflated and went straight into the changing rooms. He had finished second to Sebastian in yet another contest.

Rion's home was situated in some council flats in a part of north-east London called Hackney. Outside Rion's flat, there was a concrete football pitch with a tall fence around its perimeter. On regular occasions, Sebastian would play football there with Rion. Sebastian though, would have to travel there from his rather luxurious home situated just a couple of miles away, near Canary Wharf.

Lunchtime at school was a time to play a completely different type of football. A hardcore game. A game which Rion did not look forward to. The game was called Nutmeg Rush. In the playground, Rion and his friends Sebastian, Charlie, Michael, Yusuf and Kieth would play this hardcore game called Nutmeg Rush, invented by Sebastian.

The rules were simple. There was one football, and many players, no set amount of players, just as many that played. Everybody had to try to tackle and steel the football from each other. The ultimate aim was to kick the football between the legs of any other player. If successful, then that was called a *nutmeg*. The player who allowed the ball go through his legs, or was *Nutmegged*, would face a punishment called *Rush*, hence the name Nutmeg Rush. The punishment called rush was when the victim would have to stand by *the brick wall*, so that he could receive his punishment. The punishment involved a process where everybody could kick the ball at the victim's body as hard as they wished, for sixty seconds. The recipient of all this aggression had to stand still against the wall, and not even attempt to flee. If the victim did try to run away from the punishment, then he would be hunted down by all the players, until the victim was beaten up with rounds of punches instead.

After years of playing this game, the game seemed to have become a regular part of school break times. All the players joined Sebastian in a circle like hungry lions. Sebastian threw the ball up into the air. As the ball came down, everybody's eyes were on the ball in readiness to gain possession of it. Sebastian got hold of the ball first, he tried to nutmeg Rion, but failed. Rion had the ball, Michael tackled him and tried to nutmeg Charlie, but Charlie closed his legs just in time. Yusuf was just running after the crowd, he was lucky if he got a touch of the football. Like this, the game continued. After five minutes of thrilling action, the football went through a player's legs. The first player to be nutmegged, was Kieth.

Kieth was a simple, reserved kind of character. He would always be in a world of his own, and would always get in trouble with his teachers for not achieving the same standards as everybody else in his school work. Kieth had almost no friends, in fact that's the only reason he would play Nutmeg Rush, so that even though it was temporary and somewhat fictitious, at least he could experience companionship and friendship for a few valuable minutes. He would hang around with Yusuf most of the time, who his only real buddy. Yusuf and Kieth were similar in their personalities, both very simple, straightforward characters, with no real agenda other than to continue living life. Once he was nutmegged, Kieth accepted his fate, he went and stood by the wall. He knew what was about to happen to him. Rion was watching. Sebastian put the ball down on the floor. He took five steps back. Sebastian took a run up to the ball and kicked it as hard as he could at Kieth. The ball hit Kieth on the chest. Kieth covered his chest with his hands, everybody laughed at him.

Meanwhile Jenny was sitting on the swings with her friend Christine, and she saw how dejected Rion looked while all this was going on.

Kieth was in pain, but tried to hide the pain from the others watching him by putting on a fabricated smile. Then Charlie kicked the ball as hard as he could, it smashed Kieth on the Knees. Like this, the ordeal continued. Michael Kicked the ball which landed Kieth on his face. Kieth covered his face in sheer pain. Everybody continued to laugh at him. Kieth didn't want to seem like a wimp, so he just looked up and smiled.

Then it was Rion's turn. Rion was not so certain as everybody else, he was hesitant, but he put the ball down anyway. Jenny was watching. Rion took a few steps back and looked down at the ball. He looked around him, and saw all of his friends staring at him, it was as if everything was in slow motion. All he could see was his friends cheering him on, and he could feel his heart pounding. For the first time, Rion experienced something he had never experienced before, peer pressure. Rion began his run up, looked down at the ball, he took aim at Kieth, and closed his eyes just as he kicked the ball. The ball travelled at high speed towards Kieth, who was still recovering from being winded in the stomach after the ball hit him last time. The ball hit Kieth on the chest. Kieth was in agony once again, this time, it was because of Rion. After a few moments, Kieth put on a brave face, and pretended that he was okay. Kieth's punishment was over, sixty seconds had elapsed.

After that, although the game continued as normal, Rion had a look of contemplation on his face. For the first time, he experienced guilt. Guilt, of doing something wrong.

In the evening when Rion was at the dinner table, Rion's mother and father looked a little sympathetically at him.

His father said "I know you may be sad, but we have some bad news to break to you."

Rion looked puzzled, and asked "What bad news dad?"

His father replied "Son, we're thinking of moving house."

"What? But why?"

"I know you are really upset by this, but we are going to move to America, me and mum decided that we should move there because there are much better prospects in America for my work."

Rion looked at his parents and said "I just need to go to the toilet." Rion went to the toilet, closed the door... and celebrated! "Yes! Come on!" He said to himself. He was so happy that now he could get away from all his problems at school! His parents thought he was saddened by their decision. Rion returned to the table and said "It's okay mum, dad, I understand if we have to move." His parents were sympathetic but little did they know how excited Rion was in his heart.

The next day, the moment which Rion dreaded the most arrived once again. It was lunchtime, and therefore it was time to play Nutmeg Rush again. Nevertheless, as it was destined to be, the game began. Jenny was sat on the bench with Christine watching their game once again.

Sebastian kicked threw the ball up in the air. As it landed, the scene was as if a pack of wolves were preparing to catch their prey. Charlie had the ball, he made a dummy move to make his friends think he's going one way and then went the other way to try and nutmeg Rion, but Rion was too smart for that and tackled him instead. Rion kicked the ball towards Michael's legs, but Michael took the ball from Rion, and then chased Kieth. Sebastian tackled Michael, and then he ran towards Kieth. Kieth was too slow, and Sebastian kicked the ball through his legs. The first person to be *nutmegged*, once again, was Kieth.

Kieth knew his fate. But this was the only time that he got some attention from his friends. Kieth thought to himself *at least everybody laughs because of me, even though they are laughing at me*. Kieth stood at the wall. Sebastian put the ball down first. He took a few steps back, took his run up, and kicked the ball. The ball couriered into Kieth's face. Kieth bent down towards his knees and felt severe pain. Rion wanted to go and help him, but Sebastian stopped him and said "He's okay, he's getting up." Kieth slowly stood back up, to take the next hit.

Sebastian said to Rion "Now it's your turn."

Rion faced a moral dilemma. However, he looked at the wall, and his intention of kicking the ball at Kieth had not changed. His whole body felt numb, and he started to feel dreadful, his heart was pounding, once again. Yet, he continued to place the ball on the floor. Rion's body was just moving as if he had no control over it. His friends were all looking at him, the peer pressure was immense, and growing by the second. Rion's mind was blank, he took five steps back, and placed his hands on his waist. He looked up at Kieth to take aim. Like a flashbulb moment, Rion suddenly remembered something. He remembered the assembly Mr. McClymont gave. His words echoed in his mind, "If one of your team mates falls over or hurts himself, it's important that you all stop and see if your friend is okay." Rion looked around him, and all his friends were waiting for him to kick the ball at Kieth. Rion remembered Mr. McClymont saying "stopping and saying *are you okay?* is one of the most important gestures of mankind. Saying *Sorry* is a very easy thing, but sometimes, it could be the most important thing that you could ever say, it might save your relationship." Rion looked down at the ball. He ran towards the ball and took aim, he lifted his right foot to kick the ball. Rion followed through with his motion and kicked the ball as hard as he could. All his friends were amazed at the force with which Rion struck the ball. Kieth closed his eyes as he saw that Rion kicked the ball which was coming furiously towards him. A couple of seconds later, Kieth opened his eyes, and he saw that there was no football in sight. Rion was standing next to him, because Rion, had kicked the football as hard as he could over the wall, meaning that it couldn't possibly hit Kieth. "Sorry Kieth, are you okay?" said Rion. Kieth looked down as if his soul was sinking down into the ground at thousands of miles per hour. He started to cry. Rion gave Kieth a hug, took him to one side, and sat him down on the bench, "Wait here," he said.

Rion walked towards Sebastian with a stern look on his face. The playground was shocked into silence. Everybody was watching, including Jenny. Rion was walking towards Sebastian with sheer determination and after reaching within one foot of him, he said "Why did you pick on Kieth?"

"It's not my fault he's rubbish at football," replied Sebastian.

"Are you strong?" asked Rion.

"I'm stronger than Kieth, I'll knock him out any day, tell him to meet me after school, see what happens."

"Picking on somebody just because they are weaker than you, is not strength, why do you want to see him after school? See me now," challenged Rion.

Sebastian was surprised, and viewed Rion's comments as an immediate attack on his strength. Sebastian pushed Rion and said "You think you're hard?" He pushed Rion a second time, this time Rion was pushed a couple of steps backwards and tripped onto the floor. Sebastian said "Do you know who I am? I am everything you are not. I am successful, I am rich. My dad is a businessman, not like your dad..."

On hearing this Rion stood back up.

"Your dad is poor, he is good for nothing. You are the son of a..."

Rion looked up at Sebastian, he took a run up to him, and gave him a powerful punch on his face. The whole playground was in pin drop silence. The most popular boy in the school had been smashed. Everybody looked eagerly to see what Sebastian would do. Burbage school was shocked. But what happened next was something nobody expected. Sebastian indirectly admitted defeat and walked away from the situation, and then he started to cry. The whole playground was looking at Rion. Everybody started cheering!

"What did you have for breakfast?!" said Charlie.

"I didn't know you could do that!" said Michael.

Yusuf asked "What made you do that?"

Rion replied, "Remember Mr. McClymont's assembly? If any of my friends are going through pain, then how can I watch? Sebastian was picking on Kieth. That's the last time we will play Nutmeg rush." Everybody cheered for Rion, and lifted him into the air. The scene was unbelievable. It was as if there was a victory parade taking place.

Jenny was mesmerized by Rion, she was looking directly at him. She walked towards Rion and said "I like what you did for Kieth."

"Thank you," replied Rion, as he tried to separate himself from his friends who had surrounded him.

"I like you," said Jenny as she displayed a shy smile, looking up at Rion.

Rion couldn't believe it, he replied, "I like you too." They both stared into each other's eyes for what seemed like an eternally valuable few seconds. This was an enchanting moment, where they were lost in each other's eyes. But somewhere in their deep subconscious, they knew something was about to spoil the moment, and just on queue the school bell rang reminding everybody that lunch time was over. Jenny proceeded to the classroom leaving Rion with a smile, and the most blissful sensation he had ever experienced.

That evening, Rion felt a sense of pride of doing what was right for Kieth. However, he also felt a deep sense of guilt for hitting Sebastian, which meant that their friendship was most likely over. Rion was also happy that the girl whom he loved for so long, Jenny, finally came to him and told him that she likes him. Later that evening Rion's parents reminded him that it was the last day in school for him tomorrow, after that, they had to move to America. Rion's day went from being a day of mixed emotions, to being an extremely sad day. He would possibly never be able to see Jenny again, and that was heartbreaking. Rion worried the whole night about what was going to happen the next day.

On his final day at school, Rion was nervous. His heart was still. He felt emptiness, as if somebody had removed all his abilities to face the world. A completely different Rion to the one everybody saw at school yesterday. After Mr. Uddonseh's English class, it was break time, he was sitting separately from his friends and looked like a confused soul.

Jenny saw Rion, she saw that he seemed upset. Rion was hoping she would come and speak to him, because today he just did not have the energy or courage to make the first move. Jenny walked slowly towards him and asked in a shy voice "Hi Rion, how are you?"

Thank god she came to me, thought Rion to himself. "I'm okay, how about you?" he replied in a dull, depressed voice.

Jenny felt as though something was not right. She asked "What happened? Why do you look so sad today?"

"I need to talk to you, can we go somewhere quiet?" asked Rion as if he was begging her.

"Okay, sure." said Jenny. They both went to the emergency exit stairs, where hardly anybody ever went. Both Rion and Jenny were silent, they were both too nervous to speak first. Jenny was anxious, wondering what Rion was going to say.

"I love you Jenny," he said with a heavy heart.

Jenny had a feeling of pure bliss as Rion spoke those words. In a way, she was relieved.

She replied with a sparkle in her eyes "I love you too."

For eight years he had struggled to express his love to Jenny, and now she herself declared her love for him. Rion experienced a form of joy which couldn't be described. He took Jenny's hands and gave her the most loving and caring hug. In that moment, where Jenny was hugging Rion, he felt as though he had forgotten all his pains, sorrows, and challenges. He felt like he was in heaven, an indescribable feeling of warmth in his heart. Jenny felt as though she had everything, and she needed nothing more to be happy in life. After this magical hug which seemed to finish so soon, Rion told her "I'm sorry." Jenny was looking into Rion's eyes with a feeling of insecurity, she had everything, and now she was scared of losing it all. He went on to say "Today... is my last day at school. Tomorrow me and my family are moving to America."

Immediately, as though somebody had pushed a button, Jenny's eyes filled with tears. She just could not stop herself, as her tears began to flow from her eyes like an overflowing dam. Rion felt as though he was guilty, and seeing Jenny cry, his eyes also began to water. They hugged each other again, before Jenny could no longer bear the pain. She left Rion, and rushed into the girl's toilets to cry her heart out. Rion knew she was disappointed with him. He looked up at the boy's toilet sign and walked in like a half dead body. He looked at himself in the mirror, and asked his conscience if he had done the right thing. He felt guiltier than he had ever felt before.

The bell rang, it was time for assembly, and today it was time to enjoy Mr McClymont's wisdom filled talk again. This gave Rion some hope, perhaps he could learn something that could guide him out of this cloud of confusion that he was in. Line by line, class by class, everybody sat down. There was silence as the assembly was about to begin, Rion was listening intently.

Mr. McClymont began speaking "There was a little boy, and girl. They both lived next doors to each other. They had never seen each other. The boy's bedroom shared a wall with the girl's bedroom. One day the boy heard a knock from the girl's bedroom wall, the boy knocked back in reply. Then the girl knocked on the wall again, and so the boy replied by knocking again. Like this, the boy and girl would knock on each other's wall before going to sleep every night. It was their special way of being friends. One day the girl knocked on the wall, but this time there was no reply from the boy. The girl kept knocking all night long but there was no reply from the other side of the wall. In fact, there was no reply for the next three days. The girl was sad, and frustrated. Suddenly, there was a knock on the wall. The boy was knocking. But this time, the girl decided that she would not reply, she was angry. The boy kept knocking all night long, but the girl didn't reply. She thought to herself *If he doesn't reply to my knocking, why should I?* So she ignored him all night long. From then, the girl did not knock on the boy's wall, and there was no knocking from the boy either. A couple of months passed by. The girl was happy in her own world, and had forgotten about the boy. But one day the girl found out that the reason the boy didn't knock on the wall for three days, was that he went to the hospital because he was unwell. The boy knew that the doctors diagnosed him with cancer. And even though they didn't give him long to live, he wanted to come home one last time, so that the girl didn't think that he let her down. The girl regretted what she did, but it was too late, the boy had died." Mr. McClymont's eyes were moist after narrating this tragic tale. "From this story, we can learn, that we should never jump to conclusions in life. We should always find out the whole truth, and only ther, we should make a judgment."

Everybody gave Mr. McClymont a round of applause. Rion was moved by this story. After the assembly, he went back to the boy's toilet. He looked at himself in the mirror. This time, he was proud of was he had done, because he told Jenny the truth. Today he realised, that as long as he told the truth, he could be proud of himself when he looked at himself in the mirror.

As Rion came out of the toilet Sebastian and his three friends confronted him. "Here's the lover boy," said Sebastian.

"What do you want Sebastian?" asked Rion sternly with his arms crossed.

"I want revenge, and I want it now. Who do you think you are? Punching me in front of the whole school?"

"I didn't mean to humiliate you in front of the school. I just didn't want you to bully my friends," explained Rion.

"Oh did you hear that guys?" said Sebastian while laughing to his friends. "He didn't mean to humiliate me in front of the school!" Sebastian walked so close to Rion that they could feel the heat from each other's faces. "If you didn't mean to humiliate me in front of the school, then tell me how you'll make up for it?"

"What do you want me to do?" asked Rion out of curiosity.

Sebastian gave Rion two options, "Either you say sorry to me in front of the whole school, or…"

"Or what?" said Rion more seriously.

Sebastian smiled, and said "or you let me humiliate you in front of the whole school."

Rion was astonished. But he calmly considered his audacious proposal and concluded "On one condition."

"What condition?"

"If you want me to apologise in front of the school I will. But you have to promise me one thing."

"Promise you what?" asked Sebastian with arrogance and intrigue.

"You have to promise that you will not play Nutmeg Rush again, and you won't bully anybody anymore."

Sebastian thought for a moment while chewing his gum smoothly and then said, "Deal, meet us outside, now." Sebastian and his three accomplices walked away from Rion after giving him the most vengeful look.

Outside, Sebastian was waiting for him. He had announced to the whole playground that Rion was about to apologise to him. Everybody was waiting to see what would happen.

Rion emerged from the entrance, and walked down a long flight of stairs. He walked up to Sebastian in front of everybody. The playground was still, each and every pupil was watching in anticipation. Rion said "Sorry for punching you." The students were amazed to hear this.

"I didn't hear you properly, say it louder," demanded Sebastian.

"I'm sorry for punching you." Said Rion a little more loudly this time.

"No, not *sorry for punching me*, just say sorry," said Sebastian.

"Okay I'm sorry." Said Rion with his arms folded as if Sebastian was taking liberties.

"No, not *okay I'm sorry*," explained Sebastian, "Just Sorry."

"Sorry," said Rion agreeing to his demands.

"Good. Now there will be no more Nutmeg Rush." Sebastian wore his sunglasses in style, and looked around at the other students like he had taught his arch rival a lesson.

Rion walked away from the situation. But Sebastian continued to speak behind his back, "Love is in the eyes, love is in the heart, love is in the soul, yeah right. Money is much more powerful than love."

Rion turned back around and looked at Sebastian while he was laughing and saying to his friends. "Money can squash love like the insect that it is!" Sebastian saw Rion looking at him and said "Money is what makes the world go around Rion, not love."

On hearing this, Rion walked towards Sebastian. Everybody was quiet again, watching with intrigue, and so was Sebastian. Rion reached Sebastian and said "Love is more important than money, money cannot buy love."

"And love cannot buy money either Rion," replied Sebastian. "Your quest for love will give you nothing but pain and suffering."

Then Rion said something quite remarkable, "In this lifetime, I will prove to you that love is more important than money. And at that time, when I prove this, you will have nothing around you, except money and a feeling of shame. But don't worry, god is very kind, he might give you love too, if you have the intelligence to accept it."

Sebastian was amused, "It's a prophecy, is it?... Rion?"

"No, it's a challenge."

"May the best man win." Sebastian extended his hand to shake hands with Rion.

Rion shook his hand in return and said "No, may the right man win." Rion walked back to class, with a look of real determination and purpose on his face. The war between Sebastian and Rion had been announced to the whole school. But the battle grounds were not the school, it was actually their entire lives. Sebastian's mission was to prove that money is more powerful than love. But Rion represented true love, his aim was to prove that love can win all wars.

It was time for Rion's final class of the day with Mr. Uddonseh. There was a knock on the door. It was Mr. McClymont, he whispered something into Mr. Uddonseh's ear, who said "Rion, your parents have come for you, you're moving to America aren't you? You need to go." Rion was surprised, he didn't expect to be leaving school early. He didn't even say goodbye to all his friends. And what about his last chance to speak to Jenny? His final opportunity to bid farewell to his first true love, and his friends vanished in an instant. Jenny, Charlie, Kieth, Yusuf, in fact even Sebastian was surprised that Rion would be leaving early. Everybody wanted to say goodbye to him. But Mr. Uddonseh was adamant that Rion should leave and not keep his parents waiting. Rion reluctantly stood up from his seat very slowly. He looked around at his friends. They all looked solemnly at Rion, his mind was blank, and his heart was heavy. He looked towards Jenny, he wanted to stop and say so many things, but his feet kept moving towards the door. Rion really wanted to stop, but found that he couldn't. One last time he looked towards Jenny. Jenny looked like her eyes were in pain, she wanted to cry her heart out, but she smiled for him. Rion caught a final glimpse of Jenny, and left that classroom… forever.

Before leaving the school, the headteacher Mr. Hill invited Rion into his office. Rion was sitting on the chair waiting to hear why he had been called into the office of the head teacher.

Mr. Hill said "Your search for love should not end at the first hurdle, your search should continue." He looked at Rion with real purpose, but Rion wasn't sure what he meant. Mr. Hill continued, "I wanted you to win that speech competition Rion, what you said was right, Love is more important than money. Off course love is more important than money. Love is the most important thing in the whole world, in history, ever. However, due to reason's I can't discuss with you right now, Sebastian won the competition. But don't worry, that competition means nothing to me. The real competition is in life, and now it is up to you to prove, that the most powerful thing not just in this world, but in the entire universe, is not money, but love.

Rion looked up at Mr. Hill with hope. He received invaluable guidance from Mr. Hill which nobody else in the world could give him.

Mr. Hill said "Promise me you'll prove it Rion, promise me!" Mr. Hill shook Rion by the shoulders as he urged him to reply.

"Yes Mr. Hill, I promise. I will prove that love is more powerful than money. I will show the world that winning a war does not require strength, it requires only love. I promise Mr. Hill, I promise" said Rion with humility and utter resoluteness.

"Good, I will remember your promise…"

Rion smiled in agreement.

"Now you must go. Your parents are waiting for you outside."

Rion thanked Mr. Hill for his guidance, "Sir, I will always remember your words, I won't let you down, thank you."

Before Rion left the office Mr. Hill said "One more thing." Rion stopped and looked back. Mr. Hill walked Rion and gave him the biggest hug and said, "All the best."

Rion left Mr. Hill's office with fearlessness in knowing that the path on which he was treading was the one that Mr. Hill blessed him to continue upon. He knew that love is the foundation of life, and with the power of love he could achieve anything in the world. Rion wanted the power of love. And with that, Rion proceeded to a new life in America, where he did not know how, but he knew that he would embark upon a mission to prove love is more powerful than money.

Chapter Three

Quest for Love

Eight years later, Rion had grown into a handsome young man. He was studying in the third year of his undergraduate Psychology degree at Harvard University in America. Rion was an all-rounder, with skills in many different aspects of life. He enjoyed many sports including basketball, football, baseball and cricket. But he had just one main purpose, to find true love. With just one more year left of university education, his quest to find true love was still not over.

Rion had three good friends who studied at the same university, Harvey, Hannah and Eddy (short for Edward). Rion had many other acquaintances, but these were three of his closest, most reliable friends.

After Just a ten minute drive from the university in Rion's car, Harvey, Hannah, Eddy and Rion were all sitting on a hill looking down at the most beautiful view of the ocean. They had arrived at the Eastern part of Boston, where the most stunning views of the North Atlantic Ocean could be seen. Everywhere they looked, from the East to the West of the horizon, there was just the deep blue colour of the water. It was a warm summer's day, with a slight breeze. Birds were flying in the sky, there was the smell of fresh green grass, the scene was set, but for what?

"So, why did you bring us here Rion?" asked Eddy.

"Yeah, we could have discussed what you wanted in University!" said Harvey.

"No," interrupted Hannah. "If Rion has brought us here, there must be a reason behind it."

"Yes, I have invited you all here for good reason."

"What's the reason?" asked Eddy.

"Yeah what happened?" asked Harvey.

"I want to tell you all something, which I haven't told anybody until today. I am searching for something, my heart is searching for something..."

"What are you searching for?" asked Harvey.

"Since I was young, there has been a vacuum in my heart, which nobody could see, and nobody could heal for many years."

Hannah really wanted to know what Rion was so worried about, "What is your heart searching for?" she asked.

"Love." Said Rion. Harvey, Eddy and Hannah were intrigued, intent on listening to what Rion had to say. "I have been searching for my true love for many years, but I can't find her. It is the biggest regret of my life."

Hannah asked Rion "Haven't you found a girl who you like?"

Rion smiled to himself and said "I found a girl that I liked, in fact we both loved each other. But destiny took us away from each other."

"I know you're still upset about Jenny," said Hannah. "But you have to move on."

"Yes, how long can you keep thinking about one girl? You have to find someone new!" added Harvey.

"Didn't you find any other girl who you like? Any other girls who make you feel something special?" asked Hannah.

"Well actually, now that I think about it, there have been one or two occasions when I felt a little attracted towards a girl."

"There you go! Then what happened?" asked Hannah. Harvey and Eddy were listening carefully.

"Well there's just one problem…"

"What?" asked Hannah.

"I found many girls I like, but I couldn't develop a relationship with any of them."

"Why couldn't you develop a relationship with them? You're a great guy," said Eddy.

"Yeah, any girl would be lucky to be your girlfriend," said Hannah in a persuasive tone.

"Well, I never had the courage to ask any of them out."

"Huh!" said Harvey as Eddy joined him in laughing at Rion.

"How comes you don't have the courage to ask out a girl?" asked Harvey.

"You're such a confident guy, you play sports, you work out, you're the most confident speaker I've seen. Whenever you need to give a presentation in class, you're the best. So why…"

"I don't know," interrupted Rion. "I can compete in sports, I can be confident if I need to give a presentation. I even have no problems with my studies, but when it comes to talking to girls, I don't know what happens to me. When I see a girl I like, my heart starts to beat twice as fast, I feel as if the earth will eat me up alive. As I'm about to speak, my mind convinces my body to run away from the situation."

"It's called approach anxiety!" said Eddy. "Don't worry I'll help you overcome it," he insisted. "All you have to do is…"

"Never mind that, first tell me who is the perfect one Rion? What are you looking for?" interrupted Hannah.

Rion stood up, put his hands in his pockets, looked towards the horizon, walked a couple of steps forward and said "I want a girl who is so beautiful she makes my heart beat when I see her. I want a girl who can make me a stronger person. I want a girl who is pure love."

"You can't have three separate girls all at the same time!" said Harvey.

"Yes he can, if he moves to Afghanistan!" said Eddy, laughing at him.

Hannah took control of the conversation again "Look Rion, you can't be selfish in love. Do you want a girl who makes your heart beat, who makes you stronger, or do you want a girl who is pure love? Do you want beauty, strength or love?"

Rion paused for a split second and made up his mind, "I want love."

"Right then, so now at least we know what to find for you," said Hannah reassuringly.

Rion disagreed, he said "Love cannot be found, love will find you."

Eddy could not resist, he said, "Then you sit on this mountain, and wait for love, when love finds you, call us, we'll come to your wedding with a huge bouquet of flowers."

Harvey added "No I have a better idea, wear a t-shirt saying I'm looking for love, please come and find me!" Harvey and Eddy both ridiculed Rion.

Hannah tried to steer the conversation in a positive direction, "Rion, if one day you find true love, what will you say to her? Imagine she is standing in front of you, what would you say?"

Rion smiled, he imagined that his true love was in front of him, and he said passionately "I would look in her eyes, hold her hands and say to her; *I am your love, it's me who you have been looking for, my heart is yearning for you, and I can feel your heart is yearning for me, give us one chance and see how magical the world becomes.*"

Harvey and Eddy burst into laughter. Even Hannah couldn't control herself! Eddy repeated "My heart is yearning for you!" And was in stitches with laughter.

Harvey also couldn't control himself and said "No, no… I know your heart is yearning for me!" They both laughed in Rion's face, and then even Rion couldn't hold his laughter in and smiled!

Deep down however, Hannah, Eddy and Harvey knew that Rion's love was pure. However perhaps he needed to be dragged into the modern era, so that he could attract girls more successfully.

Eddy suggested "Look Rion, girls nowadays don't want to hear all of that."

"Why not, is what I said not right?"

Eddy tried to explain "Yes it is, but…"

"Well then why wouldn't a girl want to hear that?" interrupted Rion.

Harvey put his hand on Rion's shoulder and said "she would, but not in that way. If you tell a girl what you said, she will run away."

Rion was confused, "If love is real, then it should be expressed in a real way. If it is not expressed in a real way, then it's not real love," he said.

Eddy joined in, "Listen Rion, you have to be cool. You have to..."

"What do you mean by cool?" asked Rion.

Eddy said "Cool man, cool! You have to be smooth as silk, you have to go up to a girl and say to her, *hey girl, you looking hot.*"

"No no no" interrupted Hannah. "If you do that the girl will run away too. Just go to a girl you like, and give her a compliment."

"A compliment?" asked Rion

"Yes, a compliment," confirmed Hannah. "Tell her how beautiful her dress is, or say how cool her style is, keep it simple."

"And then what should I do?" asked an educated Rion.

"Then you should ask her out on a date," suggested Eddy

"Where should I take her?"

"On the first date it's best to take her to a restaurant or a place where you can both do something, an activity, you know."

"I have an idea, tomorrow, why don't you approach girls!" suggested Harvey.

"Approach girls?" Rion was confused.

"Yes! That's a fantastic idea! Rion! Tomorrow you approach girls all day, surely one will fall for you," added Harvey.

"Yes, and we can have fun watching you get rejected!" said Eddy.

"But where? How? I don't even know how to approach," said Rion fearfully.

"Don't worry," said Hannah, "I will be with you, we will all be with you, but tomorrow, we will help you in your quest for love."

Hannah, Eddy and Harvey looked at Rion to see if he would agree. Rion was considering it when Eddy interrupted "Are you sure you want to approach girls tomorrow? I mean women are really difficult creatures to understand you know!"

"Shut up Eddy!" said Harvey, "Let Rion speak... So tomorrow, we find your love... What do you say?"

Rion said "Okay guys. I trust you. Tomorrow, I will approach girls." Hannah, Harvey and Eddy cheered. The four friends left together, looking forward to tomorrow, a day when Rion was hoping to find true love.

Secretly however, Hannah had a plan. She was hoping that Rion could find his true love, and be happy. But she decided, that tomorrow, if Rion didn't find a girl, then she would declare her love for him. Hannah secretly admired Rion, but never had the courage to tell him. She didn't know if he'd be interested. But today, seeing how romantic he is, made Hannah feel that maybe she could be happy with Rion because she felt that they were very similar in their personalities. She felt that she could complete

Rion's heart and give him all the love that a girl should give to her lover. Hannah loved Rion, and if Rion didn't find love tomorrow, then she wanted to give it to him. But she wanted to give him one day, to explore his love, maybe he would find somebody new?

The next day, Rion, Hannah, Harvey and Eddy all went to the Harvard University Campus, where Rion was planning on approaching girls who he had never spoken to before.

"Go Rion, good luck," said Harvey.

"Yep, we're all with you…" Eddy put his hand on Rion's shoulder and completed the sentence, "…from a distance."

"I have to love a girl before I speak to her!" objected Rion.

Hannah answered back "No! You have to speak to a girl before you love her, don't be so picky, have you forgotten what we discussed yesterday?"

"Okay, I'll try if you say so," compromised Rion.

Hannah scanned the horizon, and it didn't take her long before she spotted a girl "Her! You see that girl going towards the canteen? She's perfect, go and speak to her."

"But I don't love her!" protested Rion.

Hannah pushed Rion and said "Just go!"

Rion walked towards that girl hesitantly. As he reached closer and closer to her, he walked faster and faster, he looked at her as they were about to cross, and the girl smiled at Rion, Rion kept a serious face and continued walking past her.

Rion went back to his friends and said "she smiled at me!"

"Yes so you should have said something to her!" exclaimed Hannah.

Rion refused "No, she smiled because she thought I was a nice person, if I spoke to her, she would have thought that I'm a bad person.'

"Oh my god! No! She won't think you're a bad person if you say *hello* to her," said Hannah.

"Yes Rion, you can't think like that, otherwise you will never be able to find love," suggested Eddy.

"Be brave, just go there and say Hi, I think I like you, can I ask you your name?" said Harvey.

Hannah agreed "*Yeah*, that's a good one, just say that!"

So Rion repeated "Hi, I think I like you…"

Hannah confirmed, "Yeah, can I ask your name?"

Rion completed the sentence "… Can I ask your name?"

"Perfect," said Harvey and Eddy.

"Now keep practicing," said Hannah.

Rion reiterated to himself "I think I like you, can I ask your name? I think I like you, can I ask your name? I think I like you, can I ask your name?"

Just then, Rion saw a girl he thought was attractive, he said to Hannah "Shall I ask her?"

"You don't have to ask me! Just go!" said Hannah.

Rion started walking towards her, this time didn't walk as fast as last time, he slowed his pace a little. As he approached her and got closer he was in a dilemma of whether to say something or continue walking like last time. He mustered up all his courage and asked the beautiful girl "Ex, Excuse me."

The girl responded "Sorry, I don't have any change."

Rion was left on what felt like a stage where the spotlight was shining on him and the whole world was watching. He walked with embarrassment back to his friends.

"What happened?" asked Hannah.

"I said excuse me to her, and she said *sorry I don't have any change* to me."

Eddy and Harvey burst into laughter! Rion said "If you guys think you can do better then you approach."

"No no, sorry Rion, we don't mean that. We want you to be confident, we don't want you to fail," said Harvey.

"Yes, we want you to succeed, but it is funny how she said *sorry I have no change!* I don't know what we can do for you, if we can help tell us. Just be confident, don't hesitate, or the girl will think you're a beggar. Just be the man, own her and tell her how you feel," said Harvey.

Rion said, "You're right, I have to own her and tell her how I feel."

Hannah saw a girl and suggested to Rion, "what about her? Do you think you can go up to her?"

Rion liked the look of this girl, he nodded his head with confidence and said "yes." He walked towards the girl he saw fifty metres in front of him with utmost confidence. It seemed as though nothing would get in his way. Rion could only see her and nothing else. Just then a guy popped up in front of him and said "Have you or your anyone you know been involved in an accident resulting in an injury that's not your fault? If you have then we can get compensation for you faster than…"

Rion interrupted "Sorry I'm busy right now."

The compensation guy moved out of his way and said "have a nice day." The girl Rion wanted to talk to couldn't be seen. He looked left and right in a hurriedly. His eyes were searching for this girl like a camel searching for water in the desert. Just then he caught a glimpse of her again, she was walking away from him. Rion recalled his thoughts again, mustered up his confidence and gathered his momentum towards her once more. He was walking towards her like no man's business, as Rion got close to her, he experienced a feeling of nervousness like never before and felt like aborting the whole operation. But instead Rion turned his fear into confidence, and walked up to her with even more confidence. He said to her "Excuse me, I think I like you, what's your name?"

The girl smiled and replied "Oh that's really sweet of you, I'm Anastasia, what's your name?"

Inside Rion's heart, fireworks were going off, he was rejoicing the new year, Christmas and his birthday all at once. Rion kept a calm exterior while on the inside he was jumping for joy. "I'm Rion," he extended his hand to shake hands with Anastasia. Eddy, Harvey and Hannah couldn't believe their eyes, Rion successfully spoke to this girl he never met before. Eddy said to Harvey "Lucky dog, can't believe she fell for him!" Harvey said "Nah, he's confident, I knew he'd do it."

"You have a lovely name," said Rion trying to stay calm.

"Oh thank you, and what is your name?"

"I'm Rion," He extended his hand to shake hands with her.. Anastasia reciprocated.

"Oh, what do you study here?" he asked.

"I study Economics," she replied. "So what made you come up to me all of a sudden, I'm really curious to find out?"

Rion smiled, thought for a moment and replied "Well I think you have nice hair, nice eyes, and I just thought maybe if we..." Just then Rion saw another girl in the distance, the girl had two long blonde ponytails, and the most beautiful smile he had ever seen. Rion was enchanted by this girl and was staring at her while Anastasia was waiting for him to answer. Then all of a sudden Rion left Anastasia and rushed towards this new girl he had never seen before. Anastasia was left amused and surprised, as Rion ran uncontrollably towards this other girl. Hannah, Eddy and Harvey couldn't believe what was happening.

Rion walked in front of this new girl, and with the utmost confidence he took her hands into his own hands. He looked directly into the girls' eyes and said "I am your love, it's me who you have been looking for, my heart is yearning for you, and I can feel your heart is yearning for me, give us one chance and see how magical the world becomes."

Hannah, Harvey and Eddy were looking from a distance. Eddy said "She will slap him now."

"No she will kiss him now!" said Harvey, they both laughed. Hannah was like a godmother of Rion's who told them both to be quiet while Rion's fate was being decided.

In actual fact the girl's response was a surprise, she said "That's very brave of you, what's your name?"

At this point Rion introduced himself with a cheeky smile, "I am your true love, I am Rion."

The girl was suddenly frozen, it was as if her heart and body were completely separated, she was not a part of the world any more. She came closer to Rion, and hit him on the chest with her hands a few times. She then started to cry while hugging him with great affection.

At this point Rion didn't know what to do, so he just hugged her in return and let her finish crying her heart out. The girl complained to Rion, "Do you know how long I looked for you? Do you know how many places I searched for you?" Rion didn't have a clue what was going on. Although he did feel real love for this girl when he saw her, he didn't know his words would be this successful. "Why didn't you come looking for me before, do you know how lonely I felt without you?" continued the girl. At this point Rion's heart sunk, he thought to himself of who this girl could be. Meanwhile she continued bellowing "Why didn't you come looking for me, even once, not even once?"

He looked at this girl in the eyes, filled with tears. Rion asked the girl hesitantly, "Jenny?"

She nodded "yes." This was Jenny, the first girl Rion had ever loved, his first true love. It felt as though the Earth had shattered beneath their feet. Rion and Jenny both hugged and kissed each other multiple times. Both Rion and Jenny were in tears. Their whole life suddenly made sense, the pain and emptiness in their heart had been restored, their lives had a new meaning, and most importantly of all they found their true love.

At this point, Harvey gave a tap on Eddy's head and said "See, I told you he would kiss her!" They were both happy for Rion.

Hannah however had tears in her eyes. Eddy asked Hannah "What happened, why the tears?"

"Nothing, I'm happy for Rion, at least he found his true love."

Rion and Jenny were in a world of their own, nothing would distract them. They walked off together, holding hands, looking forward to their future filled with joy, happiness and love.

That evening, after Eddy and Harvey went home, Hannah tried to call Rion. She was still waiting for him at the University campus. But for the first time, he didn't answer her phone. Hannah looked down at her phone, and her eyes were about to fill up with tears. Just then, someone tapped her on the shoulder and said "Give me a hug."

Rion hugged Hannah, he was really happy, and Hannah was relieved to see him. She had a feeling of immense sorrow in her heart, which she couldn't express while Rion hugged her. She composed herself quickly and asked "How did it go?"

"Do you know who she is Hannah? You will never believe it! Guess who she was?" Hannah looked confused. Rion said "It was Jenny! Can you believe it? That was Jenny, after eight years I saw her Hannah, eight years! I'm so happy!"

Hannah was surprised "It was Jenny?"

"Yes!" Replied Rion, still excited.

"I'm so happy for you," she said.

"Thank you Hannah, if it weren't for you guys, I would never have met her."

"Won't you meet her again?" asked Hannah.

"Yes we're meeting tomorrow."

"Oh great... Where are you taking her?"

"I'm not taking her, she's taking me, to a restaurant a few blocks away, I've never even heard of it!" replied Rion.

"Well I'm sure it'll be great." She went on to say "Just one more thing..."

"Sure, tell me..."

"Please don't forget me," requested Hannah with a feeling of guilt. "I know Jenny is your love, and you were both made for each other, but I can still be your friend, right?"

Rion was touched by Hannah's feelings and said "Hey, Hannah, don't say that." He wiped her tears, held her face, looked her in the eyes and said "You know something? You are the best in the world, and even if I found Jenny, I think god was even more kind to me, because I found you." He gave Hannah a gentle hug filled with emotion.

The next day Rion arrived at the restaurant to meet Jenny on their first date. He saw Jenny, and immediately hugged her. This time there was a certain shyness in Jenny's eyes. They both walked into the restaurant together.

After sitting down at the table, there was a moment of silent respect for each other, which was a stark difference compared to yesterday when they were both so animated on reuniting after so long. Rion was the first to break the silence "Nice weather today huh?"

Jenny replied "Yes, very nice, and the breeze is so nice."

Rion continued the small talk "So what are your plans for today?"

"Oh nothing, I'll just have this meal with you and then probably go to the beach for a walk," she said. On the inside Jenny was thinking how much she just wanted to take Rion to her house and unleash her romantic side. But instead she had to stay formal and ask "How about you, any plans?"

"Yeah a few, after this I have to meet a few friends of mine..." He paused for a moment and said "Ah who am I kidding, I have no plans! I just came here to meet you, my whole day, my whole life if for you Jenny, I love you!"

Jenny asked a question which she had in mind for a while "If you love me, then why didn't you come back for me? Why did you leave me?"

"You don't know the whole story... Let me tell you what happened." At this point Rion narrated his story as if going into a flashback of the past "That day when you told me that you like me, the same evening I asked my parents many times why we were going to move to a different country. My mother and father didn't tell me anything despite me asking and arguing the whole evening. My father was a hard-working craftsman, he toiled away making hand crafted shoes for a large shoe manufacturing company in London. He would often work for twelve hours per day, and still come home with a smile on his face. After nagging him, my father told me the truth. He had received a death threat from somebody who threatened him to leave London. But he didn't tell me from who or for what reason. So, my dad just said that we have to go. After coming to America, I asked my parents many times to go back to London, if not to move there then at least to see you. But my dad always said *No Son it's not safe*. So do you know what I did?"

"What did you do?" asked Jenny.

"My mother would give me spending money for lunch every day. I wouldn't spend that money, and instead put it in my locker. After a very long three years, when I was fifteen years old, I saved up enough money to come to London by flight. I lied to my parents and said I'm going for a school trip, but actually I came to see you." Jenny was emotional, and listening carefully. "When I arrived, I asked our old teacher Hillary where you were. But she said you had moved school. I asked her many times which school you moved to, but she never told me. By the time I came to London, you had gone Jenny, you had gone."

"But Rion, I left Burbage school to come to America when I was sixteen, if you came to London when you were fifteen, then why did Hillary tell you that I had gone?"

Rion wondered "Really? Are you sure you left London when you were sixteen?"

"Yes!" replied Jenny "Are you sure you came to London when you were fifteen?

"Yes, positive," confirmed Rion.

Then they both asked each other at the same time "How old are you?" Then they both answered at the same time "Twenty-one!"

So Rion continued to assess the evidence by saying "If I'm twenty-one, and you're twenty-one, then either I'm lying about when I came to London, or you're lying about when you left London, or Hillary's lying about you leaving London."

They both concluded together "Hillary's Lying!"

Jenny halted the conversation and said "don't worry she probably didn't realise how much we love each other. An eye for an eye makes the world go blind, just forgive her."

"Wow, my father used to say that too!"

"What did he used to say?"

"An eye for an eye makes the world go blind."

"What do you mean used to?" asked Jenny inquisitively.

"Well you know how my father received a death threat in London? It seems as though destiny never changes no matter how much you run from it."

"What do you mean?" Jenny was worried.

"My father died in a car accident after we moved to America. He always used to say that an eye for an eye makes the world go blind, never use violence, just forgive and forget. But it seems that life didn't forgive him."

"I'm sorry to hear that," said Jenny compassionately.

"It's okay."

Jenny searched for some words in her mind and said "Your father loved you, and taught you a lot. I'm sure he's an angel in the sky, and he's looking out for you now."

"Thank you. You know Jenny, whenever I remember my father, I always remember how hard working he was. He always used to teach me, '*son, if you work for anybody, it doesn't matter what they do for you, the only thing that matters is how hard you work for them, and how honest you are.*" Jenny was impressed by such high morals. "How about your parents, how are they?" asked Rion.

"They're okay, my mother also passed away. She suffered a heart attack after we came to America. She always used to say that I am her little princess. But after she left this world it seemed as though god had taken away the protective bubble she kept me in."

"Don't worry Jenny, I am with you now, I will protect you, and keep you in a new bubble, safe from the world." Jenny felt a little more reassured by Rion's words. "But to make that bubble, I need to order some food, so can we order something?" he said.

"Sure," Jenny smiled.

Rion called the waiter "I would like to place an order please."

"Sure sir, what would you like?" asked the waiter ready to take instructions.

"I would like a large chicken burger with fries and a coke please," stated Rion, "how about you Jenny?"

"Sorry sir this is a vegetarian restaurant," replied the waiter.

"What!?" Rion looked at Jenny and questioned her "A vegetarian restaurant?"

"Yes, I'm vegetarian," she smiled.

"Why? I mean when? When did you become vegetarian?" Rion was surprised, the waiter left to give them more time to think.

"You inspired me to become vegetarian Rion…" explained Jenny.

"Huh?! How! When?" Rion was shocked.

"Well do you remember when you challenged Sebastian in school and you said it's wrong to treat another person with injustice by playing Nutmeg Rush?"

"Yes, I remember, but what about that?"

"That made me think…"

"Huh! Think? Think what?" asked Rion hyperactively.

"It made me think that we should not just think about the pain we cause to other humans, but we should also think about the pain and suffering we give to animals," said Jenny.

Rion said "Oh, right, yeah, I guess so. Well I guess I can eat vegetarian food for today, where's the menu?" Rion picked up the menu, and started browsing.

Jenny asked like she wanted something "Rion, you know how you said you love me?"

"Yes Jenny I love you a lot," said Rion while looking at the menu.

"Can you become vegetarian for me?" she asked with the sweetest, most innocent face in the world.

"Sure dear," said Rion without thinking and then suddenly said "What! Huh! Where am I! Vegetarian? How can I become vegetarian?"

Jenny tried to calm him down "Sorry Rion it's okay, if you don't want to be vegetarian, I understand."

Rion was relieved "Thanks Jenny, thanks, I really appreciate your understanding." He took a deep breath to relieve his tension.

Then Jenny continued "But if you could become vegetarian, it would make me feel really happy, like you really love me a lot. But It's okay, if you don't love me a lot, then I'll settle for a little love, it's okay."

Rion gave in to Jenny's emotional blackmail, took a deep breath and said "Okay, I will try my best to become vegetarian. Happy?" Jenny smiled and leapt onto him like a baby monkey on a tree. Rion said "But you have to give me some time, I'll give up slowly okay. It's been a lifetime of meat."

"Thank you Rion, you don't know how much that means to me," said Jenny appreciatively.

Then Rion looked at the menu again, and asked her to suggest something. Since this was an Indian restaurant, Jenny knew that Rion might not know what to order, so she placed the order for them both. She beckoned the waiter again.

"Yes mam are you ready to order?"

"Yes, can we have two Chole Bhature, Rass Malai, two Lassi, Poppadum and one Masala Dosa please?"

Rion just stared at Jenny like a water buffalo in shock when she was ordering, as he didn't have a clue what was going on. "Where did you learn all that?"

"Top secret!" replied Jenny. "I will tell you on our third date."

"Wow! Our third date! When is our second date?!"

"Tomorrow," she replied.

"Where?"

"Top Secret, I'll tell you where to meet me tomorrow!"

Rion muttered to himself "Now I know why Eddy was saying women are so difficult to understand."

"Did you say something?" asked Jenny.

"Oh, no, I was just wondering how long the food will be!...."

Soon enough the waiter brought out all the food that Jenny had ordered. It looked like the dining table of a king. Rion asked "What's this?" After pointing towards what looked like a giant king sized pancake.

"That's Masala Dosa."

"Mister who?"

"Never mind, try it, what do you think?"

Rion commented, "I never knew vegetarian food could be so tasty!"

"Oh thank you, what you're going to do means a lot to me," said Jenny.

Rion was confused for a moment and then remembered "Oh, you mean the vegetarian thing?" Jenny smiled and nodded. "Oh it's nothing, I can do anything for you," said Rion politely. Although the food was actually delicious, and Rion didn't have a clue how he was going to keep his promise of becoming vegetarian, there was only one question on Rion's mind, where was the second date with Jenny going to be?

That evening, after dropping Jenny home, Rion called Eddy, Harvey and Hannah to have a conference meeting in the usual meeting spot on the hill.

"Don't worry, she probably just wants to give you a surprise," said Hannah.

"No, she probably wants to take you back to her bedroom and then…" said Eddy.

"No," interrupted Harvey, "she just wants to show you how poor she is, and then ask you to work with her in the circus with hyenas." Harvey stared laughing to himself when he saw everyone looking sarcastically at him. Harvey withdrew his comment "On second thoughts she probably just wants to go on a romantic date with you."

"What should I do?" asked Rion.

"Don't worry," said Eddy, "She's your childhood love right?" Rion agreed.

"So, you should be happy! She is surprising you instead of you having to surprise her!" added Harvey.

"Yes, don't worry, just go, and if there are any problems, call me, I'll tell you what to do," said Hannah.

"No call me, I'll rescue you!" said Eddy.

"Don't worry guys I'm not exactly scared of her, she is my love after all."

"Then what's the problem?' asked Hannah.

"I just wonder why she's so secretive… Are all women like that? Eddy even said that women are difficult to understand…"

"See I was right!" laughed Eddy.

"Maybe he has a point?" said Rion.

Hannah concluded "I know a woman's heart, she will surely take you somewhere romantic, where you two are both alone and can't be disturbed. But she doesn't want to tell you because she is shy. Just make sure, that tomorrow, once you arrive on your date, act like you're really surprised and happy to be there. Make her feel special. Very few girls get the chance to be looked after by the man they love."

After hearing this, Rion felt better, "Thanks Hannah, I'm sure you're right."

Then Hannah asked him "Do you love her?"

Rion looked sympathetically towards Hannah and said, "Yes, I feel like she has completed my broken heart."

Hannah said while keeping a brave exterior "Oh, I'm glad to hear that."

"But you are also a special part of my life Hannah, and without you, my heart would also be incomplete," said Rion. Hannah felt emotional, her eyes filled with tears, so Rion hugged her.

"What about us?" said Harvey.

"Yes, you both too," and Rion gave them both a hug too. This was a special moment of true friendship, a moment that felt like a warm light that shone down on them all. Now, for Rion's sake, they all looked forward to tomorrow and his second date with Jenny. But one thing was for sure, Rion knew in his heart, that Jenny was not an ordinary girl, and his second date would not be ordinary either.

Chapter Four

The Second...

The next morning while Rion was asleep, the phone rang at 7am. He looked at the phone, it was Jenny, after quickly sitting up he picked up the phone "Hi, Jenny."

"Are you ready?" she asked.

"Ready? For what?"

"For our second date!" she replied.

"Now?"

"Yes, now! Why?" she asked.

"Oh, I mean now, so late, I was waiting all night," said Rion ingeniously.

"Come on silly, I'll pick you up in twenty minutes."

"Okay sure, Huh! Twenty Minutes?" he was surprised.

"Yes Twenty minutes, be ready okay bye," Jenny hung up.

"Okay, bye," said Rion to himself as he jumped out of bed and got ready as soon as he could.

Jenny picked up Rion twenty minutes later as promised, and they were on their way to the second date before they knew it.

Rion was wondering what on earth was happening to him while Jenny was happily driving along. "So... where are we going?" he asked hesitantly.

"Well, it's a surprise, I told you!"

Rion remembered Hannah's words from yesterday. *Once you arrive on your date, act like you're really surprised and happy to be there.* "I look forward to your surprise Jenny, I'm sure it will be really nice. Wherever you're taking me, I will come." Jenny smiled just as they arrived at their destination.

However, the place where they came didn't initially seem like a romantic place at all... Because Jenny had brought Rion to the Cambridge city centre in Massachusetts! Although Rion wondered in his head why Jenny had brought him to a city centre, he stayed quiet and politely expressed how happy he was to be there. As Rion and Jenny got closer to the clock tower in the city centre, Rion realised that there was some sort of rally going on. Thousands of women had gathered in the town centre. They were shouting a slogan *"Justice for girls, say no to slavery, justice for girls, say no to slavery."*

"Don't worry Jenny, I'll protect you," said Rion as he held her head in his hands.

"It's okay, I'm here to take part!" said Jenny.

Rion let go of her head and said "Take part? In this? Why what happened?"

"Yes I believe that all people should be treated equally, including girls," said Jenny. She started marching alongside other women who were shouting slogans.

"Can I ask you a question if you don't mind Jenny?" he asked while walking alongside her.

"Sure go ahead."

"Don't you think women are treated equally to men already?"

"No, not really, do you know that women get paid up to twenty percent less for doing the same job as men?"

"Really? But did you know that there is the bill of human rights to which all human beings are entitled, and in that it is clearly stated that all people are equal?" replied Rion.

"Yes the bill of human rights does state that all people are equal, but not all people follow it."

"Okay, I agree, perhaps some women are paid less for some jobs. But how about the criminal justice system?

"What about it?" she asked.

"Women who commit the same crime as men are often given much lesser jail sentences, just because the judge is sympathetic towards women. You can't choose to keep the good parts of equality and then leave out the bad parts can you?"

"I agree with you Rion, but…"

Rion interrupted "But what Jenny? Do you know that women get charged lower entry fees in night clubs, and they get charged much lower rates for their car insurance, isn't that sexist? Isn't that unfair?"

"Yes but…"

"And, don't you know that all women who treat men badly, get away free, and nothing happens to them. What's more the courts award the rights of keeping the children to the mother in most cases?" Continued Rion.

Jenny said "I agree with you but…"

Finally Rion asked "If you agree with me, then why are you here fighting for women who have too much arrogance and selfishness under the guise of self-respect?"

Jenny finally completed what she wanted to say, "The truth is that I'm not here fighting for the women who have too much arrogance and selfishness under the guise of self-respect!"

"Then why are you here?" asked Rion.

"Come with me." Jenny held Rion's hand and walked to the front of the march, where she introduced him to a little girl. "This is Natalia."

Rion kneeled down and was touched by the most magical smile from this little girl who looked so adorable. "Hello Natalia," said Rion.

Natalia replied, "Hello, are you uncle Rion?"

"How did you know my name?" Rion was surprised.

"Mother Jenny told me about you yesterday, she said you would come and visit me today, and you look just how she described you."

"I can't believe it!" said Rion. "You already have a child Jenny? I could never have imagined. I loved you so much, and you already have a little girl! Where's your father Natalia? Where's your father?" he asked.

Jenny interrupted, "She is not my real daughter!"

"Then who is she? Why is she calling you mother?"

"Because I have made her my daughter," she explained.

"I don't understand Jenny," exclaimed Rion.

"Rion! Natalia was being trafficked by a gang of criminals from Slovenia, in Europe, so that she could be sold for money and become a slave for the rest of her life. The authorities saved her, and the police are going to return her to her family. We are all marching in protest for the safety of children like her," explained Jenny.

Rion was relieved and started to smile "Oh, phew, for a second I thought that you have a daughter!"

"No, I'm not even married yet!"

Rion looked towards Natalia with extreme compassion. He asked Natalia "If Jenny is your mother, then can uncle Rion be your father?"

Natalia smiled and nodded her head to say yes. Rion opened his arms, and Natalia jumped into his arms, as he picked her up. Rion experienced a magical moment where he felt as though he had his own daughter in his hands.

Rion looked at Jenny and said, "I'm really glad to see how special you are. I'm happy to witness how much you care about these girls. The work you're doing is amazing. I'm sorry I doubted you, I won't make that mistake again."

"Thanks Rion, that means a lot to me." Jenny was touched.

"But I'm also glad that you're not one of those!" Rion pointed towards the crowd of women.

"It's okay… One of those, what do you mean one of those?!" asked Jenny.

"Oh Nothing, let's take part in the march, *justice for girls, say no to slavery, justice for girls, say no to slavery.*" Rion continued chanting. Jenny smiled and continued the march.

At the end of the day, they were both hungry. Without proper food the whole day, Rion was craving for some meat.

"Jenny, can I have some meat today? I'll give up slowly I promise?"

"If you want you can…"

Rion began rubbing his hands in anticipation, "Oh thanks Jenny it means so much to me. Oh man Jenny's so cool! Today I'll have…"

Then Jenny interrupted "but if you could control yourself, it'll make me feel like I'm really special, just like a princess."

Rion sighed, and prepared himself "Oh okay, let's eat wherever you want," in a monotone voice.

Jenny leapt up onto Rion and gave him a sloppy kiss! They both sat down at the vegetarian restaurant, and ordered their food. Rion said "It was a really nice day Jenny, and it was very nice to meet Natalia."

"Thank you. I felt much stronger today because you were with me. But, can I ask you something?" said Jenny.

"Sure go ahead…"

"You know how earlier you said that you're glad I'm not one of those, did you mean you're glad I'm not a feminist?"

"Huh?! How come you remembered that all of a sudden?"

"I just thought I'd ask you, but never mind, it's okay if you don't want to discuss it," said Jenny.

"No it's okay, you can discuss it. You know Jenny, I've seen women's rights activists for a long time, and I've seen them from real close.

"Where did you see them?"

"Because of my mother. She used to take part in women's rights marches. She would take part in these marches because when she was in University, she faced a lot of abuse from her family when she was young. My mum had such a negative image of men by the time she got married, that she thought all men were the same. My mum would go to work, and when she came home, unconsciously, she would bully my father."

"Oh no, how did your father react?" asked Jenny.

"My father was a simple man. He was hard working, honest, never wanted too much in life, he just wanted to look after his family. But my mother wanted him to earn more money, she wasn't satisfied with the lifestyle that my father provided her. So she always threatened him. She said that she has a right to work where she wants, and do what she wants. She didn't want to be a bird in a cage. But by running after the world, my mum lost the person who loved her the most in the world. I still remember that morning, my mum left for work saying that if my dad didn't leave his job and find a higher paid job, then she would leave him, take me with her, and never come back home. My mum put so much pressure on my dad... He died in a tragic accident later that day." Rion felt hurt remembering the past.

"I'm sorry to hear that Rion," said Jenny sympathetically.

"Jenny, it's okay to have dreams about equality. But women have changed so much over the past years, that now it's the men who suffer injustice," he explained.

"What about your mum, is she still the same?" asked Jenny.

"No, since my father passed away, I think she really realized what she's lost. Now she always teaches me that a woman doesn't become less important if she is a housewife, but instead she can support herself and her family to prosper. She can give her children the education and love that only a mother can give. But now my mother is always lost in her thoughts, remembering my dad. She says to me that if she could turn back time, then she would just want to spend her life with my dad without arguing. She would give up her career ambitions, her money, everything just to live with my dad happily again. But unfortunately, that dream can never come true."

"I'm sorry to hear that Rion..." said Jenny sympathetically. "Oh by the way, I agree with you. Women always campaign for the good parts of equality, they never think about how much injustice there is against men. Many men are also stuck in abusive relationships, but nobody stands up for them."

"I'm glad you understand... Oh by the way, where's Natalia?" remembered Rion.

"She's gone to her care home, tomorrow they'll prepare to take her back to her real parents."

"I'm going to miss her..." said Rion.

"Yes, me too, I don't know how to live without her," agreed Jenny.

"I have an idea!" said Rion suddenly.

"Tell me?"

"Why don't we become real parents? That way, we can have our own children, and then we never have to miss Natalia again, right?"

"Rion! You..." said Jenny like a teacher.

"Jenny, I think it's a good suggestion! Think about it pleeeease!" said Rion mischievously.

"Okay I have to go now!" She stood up.

Rion said "I know you are very busy, but shouldn't we…"

"Go on another date?" said Jenny.

"Yes, if we could go on another date when you're free, that would be…"

"Sure we can, how about next Saturday?" she interrupted.

"Next Saturday, that's perfect, it'll give me enough time to…"

"Okay great, I'll pick you up next Saturday morning at 8, be ready okay, bye dear." Jenny kissed Rion on the cheek and ran off towards her car. Rion was left to say "bye" to himself before he could realize what had happened!

But he celebrated alone by cheering "Oh she loves me, she loves me!" and then as he realized that it's another 8am wakeup call he needs to prepare for, he slammed his head on the table, covering it with his arms and called for the waiter "Can I have the bill please?"

The next day it was time for another conference meeting with Eddy, Harvey and Hannah.

Rion told them what happened on his second date with Jenny and asked "What do you guys think?"

"She's a really sweet girl," expressed Hannah.

"She's a good girl, she stands up for what's right," said Harvey.

Eddy disagreed "I think she's weird."

"No she's not weird," interrupted Hannah. "Rion, you're really lucky to find someone like her, you won't find anyone like her in the world. If I was in her place, I would go to the cinema, or have fun with you, but she wants to share life's struggle with you."

"See, I told you she's weird!" said Eddy.

"Be quiet Eddy!" said Hannah, "Rion, listen," Hannah held Rion's hands. "The girl you have in front of you is every man's dream, a girl who stands up against injustice, and doesn't just care about make-up and shopping every day."

"I know Hannah, I know. Jenny is the best girl I could have ever wished for," explained Rion.

"Then what are you thinking so much about? Are you unsure of something?" she asked.

"I just wanted to ask you guys where she might call me on our next date," explained Rion.

"Hasn't she told you?" asked Harvey.

"Nope, it's a surprise, and it's another 8am wake up call, this time on Saturday!"

"I think she's from the army!" confirmed Eddy.

"Don't be silly," interrupted Hannah. "I think this time she'll take you to her house Rion."

"Really? I hope so! Okay, Hannah, if it was our third date, where would you take me?"

"Me? I would have taken you home on our first date!" said Hannah.

"See you're so simple, why aren't all girls so simple? Why are all girls so unpredictable?" asked Rion.

"That's how girls are. They feel like if they give everything to a boy straight away, then they will have nothing left to give them. That's why they reveal their mystery slowly. It's hard to understand, because most of the times even girls don't know what they are doing, and why they are doing it."

"It's a headache I tell you. Sometimes I think it's better to keep a pet dog, than to love a girl," complained Rion.

Hannah looked at Rion the same way as Jenny does when she looks at him like a teacher.

"Sorry…" he said like a little puppy. Rion went on to say "You know guys, I really miss Natalia. She came for a brief moment like my daughter, and now she's gone. I hope she's safe."

"Don't worry man, I'm sure she's happy wherever she is," said Harvey.

"Yes Rion, and what you did for her, she will never forget," added Hannah.

The next date with Jenny was just a couple of days away. Saturday came soon enough, and before he knew it, Rion was sat with Jenny in her car on Saturday morning at eight o clock, on his way to date number three.

Chapter Five

Third time Lucky?

As Jenny drove to their third date, Rion was more prepared than last time, and more awake, having rested properly the night before. He wasn't sure what to expect, but he knew what he might. In the mean while Rion asked Jenny "How is Natalia? Is she okay?"

"She's fine, I checked up on her yesterday, she's going to leave for Slovenia in a week."

"It would be great to see her one more time, I'll miss my daughter," expressed Rion.

"You mean, before we have our own children?" said Jenny.

Rion cheered "Our children, our children!"

Jenny Smiled and changed the topic "Don't worry, we have one more chance to visit Natalia, before she goes, probably Wednesday if you're free?"

"For you and our daughter Natalia, I'm free any day! Jenny... Our children?" asked Rion cheekily one more time. Jenny looked away and smiled, she didn't say anything. Rion cheered to himself to celebrate.

They arrived at their destination. She had brought Rion to the same place as last time! But this time Jenny asked for some assistance as she walked to the back of her car and opened the boot "Can you help me to pick up this box dear?"

"Sure," he replied, wondering if Jenny had brought him to yet another protest march. But she asked him to carry the box a short distance away. After reaching the clock tower in the centre of the high street, Rion was relieved to see that there were no people marching up and down the street this time. But it seemed as though Jenny was looking for something, then suddenly she said "Oh, there's our stall!"

"Huh? Stall?" wondered Rion. Jenny took Rion's hand and rushed towards an empty stall, where she asked him to put the box down, and began to unpack it. Before you knew it, Jenny had unpacked the box and set up her stall with a big poster that read "Meet who you eat."

Rion was a little surprised and asked "What's this all about Jenny?"

"I'm organising a protest!"

"A protest? Now what happened?" asked Rion.

"A protest to save the animals," said Jenny.

"Animals? Which animals? I don't see any animals," he said.

"The animals that people eat! Until people can meet the animals that they eat as meat, they will never have any feelings for them. So today we will introduce the people to the animals that they eat, and maybe people will wake up?" she explained.

"So you were serious about that vegetarian stuff huh?" he asked. Jenny smiled, while Rion continued to speak "You mean, you're going to have some real animals here in the middle of the city centre, and get people to touch them?"

"Yes!" said Jenny with enthusiasm.

Rion laughed at her and said "Jenny, nobody's going to become vegetarian just because they meet a few pigs!"

Jenny was upset, she said "It's my duty to try my best, whether people change or not, is up to them, you just decide if you will help me or not."

"Off course I will help you. No matter how strange you become, I'll always stand by you," he said.

"What?" she asked, with her hands on her hips and eyebrows raised.

"Nothing, you just tell me what you want me to do, and I will be the best helper ever!"

Jenny instructed Rion, "Could you please hand out these leaflets to the public, and if anybody asks any questions, try to explain to them why they should consider vegetarianism."

"Sure, for you I will do anything," he said. Jenny seemed reassured.

Rion started to hand out leaflets alongside her. After just an hour of handing out leaflets to the public, he was feeling exhausted, he asked "This is quite demanding work, what keeps you motivated to keep going?"

"I just think of you," she replied.

"Oh really? Why is that?" asked Rion with a smile on his face.

"Yes, you're the one who inspired me to do this remember?"

"Oh yeah you told me, but how on earth did I inspire you?" he asked looking confused again.

"Your courage in school to fight against injustice when you saw Sebastian bullying Kieth was amazing.

That day spurred me on to fight against all injustice in the world," she explained.

"Wow! If I knew that would leave such a lasting impression on you, I would have let Yusuf be hit. Heck I would have hit him myself."

"What do you mean?" asked Jenny.

"Just kidding!"

"Then hand out leaflets, every person is important," she ordered.

"Yes boss!" replied Rion.

Around two hours later at 11:00, as the morning rush of commuters was over, an old gentleman came to Rion and asked him a question, "Excuse me young man, what are you doing?

Jenny was busy handing out leaflets, so Rion answered his question, "We're handing out leaflets sir, about why it's a good thing to become vegetarian." He gave the old man a leaflet.

The old man literally scratched his head while looking at the leaflet and asked "But why would someone want to do that? Where would I get my vitamins and protein from?"

Rion could see the old man's point of view so he said "Yes that's true sir, a..." he searched for an answer in his mind, but couldn't find one.

The old man continued to speak, "And isn't it human nature to eat animals? Isn't that the reason animals were made?" Again, Rion had no answer to the question, but the old man continued questioning "Who will control the population of these animals if we don't eat them?" After just thirty seconds of questioning from the old man, Rion was flustered and didn't have a clue what to say. He looked towards Jenny, but she was still busy talking to another person. So, he looked at the old man and just as he was going to say something, the old man interrupted him again and said "It's okay young man, you can keep this leaflet, I think *you* should consider becoming a meat eater, it tastes darn good!" The old man returned the leaflet to Rion, tapped him on the shoulder and continued walking.

Flattened from the whole ordeal, Rion waited till Jenny was free and then asked her "Hey Jenny, I missed breakfast this morning, and I'm sure you're hungry too. Can we have some breakfast first, before I continue helping you to wage this war?"

"Sure where you gonna eat?" asked Jenny.

"McDonalds, why aren't you going to come?"

Jenny looked at Rion like a teacher.

"Just kidding, I'll look for some vegetarian restaurant okay?" said Rion.

"No you go ahead, I'll finish setting up until then. If you go down that street, there's a nice fast food place called *Naturally Food*, they do nice vegetarian breakfast," Jenny pointed him in the right direction.

"Thanks for letting me know," said Rion sarcastically, "do you want anything?" he asked.

"Yeah sure, can you get me some Handwo and a samosa please?"

"Hand what?" asked Rion.

"Never mind!"

"No, tell me, hand…"

"wo, handwo!" completed Jenny.

"Handwo?" Said Rion.

"Yes that's right! Handwo and samosa," she confirmed.

"Okay sure, I'll get you a hand and a sosa," she looked at Rion like she was worked up again.

"Just kidding, I know, handwo and samosa!"

Jenny smiled, "Don't be long, I have a surprise for you."

Rion began walking very slowly towards the vegetarian restaurant *Naturally Food*. A minute later, around 100 metres down the street, just as Jenny looked away, Rion saw a McDonald's restaurant on his right. He could see it come in slow motion. He looked back, checked if Jenny was looking or not, she wasn't so with haste, he ran into the McDonalds restaurant. He asked the assistant behind the counter in a hurry "How long will you take to give me a Big Mac and Fries?"

The assistant said "around four minutes."

"Okay, as quick as you can. It's a matter of life and death!" said Rion.

The assistant prepared Rion's breakfast in under four minutes, and Rion scuffed it down in less than two! After finishing his breakfast, he tip toed out of McDonalds while making sure that Jenny wasn't looking, and then ran towards the vegetarian restaurant *Naturally Food*.

Rion entered the restaurant and there was a big line of customers, he couldn't believe his bad luck and waited reluctantly. After an excruciating fifteen minutes, Rion reached the front of the line and suddenly forgot what Jenny wanted, so he said "My girlfriend wants something, she told me what she wants but I can't remember. I think it's hand, something, hand…"

The old man behind the counter said "Is it Handwo?"

"Yes that's the one, well done!" said Rion. He continued to recall "And she also wanted a sam, something, sams.."

"Samosa? Asked the old man.

"Yes that's it, how did you know?" asked Rion as he was pleasantly surprised.

"Is your girlfriend's name Jenny?"

"Yes it is, how do you know her?!"

"She often orders handwo and samosa for breakfast, I am the owner of this shop, and she is our loyal customer," said the old man.

"Does she do protests against non-vegetarians regularly too?" asked Rion.

"Yes young man, she does. What she is doing is great work, may god bless her soul."

Rion smiled to himself thinking what a crew Jenny had built up around her. It took around ten minutes for them to prepare the breakfast, and the old man gave it to Rion at which point he went on to suggest "Why don't you take some buttermilk too, she likes it with her breakfast."

"Okay sure, if you say so, then I'm sure she'll love it." said Rion trusting the old man.

"She is a good girl, I'm pleased to know she has a good boyfriend like you, make sure you look after her," said the old man.

"Yes sir, I will," replied Rion, as he took the food hurriedly and left the restaurant to get back as soon as possible.

Rion was walking towards Jenny just as he saw something astonishing on the floor near her. He saw a beautiful brown baby calf. It felt as though the world had slowed down, he saw the most heart touching thing he had ever seen. The little calf was sitting there on the floor, and just looked like the sweetest and softest creature. Rion smiled, and instinctively kneeled down near the calf, and stroked it on the head. He said, "Wow Jenny, when you said you would bring animals, I didn't know you would bring the most adorable animal in the whole world."

"Her name is India, and she is my favourite little cow."

"Oh wow, hello India," said Rion, as he looked at her in the eyes. She looked innocent, much like a child. Rion stood up and spoke to Jenny "I admire what you're doing, but don't you think what you're doing is... a lost cause?"

"Nothing is a lost cause," replied Jenny.

Rion pointed out "But you're working so hard, you'd be lucky if even one person becomes vegetarian."

Un-phased, Jenny asked "If one person becomes vegetarian, do you know how many cows I can save?"

"How many?"

"At least one hundred. And that's just the cows, think how many chicken, sheep, and other animals people eat during their lifetime. At least one thousand animals have to die to satisfy the tongue of one person. And I haven't even counted the needless animals that lay down their lives for leather sofas, leather interiors in cars, airplanes and needless leather handbags that people buy," she said while handing out leaflets to the public.

"But Jenny, just a small question I have…"

"It's okay, you don't need to hesitate, I get asked all sorts of questions all the time, just ask."

Rion gave Jenny her breakfast and as she took it out of the bag she asked Rion "Where's your food?"

"Oh… I ate it already in a…"

"Never mind what were you going to ask?" said Jenny.

"Oh yes, if we don't eat meat, then won't the population of those creatures spiral out of control? Won't they practically take over our earth?"

"Our Earth? This is their earth, and we've taken it over. The single species that hurts mother earth the most is human beings, so should we go around killing people to reduce the population?"

"No I guess not…" agreed Rion.

Jenny continued saying "Did you know that cats and dogs have just as many children as pigs do when they give birth? The only difference is that we keep one animal because it's useful to us, and kill the other because we label it as less intelligent. Nobody is less intelligent Rion, every living being has equal intelligence, whether it's an ant or an elephant, whether it's a student from Harvard, or a hard-working immigrant from abroad, everybody is equally intelligent, it's just that we all have different types of intelligence. Some have more intelligence here…" Jenny pointed to her brain, and went on to say "…and some have more intelligence here…" she pointed to her heart, "…and nobody should be punished for that."

"I agree with you, every living being has equal intelligence, but don't you think we need animals to survive, like where do you get your protein from?" asked Rion.

"I get protein from lots of places, like beans, cheese, milk, rice, soy and quinoa," Jenny clarified.

"Well, I guess you're right, and you don't look too malnourished. Well, don't you think god made animals so we can eat them?"

"What if I said god made you so I could eat you, how would you feel?" Jenny looked at Rion like a hungry lioness.

"Wow can you stop looking at me like that!" he was freaked out.

"Look at India, does she deserve to be eaten?" asked Jenny. Rion looked down towards India sympathetically.

"Yes, but India can't even talk. She can't understand what we're saying. She doesn't have any intelligence."

"Who says she can't talk? Who says she doesn't have any intelligence? All animals have their own language. You can't understand her language and she can't understand yours, simple. But all animals have their own type of intelligence and their own language. It's not up to you to decide which animal deserves to live and which doesn't," stated Jenny decisively.

"But animals like this, who have such a low level of intelligence are no use to us, so, isn't it better to just..."

"Just what? Just what Rion?" Rion was listening whilst she was staring at him up close like a zombie. "What about humans with low levels of intelligence? Should we just eat them too? What if we kill and eat the humans who are no use to us, is that okay?"

"No, I guess not," agreed Rion, but he went on to say "what about other animals in the wild? They eat each other too, so what about them, is it okay for them to eat each other? Why can't we do the same?"

"Animals also steel from each other in the wild. They kill each other, and they also do lots of other things which we don't. Are you an animal?" asked Jenny.

"I know what you're saying but..."

"Just answer my question, are you an animal?" interrupted Jenny.

"No, I'm human." concluded Rion.

"You can't choose when you want to be an animal, and when you don't. You can't say that we are all human beings and we deserve the bill of human rights because we are not animals, and then kill and eat animals because they kill each other. In the same way that women can't choose the good parts of equality and leave out the bad parts, you can't wear clothes, use soap, drive a car, watch TV, use the internet, go to school, turn on your heating and sleep in a comfy bed because you're a human being and then suddenly kill and eat animals, because you're an animal. Choose, and decide once and for all, are you an animal, or are you a human being?"

"I'm human," agreed Rion.

"Then please, help me to make other animals realise that it's time to become human," pleaded Jenny.

"Sure", said Rion. He went on to say "Jenny, I love you."

Jenny looked relieved and said "Thanks. If you're by my side, then I can achieve anything in this world." Rion hugged Jenny as they both cherished this strong bond of trust.

Rion looked with fresh eyes towards India, and said to her "You know what India?" The baby calf looked at Rion. "India doesn't deserve to die for anybody's tongue. From today onwards, I'm going to join this fight for animal rights, for your rights. And shall I tell you something else?" Rion looked at the baby calf while Jenny was watching. "From today onwards, either you are a human being, or I am an animal. Because from today, we are both equal, and whatever it says in that bill of human rights, applies to both of us!" Rion hugged India affectionately. Jenny had tears of happiness in her eyes. Rion held Jenny in his arms, and said "From today, your fight is my fight, your struggle is my struggle, and your animal friends... are my human friends." Together they felt an emotion of strength and courage to be able to take on the world without fear like they had never felt before.

This time, Rion didn't need to hold a conference meeting with his friends. The feeling he felt in his heart was the same as Jenny's. Rion realised that there was still much wrong in the world despite how far society had progressed. He felt the need to fight against injustice and he wanted to engage in every battle with Jenny, because together, they were stronger.

At the end of the day when their campaigning was over, Jenny was really impressed by Rion's passion for her cause. He toiled away for her all day, and didn't complain even once. Rion took Jenny to the place where he often met with Hannah, Harvey and Eddy. As they both put their arms around each other staring into the horizon, looking at the warm glowing sun about to set, Jenny said, "You must be tired of me..."

"Why do you say that?"

"A normal girl would ask you to take her travelling to some romantic place, where it's just her and you. And I take you to the city centre, to hand out leaflets. You must be tired, Right?" She looked up to see his response.

Rion thought for a moment and replied "How can somebody get tired of god?"

"God? Who?" asked Jenny immediately.

"You Jenny, you. My mother always told me that somebody who makes you a better person, somebody who shows you the right path, has the light of god inside them. For me, you are my god."

"No Rion, in this lifetime, if we can just live just like human beings, that is enough. God is too high, to be compared to god is not something I am worthy of," said Jenny.

"You have the power of god in you. I have the power of god in me." Rion pointed towards an ant walking on the ground. "This ant crawling has the power of god inside it. Every living being is a representative of god's power, and today, *you* have made me realise this. You made me realise that I cannot decide whether another animal lives or dies. You've lifted my level of thinking. You've lifted my soul, thank you."

"Actually Rion, I learned a lot of what I know from my teachers…" confessed Jenny.

"Who are your teachers?" asked Rion.

"I visit my teachers every Sunday, I can introduce you to them if you like."

"Okay, I'd love to meet them. But for me, you are the one who showed me the right path first, so you are my teacher, you are my god, and you are my love." At the setting of the sun, while the birds were flying above them, the scene was perfectly set, as Rion and Jenny both leaned slowly towards each other, and kissed each other passionately.

Chapter Six

Meeting with Gurus

On Sunday morning, Rion set off with Jenny to meet her teachers. While driving she said "My teachers taught me everything I know, if possible please respect them."

Rion was wondering why Jenny would say this, "The question of me not respecting your teachers does not arise. I love what you taught me, and I have to respect the teachers that taught you."

"Thank you, you don't know how much that means to me." Jenny parked the car outside a Church and said "Come Rion, let's meet my teacher."

"Your teacher is in this Church?" asked Rion.

"Yes," said Jenny "I hope you don't mind coming in?"

"Why would I mind coming in? Your teacher is my teacher." Jenny was pleased as Rion entered the Church with her. "Wow, this church is beautiful," said Rion. They both sat down on the front row bench. While Rion's eyes were wondering around marveling at the architectural genius of the church building, Jenny was in a world of her own, with her eyes closed, focused on prayer. He suddenly looked at Jenny while she was praying, it seemed as though time stood still, there was peace, there was bliss, and there were no worries on her face. When Jenny finished her prayer, she opened her eyes, and looked at Rion. He was gazing at her as though there was nothing else to see in the whole world.

"Do you know what I learned here?" asked Jenny. Rion was still lost in Jenny's eyes, looking at her, without blinking. Jenny said "Rion, Rion!"

Rion had a sudden wake up call, and snapped out of paradise mode. But he was still in a trance like state, "Jenny, I love you," he said, Jenny smiled, Rion leaned forward to kiss her.

Jenny stopped him by slapping him hastily "No, not hear, it's not respectful !" Rion was hurt but Jenny consoled him quickly. She went on to say "Do you know what I learned hear Rion?"

"What, how to slap people?!" asked Rion mischievously.

Jenny smiled off his comment and said, "I learned that you should love your neighbor as yourself."

"Oh wow, that's interesting."

"If the whole world understood this one quote, then there would be no wars, and nobody would fight for their own religion," explained Jenny.

"Why would there be no wars?" asked Rion out of interest.

"Because problems in the world arise when a person thinks to himself, *I am better than other people because...* And any number of words can complete the sentence, but the problem lies with the first half. People think they are better than others because of their knowledge, their religion, their power, their wealth, their intelligence. But if people stop saying *I am better than others because*, and if people instead say *others are the same as me because.... Others have the same*

*soul as me. Others have the same heart as me. Others have
the same blood as me. Others have the same feelings as me.*
If everybody understood that *I should love others just as
I love myself.* Then there would be no more wars in the
world." Jenny smiled at Rion after saying this.

Rion was in awe of her words, "What you said is so
true, and I don't know if anybody has said something
so powerful to me before. I want to meet the person
who gave you this knowledge, where is your teacher? I
want to thank your teacher for…"

Rion stopped talking, as Jenny pointed in front of
her, in the direction of her teacher. Rion looked where
Jenny was pointing and noticed the huge statue of
Jesus Christ in front of them. Rion was intrigued, and
asked "Jesus?" Jenny nodded her head slowly to say
yes. Rion looked at the statue in awe, as a feeling of
immense fear shimmered through his veins while he
tried to take in the sheer magnitude of the teacher in
front of him. Rion was speechless, in a moment of
complete surrender to the magnificence of Jenny's
teacher. Rion closed his eyes and offered a prayer to
the idol of Jesus Christ. He surrendered his pains,
fears and wishes at the feet of Christ.

With that, Jenny and Rion left the Church. After
Jenny started driving, she said "Thank you Rion."

"Why?"

"Thank you for coming to see my teacher."

"No Jenny, thank you for allowing me come into
your world."

"What did you think of my world?" she asked
humbly.

"I think your world is beautiful, it is like the moonlight, it's cooling, peaceful, and yet enlightening." Jenny's face was a true reflection of how happy she was within. Just then she stopped the car, parked and said "Let's go."

"Where are we going?" Rion was intrigued.

Jenny opened the door and said "to meet my second teacher, I have seven teachers, remember?!" Rion was interested, he stepped out of the car and followed Jenny into a building which looked like a Church but had some distinct features. Jenny took out two items from her handbag and said "First put this on."

"What's this?" asked Rion.

"This is a Kippah, and it is worn in the Synagogue to cover your head in front of god."

"But I'm not Jewish!" said Rion.

"It's okay, every human being is welcome to come in, you can come too." Explained Jenny.

Rion smiled and said "Okay."

After this Jenny gave him a shawl and said "Wear this too, it's called a Tallit, you have to wear it for Shabbat."

"Shabbat?"

"Oh sorry, Shabbat means a day of prayer. Can you say a prayer for me too?" Rion agreed and then Jenny went on to say "Repeat after me, Barukh ata Adonai Eloheynu Melekh ha'olam, asher kidshanu b'mitzvotav vitzivanu l'hitatef ba'tzitzit." Rion was impressed. He tried to repeat the prayer, and although first time he couldn't quite pronounce the words properly, but after a couple of attempts from Jenny,

Rion understood the prayer and repeated it successfully.

Then Rion asked her "Have I been converted now?!"

Jenny said "Don't be silly, how can you be converted with just a…"

"I'm joking, I'm joking!" interrupted Rion.

"Let's go in," Jenny lead the way.

Rion then stepped in cautiously, weary of the environment that would come before him. Jenny described the various things he could see as he entered the Synagogue. She said "These are the pews."

"Pews?"

"Benches! From where people can listen to the service prayers." As they walked slowly towards the front, Jenny whispered "The stage at the front of the room you can see is called the Bimah which means high place of worship in Hebrew. In the middle of the stage is the Ark where the Torah is kept." Rion looked at Jenny confused, Jenny said "Oh, the Torah refers to the first five books of the Hebrew Scriptures. It is believed by Jews that those five books contain sacred messages given to Moses from god."

"What's that light shining on the Torah?"

"Good question, that symbolizes the Ner Tamid or Eternal light shining down on the Torah."

"Can I ask you one more question Jenny?"

"Yeah sure go ahead," she said.

"Are you Jewish?"

"Why!" Jenny was surprised.

"How do you know so much?!"

Jenny looked mischievously at Rion, changed the topic and said "Come on, I'll show you more!" She went on to explain "The person standing at the front is the Rabbi, he will lead the prayer service."

"When will the prayers begin?"

"Soon, let's sit down."

The Rabbi walked up to the Ark, and opened the curtain, revealing five religious scrolls, approximately two and a half feet tall. The Rabbi took one scroll and walked back to the left of the stage, from where he would begin speaking. The Rabbi commenced the prayer ceremony. Rion and Jenny read from the book, and tried to follow along.

At the end of the service, Jenny asked Rion "Would you like to meet the Rabbi?"

"I'm scared of him, but if you want then let's go." Jenny smiled as they both proceeded to greet the Rabbi.

"What's your name young man?"

"Rion, I'm Jenny's…" The Rabbi put his hand up and stopped Rion from continuing.

"I know who you are. I can see from your eyes how much you love Jenny." Rion felt shy and looked down in agreement. The Rabbi continued speaking "Jenny, you are very lucky to have such a kind and caring boy. Such men are not made any more. And Rion, you are lucky to have such a lovely girl. May god bless you both. I can see from your eyes that you have a question young man." Rion was a little surprised as to how the Rabbi could know that he wanted to ask something. The Rabbi said "You don't have to hesitate in asking your question Rion, just ask."

Rion spoke "Sir, I just wanted to say that you are all doing such amazing work, how do you get the inspiration to do it?

"That's not your real question son, what were you really thinking about? What did you really want to ask?"

"Yes sir actually, I wanted to ask something else. Mr. Rabbi sir, Jenny has so many teachers, all from a different religion, but they are all beautiful in their own way. What I wanted to ask you is…"

"Don't hesitate son, you can ask…"

"I wanted to ask you which one is right, which path is the best path?"

The Rabbi replied "Would you like me to tell you the truth, or would you like me to be politically correct?"

"I would like to find the truth sir."

"Then prepare your ears to hear the truth my son. Judaism is the best path to god. In our religion we have ten simple commandments which are easy to follow. For example, one commandment *remember the Sabbath day, to keep it holy* means that one day of the week, Sunday should be dedicated to god, not to your personal work. God constructed this earth in six days, and on the seventh day he rested, so on the seventh day of the week, you should also rest and think only about god. Another commandment is *honour thy father and thy mother*. Another is *thou shalt not kill*, and *thou shalt not commit adultery*.

Rion asked, "Is adultery to…"

"Yes son," interrupted the Rabbi. "adultery means to cheat the person with whom you are married.

Another commandment is *thou shalt not steal, thou shall not bear false witness against thy neighbour* and *thou shalt not covet a neighbour's house, wife, slave, animal or anything else.*"

"I'm sorry to interrupt, but what does covet mean?"

"Covet means to desire, so it means you will not desire to possess anything that belongs to somebody else."

Rion was feeling as though a light was shining on him, and was really enjoying listening to the commandments. He asked the Rabbi, "Are there any more commandments sir?"

"Yes," said the Rabbi, "there are three more commandments. *Thou shalt have no other gods before me. Thou shalt not make unto thee any graven image,* and *thou shalt not take the name of thy lord thy god in vein.*"

"May I ask you what these commandments mean?"

"Yes son, it means that *I am your god, so do not bow your head in front of any other god, do not carve any idol of me, and do not take my name for no reason.*"

"Does this mean that if I have another god then I cannot go to heaven?"

"Look son, basically what the commandments say is that the way to reach heaven is to pray to the god and..."

"Please sir, please answer my question, does this mean, that if a person prays to another god, then that person cannot go to heaven?"

"Yes Son, it does."

Rion looked down in disappointment, then he folded his hands into a prayer pose, and said to the

Rabbi "Thank you sir," then he left the Synagogue. Jenny thanked the Rabbi and followed Rion outside.

She asked him "Why did you suddenly come out?"

"I'm sorry, maybe I shouldn't have come out like that, but there's something I'm thinking."

"What happened?"

"Tell me something, do you have more teachers you want to introduce me to?"

"Yes, five more."

"Then let's go to see your next teacher I don't want to jump to conclusions just yet." Said Rion.

"But why? What happened?"

"Nothing, I just feel positive and negative at the same time. Let's go to your next teacher."

Jenny drove Rion to her next teacher. This time she parked outside a mosque.

Rion followed Jenny into the mosque. They both removed their shoes. Jenny requested him to go into the men's *Wudu room*. She explained to Rion "The Wudu room is where you should wash your hands, feet and face before entering the mosque. I'll go to the ladies' Wudu room, and you go to the gents'."

"But why do we have to wash ourselves before going in? I already had a shower this morning!"

"Muslims believe that it's important to wash your hands, feet and face before presenting yourself to god. It's an extra step in purifying yourself and getting into the right frame of mind."

"Interesting, okay, cool, see you in five." Said Rion.

Rion went into the Wudu room, and used the facilities to wash his feet, hands and face.

After he was done he met Jenny outside the Wudu room, she said "Now we will both go in separately," Jenny wore a scarf and covered her head. She said "If you have any questions you can ask the person at the front of the mosque, he is the *Imam*."

"But I can't go in alone, where are you going?" asked Rion.

Jenny continued walking towards the female entrance, and said "It's okay, we'll meet here in fifteen minutes."

Rion was left alone, and walked slowly towards the male entrance. He stepped in and saw some people offering prayers by kneeling on their knees and then bending down towards the front of the prayer room. Rion sat down and waited patiently." After the prayer was over, the imam at the front of the room noticed that Rion's face wasn't a familiar one. He walked up to him and said "Asalaam alaikum, what is your name young man?"

"My name is Rion sir, are you the Imam?"

"Indeed yes I am. I've not seen you here before."

"Actually my name is Rion, I'm here with my girlfriend Jenny."

"Oh, Jenny is your girlfriend? She is a very sweet girl, she comes here many times to pray."

"Thank you, sir. I'm sorry you said something to me when we met, I didn't understand?"

The imam smiled and repeated "I said asalaam alaikum, which means may peace be upon you, it's like a greeting."

"Ohh, so what should I have said in reply?"

"Wa alaikum asalaam, which means that you also wish that I may be peaceful."

"Wa alaiku…" Rion attempted to say it.

"Yes, wa alaikum asalam," the imam said.

"Wa alakum asalam," said Rion finally.

"Well done young man. Do you have any other questions for me, is there anything else you'd like to know?"

"Well sir Imam, I was actually wondering why Jenny went in through a separate entrance?"

"That's a very good question. You see, in Islam women are given certain rights to privacy. Because this is a place of worship, it is our belief that men and women should focus on only god and nothing else when they come here. As there is a natural attraction between men and women, if they pray together in the mosque it can cause the attention to be diverted in a different direction than towards the all mighty Allah."

"Oh that's interesting, I never thought of it in that way. Is Allah the god in Islam?"

"Yes young man, he is the all mighty, he is not just my god, he is also your god, in fact he belongs to every human being."

"But why is there no picture of him anywhere Imam?"

The Imam smiled and replied "Because Muslims believe that god has no form, he is beyond description. How can the human brain conceive something which is beyond its conception?"

"But sir, let me ask you this, you said that Allah is my god and he is everybody's god?"

"Absolutely son."

"I would like to thank you for saying that, and I'm humbled that I can also call your god my own. But what of all those people who pray to different gods?"

"Well in our religion we believe that praying to Allah is the only way to heaven, and anybody who practices a different religion will soon come to realise the truth of the beautiful almighty Allah."

"But sir, if a person prays to a different god, does this mean that they will go to hell?"

"Well, in our religion we believe that Allah is the most beautiful and ultimate truth in the universe. We believe that anybody who doesn't believe in this truth is a *Kafir*, or *non-believer*."

"And what happens to a non-believer in Islam sir?"

"If a person dies and despite hearing of Islam, he did not believe in Allah, then we believe, that they will go to hell."

"Thank you for clarifying that for me."

"Do you have any more questions?" Rion looked down at the floor, and was thinking what to say, the Imam said "Listen Rion, I know what you are trying to say. But we Muslims believe that Allah is the ultimate truth in the whole universe. Do you know, the description of Allah in the Qur'an is so beautiful and deep, that it cannot be configured into one name. Allah is so magnificent, that there are 99 names for him in the holy scriptures."

"He has 99 names?"

"Yes Rion!"

"Can you give me some examples?"

"Sure, Al-Rahman, it means the compassionate one. Al-Rahim, the merciful one. Al-Hakam, the judge…"

"Can I ask you something?" interrupted Rion.

"Yes, off course."

"If there can be 99 names for the same god in the Muslim religion, why can't there be thousands of names for god in the world?" The Imam was presented with a question he had never thought of before. Rion continued "If you can see 99 different qualities to the same god, like supreme judge, merciful one and compassionate one, then why can't the world see different qualities in the same almighty god? Is it not just going to glorify god more, if humans worship god, regardless of the different names and forms?"

"Maybe…" thought the Imam. "Actually… what you said makes sense. I never thought of that before… But now that I think about it, I wonder why more people don't think like you."

Rion thought for a moment and asked "What is the most beautiful teaching of Islam?"

"There are many teachings, but what you might find interesting is that during the holy month of Ramadan, all Muslims fast for 30 days. They don't eat or drink anything, from sunrise to sunset, for the whole month."

"Wow, that is impressive… I find it difficult to go without food for a few hours let alone the whole day."

"It's not easy to fast young man, specially in the heat of middle eastern countries, where many Muslims reside."

"I can imagine. But what's the reason behind the fasting Imam?"

"It is to exercise self-restraint, and rise above the worldly pleasures. Also, during this month Muslims donate to charity, it's a time to remember those who are less fortunate in the world."

"That's very powerful thinking, thank you for explaining it to me."

"May god give you everything you desire," blessed the Imam.

"Thank you sir," Rion respectfully took the Imam's leave, stood up and walked out of the prayer hall. He saw Jenny waiting. Jenny smiled at Rion as he also was taken aback by the experience. They both made their way outside.

"What did you think of the Mosque?" asked Jenny.

"I think it's beautiful, and the Imam is very kind, he gave me his blessings!" said Rion excitedly.

"Well, did you get the answers you were looking for?" asked Jenny. Rion seemed little reluctant to speak, Jenny asked again "Tell me, you can tell me what you really think, did you get your answers?"

Then Rion broke his silence, "Every religion Jenny, every religion wants us to prey to their god. *Prey to our god, and you will go to heaven, if you prey to anybody else you will go to hell.* Do you know how divisive this is?"

Jenny was looking into Rion's eyes contemplating his words.

"Don't think that I don't like religion, every religion is good. They all teach good things. Don't steel, don't kill anybody, be peaceful, be charitable.

But when it comes to the name of god, they argue with each other like little children."

"I know what you mean," she said. "Every religion has its own god and its own way of thinking. It's like an institution Rion. No institution can be successful without giving its followers a set of rules and guidelines. Even if it's Manchester United football club, Harvard University, or even a small nightclub, every institution has its own rules. We can't say that the rules of any institution are wrong can we?"

"We can. Let me ask you, a Muslim who lives a very good life, peaceful, caring, kind, according to Christians he will go to hell because he doesn't prey to their god. And a Christian, a decent loving peaceful Christian, he cannot go to heaven according to Muslims because he doesn't prey to Allah. It's like two separate football clubs arguing with each other, when the truth is that they both belong to the same religion, football. In the same way, the Christian and Muslim gods are both the same god, just different names. So who is right Jenny? Who is right?"

Jenny put her hand on Rion's shoulder and said "They are both right."

"How could they both be right?" wondered Rion.

She said, "Religion can only be found in an individual's heart, not in the textbooks of any religion. An individual can pray to any god that he wishes. As long as his heart is pure, the gates of heaven will always be open for him."

"Yes that's right Jenny. But *you're* saying this, none of the religions say this, none of them."

"They do Rion. There are many religions that say this."

"Well? Why haven't you shown me?"

"Because I believe all religions are equal. Now let's go to the next place. Their approach to god is a little different than you might expect."

Next thing he knew, Rion was standing in a Jain temple with Jenny.

"They don't believe in any god," whispered Jenny.

"They don't? But why? I thought every religion had a god?"

"I'll tell you, but first let me show you inside," said Jenny mysteriously.

Rion walked in with her and saw a peaceful, serene prayer hall. Jenny explained "Jains believe that the soul is eternal. There was never a time when the soul didn't exist, and there will never be a time when it will not exist. They believe in re-incarnation, where the soul goes through many births and deaths in living form. They believe that the aim of life is to escape the cycle of birth, death and re-birth, which means to attain salvation. Jains believe that the power to achieve eternal salvation lies within one's own self and they don't depend on a supreme power to show them this path."

"This is a different way of thinking completely, it's uplifting. Is this the only religion that thinks like this?"

"Well, the answer is… yes and no. This is the only religion where they don't believe they need a supreme power, like a god to attain the ultimate, which in this case is salvation. However there are many other religions which believe in the soul being eternal and the aim of life being to achieve salvation."

"Which other religions?"

"Sikhism, Buddhism and Hinduism, they also believe in the soul, reincarnation, karma and salvation."

"What is karma?"

"Karma means action. These religions believe that life can't be lived without action, and one must bear the fruits of his or her actions, whether they are positive or negative."

"I suppose you're going to take me to those religious places next?"

"Yes!"

"I thought so!" said Rion predictively.

"Shall we go?" asked Jenny.

"Wait, before we go, tell me one of the most important things you learned from Jainism."

"Well, in Jainism everyone is vegetarian. In fact Jains believe that even plants have souls, so they only eat the plants which have fallen from the trees above, and they never kill living plants."

"Really! I thought being vegetarian was hard enough. This is some next level sh…"

"Control yourself," interrupted Jenny. "This is a place of worship. We have to respect it. Jain's believe that animals, humans, plants, they all have a right to life, and that is the thing I respect the most about this religion. Now let's go."

"Oh okay, sure, sorry, let's go."

Soon enough, They were standing in a Sikh Gurudwara. Jenny had once again covered her head, but this time she used a cloth found in the Gurudwara, Rion did the same. He saw many people praying who wore turbans and kept long beards. "I think I know their religion, are these Sikh people?" asked Rion.

"Yes," said Jenny. "They keep long hair in their turbans to symbolize a high level of spiritual thinking, above the low level everyday concerns of the human body."

"Wow that's cool, so they never cut their hair?"

"No, they also wear a round bracelet on their wrists called a *Kara*, to symbolize how there is no beginning and no end in this eternal universe."

"Is there anything else that they do?"

"Yes, they have a *Kanga*, which is a comb they use to tidy their long hair. It represents a clean mind and clean body. They also carry a *Kirpan*, which is a small knife or dagger."

"Why do they carry a knife?" asked Rion worriedly.

"Sikhs practice peace, however they believe that they should be like soldiers, ready to defend the rights of those who are weak and suffer injustice, at any time."

"Oh wow! I think I should carry a dagger with me wherever I go!" said Rion jokingly.

"If you want to protect those who are defenseless, then that's a great idea," said Jenny in agreement.

Rion was speechless.

Next, Jenny showed him, "this is the holy book of the Sikhs, it's called the Guru Granth Sahib."

"What does their holy book teach?"

"It teaches *Ik Onkar*."

"What does Ik Onkar mean?"

"It means one god," she explained. "Sikhs believe that there is one god, but god can take many forms, and resides in the heart of every individual. The Guru Granth Sahib teaches that every human being is fundamentally good because of the indwelling god, and no matter how bad that person is, they are capable of change."

"What is an indwelling god?"

"The indwelling god is a concept where the god lives inside the heart of every individual."

"That's high level thinking... so you mean, in Sikhism all human beings have a direct link to god?"

"Absolutely, and every human being is equal in front of god. Now let's meet my sixth teacher."

Rion's tour of the world's religions continued next at a Buddhist temple. When he was stood outside, for some reason it reminded Rion of something "Is this temple similar to the way ancient Chinese buildings were designed?"

"Yes you're right. They were designed keeping in mind the five elements of fire, air, earth, water and wisdom. Buddhism was founded by the saint Siddhartha Gautama in what is present day Nepal. Due to its location between China and India, there was a lot of influence from Chinese building styles."

"Who was Siddhartha Gautama?"

"He was a prince, his father was the king, and one day after seeing pain and suffering of ordinary people in the real world, it made him realise that the way to god was through simple living and high thinking. He gave up his kingly luxuries and became a sage, practicing meditation and non-violence. He was referred to as *Buddha* or the *enlightened one*, by his disciples."

"I feel ashamed of myself listening to that," said Rion guilt fully.

"Why?" asked Jenny.

Rion turned to Jenny and said, "If a prince can realise that the materialistic world is not worth what it seems, then why do we get so caught up in it?"

"The denunciation of materialistic life is not for everybody. Sometimes we must live in our normal lives and still accomplish spiritual upliftment. Becoming a sage is just one path to enlightenment, there are many ways. You can stay a part of this world and yet you can stay separate from it."

"How can I stay part of something and yet separate from it? It doesn't make sense."

"You can, like a lotus flower. A lotus flower stays in water, yet it separates itself from the water. You can do the same. You can live in this world which seems like a rat race, and yet you can live your life like a yogi, who is not disturbed by the chaotic world, like Buddha. You can be non-violent, and only raise your arms when you need to, like the Sikhs. You can sacrifice yourself for the world, like Christ, and you can be charitable like a Muslim. You can be vegetarian, and harm no other living creature like the Jains, and you too can love your neighbor as yourself, like the Christians."

Rion was in awe of her words "Jenny, you are not a normal human being…"

"What, why am I not normal?" she interrupted.

"You're special. If only everybody knew what you just said. You see, you don't want to be blinded by just one colour of the rainbow, but you want to take in the beautiful colours of every religion and become the rainbow. I am truly honoured to have a friend like you."

"Friend?" asked Jenny in a surprised tone.

"I mean… girlfriend, like you!"

Jenny was in a mischievous mood, "I guess that makes me the most colourful girl in the world!" she said with an angelic charm.

"Yes!" he smiled.

"Well, wait till you meet my final teacher, he's the most colourful teacher in the world, even more colourful than me!"

"Really? You're final teacher?"

"Yes, my final teacher. He belongs to the Hindu Religion."

"The Hindu religion?" asked Rion.

"Yes. The Hindu religion was the first ever religion. It is the oldest of all religions, it's more than 5000 years old. The believers say that whichever god you believe in, and whatever name you call god by, it is the same god that responds, because ultimately there is only one god. Hindus believe that you can call god by any name and give god any form, but in the end there is only one creator. In fact in the Hindu religion there are millions of different gods. This is the very core of Hindu belief, that everybody in the world can worship a different god, and yet everybody can still go to heaven. Because we have the power of god within us. Hindus believe god incarnates himself from time to time in human form to set an example of how an ideal human should live life."

"Is it possible for god to limit himself in the confines of the human body?"

"There is nothing which is impossible for god. If god wishes to demonstrate to us humans how an ideal person should live their life, then off course it's possible for god to do that."

"Wow that's deep thinking." Rion felt as though he had seen everything there was to see in the world, a feeling of enlightenment. He expressed his emotions, "This morning you showed me one colour of the rainbow. Bow now I feel like I've seen all the colours of the rainbow. Thank you, Jenny. But, I am curious to know, you're like unbiased towards all religions, right?

"Yeah…"

"And you're not Hindu either right?"

"Nope…"

"Then why is your last teacher the most colourful?"

"I don't know why Rion. I guess there's something which draws me closer to him. He is fun, mischievous, and yet fulfills his duty as an ideal human. He is vegetarian, and yet he is a strong warrior. He stands up for what is right, and protects those who are vulnerable. He guides people, but leaves it up to you, whether you follow his advice or not, you are responsible for your actions, that's what he says. And that's why I feel as though he has parts of every religion inside him. Maybe that's why for me, he's the most colourful."

"Really, who is he?" Rion was inquisitive.

"I'll introduce you to him tomorrow evening, there is a special Holi festival taking place."

"A special Holy festival?" He asked.

She smiled and said "No, *Holi* festival, it's the most colourful festival of the entire Hindu calendar, *Holi*. If you'd like to, you can bring your friends too, they will love it."

"Really! Can I bring them? They haven't been invited?"

"Nobody needs an invitation to take part in Holi, it's a festival for everybody who wants to join in."

"So why don't you tell me who he is now?"

"I'll introduce you tomorrow evening," said Jenny. "It's best if you see him for yourself…"

Rion was left hanging, as the seventh teacher of the most colorful girl in the world would be revealed to him tomorrow.

Chapter Seven

Holi

The next evening, Rion, Eddy, Harvey and Hannah all embarked on a mission to take part in the *Holi* celebration. This was the first occasion where Rion's fellow comrades could meet Jenny properly. While driving, Rion asked Eddy and Harvey "Why are you guys wearing suits?!"

Eddy said "Today, we will meet your future wife for the first time, so…"

Harvey completed the sentence "so when we heard that tonight we will meet Jenny, we went out as quickly as possible and bought these expensive designer suits to impress our sister In-Law," explained Harvey.

"Sister In-Law?" Rion was surprised.

"Yes, Sister In-Law. You're just like our brother Rion, so she is our sister In-Law!" explained Harvey.

"Ahh that's so sweet guys!" said Hannah.

As they all arrived at the Holi festival, they were greeted by a host at the entrance, who formed his hands in a prayer position and said "Namaste, Happy Holi." The four friends responded by doing the same in return. Then the host put some red coloured powder on Eddy's cheeks. Eddy wasn't sure why he did that, but then the host went on to put red powder on Rion, Hannah and Harvey as well. Eddy was relieved to see that there wasn't any colour on his suit so he said to the host "Thank you, I like the colour."

"You're welcome," replied the host, "this is just the beginning, please come in." Wondering what the host meant, the four friends entered the Holi festival. Then, they saw Jenny coming towards them. She looked beautiful yet simple. She wore a white Indian dress, and adorned herself with simple yet elegant jewelry, coloured bangles, a golden necklace, and a golden nose ring.

Jenny greeted Rion's friends and invited them to come in. "Hello, it's a pleasure to meet all of you, Rion had told me so much about you."

"What did he tell you?" asked Hannah anxiously.

"That you guys are his closest friends, and if he had to trust anybody with his life then it would be you guys," said Jenny.

"That's true, you can trust me with your life, I'm not sure about Harvey though!" said Eddy jokingly.

"So you must be Eddy?" Jenny laughed.

"Well my full name is a bit posher, it's Edward, but yeah everyone calls me Eddy. How did you know I'm Eddy?"

"Because Rion told me that although you and Harvey are both mischievous, you are slightly ahead in that department!"

"Well thank you, I'll take that as a compliment!" said Eddy like a snobbish comedian.

"If you all don't mind, I'd like to discuss something with Rion for a moment."

"Oh sure you have Edward's permission," said Eddy jokingly while pointing his hand to his own chest.

Jenny smiled and said "thank you Edward!" as she took Rion to one side away from his friends. She showed him a statue of a handsome man playing a flute and asked "what do you think?"

"Well… he seems like a cool guy. He seems playful and peaceful. Why, who is he?"

"This is my seventh teacher," said Jenny.

"Oh so this is the colourful god… Introduce me," said Rion.

"It's Lord Krishna. He's one of the god's in the Hindu religion."

"Wow… He seems quite cool, but why did you say he is colourful?" asked Rion.

"Let me show you why…" said Jenny with a mischievous smile.

As they all walked in, the celebration had started and there was a big outdoor field in which the festival took place. It was a chaotic scene. Many people were throwing coloured powder on each other. There were lots of different colours being scattered around, yellow, green, blue, orange, red, purple, pink, in fact all the colours of the rainbow could be seen in one place or another. Rion and his friends were looking in amazement. Eddy asked Jenny "This seems like quite a fun activity, is there an application process to take part?"

Just then a stranger came up to Eddy, and said "Happy Holi," he gave Eddy a hug.

Eddy also responded by saying "Happy Holi," and shaking hands. The stranger then threw lots of colour on Eddy, his whole suit was covered in colour. Then another group of people threw colour on Jenny, Rion, Hannah and Harvey.

Rion asked Jenny "Is this just a one way process?"

"No, there's colour on that table, you can throw some colour on them if you want."

Rion said "Thank you Jenny, you can't get away with that this means war! Team, lets go!...."

"Yeah, they were our designer suits those people just ruined!" said Harvey

Rion, Harvey, Hannah, and Eddy walked towards the table of powdered colour with a look of determination on their faces. They picked up as much as they could in their hands. Then, as if from a Hollywood action movie, they were all set to get their revenge and they let loose on the other people by throwing colour on them. This turned quite quickly into the most spectacular celebration they had ever seen. Throwing colour on others, and on each other. Soon, their faces couldn't be distinguished. Their hair, face and clothing was completely covered in one colour or another. This was the true spirit of Holi, where all people were covered in the colours of love equality and happiness.

At the end of the night, as the celebrations came to a close, Rion, Hannah, Jenny, Harvey and Eddy all sat down so that they could gather each other's thoughts on their experience. Rion said "I had an amazing time today, specially seeing Eddy and Harvey's suits get ruined!"

"Don't worry, next year I won't wear a suit, but I'll definitely get you back Rion!" said Eddy.

"But Jenny, is there a reason why this festival is celebrated in this way?" asked Hannah.

"Yes," said Jenny. "When we throw colour on each other, we can't see who they are, and because we can't see who they are, we can't judge them. On the day of this festival, no matter who you are, you are equal, it doesn't matter if you have money or not, it doesn't matter which religion you belong to or where you come from, but on Holi, we are all equal."

"That's wonderful Jenny," said Hannah "You're very knowledgeable," she added.

"Thank you, you are very beautiful," Hannah smiled, there seemed to be an instant connection between them.

"Hannah and Jenny are both equally beautiful," said Rion.

"Why?" asked Hannah anxiously.

"Because you both have colour on you!"

Hannah smiled on the outside, and was a little relieved to hear that explanation. But in her heart there was a vacuum, which she felt at this moment more than ever before. It seemed as though that vacuum couldn't be filled in her lifetime, because that vacuum could only be filled by Rion, who was deeply in love with Jenny.

Jenny said "Rion, can you take me home?" She saw all of a sudden Hannah, Harvey and Eddy staring at her like hungry children so she added "I mean, right after you drop off your friends."

"Sure," said Rion, I'll drop you off first, then I'll take my friends."

"I don't want you to drop me off, I want you to come home with me," said Jenny.

Rion was gob smacked. The rate at which Jenny was progressing each date, he felt as though he would never be invited to Jenny's house, but suddenly, she wanted to take Rion home. He Said cautiously "Okay, let's go."

While Rion was driving the car, Jenny was sat in the front next to him, and Hannah, Harvey and Eddy were sitting in the back. This was a very good opportunity for Harvey and Eddy to ask Jenny anything they wanted, so Harvey kicked off proceedings "So Jenny, we heard that, I mean Rion told us that you knew each other in primary school in London, is this true?" Hannah slapped Harvey on the arm, he changed his words "I mean, did you two love each other back then as well?" Hannah slapped Harvey on the wrist and he tried one more time "I mean, what was Rion like in primary school?"

Jenny smiled, "Rion was very kind, when we were in school, he would always help others, he was brave. But when it came to telling me that he liked me, he wasn't brave at all. And because of this by the time he told me that he liked me, his parents had decided to move house, and it was too late."

"Why did your parents move house Rion?" asked Eddy.

Rion didn't want to go into too much detail, so he just said "My dad found better working opportunities here, in America, so we moved here."

"But Jenny, how about you? Why did your family move to America?" asked Harvey.

"And not only that, how did you choose Harvard University?!" added Eddy.

"Well my dad also found better working opportunities here, in America, and I wanted to study sociology, and Harvard University is a good university is a good one for Sociology, not only that, it's also close to our home."

"Wow, not only did you come to America, but you also came to Harvard University, what a coincidence…" said Hannah.

Rion dropped off Eddy and Harvey to their homes, and then drove to Hannah's house. On the way, Hannah asked "When Rion told you that he liked you what did you say?"

"At first I didn't say anything," said Jenny.

"Yes and I was heart broke for many years!" said Rion.

"Sorry baby," Jenny said to Rion. "Maybe I wasn't mature enough to see his love. But one day when I saw him standing up to Sebastian when he was bullying other children, I fell in love with him. Then I myself told him, that *I like you*. I told him how I feel, but the next day, he broke the news to me that his parents needed to move home, I felt helpless, and sad."

"Then destiny brought us together again," said Rion.

"Yes… destiny is very kind," said Hannah, knowing how opposite that statement felt to the truth.

Hannah's home arrived. As she left the car, Hannah felt a sense of helplessness, as she knew where Rion was going with Jenny next. Hannah wanted to stop this moment if she could, but knowing how much Rion loved Jenny, she controlled herself and said "I hope you have a good night, it was nice meeting you Jenny."

"It was nice meeting you too Hannah, I hope we can hang out some time when you're free?"

"Sure any time," said Hannah reluctantly. "Good night Rion," she said.

"Good night Hannah, sweet dreams," said Rion as he drove off with Jenny. Hannah was left outside her home alone, waving goodbye to Jenny and Rion.

"Hannah's a nice girl," said Jenny.

"Yes, she's my best friend," said Rion.

"Only friend?" she asked.

"Oh yes of course, only friend. She's always there for me. When I need a true friend, I always remember her."

"Are you remembering her now?" asked Jenny.

"No off course not, now, I'm with you! And Jenny time, is only Jenny time!"

Her house was quite a distance from the city, "I never knew you live so far from the University. Do you drive every day?" he asked.

"Yes," said Jenny, "my father didn't want me to live in university accommodation, so I drive an hour every day."

How comes your father doesn't want you to live in university accommodation?" asked Rion.

Just then, they arrived at Jenny's home.

"Wow, your house is lovely," he said.

"Thanks, actually my father's a little strict. To be honest he doesn't like me going anywhere, that's why I drive so far. I just hope he doesn't mind too much when he finds out about you."

"You haven't told your father that you have a boyfriend?!" asked Rion.

"No not yet," confirmed Jenny hesitantly.

"Does he have a big moustache? He won't come running after me with a gun when he finds out about me will he?" asked Rion in a joking tone.

"I'm not sure," replied Jenny.

Rion stopped smiling and said "How can you not be sure if your dad will shoot me with a gun or not? I can't come in your house. I'll just drop you here and go home."

"Don't worry!" said Jenny, "My dad's gone away for the weekend, he'll be back tomorrow!"

"What if he comes home early?"

"He won't come early, he needs to buy food from the wholesale market tomorrow, and today is Sunday!"

"No way, I don't want to die, I don't even have any children yet."

"Don't be silly, we will have children together."

"Really?" said Rion romantically as he moved closer to Jenny and looked in her eyes.

"Yes! Now come in," said Jenny while getting out of the car confidently, knowing that Rion would follow.

Rion hesitantly stepped out of the car. He walked like James Bond, taking every step as cautiously as he could. Suddenly he heard a loud noise. Rion gave

Jenny a hug from behind. Luckily, it was just Jenny's pet dog that made that noise. Rion was relieved. He looked at Jenny in the eyes, and leaned forward slowly to kiss her, just as he was about to, Jenny said "Later, let's go in."

"Yeah you're right, it's better to be shot by your father inside your house rather than out here in the cold," said Rion sarcastically. Jenny smiled and unlocked her door, as they entered her home for the first time together.

"Nice dog," said Rion, he stroked Jenny's pet Labrador while she was putting some food for the dog in its bowl. His name is Victor, and he is my friend."

"Anybody that is your friend, is my friend!" said Rion.

"Then you have lots of friends from today," Jenny said, as she smiled secretly.

"Why, how many friends do you have?" Rion asked.

"Around 1000," said Jenny casually.

"Wow that's impressive, you have a thousand friends, are they all on Facebook?" he asked.

"No they don't use Facebook," she replied.

"Oh okay, so what do they use? Twitter?"

"No they don't use the internet, they are a little old fashioned."

"Oh brilliant! I always wanted to get away from technology and stuff. My mum always says I should go on a retreat or something. But your friends must feel quite liberated by now, they've escaped the rat race of us city people, right?" Jenny nodded her head in agreement with a mischievous smile. "It would be a real pleasure to meet your friends."

Jenny immediately said "Would you like to meet them now?! Or tomorrow morning?"

"It's a bit too late right now, your friends must have fallen asleep, and we can't meet all 1000 now can we? Let's meet them tomorrow," said Rion... Jenny agreed. Rion said "Right now, the only person I want to meet is you."

Jenny came a little closer to Rion and whispered "I have a better place where we can meet each other..."

"Where?" asked Rion softly like a zombie.

"Upstairs," Jenny took Rion's hand and led the way. After walking upstairs while looking into Rion's eyes, Jenny entered her bedroom. Jenny, still holding Rion's hand, sat him down on her bed. She then went to close her door. She locked her door from inside, and came back to sit on the bed next to Rion. She rested her head on Rion's shoulder. He put his hand around her. Rion felt a warm feeling near his heart, he could feel Jenny's love, and she could feel Rion's heartbeat. He experienced love currents flowing through his body which he never experienced before. Jenny was sensing a feeling of warmth and safety for the first time ever. Rion stood up, and offered his hand, he wanted to dance with her. Jenny accepted his hand, and stood up to dance with him. Rion put one hand around her waist and took her other hand in mid-air. They gently waltzed, dancing with unity. Two bodies, but what felt like one soul. Jenny had a tingling feeling through her body and heart while Rion danced with her. She never wanted this feeling to end. Rion allowed her to lean back while he held her by her waist. He then kissed her neck, and then admired her from this unique position, while Jenny lied in what felt like thin air, taking deep breaths. Rion picked up Jenny in his hands and lied her down on the bed. Jenny's eyes were closed the whole time, she was ready to allow Rion to do whatever he wanted. Jenny was in a bubble of her own, she felt as though nothing in the world could harm her. Rion kissed Jenny on her neck, and then on her lips. Rion went down slowly to kiss Jenny on her waist, which was exposed due to her wearing an Indian saree. As Rion kissed her waist, Jenny began to breathe more deeply. She held Rion by his hair, and wanted him to continue touching her. Rion came up slowly near her face and kissed her lips again. Then Rion covered both himself and her with a duvet. Rion hugged Jenny with compassion, her eyes still closed, experiencing everything in as much depth as her senses could allow. Rion put his hand on Jenny's forehead, stroking her with affection. Just as Rion did this, Jenny began to drift off into a dream world. She felt as though she was sleeping on clouds, with the gods protecting her, and yet a feeling of warmth, coziness and comfort that can only be experienced in the womb, by a mother's child before coming into the world. At this time, Rion was everything for Jenny, and Jenny was everything for Rion. The power of Rion's touch was immense. Her heart, mind and soul were completely one with Rion.

The next morning, only the rays of sunlight that fell slowly on her eyes allowed Jenny to become aware of her surroundings. She was gently woken from the best night's sleep she had ever experienced. As she woke up, she noticed that Rion was sleeping on the chair, not on her bed. Though a little surprised, Jenny just looked at Rion, while he was asleep, and admired his innocent, charming face. She stood up, and stroked Rion's cheeks. She cherished this precious time where she was still in complete control of him while he was deep asleep. Jenny touched Rion's beautiful, long eyelashes, his lips, and then his cheeks. Jenny could not stop looking at Rion. She had a feeling of weightlessness, a feeling of looking after the person who she cared about most in the world. She couldn't control herself, so she leaned forward and kissed Rion. She whispered to him "I love you Rion, I love you," then, Jenny slept on Rion's chest, next to him, where she fell asleep once more. The next time that Jenny woke up, it was Rion who was looking at Jenny, admiring her. As Jenny opened her eyes this time, Rion took her cheeks, and kissed her on the forehead, allowing her to feel like the most special person in the whole world.

Jenny asked, "Why didn't you wake me up?"

"Because when you sleep, I feel like there is nothing else in the world except you."

Jenny went on to ask "But why did you come on the chair? Don't you like sleeping with me?"

"I do but…"

Jenny interrupted "Then why did you come on the chair?"

"Because I don't want you to think one day in the future, that I loved you only for your body. I love *you*

Jenny, and until you are completely happy to give me everything you have, how can I take the most precious thing from you without asking you first?" explained Rion.

Jenny was emotionally touched by Rion's words and snuggled up into his arms once again. She asked, "You will never leave me will you?"

"I promise, unless you leave me first, I will never leave you. How can a flower leave the soil it is joined to? You're my world now, and I can't leave you even if god comes to me and tells me to leave you. From today I'm yours, this heart is yours, this body is yours. We may have two bodies, but from today, our soul is one." Rion took Jenny's hand, and said "If I mean so much to you, then how can I leave you? From today, Rion is yours, his mind, his body and soul are all yours. I love you Jenny, I love you."

Jenny had no words to explain her emotions at this time. They both felt as though they had promised their lives to each other. Now, their life would be full of so much love, religion and laughter. This happiness could never desert them, as long as they were together.

Jenny suddenly remembered "My father! What if he comes? He could come any time."

"Don't worry," said Rion, "I love you, and true love should not be afraid. I will meet your father, and tell him everything."

Jenny expressed her concern again "But Rion, you don't know my father, he..."

"Your father doesn't know me!" interrupted Rion. "After he sees how much love I have for you, his anger will also turn to love."

"Do you love me that much?" asked Jenny.

"I love you so much, that now even if god tells me to leave you, I will not listen."

Jenny remembered something, she said "What about my friends? Will you love them just as much as you love me?"

"Your friends?" he tried to remember. "Oh, you mean the 1000 friends you were going to introduce me to?" Jenny nodded and smiled. "Jenny, your friends are my friends, and if you love them, then I will also love them."

"Can you promise me that you will always keep my friends in your heart?" said Jenny.

"Sure I'll always keep them in my... wait a minute, who are your friends? And why are they in your heart?"

"Let me introduce you to them, maybe then you'll understand my feelings better, come with me." Jenny stood up and took Rion's hand to show him something.

"You mean you want me to come with you now, and meet 1000 of your friends, without taking a shower, brushing my teeth, in my shorts?"

"Don't worry, you don't need to be so formal to meet my friends." Jenny took Rion's hand and stood him up, pulling him to go downstairs.

As Rion was being dragged against his will he said "Wait at least take a shower before we go, let me grab my wallet, my car keys!"

Jenny would not listen to anything and continued to escort him downstairs like a child. Jenny took Rion to the back door, where he wore his shoes, and then she opened the door for him. Rion witnessed the most spectacular site he had seen in his life.

Chapter Eight

The Revelation

In front of him was a panoramic view extending beyond the boundaries of vision. A huge farm. He saw a diverse range of animals. Rion saw hundreds of cows, pigs, sheep, horses, and that was just what he could see with his eyes.

"So, these are your friends?!" asked Rion with a big grin on his face while walking out onto the farm.

"They are my best friends, come with me, I'll introduce you," said Jenny.

As Rion followed her, he was astounded to see so many animals. "I know you love animals a lot, but why do you have such a large collection of animals? You can't take them all to protest with you on the streets, can you?"

Jenny said "No Rion, these aren't mine. These are my father's animals, it's his farm."

"Oh I understand. Wait let me guess… So does your father keep these animals so that he can sell the milk, eggs and the wool of the sheep?"

"Yes… but that's only half of the story."

Rion stopped walking and asked "What's the other half?"

"Don't worry, I'll tell you later, first let's go and meet the animals." Jenny showed Rion all the cows. Half the cows were kept in a special enclosure the size of a small factory. The cows were of predominantly black and white colour, quite large in size, much bigger than Rion had ever imagined cows to be. Each cow had a serial number tag on its ear. The cows were kept in specially designated areas, which seemed just about big enough to allow the them to stand up and sit down. Jenny introduced Rion to a few of them, she said "this is Angel, she's a real sweetheart, and this is Catherine, her friend, they always hang out together, don't you Angel?" said Jenny while shaking the cow's cheeks from side to side.

Rion stroked both Angel and Catherine, while asking Jenny "Have you named all of these animals?"

"Yes, and I remember them too!" smiled Jenny proudly.

"But why have you named all of them?" he asked.

"Everybody treats animals as commodities these days, I think that they all deserve a name instead of a barcode. After all animals have the same feelings as us, they just can't speak English right?"

Rion looked at Angel and Catherine in the eyes while stroking them. This moment fundamentally reminded him of a little three-year-old child. So simple, so innocent, so sweet.

Jenny suddenly remembered "I almost forgot, I have to milk the cows."

"Milk them? You're going to milk the cows with your hands!" Rion laughed.

"No, with a machine!" Jenny attached the milking machines to the udders of each cow, and then turned on the automatic milking system.

"What are you doing?" asked Rion.

"I'm milking the cows..."

"Don't these machines hurt the cows?" Rion asked.

"Well we are attaching a machine to a female cow's breasts, and sucking the milk out, they are painful, but we have no other option." Explained Jenny.

Rion was surprised by this milking process. He couldn't comprehend the cows' pain, standing with an industrial machine sucking the milk from the breasts that is supposed to be for the cow's children, which he noticed were being kept separately from their mothers. Rion noticed a cow *mooing*, and he thought he could see her baby calf in the cage opposite *mooing* for its mother. He asked Jenny "Are those the children of the cows?"

"Yeah, they're the baby calf... why?"

Rion asked hesitantly "Well, I was just wondering if it's fair to keep the animals separate. I mean, shouldn't the milk be for the calf, and not for us?"

Jenny stopped working and looked at Rion, "There are a lot of things that happen to animals which are not fair, but what can they do? They're helpless. You never think about it when you eat meat or drink milk do you?"

Rion kept his feelings suppressed, he continued the tour of the farm.

Jenny went on to introduce him to the other animals, she took him to the chickens next.

The chickens were housed in a separate shelter. As Jenny and Rion walked in, it felt considerably warmer. Rion noticed light bulbs quite close to the chicken. A large number of chicken were kept in a relatively small space, cramped together. Jenny introduced Rion to the different chickens, she said "This is Velma, this is

Dorothy, this is Shelly, this is Martha, this is Terry, this is Crystal..." Rion listened to each and every name. He was admiring Jenny's devotion towards her animal friends. Even though the introductions took a long time, Rion patiently listened.

"I'm guessing these chickens lay eggs?"

"Yes, they lay many eggs, and I will collect them later."

"Can I eat some?" asked Rion.

"Rion!" said Jenny in a cheeky voice.

"But why can't I eat egg? Eggs aren't living animals are they?!" he protested.

"No, but they are a symbol of what could have been the mother's child. It's like eating the child of a mother while it is still in the womb."

"Jenny... please don't say that!"

"Why? You're having so much difficulty listening to me, but what about those mothers who have to give up their children for us?"

"But I heard that there are artificial methods to make chickens lay eggs, and the eggs would never have hatched anyway."

"Yes you're right. In the wild, on average these hens lay 30 eggs per year. But after being given artificial enhancers to boost their rate of egg production, do you know how many eggs they produce now?"

"How many?"

"On average, 300. Laying eggs is a painful process, and each hen goes through hours of hardship to lay an egg, and because of human greed, their whole lives are becoming nothing more than a life of pain."

"Really? I didn't know that… But Jenny, they look quite healthy? They must live a decent life right?"

"Depends what you call decent," said Jenny.

"What do you mean?"

"The reason they look healthy, is because my father gives them poultry feed which fattens them up. They eat less, but put on more weight, because their food contains antibiotics to make them bigger and lay more eggs. Because of this, their legs cannot support their own weight." Jenny demonstrated by walking up to one of the chickens, and showed Rion. She looked at him, and then slowly lifted the chicken, it could hardly support its own body weight, and sat back down. "Does this look like a decent life to you?"

"Unbelievable, I thought that animals were given a good life on farms," said Rion.

"These are just the ones who are alive, because they are useful to humans."

"What do you mean?"

"Let me explain. Chickens are just the names for the birds. The female birds are called hens, and the male birds are called roosters. The hens are like a goldmine for the farmers because they lay eggs, so the hens are kept alive to lay eggs for their whole lives. But the roosters, when they are little sweet chicks, they are…"

"They are?" Rion' heart began to beat faster.

"These baby chicks, who have just been born, whose mother gave birth to them to live a happy life in this world. Those chicks are… never mind, I'll tell you some other time."

"What? Newborn chicks are what?" Rion looked concerned.

"I've lived on a farm all my life, I don't want you to know everything. But just understand this much, living life on a farm as an animal, is worse than being a slave. Come, let me introduce you to the horses."

Rion was disturbed at the revelations. This was a world away from what he thought farms were like in his imaginations. "What happens to the baby chicks?" he stopped Jenny and asked her more seriously this time.

"Okay, if you're insisting I'll tell you. The baby chicks are put in a giant shredder, alive. Their bodies and cut into thousands of pieces, and then thrown away, because they're useless to us humans."

Rion was shaken from Jenny's revelations. "Unbelievable," said Rion. "We humans enslave female chickens their whole lives, to take their eggs, and shred the young chicks alive, just because they're no use to us? Unbelievable, and it's unforgiveable."

Jenny understood Rion's reaction at hearing the truth and said "Yes, it's unbelievable, and that's why I'm trying to make a change in the world."

"Don't worry, I'll be with you," said Rion resolutely.

"Thank you, my love," said Jenny gratefully.

Next on Rion's tour, he noticed how the horses were kept in significantly better stables compared to the cramped spaces of other animals. Jenny walked up to a horse and said, "This is Legacy, would you like to take him for a ride?"

"He won't make me fall, will he?"

"No off course not, Legacy's my best friend, he'll never do such a thing!" said Jenny confidently.

Rion looked cautiously, but he accepted the challenge, "It's all up to you now god!" He said while looking in the sky. Jenny took Legacy out of the stable and helped Rion mount him. She held the reins of the horse, and took Legacy on a slow walk. Rion warmed to the experience, "Legacy is cool! How do I make him go faster?"

"He isn't a car! He's a horse. Don't do anything yet, I'll teach you another time, let Legacy get used to you first…" insisted Jenny.

Rion looked down and said "Legacy and me are friends now, aren't we Legacy?" Legacy nodded his head. "Do you know how to ride him?" asked Rion.

"Me?" Jenny smiled.

"Yes you must be good since you have Legacy in your back yard whenever you want to take him for a ride."

"Well I'm okay I guess."

"I'd like to see!" suggested Rion. Then Jenny took the opportunity to show Rion how she can ride a horse. Jenny mounted the horse with confidence. She pulled on the lead, and Legacy stood up on two feet making a loud announcement. Jenny took Legacy all around the farm as fast as a horse could go. Legacy was a real beauty and raced along like a breeze. Jenny returned to see Rion's astonished look, "Impressive," he said.

"See I'm not just a pretty face!" insisted Jenny.

"Yes, you're a very very pretty face!" Jenny gave Rion *the look* again, before he changed his words "Just joking!"

After returning Legacy to the stable, Jenny proceeded with the tour.

"These are my favourite friends!" said Jenny.

"Aren't they all?" Rion muttered to himself.

"Did you say something?"

"Oh no, I was just saying, you have so many friends, who you can call your best friends." Said Rion while changing his story.

Jenny smiled and replied "You're right, but the animals I will show you next are all extra special, because they never want to hurt anybody." Rion could see countless sheep in front of him. "they are soft, simple, and in a world of their own," said Jenny as she introduced Rion to a few of them "This is Emma, this is George, and this is Sheela." Rion stroked the sheep. As he looked at them, it reminded him of innocent children, much like the other animals, no agenda, no greed, simply interested in living, nothing else. As Rion stroked Sheela another sheep put his head in the way. "I think that George likes Sheela!" pointed out Rion.

"Really! I thought there was something going on between them two as well!" said Jenny.

"Yeah look, every time I stroke Sheela, George gets jealous and puts his head in the way to stop me from touching her! Wow, I didn't know that even sheep can feel jealous." said Rion.

"Animals are more like us humans than we think," Jenny said while stroking Sheela.

"See when you stroke Sheela, George doesn't care! When I stroke her, he butts his head in the way!"

"It's because George knows I'm a girl!" Jenny stuck her tongue out at Rion.

"Sheep are more intelligent than I thought," he realised.

After Jenny completed her tour of the farm, she asked Rion, "So what do you think of my friends, do you like them?"

"I like your friends, but... I don't like your farm," admitted Rion.

"Why?"

"I know you really like animals, but in your farm, you treat them like... Now I know why people say that they don't want to be treated like animals, because this is how animals are treated. In your farm, cows and chickens are fed antibiotics to make their bodies extra large, so that an industrial machine can suck the milk from cows and chickens can be forced to lay eggs. And when they stop laying eggs after a lifetime of pain, they don't get a chance to rest. Jenny, I thought you wanted to protect animal rights, but you're putting animals through such pain and suffering, it's terrible."

"I'm happy to see that you have feelings for these animals. If I couldn't protect these animals, at least you might one day. But before accusing me of causing this pain, at least ask me whose farm this is."

"It's your father's farm isn't it?"

"Yes it's my father's. But my father's not a normal man. He is a stone-cold man, he has no heart. If he cares, he only cares about money, if he loves, he only loves money, and if he listens, he only listens to money. You don't know how many times I've tried to explain to him, he just doesn't understand."

Rion felt a little guilty "I'm sorry Jenny, I didn't know that your…"

Jenny interrupted "But just think for a moment. You are so hurt after seeing just this one farm. Think how many farms like this there are in this city. Just think how many farms there are like this in this country. And just think how many farms like this there are in the world. None of those farms have any cameras to show what happens behind closed doors. People just pick up meat from supermarket shelves as if it's just food, not as if it's the dead pieces of once alive animals. If you want to change then first change yourself. You yourself eat meat, you never think about animals then. It's very easy to point fingers, but to make a change in the world is very difficult. Can you make any difference? Can you give up meat? You can't can you?" Rion said nothing, Jenny began to cry, she said "Then how can farms like this change, until there is a demand for meat from people like you?"

Rion walked up to Jenny, held her hand, wiped her tears and said "Jenny, from today, I promise you, that I will stop eating meat. From today, animals and me are the same. Your animal friends are now my animal friends. And from today, I will fight for the rights of these animals, I will try my best to wake up the sleeping human population."

Jenny was emotional because of Rion's promise, and leapt onto him as tightly as she could, she felt cold and was shivering. They both felt as though they had become one, with one goal, to protect animals. No longer were they on separate pages, rather singing from the same hymn sheet.

Just then they were snapped out of their bubble of love as a loud voice shouted from behind them "JENNIFER!"

Rion and Jenny both looked to see who shouted. There, a distance behind them, were five men. Jenny immediately let go of Rion, and took a step away from him. Rion looked at her but Jenny's gaze was firmly set on those five men, who were walking towards them with great authority and fearlessness.

Rion wasn't sure what he should do. Jenny wouldn't flinch. The five men wore suits, with the one in the middle wearing a different coloured suit to the rest of the men. As they approached closer, the man in the middle shouted "Jennifer, who is this man?"

Chapter Nine

The Brown

Rion said "we are…"

But he was interrupted by the man again who said "uh, Jennifer, tell me, who is this man?"

Jenny explained "This is my friend dad, I was upset because I got a low grade in my paper, so he was just consoling me. He's going to help me with my dissertation."

Rion was astounded to see that this was Jenny's father. He was even more surprised at why he was calling her Jennifer. Rion allowed Jenny to complete telling *her version of the truth*.

"What's his name?" asked Jenny's father.

Jenny interrupted Rion from speaking again "His name is David, he's very clever and he's my best friend."

Jenny's father looked at Rion inquisitively. He analysed Rion like a private detective, and circled him slowly like a crocodile. He said suspiciously "Nice to meet you young man, I am Mr. Brown," he extended his hand. On shaking hands with Mr. Brown Rion felt a strange sense of impending doom.

"So you study with my daughter?" asked Mr. Brown.

"Yes sir," replied Rion politely.

"It is with gratitude that I thank you for your kindest attention towards Jennifer. How can I repay you for your efforts?"

"Oh it's nothing Mr. Brown, I think it's my duty as Jenny's..." Jenny looked at him sternly. Rion changed his sentence "I mean as Jennifer's friend to look out for her and to make sure she is okay," said Rion informally.

"Well David, the very least I can do for you is give you a tour of our farm."

"I've already shown him," interrupted Jenny.

"Oh have you?" asked Mr. Brown in a foxy voice.

"Yes I showed him how we milk the cows. I also showed him the chicken hut, the sheep and the horses.

Mr. Brown laughed and said "Have you also told your friend..." Mr. Brown looked towards Rion as if he had forgotten his name.

Rion looked at Jenny and then said "David, Sir."

"Ah yes David, have you also told David the names that you have given to all your animal friends?"

"Not all the names dad," said Jenny. I told David some of the names."

"Well, have you shown your friend David where your friends will end up one day?"

"No dad, David is vegetarian."

Mr. Brown looked at David and said "David sounds like a Christian name, how can you be vegetarian?"

"I believe a person shouldn't be judged by his religion, but by his actions," said Rion. "Jennifer explained to me why it's good to be vegetarian, it made sense to me, so I adopted the new way of living."

Mr. Brown thought for a moment and said, "So, Jennifer explained to you that you should become vegetarian, and you became vegetarian? If she asks you to jump off a bridge will you jump off a bridge?"

"I can do anything for Jennifer Sir," said Rion without hesitating.

Mr. Brown repeated what Rion said very slowly "Ohhh, so you can do anything for Jennifer? You can become vegetarian for her, you can jump from a bridge for her…"

Rion and Jenny were both silent, anticipating what Jenny's Father would say next. Mr. Brown continued "Well perhaps some day we will put your devotion towards Jennifer to the test. But let's have lunch for now shall we?" They all made their way back towards the house where Rion would have lunch with a man who may one day be his father in-law.

As they sat down at the table to eat lunch, Mr. Brown asked "So David, tell me, what does your father do for a living?"

"My father passed away when I was young sir," said Rion politely.

"Oh, I'm terribly sorry to hear that. How about your mother?"

"My mum's a teacher sir, in a school."

"Oh, that's a very noble job isn't it? Looking after the future of our country, giving children education is an extremely noble profession indeed," said Mr. Brown as Rion smiled in agreement. "Do you have any siblings?"

"No sir, it's just me and my mother. Although we don't live a lavish lifestyle, we're very happy. My mum always says, be happy and you'll be the richest person in the world."

"Very good young man, perhaps your mother is not fully aware of the truth?"

"Why sir?" asked Rion.

"If you have money, you can buy food, a house, a car, you can buy happiness David, you can buy happiness."

"But sir, my mum always says that money can't buy happiness."

Mr. Brown sniggered, and said "Perhaps your mother is misinformed."

Just then, Rion's phone rang. He picked it up and said "I'll call you back." Rion looked towards Mr. Brown and said "yes sir, you were saying something."

Mr. Brown continued "Yes, I was saying that…"

Just then Jenny interrupted "Actually dad, David has to go to University, his class starts soon."

"Oh is that so?" asked Mr. Brown while looking at Rion.

Rion smiled and said "Yes sir, my class starts soon."

"Very Well David, I look forward to continuing this discussion with you another time."

"Sure sir," said Rion while shaking hands with Mr. Brown. He left Jenny's house feeling a sense of freedom, as if he had just come out of a prison. Jenny however, stayed at home, and waved goodbye to him as the door was shut closed by Mr. Brown.

The whole day, Rion spent time thinking about what Mr. Brown said. He tried ringing Jenny, but her phone was switched off. That evening Rion met with Hannah, Harvey and Eddy on the hill overlooking the sea. Hannah put her hand on Rion's shoulder and said "Do you want to marry her?" Rion nodded his head to say yes.

"It doesn't seem like her father will accept you," said Eddy. "The old man is so stuck in the past that he calls his daughter Jennifer. What's wrong with Jenny? It sounds do sweet and simple. But no, he wants to call her Jennifer, sounds like he took out the flower and kept the thorn!" Eddy seemed more angry than Rion!

"So true," agreed Harvey while laughing. "I don't think that *The Brown* will agree either. But have you asked Jenny if she wants marry you?" wondered Harvey.

Rion started to laugh, he said "No that's true I haven't proposed to Jenny yet! But I think I can see it in her eyes."

"It's okay to see love in her eyes, but it's also important to ask her if she will be your wife," said Hannah.

"Most probably she will say yes, but what if she says no?" pointed out Eddy.

Rion was sat in the middle with his friends either side of him like devils advocates.

"Yes, what if her father already promised her hand in marriage to somebody else?!" asked Harvey.

"Child marriage!" added Eddy.

"Yes…" agreed Harvey.

"What if she doesn't want to get married but only wants you to be a boyfriend?" asked Hannah.

"What if she works in a circus with hyenas?!" said Eddy. Everybody stared at Eddy, so he got flustered and said "Okay maybe she doesn't work in a circus, but you get the point?!"

Rion was swayed by his friends "You know maybe you guys are right... I should ask her to marry me, what if she brings out some wacky story to tell me why she can't marry me? Okay guys, I've decided, I will propose to Jenny!"

After two days, Rion was still unable to get in touch with Jenny, so he decided to go to Jenny's house in the middle of the night.

Meanwhile, Jenny was lying in her bed thinking how lucky she was to have a boyfriend like Rion. But she was also fearful of the future. Putting all worries to rest, Jenny was holding a picture of her late mother in the hands. She hugged the picture to her chest, and gently began to fall asleep. This was the only soft, safe sanctuary she had, her mother's picture, and her bed. This was the same safety that Jenny felt when she laid her head on Rion's arms. Little did she know, Rion's safe, warm hands and his sanctuary was heading for her now.

Rion parked his car 100 metres away from Jenny's front gate. He climbed over the gate and walked slowly towards Jenny's house. He tip toed towards the house, until he could see Jenny's bedroom window above him. Rion could see a pipe fixed to the wall. He climbed up the pipe slowly but surely. He knocked on the window. Jenny was scared, she didn't know what that sound was, she tried to fall asleep again. Then, another knock sounded on her window. She immediately got up from bed and opened her curtain. She saw Rion, Jenny couldn't believe it, she quickly opened the window and let Rion come in. Rion climbed through the window. Jenny said "Rion, at this time? What happened, is everything okay?" Rion asked Jenny to sit down on the bed with him, and he showed her a box. "This is for you, my lovely Jennifer," he said.

"I don't mind if the world calls me Jennifer, but from your mouth, I only like to hear Jenny." She complained.

"Okay my dear Jenny. But does anybody else call you Jennifer, or is it just that strange father of yours?"

"Don't say that, he's my dad…"

"Only joking only joking!" interrupted Rion. "Now open the box!"

But Jenny continued to speak "You know because his status is so high up in society he prefers to call me Jennifer in front of guests. But when we're alone he always calls me Jenny."

"Okay my dear Jenny I'm sorry. I'm glad to hear that your father considers me a guest. Now please, open the box!"

Jenny opened the box to see the most beautiful pink heart shaped cake which said on it *happy birthday Jenny*. Jenny was really surprised by this, as Rion took out a candle and put in in the cake to light it, she asked him "How did you know it's my birthday?"

"When we were in school, I looked in the student register to find out when your birthday is. I even got a present for you then, but you didn't come to school on your birthday, so I couldn't surprise you."

Jenny was impressed, she had a tear in her eye. Rion lit a candle in the cake. Jenny felt as though she was in heaven and all her wishes had come true at once. Rion began to sing a song as softly as he could "Happy Birthday to you, Happy Birthday to you, Happy birthday to Jenny, Happy Birthday to you!" They both fed each other some cake. Jenny said "Thank you so much, nobody has ever done this for me, this means a lot."

"I will look after you forever my baby," Rion suddenly remembered "why didn't you pick up the phone? I've been trying to call you for the last two days, I was so worried about you."

Jenny explained "I've been helping my father on the farm, and he didn't want me to get distracted so I turned off the phone."

"Oh, now I understand," said Rion, "How much longer will you be busy?"

"We're almost done now," said Jenny. "Tomorrow I should be able to see you at university, there's just a little bit more work to do, I'll do it later in the week."

"Good!" said Rion in a relieved and mischievous way. "Because now, I want to do some work with you!" He took Jenny in his arms and kissed Jenny on her neck, and she felt ticklish and began to giggle. They both felt mischievous, Jenny touched Rion's tummy and said "How many months left?"

Rion touched Jenny's tummy in return and said "hopefully nine and a half months!" Jenny hit Rion like a baby playing in its cradle. Rion admitted defeat and let her win. Rion said "There's something important I need to tell you."

"Tell me," said Jenny softly with anticipation.

"I will tell you, but not now, tomorrow…" Rion decided it was time to leave before Mr. Brown woke up and spoiled the party. Jenny slowly escorted Rion down the stairs, and out to the front door. Before leaving, Jenny said "I look forward to hearing what you have to tell me tomorrow."

"And I look forward to telling you, please be on time, tomorrow is an important day for me." Explained Rion one last time.

"I will," she smiled and closed the door, feeling excited about what he would say to her the next day.

Rion sneaked out the same way by climbing over the gate and then he drove off in his car.

The next day Jenny met Rion in the University canteen. She was ready to hear what he wanted to say, but he hadn't said anything yet. They were both twiddling their thumbs, and then Rion said "Will you…"

Jenny thought to herself *finally* "yes, will you…"

"Will you…" Rion took Jenny's hands, he could see Hannah, Eddy and Harvey in the distance looking at him while he tried to propose to Jenny. He saw Eddy eating an ice cream and then Rion said "Will you have some ice cream with me?" Jenny was annoyed, she let go of Rion's hands. She was pretending to be a little upset so that Rion could express his feelings more quickly. Rion just got up and actually brought back two ice creams. He ate one and since Jenny didn't want one he ate hers too. Some time passed like this, and Jenny said "We've been sitting here for two hours, at least now tell me what you wanted to say."

"Give some more time!" said Rion.

"How much more time?" asked Jenny.

"I don't know, five or six… hours."

Jenny said "Why are you thinking so much? You don't need to worry about anything!"

"I don't?" asked Rion.

"No, you don't need to worry!"

"What if you say no?" asked Rion.

"I won't say no," said Jenny with a pleasant angelic smile on her face.

"Oh, well, in that case," Rion took Jenny's hands, and started to speak again "Jenny, I Rion would like to ask you Jenny, if you would like to spend…" Rion still felt he couldn't get it out so he said "if you would like to spend… the next three hours with me so that we can watch a movie? Yes that's it! Let's go and watch a movie, come on girl." He took Jenny by the hand and chaperoned her to the cinema.

"But which film are we going to watch?" protested Jenny.

"Any film that you want!" said Rion as he grabbed her hand and took her with him. As they entered the cinema screen, Jenny suggested "let's sit here," she pointed towards some seats in the middle of the cinema hall.

But Rion said "No, I don't want to sit in the middle."

"Then where do you want to sit?" she asked.

Let's sit at the front!" He took Jenny right to the front row of the cinema hall. Rion was twitching his fingers as he sat next to her, Jenny said "Don't you think this is a little close to the screen?"

"Close? No, this is too far away! I like to sit at the front because that way you feel like you're a part of the movie. Like this." Rion spread his arms in front of the cinema screen as if he was bathing in its light.

"You know Rion, you don't have to be shy, you can ask me anything you want!"

Rion said very loudly "Huh? What did you say? I can't hear you." People sat behind told Rion to be quiet because he spoke too loudly. So, using it as an excuse, he stayed quiet and didn't reply to Jenny. Rion stood up to go outside. Jenny asked "Where are you going?"

"To get some popcorn!" he replied.

He went outside, where Eddy and Harvey were waiting for him. Eddy asked "How's it going?"

"Not good, how about you guys?" asked Rion.

"We're good to go!" said Harvey.

"Cool I'll see you when the film finishes." Rion went back inside. Jenny asked him "Where is the popcorn?" Rion looked at his empty hands and said "Oh, I asked the lady to give me no sugar, not no popcorn, wait a minute I'll go and get it."

Jenny said "It's okay, let's just watch the film together." Rion sat down and twiddled his fingers, as Jenny snuggled up close to him, and they both enjoyed the film together.

"What's this film about?" asked Rion.

"In this film, the woman has to choose between her career and the welfare of a village community, because she's a journalist." Jenny explained.

"Wow, you chose a great film," stated Rion.

After the movie, they came outside the cinema, and Rion told Jenny "Wait here, don't go anywhere, I'll be back in five minutes okay!"

Before Jenny could ask anything, Rion ran off, and Jenny was left waiting alone outside the cinema. Once again, she was left feeling bemused. She didn't know what was going to happen next, she didn't know why Rion was behaving so strangely the whole day. Jenny was standing outside, alone, in the cold, wondering where Rion had gone.

After a few minutes, Jenny was amazed to see the most stunning site she had ever witnessed in her life.

A decorated elephant was walking towards her. There were many dancers performing either side of the elephant. There was energetic music playing, heard by all those witnessing this procession. As the parade of dancers and the elephant came closer towards her, Jenny saw Hannah, Eddy and Harvey among the many dancers! But she couldn't believe what she saw as the person on the elephant became visible, it was Rion! He was on the elephant enjoying the music and looking with love and laughter at Jenny. The elephant came closer and closer to her. Jenny was blushing, Rion came down from the elephant, walked towards Jenny and he took her hands. Everybody was looking at Rion and Jenny, and some were even filming them on their mobile phones. Rion took out a ring from his pocket, offered it to Jenny, and asked her "I will look after you forever, your pain will be my pain, your happiness will be my happiness, I want to spend my whole life with you, and I want to ask you, would you like to spend your life with me? Will you Marry me Jenny? Will you marry me?" Rion was on one knee as he waited for Jenny's permission to put the ring on her finger.

Jenny thought for a brief moment, everybody was frozen, waiting for the response. The party atmosphere had transformed into pin drop silence. Everybody was watching to see what Jenny would say. Then she gave her verdict by nodding her head to say yes. Everybody went up in raptures. Hannah, Eddy and Harvey were celebrating around Rion and Jenny. Rion put the ring on Jenny's left hand ring finger, and lifted her in the air, spinning her around like a princess. Even the people watching started to dance in what seemed like a celebratory festival. The entire street had been transformed into a carnival atmosphere with nothing but celebration taking place everywhere. This moment was a moment for Rion and Jenny. Although a part of their self knew that the world was watching around them, they were almost in a world of their own. A bubble which could not be burst. This was the happiest time of their life. Nothing could separate them, nothing could hurt their love, and this, was the most powerful feeling imaginable.

All the spectators congratulated the lovely couple one by one.

Eddy said to Jenny "You've taken our Rion from us! Until now, he was ours, but now, he'll spend all his time with you!"

Harvey said to Eddy, "No that's not possible! I've decided, I will be their adopted child!" He stood in the middle like a little baby.

Hannah had always felt a special bond with Rion, she said to Jenny "Congratulations, you're very lucky, please look after Rion." Jenny smiled and said "Sure, I promise." She hugged Hannah, and could almost feel her emotions.

After a couple of hours, when the festivities were over, Jenny and Rion were alone, holding hands, walking in the park.

"I want to tell you something," said Jenny.

Rion stopped walking and said "I know what you'll say…"

"What will I say?" Jenny was worried.

"You'll say that you love me, and you can't wait to spend the rest of your life with me." Jenny looked a little lost, and covered up her inner feelings with a smile. "Oh, that reminds me, how's our daughter? We have to go and see her, right?" asked Rion.

"Our daughter?" asked Jenny.

"Yes! Natalia, remember?"

"Oh, off course, Natalia…" said Jenny.

"You said we could meet her one more time, today? Let's go!"

"But I want to tell you something…" said Jenny slowly and carefully.

"Tell me later, we have to meet our daughter before she leaves forever." Said Rion in a care free manner.

Jenny agreed reluctantly, and they went to see Natalia at the children's shelter.

"What's the name of the shelter?" asked Rion as they reached the destination.

"Destiny rescue," said Jenny.

"Wow, cool name!"

"Yep, their mission is to rescue, restore, protect and empower children stuck in sexual exploitation and slavery."

"Very noble," said Rion while entering the building.

Inside, he saw a number of children as young as three and as old as eighteen, who were all engaged in learning, playing or supporting each other. There seemed to be a community spirit in this shelter, unlike anything Rion had seen before. Just then, Jenny brought Natalia to him, and she gave Rion a hug and said "Hello uncle Rion."

"Hello Natalia! How are you?" he said, as he was mesmerized by this angelic girl who had come so close to his heart.

"They will take be back tonight, I don't want to go," said Natalia.

"Where are they taking her Jenny?" asked Rion.

"They're taking her back to her parents, in Slovenia...." She said. "Aren't they Natalia?"

"You are my parents now," said Natalia as she hugged Jenny and Rion together.

Rion and Jenny looked at each other, helpless as to what they should do. Rion said, "If she wants to stay with us, then can't we adopt her?" Jenny looked at Rion mischievously. Rion said "I don't mean to flirt with you, but now that we know we will get married, can't we adopt Natalia?" Natalia was listening with hope in her eyes.

Jenny's spirit was dampened, and she said "Unfortunately not, we can't adopt her."

"But why? According to the law, we can adopt her…"

"The problem is not the law." interrupted Jenny.

"Then what's the problem?" asked Rion.

Jenny took Rion outside, where they sat on the bench with Natalia. Jenny pointed up at the moon and said "Do you know what's so special about the moon?" Rion was lost for words, Jenny continued to speak "You can see the moon, you can experience the moon, but it can never be yours."

Rion became a little more serious and said "What do you mean? just tell me clearly. Why do you say the moon can never be yours?"

Jenny looked up at the sky, and then with tears suddenly appearing from nowhere she said, "I can't marry you Rion, sorry, we can't get married."

Rion was shocked, all of a sudden, it was as if the whole world came down on him and his heart broke into a thousand pieces, he said "But just now you said that…"

"I know," interrupted Jenny "I didn't want to say no to you in front of everybody. Even when I said yes, I knew my father won't let us get married. And my suspicion came true, he just called me an hour ago, he said he wants me to marry his friend's son. He ordered me to come home as soon as possible so he can arrange our marriage." Rion was in complete shock. Jenny went on to explain "You don't know my father, he's ruthless. If he finds out that you proposed to me, then he will punish me for sure, but I'm more afraid of what he'll do to you."

Rion smiled, wiped Jenny's tears and said "What will he do to me?" Jenny wanted to speak but Rion stopped her and said "Jenny, look, every father in the world only wants his daughter to be happy, wherever she is. Your father will only say no to me because he doesn't know me yet. Once he sees how nice I am, how I can look after you, and how much we love each other, I'm sure he'll agree to our marriage."

"Do you really want to marry me?" asked Jenny seriously after wiping her tears.

"Off course," replied Rion.

"Well then there's only one way. We have to run away with each other." Said Jenny seriously.

"Run away?!"

"Yes! That's the only way, let's run away from here, so far away, that nobody can disturb our love, just you and me. Please Rion, please?"

Rion tried to calm Jenny down and said "we love each other Jenny, we haven't committed a crime…"

"But in my father's eyes love is a crime, we have to run…" she interrupted.

Rion held her cheeks and interrupted her again, "Until today your father has seen the power of money, now let me show him the power of love. Once, at least once, let me show him how much I love you, maybe he will agree."

Jenny shook her head to say "No, he will never listen…"

"He will," said Rion. "Just give him a chance. He gave birth to you Jenny, he looked after you so many years. Every father has a dream to marry off his own daughter himself. To invite the whole family to take part in the celebration. At least give him one chance to live that dream."

Finally, Jenny agreed, she said "Okay, but on one condition," Rion listened carefully. "First I will tell him that we love each other, if he agrees, then I'll call you to our house, then you can tell him anything you want." Rion was satisfied but before he could speak Jenny continued, "But if he doesn't agree, promise me, that you will take me very far away from here, so that my dad can never see me again."

Rion held Jenny by her shoulders and said "Okay I promise, if your father doesn't agree, then I will take you far away from here, and then it will be just you and me in our little world, okay?"

Jenny was still shedding tears however she was more peaceful inside. Meanwhile Natalia had fallen asleep on Jenny's lap. Rion said "But I have one condition too... You have to wipe your tears, and come with me to have something to eat! I'm hungry now! Okay?"

"Okay," Jenny smiled, they took Natalia to her room, and allowed her to fall comfortably to sleep.

On the way out, Rion spoke to one of the members of staff working at the Destiny Rescue shelter, and said "We would like to adopt Natalia, if you could postpone her trip to Slovenia, we would really appreciate it."

The staff member replied "You will have to speak to the manager regarding adoptions sir, but I can't see any issues with that, you both seem like a caring couple." Jenny and Rion smiled, the staff member continued, "Natalia won't go this week anyway, you have until next weekend, because actually her parents were also hoping that Natalia could find a new family to look after her in America. And not only you, but another couple were also interested in adopting her, so Natalia will stay here for one more week."

"That's great news, but don't her parents want to keep Natalia with them?"

"Well they do, but they also know their limitations, they know that they cannot provide for Natalia as well as perhaps you can. If Natalia can find a new family here, then they're happy for Natalia to go."

"Oh, that's great news," said Rion as he looked happily at Jenny. "We'll speak to the manager in the next few days."

Overjoyed at the fact that they still have some time to adopt Natalia, Jenny and Rion both went to have a meal together. Then when Rion dropped Jenny home he said "Speak to your father about us…"

"I will, tomorrow, when he's in a good mood, I'll tell him everything, I hope he agrees."

"Me too. But if he doesn't then don't worry, I'll take you far away."

"Thank you, my future husband," said Jenny happily.

"You're welcome my future wife!"

The next day Rion waited for Jenny to tell him how her meeting with her father went. The whole day, he was waiting, but Jenny didn't call, and she didn't answer her phone either. This wait turned from a day to two days, and then from two days to a few days. He called Jenny many times, but she wouldn't answer the phone. Rion was anxiously looking at his phone every five minutes hoping it would ring. He received a text message, it was Eddy, asking Rion "has she replied yet?" Rion called Eddy, Harvey and Hannah to the usual seaside location to discuss the situation.

"Do you think her father's going to listen?" asked Eddy.

"Why don't you just run away with her?" suggested Harvey.

"I have to try at least once guys," explained Rion. "My mum always said, do things peacefully if you can, war should be the final option."

"This isn't a war!" said Harvey.

"Yes, but this is love, and I want to win love with love, not with hate," said Rion.

Hannah added "Rion's right, we have to support him. Love is the best way to win love. And it's only been a few days, give it some time, maybe her father will agree."

Harvey was frustrated, he asked "So what shall we do? Just wait for her to call you, and say come Rion, my dad is happy for you to marry me, let's get married?"

Just then Rion's phone rang, coincidentally, it was Jenny! After a brief conversation with her, Rion ended the phone call, and looked at his friends.

"What did she say?" asked Harvey.

"She said that her father has invited me for dinner tomorrow night and he wants to discuss our marriage!"

"Really!" shouted everybody! Hannah, Harvey and Eddy cheered as they gave Rion a group hug.

Hannah came close to Rion and said "Be careful, I worry about you sometimes." Rion gave Hannah a hug and said "god won't let anything bad happen to me, because you worry about me so much." Hannah was moved by this and clung onto him.

The next day, Rion went an extra step further to prepare himself to visit Jenny and Mr. Brown. He took Harvey, Eddy and Hannah to pick out a stylish suit for him, along with a matching tie, shiny new shoes, and even a new watch. He bought a present for Jenny and her father. He rehearsed his walk, his talk and his style as much as he could to make sure that he could impress his future father in-law.

After spending the day preparing with his friends, the time came for Rion to bid his friends farewell, and face this moment alone.

Chapter Ten

Scrutiny

Finally, the moment of truth came, Rion drove up to Jenny's driveway, stepped out of the car, and walked up to her front door. After one final check to make sure he smelled okay, looked okay, and felt okay, he knocked on the door Jenny opened the door to welcome Rion. She was wearing an elegant red dress.

"You look wonderful," he said to Jenny as he gave her flowers and some presents. "I'm not late, am I?" he asked, as he walked in carefully.

"Late? You're ten minutes early! Come in, my father's waiting for you inside." Jenny showed Rion to the living room, where Mr. Brown was waiting for him.

Rion walked up to him, and said "Hello Mr. Brown."

"Ah David my boy, come in, take a seat. You're early, very punctual I see."

Rion remembered that Jenny had lied to her father and told him that his name is David, not Rion. Jenny gave Rion and her father some Tea. Rion smiled like a shy girl and sat down next to Mr. Brown. He then remembered to give him the gift he had brought for him.

Mr. Brown obliged "Why thank you, how thoughtful of you." Mr. Brown then said to Jenny,

"Why don't you go and prepare the dinner, I will discuss everything with Rion." Jenny smiled, and reluctantly obeyed her father, leaving Rion alone with Mr. Brown.

"So, you've become quite famous David?" asked Mr. Brown.

Rion was confused, "Famous? I don't understand," he asked.

"Yes, famous. You seem to have become an internet sensation." Rion was still confused.

Mr. Brown showed Rion a video from the internet, the video was of Rion proposing to Jenny. The title of the video was *Boy's stylish proposal to girl.*

Rion spat the tea in his mouth back into the cup, he was shocked to see it. He hesitantly said "that's not me sir."

The video then zoomed into Rion's face, showing him proposing to Jenny. Rion said "That is me sir, I mean..."

"It's okay David, it's okay, you don't need to explain yourself."

"I don't?" said Rion with relief.

"No!... One million views in three days, your video has gone viral!"

"Thank you sir," said Rion, not knowing what to expect next.

"That day, when I first saw you with Jenny, I had a feeling something might be going on between you two," said Mr. Brown.

Rion smiled and looked down trying to avoid eye contact.

"So, it's true, right? You... and Jennifer, hmm?"

Rion smiled and nodded to say yes.

"Why didn't you tell me that day huh? If you had told me that day, it would have been good. Because, if you told me that day, I would have slaughtered you instead of the animals."

Suddenly Rion felt as though his heart had sank. He had a feeling of a black hole in his heart, because he was insulted by a man who he thought would one day be his father-in law.

Mr. Brown stood up and asked Rion angrily "What are you trying to prove by doing all this?" Rion wasn't sure what Mr. Brown meant. Mr. Brown continued "What will you get by doing all this? Do you know how much money I have? Do you know my status in society? Do you think I will sacrifice my image in society for a little boy from London, who has nothing more than a smile on his face and love in his heart? I don't think so RION, I don't think so."

Rion's heart was pounding. Mr. Brown insulted his love for Jenny, and perhaps more surprisingly, he knew his real name.

Mr. Brown said, "A little school child from London is reunited with his first childhood love again in America. What a sweet little love story. *I don't think so Rion, I don't think so.*"

By now Rion felt as though he had lost everything, nevertheless he continued to listen, for Jenny's sake.

"What did you think? I didn't know who you were? Jennifer would tell me that your name is David and I would believe her? I was suspicious of you the moment I saw your dirty eyes looking at my daughter. I have eyes and ears everywhere. My men kept an eye on Jennifer since the first day she met you. They told me everything. I know you don't call her Jennifer, you call her Jenny. I had my eyes on you, and you didn't even know it."

Rion was speechless, he didn't have any idea what had hit him, and continued to bear this onslaught from Mr. Brown.

"Now, I will give you two options. Either you have dinner peacefully, and don't let Jenny hear a word of what has happened between us, I will let you go from here alive. Today, in front of Jenny I will accept your hand in marriage for her, but after eating dinner, I want you to tell her that you don't want to marry her, because you have found another woman who you have fallen in love with."

Rion was shocked to hear these words from Jenny's father.

Mr. Brown went on to say "There is no reason why I should be the villain in this story. You can be the villain, I'll console my daughter and tell her that we can find another boy for her, since you have fallen in love with somebody else."

Rion mustered the courage to look up at Mr. Brown and asked "And what is my second option?"

"Listen carefully..." Mr. Brown grabbed Rion by his shirt collar and said "... your second option, is that even if try to meet Jenny again after today, I will punish Jenny by putting her through hell, but you... My men will grab you and you will disappear from the face of this earth faster than if you were struck by lightning when you least expected it. It's up to you.

You choose, your love, or both of your lives, decide now."

Rion was shaken, hurt and emotionally drained because of this completely unexpected attack on his pure and true love for Jenny. Although his heart felt as though it had been stabbed a thousand times, Rion kneeled on his knees while Mr. Brown was still sat on the couch. He gathered his feelings, thoughts, hopes and emotions, and he mustered up the courage to speak, "Sir, I am sorry if I made any mistake. I am not like other boys. I don't want to run after Jenny because of materialistic reasons. I'm glad to see that you have a lot of money. I'm happy to feel that you are very successful. I'm sure you must have earned that money with years of hard work, and only you know the sacrifices you've made to get to this position."

Mr. Brown was listening intently to every word that came out from Rion's mouth.

Rion continued, "But I really love your daughter sir. Someday perhaps you must have loved a girl too. Imagine yourself in my shoes. What would you have done to win the love of a girl? I really love Jenny, I love her from the bottom of my heart. I will do everything to look after her for as long as I live. I will take care of her until my last breath. I love *her* sir, not her beauty. If one day she becomes old, I will love her just as much as I do today. I just don't want her to come with me without your blessings. I want you to bless her. I want us to be a happy family. I know I'm not rich, but I will work hard. I promise I will become successful, so successful that the whole world will see. Just give me one chance, please. I will do everything I can to earn money. I will work day and night. Please give me one chance to marry your daughter and look after her forever. Please, please, please." With these words, Rion finished speaking, he lowered his head to the floor, begging Mr. Brown for his love, Jenny.

Mr. Brown stood up in front of Rion and said "If you kiss my shoes, and beg me for Jenny's hand, then maybe I will consider whether or not she can marry you."

After just a fraction of time to compose himself, Rion said "Sure sir, my ego is not bigger than my love for Jenny. I can you're your feet, and ask for Jenny's hand in marriage. If this is what it takes for Jenny to be happy, then I'll happily do it." Rion slowly bent down to obey Mr. Brown's command. He kissed Mr. Brown's shoes, slowly rose up, still on his knees and said "Sir, now may I please marry your daughter?"

Mr. Brown leaned forward looking Rion in the eyes and said, "I don't want my daughter to marry a slave who has kissed my shoes. Now get up, have dinner, and get out of my house. And don't think about contacting Jenny again, if you do, your life will be finished."

Rion felt humiliated by the experience he had been put through. Mr. Brown gave him a tissue to wipe his tears. He stood Rion up, and gently slapped his suit as if to clean the dirt from it. Then he said to Rion in a more pronounced voice "Come my boy, let's eat, Jenny has cooked my favourite dish, I'm sure you must be really hungry." Rion agreed silently, as if accepting destiny's cruel fate. He walked slowly towards the kitchen, where Jenny had prepared the food for them.

Rion was sitting at the dinner table as if his soul had been removed from his body. But then Mr. Brown reminded him by saying, "Please have something to eat David. Jenny has made such lovely food, after all you should eat for her happiness, don't you think?"

Rion produced a fake genuine looking smile and started to take food. Jenny had prepared turkey for her father, and vegetarian pasta and pizza for herself and Rion. Jenny also took her place to eat.

After dinner, Rion said, "Thank you for the food, it was lovely," he politely took Mr. Brown's leave. Rion slowly left their home from the front door.

Jenny waved goodbye to him, and Rion waved goodbye back, but it all seemed to go in slow motion, as if this was the last time that he could see her. His heart was utterly broken, he didn't know what to do. Rion walked painfully back to his car, and felt as though the world had been taken away from him. With his empty heart, mind and body, Rion drove away slowly, like an unconscious body, that was somehow awake. After he reached home, Rion lied down in his bed, and cried more than he had ever cried before. While his tears were still flowing, he sent a text message to Jenny, saying "I'm sorry Jenny, I can't marry you, please forgive me, because I'm in love with another girl, Rion." After sending this message, he covered himself with his duvet, pushed his head into his pillow, and cried his heart out for the rest of the night.

Many days passed, painfully and slowly, yet Rion didn't try to contact Jenny, and heard nothing back from her. Rion visited Natalia at the Destiny Rescue shelter, he was depressed. Natalia looked at Rion with hope, but he could only say "Sorry Natalia, aunty Jenny and me won't be able to adopt you."

Natalia started to cry and said "but you said you will adopt me uncle Rion, I don't want to go."

Rion had no choice, he said "Don't worry Natalia, everything will be okay, your parents will look after you."

Natalia wouldn't listen to anything and started to cry while shouting and screaming in protest.

Just then the member of staff who spoke to Rion and Jenny last time spoke to him and asked "what happened sir, you were going to adopt Natalia?"

"Yes, but now, we can't marry each other," said Rion.

"Oh, I'm sorry to hear that, but if you couldn't marry her, then you shouldn't have given false hope to this child." Natalia was in tears, so a member of staff took her away. Rion was left alone to say "I know," to himself, as he also began to cry. Rion left the Destiny Rescue shelter in tears. The next day, Natalia was flown back to her country, Slovenia. Rion was left stranded, with all his dreams broken at once.

Hannah, Eddy and Harvey tried their best to console Rion, but nothing would make him feel better. They tried taking him out to have fun, to theme parks, shopping, cinema, but nothing would cheer him up. Rion felt like an empty body with no soul. He would almost look like a psychiatric patient, without emotion, without feeling, and without love. Rion found brief moments of tranquility when he went to the different places of worship where Jenny had taken him before. He tried praying. He thought that at least one god from the many faiths would understand his pain. He would pray to Jesus, to Allah, to Krishna, to Buddha, to Guru Nanak. In fact, he prayed at all these different places of worship every single day. Rion hoped that if even one of these gods blessed him, then Jenny could be reunited with him. But deep inside his heart, he knew that this wish couldn't come true. Still, to console himself, and to convince himself that somehow, some miracle might happen, he would pray to god every day. He would go home, and just sit in his bed, for hours and hours on end, without any activity, or goal. Rion began to miss university lectures, he began to binge eat, binge sleep, his whole life was beginning to derail.

One day, Rion was walking on his way to a rare university lecture, when suddenly his mobile phone began to ring. It was from a new phone number which Rion didn't recognise. He answered the phone "Hello." After two long months, it was somebody special on the phone...

Chapter Eleven

Resurrection

"Jenny, is that you?" asked Rion.

"How much money do you have in the bank?" asked Jenny.

Rion was surprised by this question but he instantly replied "Around 17,000 dollars, is everything okay?"

"Great, can you go to a bank, keep 2,000 dollars cash, and transfer the rest of the money into my name through any international money transfer service."

"Sure Jenny, but..."

Before Rion could say anything else she interrupted "I'm running away with you! Can you pick me up from the bus stop outside my house in exactly two hours?"

"Running away? But... even after I sent you that text message?"

"Rion, I know that message was fake, you love me more than Romeo loved Juliet. Now please, hurry up, transfer the money, and then meet me at the bus stop. I'll be waiting there for you in exactly two hours okay?"

"Okay..."

Jenny hung up the phone before he could say anything else. Rion was suddenly charged up with more energy than ever. He ran as fast as he could to his car, and then he drove to the bank. He was running towards the bank when suddenly somebody came in front of him and said "If you've suffered an accident or injury, we can claim compensation for you." Rion said "I'm really busy right now!" and he continued hastily towards the bank. After negotiating his way through a long line of customers by begging them to let him go first, Rion transferred all his savings into Jenny's name by international money transfer. He withdrew the last 2000 dollars in his account as cash. There were just twenty minutes left for two hours to be up. Rion drove to Jenny's house as fast as he could just under the two hour deadline, and looked for a bus stop. He saw the bus stop outside her house, and he waited at a distance.

After waiting for a few nervous minutes, Jenny came running from her house towards his car, she opened the door, sat inside, and said "quickly, let's go!"

"But where are we going?" asked Rion.

Jenny explained, "to the registry office, we should get married first, after that nobody can stop us from being together."

"But what about your father, if he catches us do you know what will happen?"

"What will happen? At most we will die? I don't care. I'd rather live with you as your wife for one day, than live my whole life separately from you. Id' rather live like an elephant for a day than live like a sheep forever, how about you, are you an elephant or a sheep? "

"Me?... aaa" Rion was wondering what to say.

"Never mind, let's go!" said Jenny. Even in this moment of pressure, Rion was astonished by Jenny's wisdom and courage. He drove to the registry office as fast as he could, where Jenny had already booked an appointment for them to get married. Inside, the registrar was completing the marriage vows for another couple. They waited patiently.

While standing in the hall for their turn, Rion asked something that was on his mind, "But how did you know that I love you so much? Didn't you think I could love another girl like I said in the text message?"

"No, you made that proposal remember, it's a YouTube sensation now, 12 million views! I still remember that day, you were so nervous at how to tell me that you want to marry me!"

"You're right Jenny, I can't live without you, I can't imagine living life without you," this time, with full confidence, Rion kneeled down and asked Jenny once more, "Will you Jenny Brown, take me Rion Rai to be your lawfully wedded husband?"

Jenny smiled and said "I do!"

"Too right you do! Jenny Rai sounds too irresistible. Now, I may kiss the bride!"

As he leaned forward to kiss Jenny, the Registrar appeared from the marriage hall and said "You can do it for real, Mr. Rion, Miss Jenny, come this way." The registrar escorted them to the marriage registry hall.

Eventually the moment of truth came, the registrar asked "Do you Rion Rai, take Jenny Brown, to be your lawfully wedded wife?" Rion smiled at Jenny, knowing that the world would be his oyster from the moment he said the following words "I do." Then, the same question was asked by the registrar to Jenny "Do you, Jenny Brown, take Rion Rai to be your lawfully wedded husband?" Without hesitation, and with complete trust in her future husband to look after her until her last breath, she said "I do." The registrar went on to say the most meaningful words to Jenny and Rion they had ever heard "I hereby pronounce you husband and wife. You may now kiss the bride." Rion and Jenny were so emotional, that after what felt like a life long journey, they were unified in this purest bond of love. Rion took Jenny's face, and leaned his forehead on hers while looking into her eyes and subliminally asking her *can you believe it, we're finally married?* Tears of happiness were rolling down Jenny and Rion's cheeks. Their happiness in this moment had no bounds. They kissed each other with heavenly bliss, and officially joined each other with their heart, mind and soul.

After the brief ceremony, they collected their marriage certificate and Rion asked the registrar "If we lose this certificate for any reason, then is there any way that…"

"Don't worry, if you lose this certificate, you can order another copy by calling us on this number," the registrar gave Rion a business card for the registry office. "Even a friend or relative can come by and take a look at the records and verify that you two are married."

"Thank you, sir," said Rion, "you have done something very special for us, and by helping us, we will always be indebted to you."

"You're welcome, and if there's anything else I can help with, please let me know," said the registrar.

"Yes, thank you sir, Rion we have to go now," said Jenny, as she took his hand and rushed him outside.

"But we're married now, we don't need to be afraid," said Rion.

"No, my father will come looking for us as soon as he finds out that I'm not at home. He locked me in the house for the past two months because I told him that I will only marry you," Jenny explained.

"What!" Rion was shocked to hear this. "You were locked at home for two months?"

"I'll explain later, let's go the airport first," suggested Jenny.

"But where will we fly to?"

"I'm not sure, but you transferred the money, didn't you?"

"Yes, I have 2,000 dollars cash, and I transferred 15,000 to you."

"Great," said Jenny, "let's go." Before getting into the car Jenny asked "Do you mind if I drive?"

"Sure," said Rion. "But why?"

Jenny got into the car, fastened her seatbelt, started the engine and said "because you drive like my driving instructor," and she put her foot down on the accelerator big time. She swerved in and out of traffic like a superwoman. Rion felt like he was sitting on a roller coaster. He put on a brave face, while hiding his fear from Jenny's adventurous driving skills. They were at the airport in less than fifteen minutes. Rion was taken back by his wife's driving skills, he said "Very impressive Jenny, I never knew you were such a good driver!" Then while getting out of the car he said to himself "I wonder why women change so much after marriage?"

They entered the Logan international airport in Boston and looked at the flights screen showing the departures. Rion was looking around casually when he saw Jenny's eyes fixated on a single point on the screen. Jenny's eyes fell on one particular destination which she wanted to travel to all her life. That particular flight, was to India.

"But don't we need visas to go to India Jenny?" Rion asked with intent.

"We do, but we can get the visas when we land, upon arrival."

"India's a very hot country... And isn't it too far, it's like a sixteen hour flight."

"But I love India," said Jenny, with an innocent smile. "Can we go to India, please?" she tried to look as sweet as possible.

Rion took a deep breath and said "Right where's the ticket desk?" Jenny leapt up onto Rion to give him a sloppy cheek kiss. They did the research and found out that the tickets weren't too expensive, and the next flight was in three hours, perfect for clearing security. So Rion bought two tickets. Once they passed the security check points and proceeded to the duty-free shopping area, Jenny ran towards the expensive perfume and make-up section like a lost child that returned home after many days. She couldn't help but stare at all these items which had some sort of magical pull gravitating her towards them. Rion tried his best to keep her away but the effort was in vain. She couldn't keep herself away. Eventually Rion managed to take her hands and tell her something, "Jenny, I know you have a lot of desires, but right now, we need to save every last penny for our trip in India. I know we just got married, but I can't buy any of these things for you now. One day, when I become rich and successful, I promise I'll let you buy any of these things, but for now, please control yourself."

Jenny smiled, looked at Rion and said "These materialistic things aren't important for me Rion, you are. For a moment, I forgot the situation we're in, and ran after these meaningless things like a little girl. I don't mind if you don't become rich. Even if one day we have nothing, I will still live happily with you." Rion kissed Jenny on the forehead, and said "thank you for understanding love." They both made their way towards the departure gate.

After boarding the plane, Jenny took her window seat, while Rion sat next to her. Then he surprised Jenny by giving her one perfume that she saw in the duty-free shop.

"When did you get this?" she asked. "How did you know that I wanted this perfume?"

Rion explained "When you were running around in the shop, there was one perfume you were looking at the most, so while you were too busy looking at everything, I went and bought this for you." Jenny was delighted.

While the plane was gathering momentum on the runway to take off, Rion put his hands around Jenny's waist, as they both looked out of the window. The sensation that was felt by both of them was inexplicable, as the roar of the engine somehow reflected the feeling of excitement and expectation felt by both of them in their hearts. As the flight took off, their honeymoon of a lifetime, had begun.

On the sixteen hour long journey, Rion explored the free-view entertainment and stumbled across an Indian movie, luckily with subtitles. He found it to be quite interesting, and tried waking up Jenny to watch, but she was too busy sleeping on his shoulder. After giving up his lazy attempts of trying to wake her up, he simply admired Jenny while she was asleep. He let her stay in this soft protective bubble that she was in, and eventually fell asleep too.

As the journey came to an end and the plane was about to land, Rion and Jenny looked out of the window, and felt a sense of freedom. Jenny said "I feel relieved, finally we've escaped the problems, and come thousands of miles away. I feel like the world's happiness is in my heart now Rion, because you're with me."

After landing, the first thing that hit them when they disembarked was the heat. It was much hotter than they had imagined. However, Jenny and Rion had more pressing concerns. They had to clear the immigration check, and get their visitors visas. The queue for this job was a long and chaotic one. But, after one hour, they reached the front of the line. Rion told Jenny "Let me do the talking, you just wear this as a head scarf," he gave Jenny a long cloth. He took the front position while talking to the official at the desk. The immigration officer asked for their passports, and then asked them, "What's the purpose of your stay?"

"We just got married, we're here on honeymoon," explained Rion.

"Have you got any proof to show that you are married?"

Rion took out the marriage certificate he was given in America, and showed the officer "Yes sir, here it is."

"Do you have any photos with family members or a marriage function?"

Rion looked at Jenny, and then looked at the immigration officer and replied "No sir, we haven't, we will have the ceremony later."

The immigration officer looked at another colleague working with him, and said something in the native language Hindi "In dono ne bhaag ke shaadi ki hai!" The colleague looked at Jenny and Rion and laughed. The immigration officer looked at Rion and said to him "let me ask you a question. Have both run away from your homes and got married?"

Rion and Jenny were scared, not knowing what to say. "What if I rip up this marriage certificate, and ask you, *what evidence you have that you two are married?* Do you have any other evidence? I can rip up your marriage certificate now, and I can tell the police that you have kidnapped this girl, what will you do?"

Rion and Jenny were both petrified and enlightened at the same time, they were completely speechless.

The immigration officer told Rion to come closer, he said "Don't worry, can you see that photocopy booth over there? Make ten photocopies of this marriage certificate, and keep them with you. Email a copy of this certificate to one or two of your most trustworthy friends. And don't tell anybody that you got married today. If anybody asks, tell them you've been married for six months and only give them a copy of this certificate if it's absolutely necessary. Okay?" The immigration officer stamped Jenny and Rion's passports and said "Welcome to India." He let them through with a pleasant smile. After a feeling of relief, Jenny and Rion both headed straight for the photocopy booth, where they made photocopies of their passports and marriage certificate.

Jenny asked Rion, "How much cash do you have with you?"

"After paying for the flights, I still have seven hundred dollars."

After changing dollars into rupees at the foreign exchange outlet, they made their way to the taxi booking counter. When the assistant asked where they would like to go, Jenny replied "I would like to go to the Iskcon Ashram in Vrindavan." Rion looked at Jenny and wondered what this place was. The assistant said it would take three hours from Delhi Airport by taxi.

"Are you sure you want to go to this place? What is it?" asked Rion.

Jenny calmly replied "Do you trust me?"

Rion closed his eyes and then said "Yes, more than myself."

"Then trust me one hundred percent. I am taking you to a place which is close to my heart."

When they left the airport, a random person bumped into Rion by accident, and didn't apologize, but instead continued on his path. The traffic on the roads was a little more chaotic and disorganized as they made their way out of the city. Rion realised that India is a little more different than other countries. On the outside at least, it seemed to be unique in some sense.

On the way, Jenny saw an international money transfer service, so she requested the taxi driver to wait while they went in and withdrew the money Rion had transferred to Jenny. The total of fifteen thousand dollars was enough money to fill up Jenny's rucksack.

While she got the money, Rion stepped outside the money transfer office for a while and noticed that the materialistic aspect of India seemed to be developing fast, with high rise buildings being constructed throughout the city. However he realised that perhaps it was not the materialistic side of India that Jenny was interested in.

After taking the money, they left for the Iskcon ashram in Vrindavan. As they reached closer to the ashram, the surrounding environment was visibly more beautiful, calming, and natural.

Jenny and Rion entered the Ashram, and checked into the room. Although he didn't say anything as he was testing the waters slowly, in his heart Rion was really pleased with Jenny's choice.

As they entered their room, Rion found that it was a simple en-suite room with two single beds and a fan. Rion was not too impressed. He pushed the two single beds together and he said "Nice choice Jenny, great hotel." in a sarcastic tone.

Jenny held Rion's hands and said "this is not a hotel Rion, it's an ashram!"

"Okay Jennifer! Why don't you tell me what the deal is with this ashram of yours?!"

"This is an Iskcon ashram! It stands for International society of Krishna Consciousness! It is a spiritual and religious place, where we can rest our mind, body and soul, to help us rejuvenate, and go back to our lives in the city with more purpose and meaning."

"You mean a retreat?" he asked with a realistic look on his face.

"Maybe, but not exactly. You see, a retreat only helps you to relax, and an ashram will help us to find out what is the meaning of life… This ashram was started by one man called Srila Prabhupada, who came to Chicago from India with nothing more than a suitcase of clothes. And from knowing nobody he established hundreds of ashrams around the world and now he has followers of all religions and all races throughout the world."

"This is why I love you so much," said Rion reluctantly.

"Why do you love me?" asked Jenny with a cheeky smile.

Rion sat down on the bed with her and said "Because you always have a sense of purpose in your life… Even on our first date, you didn't take me to the cinema, or to do shopping, or back to your place, you actually took me to a human rights rally! And even now, you brought me to an ashram for our honeymoon. You are something different aren't you?!"

Jenny laughed and said "It was really nice of you to come to the human rights rally and…"

Rion interrupted "No Jenny, it is nice of you to think about the world, and not just us. Every girl in the world thinks about how pretty she looks, about shopping, about her career, her family, about her money, that's it. But you, you think about the world. That's why I love you, because even though you love me a lot, you realise that there are much more important things in the world than just us."

"How do you know I love you so much?" she asked, looking a little more seductively at Rion this time.

"If you didn't love me so much, then you wouldn't run away from your father and from your home, and come here with me!" Jenny looked away smiling because she knew Rion was right. "That's why I love you, because you always think about the greater good, not just about you, or about me, or even our families, but you always think about the greater good of the world. And maybe that's why we're sitting here now, in an ashram in India, celebrating our honeymoon. Any other girl would have used my money on a five-star hotel. But you brought me here. In a weird way, I'm really proud of you." Rion felt extremely physically attracted to her at this moment. He leaned forward to kiss her lips. After kissing her, Rion removed Jenny's top. She looked stunning, and he put his hands on her waist, and kissed her lips. Then he kissed her neck, and slowly went down to kiss her chest. He touched her breasts, and was going to remove her bra, when Jenny interrupted. "I'm sorry Rion, we can't go further than this."

Rion was flabbergasted "Huh! We just ran away from home, it's our honeymoon, and we can't go further than this!"

Jenny touched Rion on the cheek and said "I'm really sorry, but when I was going to run away with you, I made a promise to god."

"Promise? What promise?"

"I promised to god that if we successfully get married, then I will live as a pure woman for one month after marriage, and I will not take part in any you know… activity."

Rion was in complete shock. He said "How could you make a promise like that! One month, do you know how long that is?"

"I hope you understand?" said Jenny.

"No off course I don't understand!" Rion was upset and turned around to face the other direction in protest, "I'm not talking to you," he said. After a few moments of silence, he turned back around and said "You know how I said just now that I respect you because you are selfless and you think about the world?" Jenny was listening with intent. He continued to speak "You know how I said I love you because you have a good heart and you look after others first?" Jenny was listening. Rion went on to say "Well, I love you even more now. The truth is Jenny that I love you, not your body, and so even if you did make a stupid promise to god to jeopardize our honeymoon, it's okay with me. Because at least we're here now because of your devotion to god."

Jenny was relieved, she said "Thank you my dear husband, you've lifted a big weight off my conscience. Thank you for understanding me."

"But now, there's only twenty-nine days left. After these twenty-nine days, nobody will be able to save you from me! I am getting ready now, for the twenty ninth day, you get ready too!" Jenny agreed with anticipation. They fell asleep together on a somewhat different and unique honeymoon night. Their past was intriguing, and the future was unknown, the only thing that was certain was the peaceful night of sleep they had with them at this time.

The next day they toured their new environment together. When he looked at the people in the ashram, Rion felt a different vibe from what he was used to. People seemed extremely calm, relaxed and peaceful.   Looking at other people in the ashram, they seemed much more content with their simple lives compared to the high-speed roller coaster of the city.

For lunch, Rion and Jenny enjoyed a wide variety of delicious Indian food. An irresistible dish called *Bhelpuri*, consisting of puffed rice, and thin noodles made from besan flour, all mixed together with potatoes, onions, chat masala and an optional chutney (a sweet or spicy Indian sauce). Fluffy pancakes called *parathas*, stuffed with mouthwatering tomatoes, peas, potatoes and carrots. The food consisted of all types of textures in good measure, including sweet, salty, tangy, spicy and crunchy. A heavenly desert consisting of sweet dumplings swimming in sweet flavoured milk. This was what was on offer at the ashram, and surrounding areas, because everybody here, was vegetarian. It was a heaven's abode for Jenny, and Rion was getting the hang of it as well, since the menu was actually spectacular.

Jenny & Rion took some time out to take a walk in the lush green grounds. It was an opportunity to reflect on the turn their lives had taken.

"Since I was a little girl, I always dreamed that a man would come and take me away…" said Jenny.

"In a shining armour? And wait for you while you walk with your father down the isle?"

"Yes," she replied. "But I got something even more valuable.

"What did you get?"

"You. I never thought I would find you again. After losing contact with you in Burbage, I had lost hope of seeing you. But now, finally, my dreams have come true."

Rion said "Hope is something that never dies. But what about walking down the isle with your father? Wasn't that your dream too?"

"Just because he's my father, it doesn't mean that I should stand by him if he is wrong. What he said to you that day, when he made you kiss his feet, was totally wrong."

Rion was really surprised, "Did you see what happened?" Jenny nodded her head to say she saw everything. "Then why didn't you say anything at that time?"

"Because I wanted my father to think he was successful in his plan, otherwise we wouldn't have been able to run away with each other. After you sent me a text message saying you love another woman, I behaved as though I was really sad in front of my father. Whenever he asked *why*, I would always say that it's because Rion broke up with me, he likes another girl. My dad thought his plan succeeded, but because he was more alert than before he still didn't allow me to go anywhere. But when my father told me he's going away for a couple of days, I called you straight away so we could run away with each other."

Rion's mouth was wide open in shock of Jenny's cunningness to pull off the whole operation. "You planned all this!"

"Yes, love is important, and I didn't want our love to fail."

"Now I know why Eddy says girls are too dangerous," muttered Rion to himself.

"What did Eddy say?" asked Jenny as she didn't hear.

So Rion said, "Okay never mind, let's just decide now with each other. In future, if we ever get separated by our parents, the police or anybody, then shall we pretend to be persuaded by them, wait for a good chance, and then run away again?!"

"Yes, that sounds perfect," smiled Jenny.

"You are one clever girl! But you said your father is going away for a couple of days, he'll be back by now right? Won't he look for you?"

"He should be home by now, I left a letter on the table saying that I love you and I'm going away with you," explained Jenny.

"Will he leave us alone after reading that letter."

"I'm not sure... But if I know my father well enough, then no. I think he won't rest until he finds us."

"How long can we keep running like this Jenny? We have to go back one day."

"Until we have children, nine months maybe. My heart says that after we have children, my father will bless us, and leave us alone."

"You mean nine months and twenty-nine days, right? Don't forget your promise! And children are not like planting vegetables, it can take longer. But are you sure, the way he spoke to me, I don't think he'll ever forgive us."

"Children are innocent, sweet, magical, and they have the power to melt anybody's heart. I don't think anybody in the world can be so cruel to hate children, can they?"

Meanwhile back at Jenny's home in the USA, Mr. Brown and his men were pacing up and down the hallway like a pack of wolves. Mr. Brown was fuming at the fact that Jenny and Rion managed to escape so easily, he asked his bodyguards "have any of you dimwits been able to figure out where Jenny went after leaving home?"

One of the accomplices said "No Mr. Brown, she didn't write where she's going in her letter"

"I know you genius," said Mr. Brown sarcastically. "But have any of you been to the police station?"

"How can we go sir? Jenny left a letter saying she's going because she wants to," said another accomplice.

"I know she left a letter," said Mr. Brown in a husky voice, "but the police don't know anything about the letter, unless I tell them. Call the police, and tell them Mr. Brown wants to report a serious crime... We need to stop them before they come back to us with any disgusting babies."

Chapter Twelve

Tranquility

Being in India, Jenny and Rion were enjoying their time in the protective, peaceful abode of a spiritual ashram. They cherished the simple pleasures in life. The gentle rainfall in the warm atmosphere of India was something special. Sometimes they would venture into the bazaar and buy something small and simple. Sometimes take a ride in the rickshaw to visit a new place. They were passing through the markets one day when they decided to try a new type of food they had seen before, but never had the courage to try. They tried a food called *pani puri*, small crisp spherical shells filled with potatoes, chick peas, yoghurt, and topped off with a tangy or spicy flavoured sauce. Jenny and Rion often held a competition to see who could finish the most *pani puri's* the fastest. Because of the tangy or spicy taste, who would win was never certain, but both Rion and Jenny would have water in their eyes by the end of the competition. Pani Puri was Jenny's favourite snack, but also very filling. It was available on almost every street being sold on small carts and also in shops. When it came to the main course, Rion enjoyed *Chole Bhature* the most. It was a soft thick fluffy bread which tasted better than any range of breads he had tried before, and this was served with a hot chick pea curry. He always found the meal incomplete without *salt chaas* which was a salt flavoured drink made simply by churning plain yoghurt until it was completely runny, and then adding salt. As for Jenny, her favourite main course was Dhosa, a giant long crispy shell made of rice flour rolled into a tube, filled with mild spicy potato curry. When it came to deserts however, Jenny and Rion both had a favourite, Rassmalai! Rassmalai was a soft sweet dumpling floating inside a bowl of sweet flavoured milk, the most heavenly taste ever.

One evening, after treating themselves with their favourite delicacies, Rion and Jenny noticed a cow, the cow looked like it had been wounded, and the cow looked like it had been starving for days. Coincidentally, the cow was outside an animal rescue shelter. Jenny and Rion were walking towards the cow, when suddenly they saw a man walk up to the cow. Rion noticed that the man had just walked out of a butcher's shop nearby. The man grabbed the cow by its horns and began to drag it along the ground. Rion and Jenny rushed up to him. Rion said "Hey, leave the cow."

"Is it yours?" asked the man, still holding on to the cow's horns with strength.

"No, but I said leave the cow."

"Are you going to make me? Finders keepers."

"This is not an object, which you find and keep. This is a living animal, it deserves to live," said Rion.

"If this cow lives then how will I eat such tasty flesh tonight?"

"Good point, but just think this, if you take this cow, then how will you live tonight?"

The man let go of the cow and said "You will beat me will you? For who, this cow? Millions of cows die like this every day."

"And I will stop them from dying. I am not a human being." The man looked confused. "I am an animal, who can speak English. Martin Luther king fought for his tribe, and I will fight for my tribe, leave the cow alone."

"Well then it would be my honour to fight with Martin Luther King junior." The man walked up to Rion, he had a knife in his hand. Rion rolled up his sleeves and walked towards him with only his fists. The man swung his knife for Rion's throat, but he moved out of the way. Rion used his legs to kick the knife out of the man's hands. Rion then kicked his chest as the man fell to the ground. Rion grabbed him by the neck and punched him until the man had no energy left. Rion grabbed his hand around the man's neck, and just as he was about to strangle him, Rion saw a police car approaching in the distance. He released the man slowly, who immediately ran for his life. Luckily, the police didn't see anything and they continued to drive past Rion.

Rion said to Jenny "wait here." He walked to the nearest convenience store only a few yards away, and he bought some biscuits. He tried to feed the cow and she ate those biscuits quite fast. Rion and Jenny were happy to have helped this poorly cow and they stroked her for a little while. They were about to get up and leave, but they noticed the cow was feeling sick. The cow threw up all the biscuits she had just eaten. This was a heartbreaking scene which Rion just couldn't let happen in front of his eyes. He said to Jenny "I don't understand why the government opens animal shelters when it can't help animals. Let me go inside and see, look after the cow, I'll come." Rion walked furiously into the animal shelter. He saw a lady who was next to a small piglet, he walked up to her, and said in a stern voice "excuse me!"

The lady said "just a minute," she finished what she was doing with the piglet and then turned around. As she turned, Rion's anger completely disappeared. He saw a stunningly beautiful Indian girl. She had long straight hair, and the most captivating big eyes. She said to him "Yes sir, how may I help you?" Rion was lost for words, and after a brief moment to compose himself, he said in a soft, gentle voice, "there's a cow outside, it's very sick, I tried feeding her, but she keeps throwing up."

"Oh no, where?" said the girl. Rion pointed outside the gate. The girl immediately rushed to the cow, where Jenny was waiting. The girl asked for Jenny and Rion's help to pick up the cow. The three of them lifted the cow, and took her inside. She asked Rion "Is this cow yours?"

"No, we just saw her outside. She isn't able to eat anything, if she does she throws up," he explained.

After assessing the cow, the girl said, "Thank you very much, if you didn't take me to the cow, she might have died. I'll give her an antibiotic injection for the next few days, she should be better soon." The girl asked "Where have you come from?"

Jenny explained, "We've come from the USA, we recently married each other, and we're just here celebrating our honeymoon."

"By the way my name is Selina, let me show you our animal shelter." She took Jenny and Rion to the inner part of the shelter, where they saw a wide variety of animals, dogs, pigs, cats, cows, camels, even elephants. All these, were being looked after by Selina because they had some ailment or injury.

"Do you run this animal shelter?" asked Rion.

Selina went on to explain "actually my father started this shelter. In the beginning, it was hard for him to get the necessary permission from the government, but after getting permission, he worked here all his life. My father believes that animals should be treated like humans, they deserve life. Now my dad is a little old, and doesn't feel as healthy as he used to, so I spend more time here and let him rest."

"But you just gave the animals an injection, so are you a doctor?" asked Jenny.

"Yes, I studied in the University of Mumbai. And every day when I serve these animals, it makes me proud to be a doctor."

"But if you're a doctor, couldn't you work in a hospital and earn more money? Why do you work in a charitable animal shelter?" asked Jenny.

Selina stopped walking and explained "actually this shelter is my father's dream. And to tell the truth, now it's my dream too. Money is only a means of getting by in life, it is not the purpose of life, my purpose in life are these animals. I can't work in a hospital and earn more money knowing that these animals are dying, my conscience won't allow that."

Rion intervened "But in a hospital, you would save human lives, aren't they important?"

"They are, but humans can speak for themselves, and there are already lots of doctors for people, but there is a real shortage of vets caring for animals in India."

"And a shortage of people caring for animals in the world," added Rion.

Jenny was really touched by Selina's story "There are very few people like you, and thanks to people like you, the world is still a good place."

"No mam, there are lots of girls like me in India. I am not great, India is great. In India people have very soft hearts, and the truth is even if you go to a poor person's home, if that person can, they will try to help you as much as possible. That is the spirit of India," she explained.

Selina's honesty and dedication was truly admirable. Jenny couldn't help but ask "Where did you learn such a high level of thinking? You are really hard working, it's not easy doing all this alone."

"My father and mother taught me from a young age that we should look after animals in the same way as humans. Me and my parents have visited the Iskcon ashram for many years, and we always learned that life should be about simple living and high thinking."

Selina continued showing Jenny and Rion the animal shelter, she showed them a young cow and pig. When she came close to the baby cow and pig, they both recognised Selina, and were displaying signs of excitement. They rubbed their mouths on Selina as she stroked them like little children. Selina explained "In Iskcon we learn that every animal has the power of god in their heart. The same power of god that keeps us humans alive."

"I think that's a beautiful thought… But which god is in their heart?" asked Rion inquisitively.

"There are many names, but the truth is that there is only one god, he is everywhere, he is omnipresent."

"But how can you say there is only one god? In India I have seen many different gods," asked Rion.

Selina smiled, "In your government, how many different politicians are there? Lots of politicians, right? If you want to improve education, then there is one politician, for health there is another politician. But there is only one president or prime minister. In the same way there are different gods in India for different aspects of life. For example if you really need more money in your life, then you can try to please the goddess of wealth *Laxmi*. If you want more knowledge in life, then you can try to impress the goddess of knowledge, *Saraswati*."

"Very interesting. But who is the president?" asked Rion.

"You have asked a very difficult question," Selina laughed. "I have an idea, would you like to come to my home and meet my father? He's very knowledgeable, you can meet my family, and that way you can also get the answers to all your questions."

"Oh no, it's okay, we'll come another time, we don't want to disturb you," said Rion.

"You won't disturb me at all, in fact my father will be happy to see you. Please, you are guests in our country, and in India we say *Athithi Devo Bhava*, meaning that we should treat the guest like god."

Rion and Jenny looked at each other, then they agreed. They walked with Selina to her home, only a short distance from the ashram.

At her home, Selina's mother welcomed Rion and Jenny in a traditional manner by lighting a small *divo* (Indian candle) for them. They felt as though they had come to their second home, to a warm and welcoming family.

Selina's father continued the discussion with Rion, he explained "You see, the analogy that my daughter gave you is good, but it's incomplete to a certain extent. This explanation of politicians and presidents is right, but you tell me how many presidents are there in this world?"

Rion was interested in finding out what Selina's father would say.

"There is a different president or prime minister in every country. Now this is very reflective of the fact that there are different gods in different parts of the world. In fact there are often many different views of the same god in the same religion. And that is the key word, *views*. Have you ever been to a cricket match?"

"No sir, I enjoy playing cricket, but unfortunately professional cricket is not as popular in America as it is in India," explained Rion.

"Yes you are right, in India people love cricket. Okay tell me which sport is popular in America?"

"Basketball is very popular, hockey and baseball, oh and football."

"Okay you've been to a baseball match right? Jenny have you been to a baseball match?"

"I've been once, a couple of years ago, with our class, we went as a treat at the end of term," said Jenny.

"Okay, so when you went to that baseball match, how many seats were there in the stadium?"

A little surprised by the question Jenny replied "I'm not exactly sure, maybe a few thousand."

"A few thousand, right? So, every person in that stadium has a slightly different point of view of that same stadium. But does that mean there are a few thousand baseball stadiums?" Rion and Jenny were enlightened. Selina's father continued to explain "In the same way that there are thousands of different points of view of the same stadium, but there is only one stadium, there are also thousands of different names, and points of view of the same god, but there is only one god."

"And who is that god?" asked Rion.

Selina's father laughed "I don't think you understand what I'm trying to explain to you Rion. God has no form. God is not one person locked up in a room somewhere. God has no definition, god has no conceivable form. Do you think the energy that moves the sun and moon can be defined? Your question is a clever one, yet a silly one at the same time. All these forms of god we see in the world, they are good, but none of them is completely correct. They are all right, and they are all wrong at the same time. Because god is everything. God is in me, in you. In Hinduism there is a quote *aham brahmasmi*. This means *I am god*. Do you know how powerful this quote is? The power that moves the sun and moon is the same power that is inside me. After my father taught me this quote when I was a child, not a single day of my life has gone by, when I was lazy. Because I live every day with the thought that the energy that moves this universe, is inside me. I am a representative of god's power. For some people that power is Krishna, for some it is Rama, for some it is Jesus, for some it is Allah. For some it is Buddha and for some it is Guru Nanak. All of these are correct, and yet all of these are incorrect. God is above religion Rion. God is above this world. God is above everything that we divisive humans have created in this materialistic world."

Rion felt as though he had got all the answers he needed.

But Selina's father had one more thing to say "Even though we have discussed this today, it's important that you don't go around telling everybody your god is not real, your god is not real! Because the truth is that because of god, all be it in different forms, if humans are able to live a more moral, decent and happy life, then it can only be a good thing, right? Come, let's eat some dinner."

"No sir, actually me and Jenny have already eaten," said Rion.

"Already eaten? Doesn't matter, you can eat again, besides, In India a guest is…"

"…is like god!" interrupted Rion. "Selina told us."

"Very good, now if you know that much, you will also know that you cannot leave without eating." Rion and Jenny had the opportunity to experience Indian hospitality for the first time. Selina's mother kept filling Jenny's dinner plate with *chapatis*. Although she was already full, Selina's mother didn't listen, she kept feeding Jenny and Rion. She put her hand on Jenny's head like a mother. Jenny experienced what felt like the love of a mother for the first time after many years.

"Here, have some milk," said Selina's mother, as she gave Rion and Jenny a big glass of milk.

"Oh thank you," said Rion, he didn't want to reject such love even though he didn't really feel like drinking milk. But to his surprise it tasted great, he said "Wow, this tastes fresh!"

"That's because I it's milk from the cows at the shelter!" said Selina.

"Oh really?!" Jenny was shocked, and put down her glass while drinking.

"Yes, I milked the cow myself! This fresh milk is best for your body and mind."

Jenny picked up her glass again to drink the milk. Rion said "Your parents are lovely Selina, I'm really thankful to you for bringing us here." Selina smiled while she was still cooking some hot chapattis for Rion and Jenny. Rion asked "Do you have any brothers or sisters?"

"I have one brother," replied Selina.

"Where is your brother? He must be hungry too," said Jenny.

Selina's father interrupted "His name is Johnny, he will be coming any moment, he knows what time his mother makes dinner! I'm glad you reminded me. I will go before he comes, he makes my head hurt."

"Does he trouble you?" asked Jenny.

"Oh no no, he has a very good heart, but you see his way of looking at the world is slightly different, he is the eighth wonder of the world. You will understand when you meet him. I'm going to go out for a walk!"

"Eighth wonder of the world?" said Rion to himself wondering what Selina's father meant, who had already stood up and left the house!

Selina was cooking with her mum, and Jenny and Rion almost finished their food, when suddenly entered Selina's brother, he said "Where's my food mother, I'm hungry. I've been working hard all day, I'm tired."

"I think he's the eighth wonder of the world," whispered Rion to Jenny.

Then Johnny saw Rion and Jenny and said "Oh hello, who are you?"

Selina answered the question, "these are my friends Rion and Jenny, they've come from America."

Selina's brother laughed and introduced himself "I'm Johnny, nice to meet you." He shook hands with Rion and Jenny. Johnny said "It's so nice to see such a happy brother and sister. Otherwise some brothers and sisters are like two monkeys locked in the same cage," he looked at Selina as if hinting the comment at her.

"Actually, we are not brother and sister," said Rion.

"You're thinking of getting married?" guessed Johnny. "Congratulations, but before you get married, let me warn you, wives are like chewing gum, in the beginning they are very nice, and then later you wonder where to put them." Rion and Jenny were a little amused but weren't given a chance to speak. Johnny continued to say "Don't get upset sister," to Jenny and said "Instead of getting married, it's better to get a mobile phone, you can put the phone on silent, but you can't put the wife anywhere. You can change the ringtones, but the wife always gives out the same tone. Don't take it wrongly sister, it's better to get a dog than a wife, if you give the dog some food, it will come, but once the wife gets upset no matter what you do she won't listen. I recommend that you both stay happily as friends there's no need to marry each other, don't take it wrongly sister."

Jenny said "It's okay brother Johnny, but we're already married, and we're very happy."

Johnny was surprised and said "Oh, I'm sorry, I didn't know, actually my view of marriage changed a long time ago."

"When did you get married?" asked Jenny.

"I haven't got married yet. Why? Do you know a girl I can marry? If you do then please tell me!" He joined his hands to beg Jenny if she knew any girls.

"I do, not here though, maybe in America…"

"Yes that'll do, America, India, Zimbabwe, Haiti, New Zealand, anywhere will do!" said Johnny.

"But brother Johnny, a moment ago you were saying that wives are like chewing gum?" mentioned Rion.

"I was just saying that to amuse myself. The truth is that I'm dying to get married, for the last 32 years, I've been looking for a girl. There's no place I haven't looked. Rivers, trees, towns, villages, temples, libraries, I searched everywhere. But some girls say I'm too short, some say I'm too dark, some say I'm too chubby. I don't know what to do!"

"Actually, I was going to ask, how comes you and your sister look so different?" asked Rion.

"You mean because I'm dark, and she's fair?" Rion tried to politely say that he didn't mean that, but Johnny interrupted "I am black, so why shy away from the truth. It's a long story, actually, I was born in Africa."

"You were born in Africa? but Selina was telling us that you've been in India since birth?" said Jenny.

"Not in this life, in my last life I was born in Africa," explained Johnny.

"Were you a bricklayer in your last life?" asked Rion.

"Hey! Don't insult me! I wasn't a bricklayer."

"Then?"

"Actually I was a spider, a tarantula to be precise. I was walking along the footpath minding my own business, when some school children saw me. I was excited to see them, so I ran after them to say hello, but they got scared and told their parents. As soon as they told their parents, I knew I was in trouble. These parents were my biggest enemy in my last life. The children loved me, they even played with me, but these parents are no good I tell you. In the end they stamped on me with their feet I still suffer from the trauma till this day."

"I'm surprised girls don't like you, you're such a funny person," said Jenny.

"Hey!" Johnny said.

"I mean jolly person," Jenny clarified. "When you came home you said you worked hard all day. What do you do?" asked Jenny.

"It's easier to ask what I don't do." Rion and Jenny looked at each other confused.

"There's nothing I can't do. You can try, ask me anything, I can do it…" said Johnny.

"Can you sing?" asked Rion.

"Sing, yes I can sing."

"Can you Dance?" asked Jenny

"I can dance," said Johnny.

"Can you cook?"

"Cooking, umm, congratulations!" Johnny extended his hand to shake hands with Rion.

"Congratulations, why!?" asked Rion.

"Because that's one thing I can't do! I can't cook food… But I can eat food very well, watch I will eat everything mum cooked in no time!"

"It's okay you don't need to prove anything, we believe you. Now I know that nobody is better than you at anything!" Rion and Jenny could see what a jolly character Johnny was.

On that note, Jenny and Rion expressed their gratitude to Selina's mother "Thank you for such wonderful food, it made us feel as though we're at home with our family."

"I am not just Selina's mother, I am also your mother, until you are in India, it's my duty to look after you both like my children. If you ever feel like eating home cooked food, come straight to me, you don't need to ask for Selina's permission, okay!" Selina's mother gave Jenny and Rion a hug and bid them farewell for the evening.

On the way back to the ashram, Rion saw a hairdresser and felt like having a haircut. While they sat inside waiting for his turn, Rion noticed something strange while watching TV. It was the news channel, and it showed a picture of both Rion and Jenny. Rion tapped Jenny on the knee to get her attention. They both watched the news broadcast. Luckily the transmission was taking place in English, the news reporter was speaking "Two Harvard University students seem to have gone missing from their homes in the United States of America. A young man named Rion and a young Woman named Jenny, both twenty-one years of age, have gone missing. According to investigators they have both travelled to India. It is unclear whether the girl has been taken by force. However, investigators in India are trying their best to find these two university students so that the reason for their disappearance can be discovered."

Rion signaled to Jenny that they should leave the hairdressers' shop. The hairdresser's attention was fortunately on cutting hair and not on the TV. So, they immediately sneaked out of the shop.

Jenny said "I don't understand, how can they know that we're in India? We didn't leave any clues. Even we didn't know that we were going to India until we reached the airport. How could they have known?"

"It's okay, they know that we're in India, but India is huge, they can't possibly find us here, we're safe in this ashram... Wait, do you remember that immigration officer we met at the airport?" asked Rion.

"Oh, you think he told my father?" said Jenny.

"No, if he wanted to get us in trouble he could have done anything at the airport itself. I think he helped us. But do you remember what that officer said?"

"What did he say?" asked Jenny.

"He said that we should tell a few of our trustworthy friends of our situation, and then if we get caught, at least our friends can help us."

Rion and Jenny went to the nearest telephone booth. Rion dialed Hannah's number. After a few rings Rion said, "Hello, Hannah?"

"Rion, is that you?" Hannah recognised his voice immediately.

"Yes it's me! How are you?"

"I'm fine, but how are you? Do you know how worried we all are? You and Jenny are on the news here, do you know?" said Hannah as clearly and loudly as she could.

"Yes I just watched the news now. Who is with you? Are you alone?"

"No, Eddy and Harvey are with me, we were just talking about you wondering where you were!"

"Okay Hannah I'm going to tell you something important, listen carefully. Me and Jenny got married in a court near University, and then we came to India together. When we came here, an immigration officer advised us not to tell anyone the truth about what we did. But I'm telling you... I am going to email you a copy of mine and Jenny's Passport and marriage certificate. We are staying in a place called Vrindavan in India right now. If the police here catch us, then please send the marriage certificate to the American officials so they can help us."

"Okay Rion, don't worry I'll look out for your email. I won't let anything happen to you or Jenny."

"Thanks Hannah, I knew I could rely on you!"

"Any doubt?! When will you come back here? I want you both to get married again."

"Get married again? Why?!"

"So I can come to your wedding! You didn't even tell us and got married, you should have at least told me," explained Hannah.

"I'm sorry Hannah, please forgive me. Even I didn't know until two hours before!"

"Hmm okay, first come back, then I'll decide whether I can forgive you or not," Hannah said adamantly.

"Okay, it's a deal, when I return, I will accept whatever punishment you give me," said Rion in a consoling manner.

Hannah remembered to ask "How is Jenny?"

"Why don't you ask her, she right here!" Rion gave Jenny the phone.

"Hello, Hannah?" said Jenny.

"Hi Jenny, congratulations on your marriage!"

"Thank you Hannah, I'm sorry we couldn't invite you guys, but when we return, we will definitely have a big celebration."

"That will be great," said Hannah a little more cheerfully. "How is India? You must be having a spectacular honeymoon?"

"Yes it's great. We're just getting used to the heat, but the food is so delicious."

"Really? I really want to try!"

"Once this mess is sorted out, then I will invite you to India, we will have a great time!"

"Sure, I'd love to," said Hannah.

"Look after yourself, and say hello to Eddy and Harvey.

"I will do," said Hannah.

Jenny handed the phone back to Rion.

Hannah said "Look after yourself, and look after Jenny. Only a girl can understand how it feels to leave everything in the world for the boy she loves. Jenny has left everything for you Rion. Take care of her, and take care of yourself."

Rion smiled and appreciates Hannah's kind advice, "I will look after Jenny, I promise, and when I return, I will... I will invite you to our wedding, okay?"

"Okay," said Hannah emotionally.

"Bye Hannah."

"Bye Rion."

Rion felt a huge sigh of relief having finally shared his extraordinary situation with friends. Rion and Jenny returned to the ashram cautiously.

Meanwhile Hannah was emotional, and resisted holding in her tears but eventually gave up. Eddy and

Harvey were there to miserably fail at making her smile again. Eddy said "Don't worry, Rion will be back here soon,"

"Will you cry this much when you find out that I've run away with my girlfriend!" said Harvey.

This finally brought a smile to Hannah's face, but she still couldn't express her feelings, she felt as though she had a special connection with Rion, which nobody could understand or explain.

Chapter Thirteen

Celebration Time

The following day there was a buzz around the ashram. The devotees woke up early as usual and chanted the following mantra: *Hare Krishna Hare Krishna, Krishna Krishna Hare Hare, Hare Raam Hare Raam, Raam Raam, Hare Hare*. The devotees would dance this in the open garden of the temple in the ashram. Rion and Jenny joined in, and they felt as though they could let go of all their worries, and surrender themselves to a higher purpose for a brief moment.

"I've heard them singing that in America too!"

"Have you?" asked Jenny while she was dancing.

"Yes! Actually, come to think of it, I think I've also heard them singing *Hare Krishna* in London when I was in school!"

"See! I told you they have ashrams throughout the world!" said Jenny.

Today was the birthday of Krishna, the god that the devotees worshipped.

In the afternoon, Rion and Jenny stumbled into Selina at the temple of the ashram. Selina invited them to celebrate the birth of Lord Krishna by participating in grand ceremony later that day. Selina helped Jenny to pick out a colourful Indian Saree from the market.

While Rion was waiting for Jenny to get dressed, he borrowed an Indian *dhoti* and *kurta* from Johnny.

In the evening, they were all finally ready to go to the festival of Lord Krishna's birth, called *Janmashtami*.

At this function, Rion and Jenny saw that there were lots of people playing a game which involved climbing on top of each other. The aim of this game seemed to be to get to the top of this human pyramid made up of around one hundred people. At the top was a clay pot hanging by a thread, around fifty feet from the ground. Once the person at the very top of this human pyramid reached the pot, he would smash the pot open. Upon the pot being broken, yoghurt contained in the pot would fall on the human pyramid for participants to taste.

This task required patience, skill and strength. There was the loudest drum style *dhol* being played as well as a host of other instruments to motivate and inspire the participants.

Jenny, Johnny, Rion and Selina were all spectating for a while. Selina asked Rion "Would you like to take part in the pyramid?"

"I don't think I can do it, it seems dangerous," said Rion.

But Selina had faith in him "It's okay, if those people can do it, you can do it too!"

Rion looked towards Jenny, who expressed that it was up to him to decide whether or not to participate. Rion said casually "Okay, I'll try."

Johnny laughed at Rion and said "Climbing the human pyramid is not something anybody can do!"

Rion gave him a stern look. Johnny was intimidated and corrected himself by saying "I mean where will you start? Will you form part of the base that supports other people or will you climb to the top?"

Rion looked at the pyramid to assess it "I think that if I stay at the bottom, and if I can't take the weight, then everybody above me will fall. So I think it's better if I climb. What do you think Jenny?"

"As you wish," she said reluctantly.

Rion stood near the pyramid to see how he would climb. There was a circle made up of forty people at the base of the pyramid, putting their arms around each others' shoulders. Above this circle were twenty-five people standing on their shoulders. Fifteen people were required to climb on top of the two floors of people to create a third floor. Rion wanted to be part of the third floor of people. He tried climbing up using a person on the base. With great difficulty, he managed to climb up one floor, but then he looked down. Rion felt a little scared imagining how painful a fall from this height would be. He tried his best to climb above the first floor, but no matter how hard he tried, he just couldn't make it. Jenny and Selina were cheering for Rion, while Johnny was laughing at him from a distance. Rion decided to give up and come down again. Johnny tried to control his laughter. Jenny and Selina said "unlucky," to Rion.

Johnny said "See I told you, you can't climb. You're from America, to climb this pyramid you need strength of mind and body, you're too weak!"

Then Jenny said "No, Rion is not weak." Jenny looked at Rion and said "Do you love me?"

"More than anything else in this world," he replied.

"Can you show me how much you love me? If you can climb this pyramid, then it means you really love me," said Jenny.

Rion didn't say anything, he looked at the pyramid, looked at Jenny, looked at the pyramid again and walked towards it.

Jenny, Selina and Johnny looked on as Rion walked towards this human pyramid with sheer confidence. His eyes were set on the top and he could see nothing else. Rion put his right leg on the knee of the person on the base, and then onto his shoulder. Using all his strength, Rion climbed up this human pyramid with fearlessness. As he was climbing his confidence was growing, so too was his strength. Rion climbed higher and higher, higher and higher, until eventually he reached his goal, the peak of this human pyramid. With utmost valor and bravery, he smashed the clay pot open to get a taste of the yoghurt inside. Then, the whole human pyramid collapsed under its own weight. Rion was on top, and came tumbling down. Selina and Jenny were worried. Rion was nowhere to be seen in this heap of people. However due to the structure of the pyramid, nobody was hurt and Rion appeared from the ruins of the human pyramid. He brought back some yoghurt from the top, gave it to Jenny and said "This is how much I love you."

Johnny had learned something, he said "Rion, until now I thought you were American, but now I realise how wrong I was. You have the strength of India in you, you have the courage of America in you, and you have the love of a human in you. I salute you my Rion." Johnny saluted him, Rion was humbled and smiled at him in return. As this happened, Selina felt something special in her heart, she looked at Rion in a way that she had never looked at anybody before. She started to like Rion. She liked what he stood for, she admired his love for Jenny. Selina saw how in an instant, Rion transformed himself for his love, and even risked his life for Jenny.

After the function was over, they all went to Selina's home. It occurred to Rion that perhaps Selina's father might be a good person to ask "What is the meaning of people climbing on top of each other to get a pot of yoghurt? Why do they do this?"

Selina's father answered his question "This function was based around the childhood of Krishna. When he was a child, Krishna would steel yoghurt and milk from other people in the village. Villagers would hide their yoghurt and milk from Krishna by placing it near the ceiling at height using a pot and string. But Krishna would invite his friends, and they would form a human pyramid and reach the pot of yoghurt with ease, and steel it from the villagers."

"But why did the Indian god steal from the other villagers? Surely steeling isn't a good thing," pointed out Rion.

"That is a very good question my boy. Stealing is bad, but the real thief wasn't Krishna, after all how much yoghurt can a child eat? The real thief was the king of the kingdom *Kansa*. Kansa would charge tax to the people of his kingdom, and take all of their food, milk and yoghurt. Krishna did not like this, he believed that milk and yoghurt should be for the villagers and the children, not for the king. So, as a way of protesting this unfair taxation, he would steal yoghurt and milk, so that it could be given to children, not the greedy king, who never did any good for his kingdom in return anyway."

"Oh, cool," said Rion, "that's the coolest way somebody can protest."

"Yes he was very cool, and very strong at the same time, he later grew up and defeated the king, and he also went on to do many other things in his life, this was just a small chapter of Krishna's life."

After hearing this inspiring story, Rion also felt motivated to do what was right in his life.

"If you were so motivated to do what is right in life, why did you kidnap 347 people?" asked officer Williams.

"Patience is a virtue, I am telling you the story, I think you need some more coffee, you're getting cranky." Said Rion patiently. Mr. Williams shouted to his assistant to get him a cup of coffee. The assistant entered the room, Mr. Williams asked Rion "Do you anything?"

"Tea would be good, milk with two sugars please."

The assistant left to get the beverages. Mr. Williams looked at Rion like a really angry heavyweight wrestler. But in truth, he was just holding in his tears. He wanted to be put out of his misery, and find out why Rion ended up committing such a horrific crime.

But Rion said "Good things come to those who wait, why don't you go home, it's quite late officer, and I'm not going anywhere. I'll tell you the rest of the story tomorrow."

Mr. Williams pulled up a chair in front of Rion, sat down a few inches away from his face and said "No, I want to hear the story right *now*."

The assistant officer brought beverages. Rion took a sip out of his tea and looked at Mr. Williams, who was staring at him like a hungry lion, so Rion remembered "Oh sorry, where were we?"

"You were inspired to do what is right, then what happened?"

Rion continued his story…

Chapter Fourteen

Trouble Looms

The following day, Rion and Jenny were walking along the Yamuna river. Jenny saw an old Indian priest. She really wanted to ask the priest a question, and greeted him by saying "Hare Krishna." The priest reciprocated and Jenny said hesitantly, "Sir, I want to ask you something which you may not be asked often…"

The priest smiled, "You don't need to worry, you can ask your question without giving me any introduction. Whatever you ask will stay between us."

Jenny was still a little hesitant so she rephrased her question, "Actually I'm here to ask you about my friend. She is from America, and you see, the problem is, I mean the problem was, that she loved a boy. The boy also loved her, but her father didn't agree to their marriage. So I Just wanted to know if the girl…"

"I understand," interrupted the Indian priest. "You want to know if she should run away with the boy or listen to her father, is that right?"

"Umm, yes, I just want to know if she should listen to her father, or if she should elope with the boy, because they both really love each other." Rion was watching with anticipation, He was hoping that this old man whom Jenny had asked such an important question to, didn't lead Jenny down the wrong path and jeopardize their relationship.

The priest asked "Is your friend's father a nice man, or is he bad?"

Jenny didn't need to think long to answer that question, "He's bad. Her father is really bad. He doesn't have any love or care about anybody. He's selfish, and only cares about money."

The priest said, "Let me tell you a little story which might answer your question. During Krishna's lifetime, there was a princess called Rukmani. And Rukmani's father wanted her to marry another prince, who was not a good man. The troubled princess wrote a letter to Lord Krishna, which she sent to him through one of her royal guards. Krishna rescued Rukmani by running away with her."

"Really! Did Lord Krishna run away with a girl?" asked Rion.

"Yes, young man. Lord Krishna believed that women should choose their life partner, and so he eloped with Rukmani. Your friend also has the right to choose who she marries, and I would advise, that you tell your friend to run away with the boy. If he really loves her, and then after some time, once your friend has a baby, she can return to her father. No father in the world can be so cruel to turn away his daughter and her child."

Jenny was overjoyed at this most precious advice from the priest. She thanked him graciously. He blessed Rion and Jenny by putting his hand on their heads. Just as they were leaving, the priest said to Jenny "How long has it been since you both ran away with each other?"

Jenny looked at Rion, and then looked at the priest, and then the priest said "Don't worry, it's okay, you don't have to fear anything. But one more thing I want to tell you. In life you should have enough self-confidence and faith in your own decisions. You don't need to ask anybody for advice, you have done the right thing, and I can see how much you love each other. Just make sure you are careful every step of the way."

Jenny and Rion were relieved and extremely greatful for the valuable advice. Rion was specially impressed with the priest's psychological skills. He knew who Jenny was talking about them, and not her friend.

On the way back to the ashram while walking through the shopping bazaar, Rion thought it would be a good idea to pick up an English newspaper. It had been days since they could keep up to date with world news. After getting to the ashram however, it was not current affairs, rather the bedroom affairs that were on Rion's mind. Rion said "It's been twenty-nine days since we got married. Your promise you made to god expires tomorrow, how do you feel?"

"I feel really happy my dear husband, and you?" asked Jenny mischievously.

"Shall I show you how happy I feel?" Rion cuddled Jenny passionately.

"I'm really sorry that I had to stop you for the past month, I hope you can forgive me?"

"I am the luckiest person in the world!" said Rion.

"Why is that?" asked Jenny, staring into his eyes with a day dreaming type gaze.

"Because my wife loves me so much, that she made a promise to god that she won't even try to have any children with me for the first month after marriage, so that we can both be safe and happy. I am really very lucky." Jenny rested her head on Rion's chest, where she could hear his heart beat, and just felt as though she was floating on clouds.

Rion however, was feeling peckish! "I don't know why I feel like eating something!"

"Shall we go out and get something?" asked Jenny.

"No I just feel like having a snack!"

Jenny suggested some cream rolls she had in the room, "Yes that's good," said Rion. So she opened the bag on the table, but there was only one roll left. "Don't worry we'll share it," he said.

"No, I'm not hungry, you can have it."

But Rion wouldn't give up and made sure Jenny had the first bite from the roll. Rion took out the newspaper and read it on the bed with Jenny.

Rion suddenly saw an article in the newspaper he couldn't believe. He showed Jenny quickly. He said "Jenny look! America is winning the most gold medals in the Olympics this year!" "That's really impressive!" She said. "Let's see who is second and third on the medals table."

"It says that Great Britain, China and Russia are in 2nd, 3rd and 4th places. But wait a minute, the full medal table is probably at the back, let me see." Rion began turning the pages when he suddenly saw another shocking article he couldn't believe. His eyes lit up! Jenny saw Rion's expression and looked at the newspaper too. She couldn't believe it either. Rion and Jenny saw a picture of themselves on the fifth page of the newspaper. The headline on the page read *American man abducts girl and takes her to Vrindavan, India, police on the hunt*. They couldn't believe it. "How can they say I kidnapped you?" said Rion. "We got married in the registry office."

"How can they call you a man and me a girl, we're the same age!" added Jenny.

"But the most important question is how do they know we're in Vrindavan? Did we leave any clues?" asked Rion.

"No, how about the priest on the River bank?" remembered Jenny.

"It can't be him, we spoke to him just a few hours ago! I don't understand how they found out that we're in Vrindavan... CCTV, cameras, the airport, the taxi from the airport, there's many ways they could have found out. We'll figure that out later, right now we need to move," Rion stood up and started to pack their bags.

"But it's ten o clock, where will we go? Aren't we safe here in the ashram? They won't think of looking for us here," said Jenny.

"No we can't take that chance, if they come looking for us now, we'll be trapped."

"But where will we go, to another city?" she asked.

"No, it's possible the police could be checking buses, trains and check posts on the highway. I have an idea..." said Rion.

They both checked out of the ashram.

Rion took Jenny to the place where he thought they could remain the safest. It was dark, it was raining. Police were roaming the streets along the way. But they just continued walking not to arouse any suspicion. Luckily, they weren't stopped.

Rion and Jenny finally arrived where Rion thought they could be safe, Selina's house. where she invited them in, but her father and mother were also awake. Selina's father asked "What happened Rion, all this luggage at this time, are you leaving Vrindavan?"

"Actually, I wanted to speak to you all about something if you don't mind?" asked Rion.

"Off course, take a seat, Selina get some water for Rion and Jenny," said Selina's father.

Rion's mind was like a war zone, he didn't know where to start. He composed himself to explain the strangest circumstances under which he would be asking for help from Selina's father. If he refused to allow them to stay in their home, then their hopes and dreams could be over.

Selina, her father and mother were in the living room waiting for Rion to explain his story.

Rion spoke, "Sir, actually me and Jenny didn't tell you the whole truth when we met you for the first time. We are married, but that's only half the truth. I didn't tell you the whole truth, so I've come here to apologise."

"You don't need to apologise my son, tell me, what did you hide from us?" asked Selina's father curiously.

"I love Jenny a lot, she loves me too, but unfortunately Jenny's father didn't approve of our marriage. Jenny's father, Mr. Brown, said that if I even think about her, then he will ruin Jenny's life and he'll end mine. I'm not worried about me, but I am worried about Jenny. I just read in the newspaper, it says that I abducted Jenny against her will, which is absolutely not true. Even if you need to see our marriage certificate, I will show it to you. But I just want to request that you let us stay with you in your house for a few days. The police is looking for us. If they catch us, then they'll take Jenny away, and I can't live without her. Please let us stay with you, please." Rion was distraught, he had never begged somebody for help, he had always helped others, but this verdict would decide the outcome for both Rion and Jenny.

Selina's father decided, "Rion, perhaps you misunderstood me. The first day when we met, I told you something important, do you remember what I told you?"

Rion looked up at Selina's father trying to remember what he said to him.

Selina's father said "It's important to recognise the person standing in front of you before helping them. You don't need to show me your marriage certificate. I can see truth in your eyes, every word that you spoke from your mouth is the truth. I believe you Rion, and on the first day we met, I told you that in India a guest is like god. You are our guest, and if you are in trouble, then your trouble is my trouble. I will help you. Both you and Jenny can stay here for as long as you wish, and when you feel that the danger is over you may leave if you want. But remember one thing, while you are here, Jenny is also my daughter, and you are also my son." Selina's father hugged Jenny and Rion, welcoming them into his home and into his heart.

Johnny came home late at usual, and he saw everybody hugging each other, he said "What's happening here?" in a strict voice, then he said "I want a hug too!"

"Sure! Come here my son!" said Johnny's father.

Selina showed Rion and Jenny their room, a guest room upstairs, where they could lay their heads for the coming nights without any fear. Before sleeping Rion called Johnny and told him to sit on the bed, "Johnny, we need you to keep something a secret, do you think you can?

"Depends on what the secret is," Johnny started laughing.

"Actually, me and Jenny ran away with each other and got married."

"Why? Don't you have a car in America?"

"No, we have a car, but her father didn't agree to the marriage, that's why we ran away."

"I know that already! I knew that the first day I met you!" Rion was surprised. "It happens all the time in India, parents never agree to marriages here either!"

"Really! So then what happens?" asked Rion.

"They run away, if the police catch them their life is ruined, and if they get away then they're lucky."

"Brother Johnny, we don't want our lives to be ruined..." said Jenny.

"Don't worry sister Jenny, I will sacrifice myself if I have to, but I won't let anything happen to my sister."

"Your sister?" asked Rion.

"Yes, Jenny is my sister! Only a sister can be so kind."

Jenny was touched hearing this, "Yes brother Johnny, I am your sister. And if you want nothing to happen to me, then you must look after yourself too. I don't want any harm to come to my brother."

"Don't worry, even if the police catch you, I know what to do!" said Johnny confidently.

On that note, Jenny and Rion could sleep peacefully feeling as though they were sleeping in their own home, not somebody else's. But all night long, Rion was thinking about what to do next.

The next morning, Rion, Jenny and Johnny left on a motorcycle for the nearest internet café. There, the operator asked Rion to provide his identification proof. Rion was about to provide his passport, but Johnny stopped him in time and provided his own identification saying that "actually I need to use the internet." When they sat down at the computer, Johnny explained to Rion "you shouldn't show anybody your ID, in case they investigate later and find out where you are. But what do you need to use the internet for?"

"I want to email the U.S embassy. I want to explain the whole situation, so they can help me and Jenny return home safely."

"Are you sure you can trust them?"

Jenny replied "Yes brother Johnny. The US embassy will do everything they can to help me and Rion once they see proof that we're married."

Rion emailed the United States embassy and explained the entire situation that had taken place with himself and Jenny. Rion also attached a copy of their marriage certificate. He explained in the email that Jenny's father was against their marriage and perhaps they would need protection when they returned to the USA.

"Whose phone number should I put at the bottom?" asked Rion.

"Don't put any phone number, just in case you get in trouble, let them email you, and then if you think it's okay, you can phone them." advised Johnny. Rion accepted Johnny's suggestion.

After coming out of the internet café, Rion saw a person reading a newspaper article about him and Jenny. He quickly hinted to Johnny that they need to get a move on. Later, he said "I think we need to look a little different, in case one of my distant family members in India recognise me."

"I know what you mean, I know a place," Johnny introduced Rion to a friend of his who could help. His friend spent hours with Rion and Jenny. By the time they had finished, it was difficult to recognise both of them. They also went to the clothing market, where by Johnny's suggestion they bought Indian clothes, so that they would look like local people and not foreigners. After a few hours of smart work, Jenny and Rion looked like two completely different people. Johnny then explained to them "You look different, that's good, but the way you walk, anybody can tell that you're from abroad."

"What do you mean? Do we need to walk in a more civil manner?"

"No! You need to walk in a more uncivil manner! Walk like you don't care about anything." Like this, Johnny demonstrated walking like a gangster with a care free attitude about what's going on around him. He explained "In India, people don't worry about what will happen to them, they think whatever happens, they will deal with it when it happens."

"What does it look like when you see us walking?" asked Rion.

"When you two walk, you look around like everything is new to you, as if you've never seen it before."

"But everything is new to us!" said Jenny.

"I know sister, but you can't let the world know that. The skill is in pretending that you've been here a thousand times. You have to pretend that you've been here so many times that you're fed up of seeing the place. Can you walk like you walk in America?"

Jenny walked a few steps to show Johnny.

Johnny said "Yes like that! See, now you're walking as if nothing is new to you!"

"I still don't get it," said Rion.

"Look, when you look around you, how do you feel?"

"I feel like a tourist and I want to explore everything."

"See that's the problem! That's the reason why you tourists get ripped off so much, because you behave like you want to discover everything! Look, close your eyes." Rion closed his eyes, Johnny said "Imagine you are here, for the first time, everything is exciting isn't it?"

"Yes," said Rion while thinking.

"Now imagine, that this is not a city, it's a big jail, where you will have to spend the rest of your life.

Think like you're in a jail and you couldn't care less what happens around you. Now, do you feel like exploring?"

"No, I feel like escaping."

"See, there! That's how you should think. If every tourist thinks in his mind that he wants to explore, and shows the world that he wants to escape, then he will never get a bad deal! Now I want you to walk as if you're trapped here and want to escape."

Rion walked a few steps to demonstrate, and Johnny said "No, you're walking like you care too much. Wave your hands a little less faster, be cool and relaxed. Like that guy walking there." Johnny pointed to a man walking on the street, who was walking like he had never faced any problems in his life.

"Ohh, now I know what you mean. Wait, actually, everyone is walking like that!" Noticed Rion. "So, does nobody have any problems in India?"

"Problems? They have more problems than you can cope with. But they are so used to the carnage of life, that they are immune. They have a relaxed attitude, they think *we'll see when it happens*. In America, you guys plan for everything, if it's going to rain, you check the weather and take your umbrella, right?"

"Yes don't they do that here?" asked Rion.

"Haha, no! Here if it rains then people will find a shelter or they will enjoy the rain. Now show me, walk like you couldn't care less if it rains, or shines."

Rion demonstrated walking as if there was no need for him to worry about anything.

"That's perfect, see! That's how you should walk," said Johnny.

Rion had an eye-opening experience, and said "Johnny, you are very clever, you should be a psychologist!"

"Shall I tell you one more secret?"

"Yes?"

"In India, everybody is a psychologist!" Johnny started laughing.

Then, the real test came, Johnny took them back home on his motorcycle. Rion walked into the house without saying anything. Selina's mother was in the kitchen, and heard somebody come in, so she came out to check who it was, she said "Yes how can I help you?" Rion said "Namaste."

Selina's mother replied "Namaste," and then she realised "Rion, is that you!" Rion took off the mustache he was wearing and said "Yes, it's me!" Selina's mother was pleasantly surprised at how convincing the new dress code looked. She said "Where's Jenny, let me see her," Rion called Jenny and Johnny inside. Selina's mother thought Jenny looked beautiful "you look wonderful in this *ghagra*, I don't think even your parents will recognise you now!" Content with their getup, Rion and Jenny decided to surprise Selina by visiting her at the animal shelter.

Jenny and Rion walked in the animal shelter, and then Rion went to one of the sheep, and started stroking it without saying anything. Selina saw Rion but didn't recognise him at first. She asked, "Can I help you?" Rion didn't say anything, instead he picked up the sheep in his hands and started walking to the exit. Selina was worried and started chasing Rion, "Hey where are you going with my sheep!" She ran after him and Rion ran faster and faster away from her. He managed to reach the exit, where Selina saw Jenny smiling at Rion. Selina just about recognised Jenny, and so she said "Rion, is that you?"

Rion turned around to show Selina, "Rion at your service!"

Selina was surprised at how different he looked. She laughed about this unusual disguise. "What's this Rion?!"

"Now I know nobody can recognise us, because even Selina's eyes were deceived."

Selina smiled, and Rion started talking to Jenny when Selina said to herself "You've deceived my eyes today Rion, please don't deceive my heart."

It was time to close the shelter, so Selina suggested "Shall we all eat ice cream together?"

Rion agreed "great idea, my treat!"

When they reached the ice cream shop, Jenny had chocolate flavoured ice cream, while Rion wanted something new, "I'd like to try the Indian kulfi please."

The assistant asked Selina what flavour she would like, she also chose the same as Rion.

While having ice cream, Selina felt more romantic towards Rion in her heart. she admired his courage, and love for Jenny. Deep down, she wished somebody would have done what Rion did for Jenny, for her. Selina said "The gentle breeze is very romantic."

"Yes I like it too," said Rion.

"Have you ever seen the monsoon season in India?" asked Selina.

"No, what's that like?"

"It feels amazing. It feels like the heavens have opened only for you. You don't feel like sheltering inside from the rain, rather you feel like taking off your shoes, and walking outside in the open. It feels like the drops of rain are falling on your heart, not your body."

"Wow Selina, you're very romantic," said Jenny.

"Have you ever fallen in love?" Rion asked.

"Love, I'm not sure what love is, but I think I am beginning to understand..." Selina was thinking of how afraid she was that she had started to love Rion. She snapped out of it and then said "Because I saw you two, now I know what love is."

Selina was imagining in her heart how she wished that she and Rion could be together one day.

Jenny said "If we can do anything to help you find the man of your dreams, then tell me, I will help you."

"Thank you, if there is a time when I feel that I am able to share my secret with you, then I'll tell you who I love."

"Do you love somebody already? Who is it?" asked Rion.

"Yes, tell us Selina, I will help you to marry him, I promise," said Jenny, not knowing the truth.

"You can't help me," said Selina regretfully.

"I can, you said I am your sister, right? So, tell your older sister, who is it that you love?" said Jenny convincingly.

Selina was caught in two minds, whether to tell Rion how she had started to love him, or not.

Chapter Fifteen

To escape or not to escape?

Selina started to speak "I love a person, who maybe can't be mine…"

"Don't hesitate, if you trust me then tell me your secret, I'm just like your sister, I will unite both of you if I can," said Jenny.

"I trust you, if you think you can help me, then I'll tell you, because you're my sister…" Selina looked up at Jenny one more time to see her smiling, positive face, she decided to spill the beans "I love…" Selina was just about to say Rion's name, when Rion suddenly interrupted.

"The police, quick we have to go." Rion put on his mustache, and as they all realised the danger, they hastily left the ice cream parlour together. Selina had to leave with a heavy heart. This was a moment where she could declare her love for Rion, but destiny had other things in mind. She knew it was wrong, but couldn't help her emotions and feelings for a man who she admired and loved so much. And as if in slow motion, her opportunity to come out with her secret, disappeared.

Once they were home, everybody was sat in the living room, contemplating the next move. Rion said "We can't keep running like this. What do you think we should do sir?" he asked Selina's father. "We have a disguise, but how long can we keep running and hiding? Do you think it's safe for us to stay here?" he asked.

Selina's father was always fast to respond to Rion's questions, but this time he gave it some thought, "To tell you the truth son, I don't think that you're safe in Vrindavan. The main thing to consider is that you two have both become celebrities for the newspapers. So the government, police and the media will not rest until they find you. Now they already know that you're in Vrindavan, so for you to stay here is like playing with fire. Don't think that I don't want you to stay with us, but I think it's in your best interests to leave. Especially when I think about Jenny, you both should go from here."

"I understand... Do you have any suggestions as to where we could go next?" asked Rion.

"Oh don't worry about that, I have a good friend in Gujarat, he is trustworthy, he will help you both."

"Thank you very much, without your guidance, we would be clueless in India, we will take the train to Gujarat tomorrow."

"No, not the train. There could be police checking on trains and buses, and there are lots of people reading newspapers. You could be recognised."

"If we don't go by train, should we go by taxi?"

"No Rion, when you came to Vrindavan, you booked a taxi, and maybe that's how the police found out where you are. Don't worry, I will tell Johnny to take you tomorrow morning," said Selina's father.

"But he only has a motorcycle, how can Jenny, Johnny and myself sit on a motorcycle?" wondered Rion.

"Oh don't worry about that, in India even five people squeeze onto a motorcycle. Think about your safety, that's the main priority right now."

"That's what I'm worried about too, safety! How can three people sit on a motorcycle for so long?"

"You will have to do this Rion, if not for yourself, then for Jenny. It is important to go through a little bit of pain for long term gain. A motorcycle can go where cars cannot, and you'll easily be able to avoid Highway check posts with a motorcycle. With anything else, it will be difficult."

"But what about our luggage? How can we take that on a motorcycle?"

"Don't worry, Johnny will solve that problem for you!"

Johnny laughed and said "If anybody can... Johnny can!"

Selina was listening, she interrupted "I will take Rion and Jenny."

"No. How can you drive a motorcycle for eighteen hours? You will not go, Johnny will go," said her father.

"I can, and I know how to ride a motorcycle, I'll take breaks, but I will go."

"You will go! What about the animal shelter?" her father pointed out.

"Johnny can look after the animal shelter for a couple of days." Said Selina.

"But he's not a doctor! Who will administer the injections?" asked Rion.

"He is multi-talented, he can give injections too..." Johnny's face lit up at the compliment given to him by

Selina. "Please dad, I want to go, I want to take them. Jenny is my sister, and it's my duty to drop my sister."

After considering her plea, Selina's father said, "Okay, you can go," Selina was ecstatic. but you have to take regular breaks, okay?"

"Yes off course! Thank you dad, you're the best!" Said Selina as she hugged her father.

The next morning, Rion and Jenny put their luggage in a small trailer behind the motorcycle, which Johnny had connected for them. After having their last breakfast in the home which had given them shelter at such a crucial point in their lives, Jenny and Rion prepared themselves for the next part of their journey. Jenny & Rion hugged Selina's mother and father, and thanked them for their hospitality. The person whose eyes were most tearful however, were the eyes of Johnny. He said "If you need anything, call me, your brother will come to help you anywhere in the world, I mean anywhere in India if he has to. Just promise me, that when you go, you won't forget this brother of yours." Rion and Jenny gave Johnny a hug and felt emotional at the thought of parting with people who had become like their family. Selina's mother gave Rion and Jenny a thread, which she tied on their wrists, "This is for good luck, it will protect you in times of hardship."

Then the time of farewell came, sooner than they had expected. Selina sat on the motorcycle, followed by Jenny and Rion who were in disguise. And then, they drove off, leaving the family behind who had helped them so very much.

Selina's father said to Johnny "I never said this to Rion, but in my next life, I want a son like him."

Johnny agreed with him until he realised what his father meant "What!" he exclaimed.

Selina was happy, to finally be free from the shackles of society. She was content just telling herself that she was sitting on the same motorcycle as Rion, and that gave her a type of satisfaction. However, she felt as though she was about to lose the person she loved forever, now was the time to decide whether she would save her love, or let him go. While she continued riding the motorcycle, Rion spoke loudly from the back "If you feel tired Selina, tell me, I will ride."

"Do you know how to ride a motorcycle?" she asked.

"Yes, your brother taught me."

"Okay, if I get tired, I'll tell you."

Four hours or motorcycle riding later, it started to rain. Selina stopped the motorcycle near a highway restaurant where they all took shelter.

Jenny was in the restroom, Rion and Selina were standing under the canopy watching the heavy rainfall. Selina asked Rion "Do you remember when I said that in the Indian monsoon season, you don't feel like staying inside?"

"Yes, I remember," said Rion. "But, you aren't thinking about doing that now are you?"

Selina smiled at him. She took off her shoes, and she walked out into the rain, barefoot. Selina closed her eyes, enjoying every raindrop that fell on her. Selina tapped into her heart, mind and soul and felt as though she was being showered with love. She felt as though it was not water falling on her, rather it was Rion touching her soul. Selina started to dance in the rain. She was in a world of her own, the only thing she cared about in her heart, was her and Rion. After a while she came close to Rion and extended her hand to him, as if to ask him to dance with her. Rion looked at Jenny, who smiled and gave him permission to dance, so he walked with her in the rain. Selina took Rion's hand and span around and around many times. She kept spinning until she couldn't spin anymore. She then fell into Rion's arms, he supported Selina to stand again and then started to dance with her, he lead the way this time. The spectacle was quite unbelievable, the rain getting heavier, and Rion and Selina engrossed in only each other. As the dance continued, Selina got closer and closer to Rion, until she hugged him tightly. Rion could sense Selina's love for the first time. Her heart was beating fast, and he was caught in the strangest situation. Part of him wanted to continue hugging Selina, but he knew that the love of his life was Jenny, not Selina. Despite her will to hug him, Rion slowly let go of Selina, and looked down at the ground as she didn't want to open her eyes and come out of this most beautiful fantasy. Despite the world looking at her, she stayed in this bubble in which nobody could enter, for a few extra moments, until she slowly opened her eyes and realised where she was.

Jenny was in a forgiving mood. Although she could see that Selina had perhaps crossed the line by dancing with Rion in such an intimate manner, she knew that Rion only loved her and trusted him completely.

After feeling rejuvenated with the energy of love, it was time for them to commence their journey once again.

From here, Rion offered to ride the motorcycle, Selina obliged. Rion asked Selina for directions whenever he was lost, however Jenny noticed that Selina was sleepy, so she said to her "You sit in the middle, so if you fall asleep at least you won't fall off the motorcycle. Selina sat in the middle, and suddenly felt completely awake as she had an opportunity to sit behind Rion! She soon took the opportunity to hold him by his waist, as an excuse to keep balance on the motorcycle. Rion didn't think anything of it, as he was focused on driving. Selina directed Rion all the way, until they safely arrived at their destination.

Selina's relatives lived in Gujarat, hence they were Gujarati. They were happy to receive Jenny and Rion, they said "Kem cho, avo avo, maja ma?" Selina explained to Rion "That means welcome, come in, how are you." After being fed lunch by the host family, they all sat down together. There was a husband, wife, two sons, a daughter and an old grandmother in their family. Rion and Jenny felt like gypsies, yet they didn't feel as though they had ever left their family, it was like going from one home to another. The husband, Mr. Gokani, wanted to tell Rion something, "Selina's parents have told us everything, you don't need to fear anything, we will look after you well. You see the problem you are facing, is a problem I faced when I was younger. Shall

I tell you a secret?" Mr. Gokani came closer to Rion, "My wife and I also ran away with each other!"

"Really? Why?" asked Rion, while Jenny and Selina were also listening.

"Because her father was an old stubborn fart, he didn't want to marry her to me. You see, he thought he was high in society, very rich, and I was lower class than him, that was the stumbling block."

"That's the same problem with Jenny's father!" He looked at Jenny to make sure he wouldn't get into trouble with her later.

"Don't worry, this is a common problem in India," said Mr. Gokani.

"What's the solution?" asked Rion.

"There is no solution to this problem. You see, when a boy loves a girl, and he tells the girl, sometimes the girl becomes arrogant, and sometimes the girl's father becomes arrogant. But by the time they realise how much you loved her, it's too late. This is a problem with the human race to be honest with you. When we have something, we don't appreciate it, and when we lose that thing, then we appreciate it."

"Thank you for supporting us in our times of trouble, we will be forever indebted to you," said Rion.

"Oh no, you are our guest, and in India, a guest is like…"

"Like god!" Interrupted Rion.

"Yes how do you know?"

"Selina's parents told me this when they agreed to keep us in their home."

Jenny felt like adding something, "From this honeymoon we have learned a lot about India. In future, even if we lose everything, we know that in India we will still be able to live happily, because this is a land of values and culture, where we will be well looked after."

"Thank you Jenny. By saying this you have given the utmost respect to Gijarat, our home and our country. If you would like to see our culture, then tonight is a function called Navratri. In this festival you can pray to our Indian goddess, she will surely solve your problems. Selina, you should go along too."

Although Selina was excited at the prospect of spending time with Rion and Jenny, she was exhausted from staying awake all night staring at Rion while he was dreaming, so she fell asleep into her own dream world for a few hours.

Meanwhile Rion and Jenny took out some time to make an important phone call. Rion spotted a telephone booth, he called Hannah from there. As soon as he phoned her, Hannah picked up and said "Hello, Rion are you okay? How's Jenny? Where are you?"

"I'm good Hannah, Me and Jenny are in a city called Rajkot in Gujarat... How did you know it was me?"

"I can see the dialing code from India, I'm always looking out for your call!" she said.

"You're the best friend ever Hannah! I hope you're well, I worry about you..."

"I'm fine now Rion, ever since you've left, I just worried about when you will be back."

"Soon hopefully, I wanted to ask you something, can you do me a favour?"

"Off course I can do anything for you, just tell me what to do."

"I sent an email to the American embassy in India, and in the USA, and I explained that me and Jenny are happily married."

"Did you send a copy of your marriage certificate?" asked Hannah.

"Yes I did. I want to ask you if you can check my email from there and see if they responded, because I don't want them to find out where I am by looking at the IP address from which I open my email in India. I think somebody is keeping a very close eye on us."

"Okay sure I'll check your email, but how can I tell you? Do you have a phone number I can call you on?"

"No I don't, but I'll call you back later. Now write down my password so you can login." Rion gave Hannah the password to his email account.

"Okay Rion, look after yourself and Jenny."

"Yes I will. How are Eddy and Harvey?"

"They are fine. They're with me now, do you want to say hi?"

"Sure."

Hannah gave the phone to Harvey "Rion, we miss you man, when will you be back, we want to see you as soon as possible!"

"I'm trying my best bro, hopefully soon, we miss you guys too."

Eddy took the phone from Harvey and asked "Where are you now Rion? is everything okay?"

"Yes Eddy we're just staying with a family in Rajkot. Hopefully we'll be back soon because I've emailed the American embassy. Pray to god for me man, your prayers always work."

"Sure my friend, I will definitely pray for you," said Eddy willingly.

"Okay, I have to go now, I'll speak later, can you do me a favour? Please look after Hannah, I miss her."

"Don't worry, as long as Eddy is with Hannah, she will be happy."

"I'm really greatful to you, look after yourself, take care."

"Take care Rion, Bye." said Eddy.

Chapter Sixteen

Sensual Souls

In the evening, Selina, Jenny and Rion all dressed up in beautiful attire to go to the Navratri celebration. Jenny and Selina both looked stunning in an Indian dress called ghagra choli, Jenny wearing a pink version while Selina wore purple. They both looked colourful, elegant, and sensual at the same time. They all entered a huge open ground with flood lights. There was live music on stage which made it a festival type, atmosphere. There was a circular display in the centre of the ground, which displayed pictures of Indian goddesses. Rion was looking around at everything like a tourist again, even though he wore his disguise, anybody could guess that he seemed like a lost soul.

Selina was all too aware and showed him and Jenny to some chairs where they all sat -down, and then she explained, "This is a function which is nine days long, it represents the battle that lasted nine days between the Indian goddess and evil forces in ancient times. During this festival, people dance all night long to the energetic tunes of traditional Indian music."

"Sounds like a lot of stamina is needed to dance for so long?" asked Rion.

"Yes, and this festival is all about energy and stamina. Not just for the duration of this festival, but it also represents the energy and stamina we need in the battle of life," explained Selina.

"Amazing, I hope the Indian goddess can bless me with energy to fight through my life, I feel like a homeless gypsy at the moment,' said Rion.

"At least you have your love with you. I'm sure god will solve all your problems soon," Selina realised that although Rion was in a tough situation, he had love, which she didn't have. But she changed the topic "shall we dance?"

Rion was a little cautious after the last time that Selina started dancing with him romantically. He carefully agreed.

Selina lead the way, as Rion and Jenny followed her to the centre of the ground, navigating through thousands of people who attended the event. It seemed as though the spotlight was shining on them, and the world was watching. Selina demonstrated what to do. The dance step was quite simple, "Just clap with your hands, take a step back, clap again and then take three steps forward. This was relatively simple, yet it took Rion and Jenny a while to get used to it. However, once they mastered this, they really started to enjoy themselves. Rion was dancing with Selina in front and Jenny behind him. They were part of a larger circle of people, that was going around the pictures of the Indian goddesses. As the music got faster and faster, the steps had to be done faster and faster. At this stage, Jenny gave up and sat down, Rion and Selina continued. They were dancing with each other, yet they were dancing in worlds of their own. At that time, Selina showed Rion another dancing circle which was outside the circle they were in. In this circle, they were doing a slightly different, more difficult set off steps, but after a short tutorial from Selina and some practice, Rion mastered that too. This was the peak of participation from the crowds of thousands of people. As the music got faster and faster, the stamina required to continue went up. Rion kept on dancing, so too did Selina. As the music became faster and faster, Selina soon dropped out. Rion kept dancing, more and more people dropped out, people were looking at the few people left dancing, Rion was amongst them. Rion was charged, he kept on going, dancing, round and round, clapping, moving, spinning, stopping, turning, and then going again. Jenny and Selina were both admiring his stamina to continue dancing for so long. But Rion was in a trance like state. He didn't care about the world, he was focused, he was free, and enchanted by the soul beating music. He kept going, more and more, the climax of the music was taking place, Rion kept on going, he danced until the music was being played. Finally, the music and the dancing stopped, Rion looked around him, he was amongst just a handful of people remaining. He walked back to where Jenny and Selina were sitting.

Jenny gave him some water and said "I didn't know you were so good at dancing."

"Neither did I!" he said, "Shall we go home now?"

"There's more dancing to come." said Selina, "It'll finish at 3am. That's why other people were saving their energy while you were dancing!"

They all laughed, "Now I know why you dropped out Selina, hey?!"

The night continued like this until it was time for the finale, the *Arti*. Selina explained, "This is the time when people gather around the pictures of the Indian goddesses and pray to them by holding steel dishes with a small *divo*... this candle. You have to wave the arti in circles as an offering to god." Selina showed them how to do it, it was a simple circular motion in which the steel plate or *arti* had to be moved while the prayer was being sung, with a candle on it. Rion and Jenny held the arti, but half way through the prayer, Rion felt that perhaps Selina should also join in, so he took her hand and put it on the arti. They were all praying together, to the goddess whom would hopefully give them the energy to fulfill the challenges of their individual lives, it was a truly moving moment.

After the arti was finished Rion said "Thank you, Selina."

"Thank you?! But why?"

"Because of you, we had a chance to experience some magical things in India. Because of you me and Jenny are safe. And today because of you, I'm sure god will bless all of us."

"Yes Selina," added Jenny "you have been a really wonderful addition to our lives, we will always remember what you have done for us." Selina was shy from the compliments being showered on her, so she just smiled with humility.

After going home, Jenny and Rion said "goodnight," to Selina, and went to their bedroom. The mood was upbeat, despite such a tiring day, Rion still felt he had some energy left, which was quite surprising considering he had just danced for almost five hours. Perhaps the reason behind his energy was the blessing from the Indian goddess, and perhaps also because Jenny was looking so beautiful. In fact to call her beautiful would be an understatement. Jenny was wearing a pink coloured Indian ghaghra choli, a golden nose ring, the most elegant earrings and bangles to match her costume. When she un-tied her hair, it revealed a long lock of hair like a waterfall. The most fortunate thing for Rion, was that more than thirty days had passed since Jenny had promised to the gods that she would not engage in any sexual activity for one month after marriage.

Rion was lying on the bed, Jenny, looking like a beautiful angel was standing in front of him. She was looking at Rion, differently than she normally does. She slowly came closer and closer to him, until she was only a few inches away from him. She whispered in his ear "You are my world, I am yours." Rion took Jenny into his arms, Jenny completely surrendered herself to him. Rion put his hands on her waist, and kissed her lips, he said "You are my world, you're everything for me, I love you, I am yours Jenny." Free from the boundaries of Jenny's promise, Rion could express his love to her however he wanted. Jenny felt as though she was the luckiest girl in the world. It felt as though Rion and Jenny's life of darkness had been lit up by this moment of joy. This moment was a moment where the pain and separation of many years could be forgotten, and all the suffering of the past months could be devoted to the love and feelings on this most special occasion. Tonight was a night, that would give them the true joy of love and marriage. Their devotion to each other was a real testimony of love without the shackles of lust. This was true love at its purest. Jenny and Rion completely lost themselves in each other. Their heart, mind and soul was devoted to each other. As their bodies touched each other, their minds and souls were also unified and uplifted. They touched each other from head to toe, and experienced every part of their being, with the boundaries of clothes removed one by one. They felt as though they wanted nothing else than each other. They felt that in their entire lives, all that they would need to be happy is each other. The entire night, in this divine moment, was theirs.

Chapter Seventeen

Go

The following morning was a beautiful one, where everything seemed to be new, and the world was worth discovering again. Jenny made tea and breakfast for Rion in bed, with the sun shining gentle rays of hope into their lives. The previous night gifted them the best rejuvenation they had ever experienced, it felt as though now, their honeymoon had truly begun.

After a romantic morning, Rion remembered he also had to phone Hannah and find out whether or not the American embassy had received the email. Jenny was still in a romantic mood so Rion said "You stay here, I'll make a phone call and be back soon."

"Okay, but take Selina with you, I don't feel safe letting you go alone anywhere," suggested Jenny.

And so Rion and Selina made their way to the telephone booth. Rion called Hannah and said "Hello, Hannah, how are you?"

"Hi Rion, I'm fine, I have some good news for you!"

"Good news? Tell me!" Rion was excited.

"The American embassy have replied to your email, they're asking for your address, so that they can send some officials from the embassy to you. They will bring you back safely, and even protect you from Jenny's father!"

"Really!? I can't believe it, are you telling the truth?"

"Yes! Give me your address, I'll send them an email. They'll bring you back from India today."

"Come on!" celebrated Rion. "Selina, they will take us back, can you believe it?" he said.

"Who's Selina?" asked Hannah.

"Oh," Rion wasn't sure what to say for a moment, "she's a wonderful girl we met in India Hannah, she helped us a lot…"

"That's good, I'm glad you had somebody to look after you in India. What's your address, I'll email the embassy officials."

"Okay write it down… It's number 24 Navjeevan Society, Imliwala Road, Rajkot" Hannah had some difficulty understanding the address, so she asked Rion to speel out the words. After Hannah wrote down the address of where Rion and Jenny were staying in Rajkot, India, she said "Thank you Rion, I'll look forward to seeing you soon."

"See you soon," said Rion. Hannah had some hope that soon she could see Rion again.

Rion was elated. He couldn't believe that the American government were going to rescue him and Jenny. He was so excited he hugged Selina and said "We're going back home Selina! We're going back home!" Selina was in a strange situation, she was happy that Rion could be safe again, but sad that he would be leaving. She had moist eyes while Rion continued to express his happiness. On the way home he said "Aren't you happy that me and Jenny will be safe and secure back in America again?"

Selina wiped her eyes, tried to smile and said "I'm happy Rion, I'm very happy… You will go home, Jenny and you can stay together happily ever after, what more could I want? I just hope, that once you go there, you won't forget me." Rion stopped walking. Selina said, "I know that Jenny lives in your soul. But if you could give me a little bit of space in your heart, I would really appreciate it."

Rion took a deep breath smiled, while looking into Selina's eyes and said, "You are such a wonderful human being. You love animals, you care about others, you have already made space in my heart, I can never forget you." Rion hugged Selina, he stroked her hair, and allowed her to rest her head on his chest, where she could let all her tears flow freely. Once Selina had vented her sadness, Rion wiped her tears and said "Now I want to see you smile, if you don't smile then I will be sad. She smiled, and that brought a smile to his face.

When they reached back home, Rion rushed upstairs and said "I love you!" Rion picked up Jenny and span her around many times.

Jenny was happy but also wondered, "What happened!"

"The American embassy has emailed me back, Hannah said they'll come to get us today once they receive her reply!"

"Really? Wow!" Jenny was ecstatic, this was the light at the end of the tunnel they had both waited for.

Without any delay, they both started packing their luggage. Once they finished they went downstairs to see Mr. Gokani and tell him the good news.

When they saw him however, the news first came from him. Mr. Gokani said "Have you read the Newspaper? They know that you and Jenny are in Rajkot."

Mr. Gokani gave Rion a copy of today's newspaper, and showed him the headlines *American kidnapper arrives in Rajkot with victim.*

Rion thought to himself "how on earth could the newspaper know that me and Jenny are in Rajkot. We only came yesterday, and that too by motorcycle."

Jenny said "This isn't good news, how do the authorities know we're here?"

"Did you tell anyone that you're here?" asked Mr. Gokani.

"No," said Rion. "I didn't tell anybody except yesterday when I called..." then it suddenly clicked in Rion's mind. He called Hannah yesterday and told her that they were in Rajkot. Even last time, when he told Hannah that he and Jenny were in Vrindavan, the newspaper headlines reflected this fact the following day. However, every part of his mind and body was not willing to accept that Hannah would stab them in the back like this.

Rion and Jenny went back into their room. Jenny asked "Do you think that the Indian family could have told the newspapers?"

"The families we lived with can't be traitors Jenny, they treat guests like god. Besides, if they wanted, they could have handed us over to the police by now and claimed a reward."

"Then I think Hannah must be telling the authorities everything Rion, you've even given her our address. We need to leave before the embassy officials get here. Maybe this is a trap to get us into more trouble." Rion looked at Jenny with contemplation, he was thinking if they should stay at Mr. Gokani's home or leave, before the person who gave the newspapers the name of the city, also gave the police their address. Rion considered whether or not they should leave without waiting for the U.S embassy officials.

Two hours later, the American officials arrived at Mr. Gokani's house. The lead official knocked on the door. Mr. Gokani opened the door, "Yes, how can I help you?" The official said "We are here because we have had information that two American citizens, Rion Rai and Jenny Brown are staying with you. We would like to take them back to America, can we come in?"

Mr. Gokani welcomed them in as a swarm of officials from the American Embassy walked into Mr. Gokani's house.

Jenny and Rion were sitting there in the living room, ready to be taken away by them.

The lead official said "Rion, we received your email from a *Hannah*? She sent us a copy of your marriage certificate. We would just like to inform you, that we've verified your marriage with the registry office, and we're satisfied that you two are here willingly. However we would request that you come back home, because your families, and now the whole country is extremely worried about you. But if you want to stay here, it's entirely your wish, we will respect your decision."

Rion considered his options and concluded calmly, "We would like to come with you now officer. But we have just one last request, can we have fifteen minutes? We would like to thank some of the people who have helped us so much and come so close to our hearts."

"Sure sir, take your time, we're waiting outside," the officials left the home and waited outside.

Rion and Jenny took this time to bid farewell to the host family who had been so helpful, and of course Selina, without whom their stay in India wouldn't have been so pleasant.

Rion walked up to Selina, and said "Thank you, the help you have given us, is invaluable. We will be indebted to you forever."

Selina gathered courage to speak, while holding in her tears, "I will miss you, I really want you to stay, if you can, then please stay." She looked downwards as tears were flowing from her eyes. Jenny and Rion were helpless. Selina said, "If you must go, then I have just one request, please don't forget me. Please don't forget me."

"Forgetting you is not possible Selina." Said Rion sternly. "Even if life throws the toughest challenges at me, whenever I remember the people who are closest to my heart, your name will always come first. You are the symbol of a good host and a wonderful human being. Whenever I think of honesty and real love, I will remember you." Rion hugged Selina, she vented her tears near his heart, and experienced his warm sanctum one last time.

"Me too," added Jenny. She also hugged Selina and said "You have made a special place for yourself in my heart, and I will never give that place to anybody else. I hope you can give your sister some space in your heart too?" Selina cried and hugged Jenny one more time.

Finally, Rion thanked Mr. Gokani and his family for their hospitality, and slowly moved towards the door. He was waving goodbye to one of the most special people in his life, Selina. This moment reminded him of the time when Rion was at Burbage school in London looking at Jenny before leaving to move to America. It had a sense of sadness which was beyond comprehension.

Rion and Jenny went downstairs, where they sat in the cars provided by the American embassy officials. As Rion was about to sit in the car, he waved goodbye to Selina one last time. In truth this was a moment, where Rion was bidding farewell, not only to Selina, but also to the cultures and values she stood for, as well as the country which had given him and Jenny so much, the country of India.

On the flight back, Jenny asked "How did you know that Hannah is so trustworthy? You told her yesterday that you're in Rajkot, and today it's in the newspaper."

"I know Hannah very well. She's a simple hearted girl.   She would never betray me."

"Then how did the newspapers know where we are?" asked Jenny.

"Don't worry, I know that there is a traitor, and the traitor is in America. Now it's just a case of finding out who the traitor is... I'll find the traitor when we reach America."

Chapter Eighteen

East or West

Once Rion and Jenny landed America, the embassy officials escorted them to high security government vehicles in which they would be transported. However, it came as a surprise to both of them when they weren't taken home, rather they were taken to the police station for further questioning.

The police officers Separated Rion and Jenny into different rooms. They were both weary but they had no other option.

A police officer asked Jenny whether or not she had married Rion of her own free will.

The police also questioned Rion separately to find out if his story matched hers.

They were both interrogated for a period of approximately two hours, in which the officers asked all sorts of questions ranging from their motives behind running away from home to what they did in India.

After two hours, they were both called together again to hear the outcome of the questioning. The inspector in charge, Mr. Sanders, entered the room. He said "Jenny, Rion, I have listened to both of you answering questions from my officers. When you were telling your stories, I was actually watching you through this one-way mirror, and so I had a firsthand account of your statements," he pointed at the glass.

Rion could see into the next room in which he was being questioned earlier. He looked at Jenny with surprise as earlier all he could see was a mirror.

There was a feeling of tension in the police station. Even the officers wanted to know what the verdict would be.

Mr. Sanders said "And my conclusion is this... Never in my career, have I seen two people who are so deeply in love, willing to sacrifice themselves for each other. I asked you Rion if you could choose one person to stay in jail between you or Jenny, and you said you would sacrifice yourself for Jenny." Mr. Sanders looked at him and remembered what Rion said, *"I will stay in jail, if you can guarantee that you will allow Jenny to be free."*

Mr. Sanders continued to speak, "Jenny I asked you, if you would sacrifice your life in jail for Rion, you said the same thing," Jenny remembered what she said *"If I'm free, and Rion is in jail, my conscience won't let me live, I'd rather stay here, so that my love can be free."*

Mr. Sanders continued "You were willing to stay in jail to let Rion go back home. Your love is an example of how true love should be... So I have decided, I want to set both of you love birds free. There are some people in this world who love so they can live. But you two live, so that you can love. The meaning of your lives is love. You are both free to go."

Rion and Jenny were extremely relieved to know that they could both live with each other again. Jenny was in a hurry to get up and leave the police station, but Rion had one request "Mr. Sanders, I would like to thank you for your kindness. But there's one thing which we're both concerned about."

"Tell me, we'll help you in any way we can."

Jenny answered the question for Rion, "Actually sir it's my father. He's the reason why we had to run away from home in the first place. We're worried that he may try to harm us. Specially if he finds out that we married each other against his will."

"Hmm, what does your father do Jenny?"

"He's a businessman, he has an animal farm, and some other food supply businesses but he never told me exactly what they were."

"Okay don't worry... Let's do this, we'll take you both to your father's house and request him to leave both of you alone. If he bothers you again, then we'll arrest him, is that okay?" asked Mr. Sanders.

Rion explained, "Sir, the truth is that we just want Mr. Brown's blessings, if he can bless us, then there will be nobody happier than us. Jenny will be able to have her father back, and I will have a father in-law."

"Okay, we'll try to get your father in-law back. Hopefully he understands that it's best just to forgive and forget the past. Let's go there and talk to him first... Um, Jenny is there anything you want from your house, any belongings that you need?"

"No sir, I've taken my most valued possessions and if there's anything else I need, I'm sure my husband will provide it. But I do have one small request..." Jenny explained her desire to the police inspector politely. Mr. Sanders smiled and then they all embarked on a mission to Mr. Brown's house.

Meanwhile Mr. Brown and his bodyguards were still anxiously waiting for news about Jenny. He was shouting at the employees "Wait till I get my hands on that low class good for nothing boy. He hasn't taken my daughter, he has put his hands on my family and my prestige. He will have to pay the price."

Just then the doorbell rang, Mr. Brown sent one of his bodyguards to take a look. As soon as he opened the door a barrage of police officers entered Mr. Brown's home.

Jenny and Rion waited patiently outside in the police vehicle, hoping that everything inside went smoothly.

Mr. Sanders looked at Mr. Brown and said, "You must be Mr. Brown?"

"Yes, I am, what's the reason for your visit officer?"

"We have found your daughter," said Mr. Sanders.

"Wait till I get my hands on her... She has made me and my family a laughing stock. Where is she?"

"She is outside, safe, under my protection, with your son-in law," said Mr. Sanders.

"Son in-law? He is a good for nothing, waste of space. He'll have to pay the price for taking my daughter away from me."

"*Mr. Brown!*" said Mr. Sanders with intense discipline. "Your daughter, and your son-in law are both under my protection, and under the protection of the United States law. If anything happens to either of them, then you will be prosecuted."

"Prosecuted? Who will prosecute me? Do you know who I am?" asked Mr. Brown arrogantly.

"I don't know who you are, and to be honest I don't care. But let me tell you who I am. I am Police inspector Darren Sanders, and once I promise to protect someone, nobody can harm them. Not even a measly pipsqueak called Mr. Brown who thinks he is a gift from god."

Mr. Brown looked as though he had been told off by a teacher in school. But he was raging.

"Perhaps you should forgive them," continued Mr. Sanders, "they really love each other. In my experience, I have never seen any two people in love so deeply. I think..."

"Enough!" Interrupted Mr. Brown with gritted teeth. "Inspector. You are here to give me the news that they are back, nothing more, nothing less. Thank you for the news. Now if you would like some tea or coffee, then my butler would be glad to serve you. If not, then get out of my house and carry on with your job at the police station."

"I will go back to my job Mr. Brown. However, perhaps you misunderstood the reason why I'm here. Jenny and Rion feel as though their lives are incomplete without you. They want you to be a part of their happiness. Actually, they are foolish enough to still want your blessings Mr. Brown so that..."

"Blessings! I will give them my blessings. Wait Inspector, wait for just a short while, I will give Rion and Jenny the best blessings you can imagine... I will make their lives a living hell. I will make them wish that they had never come into this world. They have not disrespected me Inspector, they have dishonored my prestige, and I will make them pay for it."

Mr. Sanders got a feeling that Mr. Brown was not getting the vibe of what he was saying, so he changed his tone of speaking "I need to get one message through to you Mr. Brown."

"Oh yeah? What?" said Mr. Brown with anger raging through his veins.

"It is possible that you may see Rion and Jenny again, after all they live in the same city. It's possible that you may hear news of them having a proper marriage ceremony with their family and friends. It's even possible that they may send you an invitation, because they have good intentions, and they still consider you a part of their family. But let me set one thing straight. If anything happens to Jenny, Rion or any of their family or friends, you will be the first suspect Mr. Brown. And I promise you, if I hear any news like that, I will not rest until I lock you up behind bars. So, it's best that you forget about any thought of revenge you may have in your little mind." Mr. brown looked directly at Mr. Sanders like a pressure cooker about to blow. He was holding in all his anger after hearing this ultimatum from the inspector.

Mr. Sanders put his police hat back on, and before leaving he mentioned one more thing "Jenny has said to us that she doesn't need anything from you apart from your blessings, but since you won't give your blessings, she also requested that she wants three animals from your farm. A cow called India, a pig called George and a chicken called lucky. Are you aware of these animals?"

Mr. Brown opened his mouth after holding his anger in for so long, "Indeed... I am painfully aware of these animals. See how mentally unstable my daughter is? She wants those bloody animals who don't even deserve to live."

"I will be the judge of who is mentally unstable Mr. Brown. But for now, Jenny has asked us to take these three animals. She wishes to keep them."

"Three animals, from my farm, no chance!"

Mr. Sanders looked at Mr. Brown with a stern face.

Mr. Brown changed his mind, "Fine. If she wishes to feed, look after and keep these three stinking animals, then take the low lives. Perhaps then she will understand how difficult it is to raise these dumb animals who just eat and sleep all day. Peter, go and get the animals for the police officer." Mr. Brown signaled to one of his accomplices called Peter to get the animals for Mr. Sanders to take away.

After waiting patiently in the car for one hour, Jenny and Rion finally saw three beautiful animals emerge from Mr. Brown's home.

The police took India the cow, George the pig and Lucky the chicken into the police van. Mr. Brown stepped out of his front door and looked directly at them. He looked angrily towards Jenny and Rion. Jenny had a feeling of guilt looking at her father. Rion felt sorry for her too. He put his arm around Jenny. Mr. Brown looked with extreme hatred at Rion. Rion looked with determination at Mr. Brown. The long line of police cars, and a police van carrying Jenny's dearest animal friends, made their way to the home of Jenny's mother in-law.

Jenny had never expected in her whole life, that the day she would bid farewell to her father after marriage, would be with a long line of police cars, almost in a state of war with her father. Rion never imagined that this is how he would get married. They had both constructed fantasies of a beautiful wedding in their hearts, with extravagant outfits, hundreds of guests, and a grand venue. But this was a unique set of circumstances for two unique lovers.

When they arrived outside the front door, Rion was holding a cow and a pig by the leash, and Jenny held a chicken in her hands. When his mother opened the door Rion said "Hi mum, This is Jenny, I fell in love with her, but her father was against our marriage. But because Jenny loved me as much as I loved her, we both ran away with each other. We spent one month in India running from the police and celebrating our honeymoon. Just now we came from Jenny's house after collecting three of her favourite animal friends. This is India the cow, George the Pig, and Lucky the chicken."

"Oh okay, come in I've made pasta for you," said Rion's mother.

Jenny was surprised at how cool and calm his mother was with that explanation. Jenny entered the house. It wasn't a very big house like hers, but she felt as though it was a warm and cozy home."

"But how did you know we were going to come mum?" asked Rion.

"I was watching the news, you two have become more famous than pop stars." Rion and Jenny saw that the TV was on, and the news did indeed show their story. It was the police officer they had met, Mr. Sanders on the TV, he was speaking "Today I've witnessed how much Jenny and Rion love each other. When questioned in separate interview rooms in the police station, they were both willing to go to jail for each other."

A journalist asked "But we hear that the girl's father has said that Jenny was kidnapped by Rion?"

"This is not true, I've seen their marriage certificate, and more importantly I've seen how much they love each other, I'm satisfied that Mr. Brown was just lying to save the prestige of his family. He was against their marriage, because Rion didn't match the social class of his family."

Rion's mother turned off the TV and said "Everything is okay Rion, I understand what you did, and why you did it. Jenny's a lovely girl and know you two will both live happily together." Jenny smiled out of shyness. "But where are we going to keep these animal friends of yours?"

Rion put his arms around his mother and said "Mum, you know the guest room we have, when will we be able to use that?"

His mother put her hands on her head, she couldn't imagine what was going to happen next.

Over the next few days, Rion and Jenny arranged the guest room in such a way, that there were three separate beds in the guest room for George, India and Lucky. They bought clothes for the new arrivals too.

George the pig wore a green jumper, and a nappy, along with sunglasses to top off his cool image. India the cow had an orange scarf to keep her warm, and a lovely orange sweater, with bright yellow shorts. Lucky the chicken received his very own little blue chicken costume, and a stylish matching cap. No longer were they farm animals, now they looked like respectable members of the family! After a short amount of time, Rion's mother began to warm to the animals. She would watch TV, and when she felt lonely she would shout for George, who would come and join her. India and Lucky would often feel lonely and come without invitation!

One day Rion's mother sat with Jenny to speak to her while Rion was out of the house. She said "Jenny, in any home, it's important that the daughter in-law and mother in-law have a positive relationship. When I first saw you, I wasn't sure how our relationship would be, specially when I saw these unique friends of yours."

Jenny was nervously waiting for Rion's mother to explain her point of view.

"But now, I am sure that Rion has made the right choice by marrying you." Jenny felt a huge sense of relief in hearing that. "Do you know what I like most about you?" Jenny looked up to hear what she would say. "I love your animal friends the most. And I love the fact that you have such kindness in your heart for these animals. It's very brave of you to bring these animals to your mother in-law. What gave you the strength to ask your father to give you George, India and Lucky?"

"I love animals aunty, without animals I feel like my life isn't complete." Just then Rion came home, and he listened to what Jenny was saying, without them knowing that he was there. Although India did notice his arrival, she kept quiet due to Rion's polite request!

Jenny said "I feel like inside those animals is a part of me. If they get hurt, it feels like somebody hurt me. I feel that animals feel the same way as humans do, and that's the reason why I brought them here. I hope you don't mind aunty?" Jenny referred to Rion's mother as *aunty* out of respect.

"Oh no dear. In fact by bringing them here you've opened my eyes. I never knew pigs were so clever." George was their, listening to the conversation. India left Rion in the corridor and sat with Rion's mother, she made a moo sound, so Rion's mother said "Oh and cows, I never knew they could be so friendly!" India didn't seem too pleased with that response. So Rion's mother added "Oh, not only friendly, they are so clever too!" Now India was satisfied and she rested her head on Jenny's lap. Lucky the chicken started flapping his wings, so Rion's mum said "And also chickens, even Lucky recognises me now when I go to feed him, don't you lucky?" Lucky came running to Rion's mother, and she picked him up and put him on her lap where she could stroke him. "Since the passing of Rion's father, I have never seen so much happiness in this house. For the first time in years, it seems like this is not just a house... but a home. Thank you Jenny."

George and India were right up close next to Rion's mother by now. When they saw Lucky sitting in her lap, the cow and pig came even closer to Rion's mother stroking their heads on her lap, "I can't keep both of you in my lap too!"

Rion entered the room and said "May I be of assistance?" He took George in his lap, while Jenny took India in her lap. It finally seemed like a complete family. The only thing missing was a photographer. The scene should have been captured, a cow, a pig and a chicken sat in the laps of three people who began to love animals so much. Rion's mother said "I can't believe this is happening!"

Jenny had settled in nicely to living with Rion and his mother. She felt warm, comfortable, and at home.

On Rion's mind however was another pressing issue, which he wanted to address as soon as possible. He wanted to meet his friends, and to be specific, Rion wanted to find out who that person was, that informed the newspapers in India about where they were. This was a question that kept repeating itself in his mind for many days. But now he felt as though it was the right time to answer the most important question of all. Who was the bloody traitor?

Chapter Nineteen

Finding traitor

"Hello, Hannah! It's me..."

She was excited, "Rion you're back! I missed you so much, how is Jenny? I want to see you both!"

"I want to see you too... Can you meet me tomorrow, at 4pm? But can you meet me alone? There's something important I need to discuss with you," explained Rion.

"Yeah sure I'll meet you at four."

"Oh and please don't tell Eddy or Harvey."

"Okay, I won't," she said.

"They aren't with you now are they?"

"No, I'm at home, in my bedroom."

"Okay then I'll see you tomorrow, at 4pm, please be on time."

The next day Rion met with Hannah. He discussed something secretive with her, and gave her a selection of detailed instructions.

From that day, Rion began to buy the newspaper every day. He would also watch the news religiously. Two weeks passed like this, but Rion still didn't see what he was looking for on the TV.

Jenny noticed that Rion's attention on the TV was much more focused than usual. She felt as though he wasn't giving her attention like he used to. One day while Rion was watching TV, Jenny asked "You don't love me any more do you?"

"Huh? I love you more than Neil Armstrong loves the moon, I love you more than Sachin Tendulkar loves Cricket, and I love you more than…" he was thinking.

"You love me more than?…"

"I love you more than a fat man loves pizza."

"Really?" asked Jenny with a gazed look on her face.

"Yes, really dear, now please don't ask yourself such silly questions."

"Then why aren't you focusing on me?" asked Jenny like a cute teddy bear.

"Because I am looking for something."

"What are you looking for?"

"I'm looking for a special news report about us."

"Oh really? Are we going to be on the news again!" Jenny asked excitedly.

"If my suspicion is correct, then yes."

"What suspicion my dear husband?"

"First promise you won't tell anyone?"

"Who would I tell? I don't even know anybody," said Jenny innocently.

"Okay, well, do you remember I wanted to find out who the traitor was that told the media about where we were in India?"

"Oh yeah, somebody kept telling the news stations where we were, did you find out who it was?"

"Yes, I thought of a way of finding the traitor."

"Really! How?" asked Jenny.

"Well I told two separate stories to two separate friends, and whichever friend is the traitor…"

"That is the friend that will give that story to the news networks?"

"Correct!"

"What were the two stories that you told your friends?"

"Well, I told one friend that you are pregnant and we're going to have a baby!"

"How sweet!" said Jenny. "What did tell your other friend?"

Just then, Rion saw what he was waiting for on the TV. The News reporter said "And we have some breaking news about the runaway couple who just returned from India. Rising tensions between the newly weds mean that they may be heading for divorce." Jenny immediately looked at Rion. Rion looked at Jenny through the side of his eyes like a little puppy, and just as Jenny was about to lash out at him, he jumped up and ran from her. She chased him around the house, before he ran out of the front door! He was laughing, and panting for breath. Then slowly his feeling changed from laughter to a more serious mood. He looked determined. He set off on a journey.

Rion knocked on the front door. Eddy opened the door. "Oh Rion, what a pleasant surprise!" said Eddy, and he invited Rion into his home.

Rion walked in, closed the door behind him, looked at Eddy and said "Ah, Eddy, such a sweet, innocent looking friend of mine. Anybody would think that your heart was made of gold. But behind this fun and humble Eddy, there was a sly, hidden character who was waiting to show his true colours all along, isn't that right?... Mr. Edward?" So you are the one who has been a traitor? Now are you going to tell me why you did all this straight away, or am I going to have to show you how angry I can get?" said Rion with aggression.

"I don't know what you mean Rion?" said Eddy.

Rion grabbed Eddy by his neck, pinned him up against the wall and shouted "why did you do this? Why are you such a traitor?"

"Traitor? What do you mean?" said Eddy.

Rion threw Eddy on the floor and said "You know what I mean. Every time in India wherever me and Jenny went, the News stations knew everything. Why did you do this?" Rion grabbed Eddy's neck and said "I thought you were my friend, you stabbed me in the back?" Rion continued to attack Eddy aggressively. He punched him several times.

"Please let go of me, I'll tell you everything," pleaded Eddy, as he was being beaten with extreme force.

Rion pulled him up, threw him onto the couch, and said "Okay, why did you tell the newspapers about where me and Jenny were? Why did you keep giving them all the information?"

Eddy was almost in tears, he was shaken, trying to compose himself, then he spoke, "It wasn't my idea Rion. It wasn't my plan. It was somebody else's."

"Whose idea was it?" Eddy had a solemn look on his face.

Did Jenny's father come to you?"

"No, it wasn't Jenny's father."

"Then who was it?

Eddy finally revealed who the traitor was behind his actions, "It was Sebastian."

"Sebastian?" thought Rion to himself.

"Yes Sebastian, the same Sebastian that you knew from your school in London." Rion remembered Sebastian from Burbage Primary School in England. Eddy continued to speak "It's the same Sebastian that beat you in a speech competition." Rion remembered the speech that Sebastian gave on his view of money being the most important thing in the world. Sebastian had said *"Money is the most important thing in the world, it makes the world go around."*

Rion said "And he's back to prove that money is more important than love…"

"Yes Rion, he's back. He wants to prove that he is the best. He wants to prove that money can buy love, but love cannot buy money," said Eddy.

"When did he come to you?" asked Rion.

"When you two love birds ran away with each other, and the journalists reported on your disappearance. Sebastian came across the news, and couldn't resist getting revenge against you. He's very rich now, he came to me and said…"

Eddy recited what Sebastian had said, *"If you give me all the information about Jenny and Rion before the world knows, then I will make you filthy rich."*

Eddy recalled his reply, *"But he's my friend, I can't do that to him."*

"Well you choose, either you obey my orders and become rich, or you don't listen and I will get revenge against you before I hunt down Rion."

Eddy said to Rion "He threatened to harm my family if I didn't listen to him. And the money was a temptation which I couldn't resist. I'm sorry Rion, please forgive me."

"Now what shall I do with you?" asked Rion with an raging look on his face.

"I know what I did was wrong. You can punish me if you like, but please don't kill me."

"Do you know the meaning of friendship?" Rion stood up while Eddy was repenting his actions. Rion said "A friend is someone who never stabs you in the back. A friend is someone who stands by you in times of happiness and in times of difficulty. You have broken all the boundaries of trust and friendship."

"I'm sorry Rion, I'm really sorry, I will do whatever you say, if you want I will leave him forever, I promise."

Rion turned around, looked at Eddy and said "Do you promise you won't stab me in the back again? You'll do what I tell you to do?"

"Yes I promise, this time I'll be loyal only to you," said Eddy with a feeling of extreme guilt.

"I do not want you to leave him," said Rion.

"So you want me to stay with Sebastian?" Eddy was surprised.

"Yes. I want you to make him think that you are his best friend. Continue taking money from him. But this time, when I tell you, I want you to betray him."

"If you want I'll betray him now," suggested Eddy.

"NO. Not now. Mr. Sebastian likes to play games doesn't he? Let's show him, he's not the only one who knows how to play chess. Let me show him, that love will triumph over money. This is not just a game Eddy. This is a war. A war between Love and money, a war between good and evil, a war between darkness and hope, where only one will be victorious. If this is what destiny wants, then let the war begin."

Chapter Twenty

Preparation

Rion came home in a thoughtful mood, he said to Jenny "You won't believe what happened today."

But before Rion could complete his sentence Jenny said "Me First! I have some news for you."

"Good news or bad?"

"Good news," said Jenny with a huge grin on her face.

"Tell me... I'm dying for something to look forward to," ordered Rion excitedly.

Jenny asked mischievously, "First tell me, if it's a boy what will you name him, and if it's a girl what will you name her?"

"If it's a boy I will name him... Wait! You're pregnant?" asked Rion eagerly.

Jenny smiled knowing that the treasure of their happiness was a secret locked inside her brain, which she was about to unlock. She nodded her head to tell Rion that she is pregnant. Rion's mood changed in an instant and he picked her up in his hands and swung her around like a beast picking up his beauty.

"I'm so happy Jenny, I'm so happy! You don't understand how much happiness you are going to give me."

"And me too. I can't wait to see our child, a symbol of our love..."

That night, while Jenny was cuddled up on Rion's shoulder, they both anticipated a complete family with their future child.

"I'll teach him everything that I know. I'll give him all my knowledge. I'll make him the best," said Rion.

"And if it's a girl?" asked Jenny curiously.

Rion recomposed himself and said, "Then I'll teach her about the world and everything that is right and wrong. I will make sure she attains happiness. I'll make her the best of the best! I'll teach her how to be an ideal woman." Then it occurred to Rion, "What about you? What will you do for my children!"

"I'll give my child all the love a mother can possibly give. I will read bed time stories every night, so my child can become strong, just like father Rion. I'll pass on the traditions and values I learned from my mother, so that my child can be a great human being, just like my mother." But there was something else on Jenny's mind. "Can I suggest something?"

"Tell me…"

"Soon we will have a baby, and that too in nine months."

"Yes Jenny, nine months is generally how long it takes for a baby to pop out!"

Jenny started laughing, and gave him a kiddy punch on his chest to protest, and said "What I mean is, soon there will be an extra mouth to feed, and…"

"I know what you mean. You know what, you're right," concluded Rion. "I'll start buying food now, so we never run out. Quick tell me, do we need more bread sticks? Nappies? Baby food? I'll go now, tell me quick! We only have eight months and a few days left!"

"I don't mean that Rion! I mean… maybe… it's time for you to get a job…" they were both silent, Jenny didn't know how Rion would react. She continued speaking "You don't have to get a job if you don't want, maybe you can do something else, but I'm just thinking because if we have this child then…"

Rion put his finger on Jenny's lips, he said "I know Jenny, I know. I have to think about our child's future, our future. Give me some time." Rion ran his fingers through Jenny's hair, and looked directly into her eyes while saying "Today, I want to make you a promise. By the time our child is born, I will earn money. I'll earn enough of my own money to support our family, I promise." Jenny rested her head on Rion's chest, and he comforted her with his hands while contemplating what he had just said.

From then on, Rion's life completely changed focus. From thinking about revenge against Sebastian, he started to think about his family, and their future. Over the next few days Rion started to apply for jobs in the local area. He would search for vacancies online, and write a tailored covering letter to each organisation and every job. It wasn't long before he was called to his first job interview. Rion practiced what he would say in the interview with Jenny. They both went through many possible questions.

However, when the moment of truth came, the first question they asked Rion was "Why did you leave University?" At that time Rion had no answer to their question. He couldn't say that he ran away with Jenny, because it wouldn't seem professional. He said "Sorry sir, I left due to personal reasons."

Unfortunately, Rion didn't get that job, but he didn't give up and kept applying. After many interviews, Rion found that he kept failing the interviews for various reasons, but he didn't know why. After many job applications, Rion soon accepted the job of a waiter in a local vegetarian restaurant. He began to work very long hours, from morning till late at night. He was determined to earn money for his family no matter what. His work involved serving customers, washing dishes, mopping the floor and he would do all this with honesty, dedication and a smile. Rion was a hard working, loyal employee, who would stay longer if he had to, but would never leave work early. Jenny could see Rion's persistence and dedication, she would stay awake for him until he came home every day, and only then she would eat dinner with him.

One night while lying in bed together, Rion said "After our baby is born, we will keep a grand marriage ceremony, and invite everybody we couldn't invite before."

"That's a great idea hubby," said Jenny.

"I thought you'd be happy... You can finally have your fantasy wedding come true. We will get married properly in front of the world, and have music, food, and all our friends around us."

"Yes, finally I will get a chance to walk down the isle with..." Jenny suddenly fell into silence.

"Your father?" said Rion.

"Once our baby is born... If you don't mind, can I invite my father to the wedding? Maybe he will come. If you don't mind, please Rion, please..."

"How can I mind?" interrupted Rion. "He is your father. Off course you can invite him. Maybe once you have a baby he'll change, and give us his blessings instead of his hatred."

"I hope so, thank you Rion, thank you," Jenny hugged Rion tightly. She missed her father, and wished that he could forgive them.

Rion continued to work hard at the restaurant. He saved as much of his monthly salary as he could in the bank for the day that his baby would be born.

One day, Jenny came to the restaurant Rion worked at to surprise him. She sat at one of the tables, and held a newspaper up to cover her face. Rion came to her table with a notepad and pen, and asked "Hello madam, what can I get for you?"

Jenny smiled to herself, and said "what do you have on the menu?"

"We have a range of vegetarian starters and main courses, spring rolls, samosas, dosas, currys, naan, a range of pastas, pizzas, Mexican tacos, fries and wraps. We also have a variety of juices, milkshakes and cold drinks..."

"Ok, umm, get me one of everything."

"One of everything? Are you eating for the first time in your life?" asked Rion.

"What are you trying to say?" asked Jenny cheekily.

"I mean are you sure you'll be able to eat so much alone? Oh, okay, I'll get one of everything," said Rion reluctantly.

Jenny removed the newspaper from her face and started laughing!

"Jenny, you! What are you doing here?"

"I just felt like giving you a surprise!" she said.

"But I told you not to go out anywhere, you're five months pregnant, you should look after yourself."

"I know but I couldn't resist. You're working very hard Rion, for us. When I see you working so hard, I feel sad," said Jenny emotionally.

"Every person has to go through challenges in life Jenny, this is my challenge. And once I face this challenge, then I'll be able to face any challenge in the world. Now tell me, what do you feel like eating, I'll get you whatever you want."

"Nothing, I don't want to trouble you. I'll go back home now," said Jenny.

"No, now that you're here, let's eat something together, I'll ask Mr. Decosta if I can go on my break."

Mr. Decosta was the restaurant owner, and he was watching. Rion stood up to ask him if he could go for a break. But even before Rion could say anything Mr. Decosta smiled and said "It's fine, take as long as you need. If your wife wants to eat anything, I will pay for you both. Now go and spend some time with her, she has come to see you!"

"Sir, how did you know that is my wife?!" asked Rion.

"You speak about her every day. I can see her picture in your eyes. Won't I recognise her?" said Mr. Decosta in a jolly manner.

Rion smiled and removed his apron to spend some hard-earned time with his wife. "Thank you sir," he said.

Another colleague, also a waiter, served them with food, and also gave them some cake, "This cake is from Mr. Decosta, for you mam."

Jenny was delighted and replied "Please tell Mr. Decosta that cake is my favourite, and he has made a pregnant woman very happy today." The waiter smiled and left.

Rion was happy to see that Jenny was munching her cake so enthusiastically. After eating, Rion helped Jenny to the taxi he had ordered for her. "See you in the evening," he said.

"Our child will be very proud of you," replied Jenny as she left in the taxi.

Rion's face was much more energetic after seeing Jenny. As he continued to work, he felt a lot more motivated. The lunchtime rush of customers started, and there was a spring in Rion's step, as he felt a strength in his stride. The sun was shining, and the customers were charming. The world felt wonderful. Once the rush of lunchtime customers had calmed down, Mr. Decosta said to Rion "Take fifteen minutes break, it's quiet now."

Rion stood outside to get some fresh air. A customer was walking into the restaurant and bumped into Rion. He dropped a newspaper, the customer said "Sorry."

"It's okay," said Rion, he helped him pick up his newspaper, and then the customer walked into the restaurant. On Rion's break, he had a chance for some self-reflection. He was thinking about how lucky he was. The love of his life Jenny, was with him, she was about to give birth to his baby. Not only that, he had a job, and although it wasn't the best job in the world, he was happy. Specially because Mr. Decosta treated him with so much respect.

Rion went into flashback, and remembered how he proposed to Jenny and the video that went viral online. He remembered the tough times he and Jenny faced while running away from home. He remembered how the news networks reported on Jenny and Rion as if they had become celebrities.

Suddenly, Rion realised that a customer had just bumped into him with a newspaper, and he had subconsciously seen a news story of Jenny and himself while they were in India. Immediately, Rion's suspicion increased, and he wondered who that customer could be.

Rion promptly went back inside. He saw a customer seated at a table, holding a newspaper and hiding his face. Rion smiled to himself and thought that Jenny came back to surprise him. He went up to the customer and said "Jenny, how did you know I was thinking of you? I'm glad you came back. I was missing you." But there was no response. The newspaper was still covering the face. Rion said "Jenny?"

Then the newspaper slowly came down, and the face became visible. "I missed you too Rion," said a man.

Rion looked at the man and tried to think who this was. Then it occured to him, it was Sebastian.

Sebastian said "I told you money is more powerful than love Rion. Just look at you. A poor little waiter, serving people in a tiny vegetarian restaurant, and I am a multi-millionaire. I can buy this restaurant and fire you if I want. But it's okay, I think I enjoy watching you clean tables instead." Sebastian started cackling like a witch.

"Oh that's very kind of you Sebastian. But I think you're forgetting something..." said Rion.

"Oh yeah, and what's that?" he asked with arrogance and intrigue.

"I have love. And until I have love, I know I can achieve anything in this world."

Sebastian continued to cackle, and said "Well good luck Rion. But while you wasted all these years running after love, I ran after money. Now, I am powerful, and you have love, but you're a weak incompetent loser. The question is not who will be more powerful in the end. The real question is, who will survive till the end." Sebastian, continued his evil look into Rion's eyes, as he stood up from his chair to leave the restaurant.

Rion's blood was boiling from this encounter, he had anger raging in his heart. As Sebastian left the restaurant, Rion went to the staffroom to get his apron and mobile phone from the locker. He checked his phone. Rion had 19 missed calls. They were all from Jenny. Rion was shocked, he tried to call her back. The phone was switched off. Rion called his mother. He asked her "Mum where's Jenny?"

"She's with you isn't she? She left home saying she's coming to see you."

Rion was absolutely shocked. He hung up the phone and ran to the front of the restaurant to see if Sebastian was there. But he had gone.

Rion immediately explained the situation to Mr. Decosta.

"Your wife is missing, 19 missed calls, you should go, maybe her life is in danger," said Mr. Decosta. Rion left to find Jenny.

Chapter Twenty-One

Rush

Rion ran into his car, and drove as fast as he could to the home of Jenny's father, Mr. Brown. On the way, he called the police, and said "My wife has gone missing, I need the police."

The operator asked "How long has she gone missing for?"

"Four hours," said Rion.

"Sir, do you think she might come back home if you give her some more time?" asked the police operator calmly.

"I hope so, but she's given me 19 missed calls while I was at work, and now her phone is switched off."

The operator turned a bit more serious and said "Okay sir, where would you like the police to come?"

Rion gave the operator Mr. Brown's address and drove their as fast as he could.

He rushed out of his car, and knocked on the door, there was no answer, so he rang the bell and knocked loudly one more time. There was no response, so Rion tried to open the door. It was already open.

As he entered the house he saw Jenny tied up with rope on a chair with tape across her mouth. Rion took off the tape from her mouth and said, "Jenny are you okay? What happened? Who did this?" Jenny was going to reply, but just then Rion was kicked to the floor from behind. It was Mr. Brown. Mr. Brown instructed his bodyguards to make an example of Rion. Rion had to fight them, he kicked one bodyguard so hard that he fell a few metres back. The bodyguards advanced to knock out Rion all at once. The fighting began, and Rion counter attacked them. Kicking one and punching the other, one by one he was knocking out the bodyguards. But because of the sheer number of bodyguards, he eventually began losing. The bodyguards beat Rion by kicking him and beating him while he lay on the floor. This was the most dehumanizing moment of Rion's life. Jenny could do nothing as her hands were still tied up.

There was a loud knock on the door. The bodyguards stopped hitting Rion. Mr. Brown said "Have a look who that is." A bodyguard looked through the window and said "It's the police sir." Mr. Brown went to open the door while Rion was held down forcefully by several of Mr. Brown's bodyguards. The policeman said "We received a report that a Jenny Brown has gone missing."

Mr. Brown started laughing and replied "Missing?! No officer there must be some mistake. Jenny is my daughter, she's inside. Actually she came to see me to discuss some personal issues with me."

"Can you bring her out please Mr. Brown?"

"Sure officer just give me two minutes I'll bring her."

Mr. Brown went into the room where Jenny and Rion were being kept, he instructed his bodyguard "the police officer wants to speak to Jenny."

"What shall we do now sir?" asked a bodyguard.

"Take her out to speak to the officer, if she says anything about being kidnapped, then just kill Rion." Mr. Brown looked at Jenny and said "Understand?." Jenny looked at Rion with tears flowing from her eyes. Rion was trying to say something, but his mouth was tied shut, so he couldn't speak. Jenny moved slowly towards the front door with teary eyes. Mr. Brown said "Wait." He wiped her tears, and said "smile." Jenny put on a fake smile and then continued to the front door. She saw a long line of police officers waiting to hear from her. One policewoman asked her "We received a complaint from your husband, he's been worried about you, saying you've been kidnapped, is this true?"

Jenny looked at her father. Mr. Brown said "Tell her Jenny, tell her, you don't need to feel afraid." Jenny looked at the police officer and said "No."

The policewoman was still not convinced, she said "Are you sure Jenny, you don't need to feel afraid, if there is anything you're worried about you can tell me in confidence."

Jenny gathered her emotions and said "No mam, I'm fine, actually I wanted to discuss something private with my father, and because I came here without telling my husband, that's why he got worried."

"Well okay mam, if you insist everything's okay, then we will leave, but if you need anything else, just give us a call." The police made their way back, and Jenny was left to bear the consequences with her father.

Mr. Brown took Jenny inside to where Rion was. He instructed his bodyguards in front of Jenny "Kill him."

Jenny fell to her father's feet, and begged him "No, please don't kill him father. He's my love, he's my life, I can't live without him. Please let him go. Please, I did what you said, I told the police, please."

Mr. Brown considered Jenny's plea and re-instructed the bodyguards, "Okay, just break his hands and legs." Mr. Brown pulled Rion by his hair, and said "You will leave here alive, but if you ever try to come back... you will die, understand?" The bodyguards started beating Rion. Twelve bodyguards, doing their best to beat the hell out of Rion, while all he could do is try and defend himself. One bodyguard would hit him with a thick metal rod, while the others would be kicking and punching him. Jenny was crying on the floor while her father held her away from Rion. Then a phone started to ring. Mr. Brown instructed the bodyguards "Stop, wait, whose phone is ringing?" They realised that it was actually Rion's phone. A bodyguard took the phone out of his pocket and gave it to Mr. Brown.

Mr. Brown answered the phone, "Hello?"

A voice on the phone said "Hello Sir, we would like to speak to a Mr. Rion Rai, he complained about the abduction of his wife." Mr. Brown looked at Rion who was being held down by his bodyguards. "Oh Rion is just in the bathroom, he will come out soon, would you like me to ask him to call you back?"

The police officer on the phone replied "No sir, that's okay, we will call back in five minutes, if he doesn't reply we'll have to come and visit you at your property again."

Mr. Brown was alert, and replied immediately "No officer, I'll check and see, maybe he's back out already." Mr. Brown instructed the bodyguard to hold a knife to Jenny's throat, and whispered to Rion "If you say anything wrong, we will kill Jenny, speak to the police and tell them that you want to withdraw your complaint."

Mr. Brown put the phone to his ear. "Hello," said Rion.

The police officer asked "Hello, is this Rion?"

"Yes, it's me," he replied.

"Sir, we got a complaint that your wife has been abducted, has everything been resolved now?"

Rion thought for a moment about what he should say, but Mr. Brown reminded him by holding a knife to Jenny's throat. Jenny was struggling to say something, but her mouth was held shut. Rion said "Yes officer, I found my wife, sorry to trouble you."

"Okay sir, we'll call back next week just to see how things are, in the mean while if you need anything else, please don't hesitate to give us a call."

"Okay, thank you," said Rion reluctantly, and the police officer hung up the phone.

Mr. Brown said "Good, I see that you love my daughter a lot."

"Yes sir, I can do anything for Jenny."

"Well then get out, and if the police call you next week, tell them everything is okay. If you complain to the police, or if you try anything clever, then I will kill Jenny, do you understand?" Mr. Brown instructed his bodyguards to throw Rion outside his house like trash. Rion was left on Mr. Brown's driveway, lying on the floor, like a homeless person. The rain was pouring down on him. His wounds were open, and blood was dripping from his head. He was left to pick himself up slowly, and painfully, back into his car. As he started the engine of his car and slowly reversed, Rion was crying. He didn't know if what he was doing was right or wrong. But all he knew, is that he didn't want any harm to come to Jenny. As he started to drive, his tears turned into more vocal crying, until he could bear it no longer and he parked on the side of the road, where he could cry his heart out at the injustice that had just been done to him.

Then Rion slowly started driving again. While driving his eyes would become blurred from the tears that kept appearing, making his vision impaired. His head was hurting, from the aggression he had faced. Somehow, he managed to drive to the hospital, where he parked, and walked slowly towards the accident and emergency department. The doctors recognised the seriousness of his situation and immediately put him on a stretcher, and then onto a hospital bed. He was put under a dose of anesthetic. After six hours of examination, Rion woke up. When he opened his eyes, Rion saw his mother, Hannah, Harvey and even Eddy was there to see how he was.

Rion looked at his friends and said "How did you guys know I'm here?"

"I told them," said Mr. Decosta, as he walked into the room. "When you rushed out of the restaurant to look for Jenny, I phoned your mother and explained that she should call the police to get updates if Jenny is okay."

"And then I called your friends," said Rion's mum, as she started to cry.

"Who did this to you?" asked Hannah.

"Yes, who did this?" added Eddy, "we will complain to the police."

Rion wasn't sure what to say, so he thought for a moment and then said "Actually, I already reported it to the police, I'm not sure who it was, they attacked me from behind, but I'm sure the police will find them."

"Where is Jenny?" asked Rion's mother.

"She's gone to her father's house. I dropped her there."

"You're lying, aren't you?" asked Rion's mother.

"No mum, really…"

"Quiet. I've raised you all your life. I've kept you in my womb for nine months. I know about your every emotion even more than you do."

Rion looked down at the floor, as his eyes started to fill with water again. He was trying to control his tears so they do not drop from his eyes. He didn't want to show everyone how much pain he was in.

Hannah could see Rion's pain. She knew Rion better than his friends, and perhaps even his mother. She asked everybody "Can you guys all go outside for a moment I just want to discuss something with Rion in private?"

"In private?" said Rion's mother with an intrigued look.

"Yes aunty, if it's not too much trouble," reiterated Hannah.

"Okay Hannah, if you can make my son feel better, then we'll give you some time." Rion's mother took Eddy and Harvey outside the room with her.

Mr. Decosta said "Rion if you need anything else please call me, I need to rush to the restaurant, I've left without telling the staff. We will find the people who did this to you, and get revenge, don't worry."

"It's okay Mr. Decosta, thank you for your help," said Rion emotionally.

Mr. Decosta said goodbye to Rion's mother and then left. But Harvey wasn't ready to go, he said to Hannah "What do you want to discuss?"

"It's top secret okay, now bye," said Hannah as Harvey and Eddy were being dragged away by Rion's mother like two protesting puppies.

As soon as they were left alone, Hannah said "It was Jenny's father wasn't it?"

"Who was Jenny's father?" asked Rion while his heartbeat went up a few notches.

"Jenny's father did this to you didn't he? And he kidnapped Jenny, didn't he?" asked Hannah like a police investigator.

"No, no it wasn't her father, I just got attacked by some strangers."

"Rion, you mean the world to me. If I mean anything to you, then put your hand on my head and swear on my life that Jenny's father wasn't behind all this."

Rion knew he couldn't lie any more, "Okay Hannah, it was Jenny's father, but please don't tell anybody. He said that if I tell anybody then he'll kill Jenny."

"Does he own Jenny that he will kill her? Don't worry I won't tell anyone. But why don't you just call the police?" asked Hannah.

"When I went there to rescue her, she was tied up, and when the police arrived they sent me to the front door. They said if I do anything suspicious then they'll kill Jenny. I'm sure if we tell the police, then Jenny's life will be in danger."

"Do you think that a father can kill his own daughter?" asked Hannah.

"He's not a father, he is a psychopath, and he can do anything."

"Hmm…" Hannah started making a plan in her mind. "Then we need to think of a way to get Jenny out of the house, and bring her back home without calling the police first."

"I thought a lot Hannah. If there was a way I would have gone back. But how can we get her back?"

"We need to get her back anonymously. The same way that I am speaking to you in private, we need to get her back the same way. By sneaking into her house, and to do that, we all need to work as a team."

"So what's the plan?" asked Rion.

"First, you get better, and wait for her phone call."

"How can she phone me? She's locked in her house…" said Rion.

"She can. Do you remember when you both wanted to get married, and Mr. Brown locked her in the house? She still phoned you right? Even though it took some time, she still phoned you. I know she will phone you, it's just a matter of when."

"Thank you Hannah, I can't understand why I can't think clearly in these situations like you. I don't know what I'd do without you. But until she phones what should we do?"

"Prepare. Until she calls you, we need to prepare… Look at your muscles… No offence Rion, but If you were stronger, you might have had a chance of fighting with Mr. Brown's Bodyguards today, don't you think?"

"Maybe you're right," said Rion with an enlightened look.

"We need to become strong. We need to train. Because this time when we go there, we have only one chance to bring back Jenny. If the plan works, Jenny will come back peacefully. But if the plan fails, then we will have to fight."

"*We* will fight? Who is *we?*" said Rion.

"Me and you! I am your best friend Rion I have to fight!"

"No, I can't let you come, it's too dangerous," insisted Rion.

"I don't care. Even if I can't become as strong as you, I will still help you as much as I can." Hannah crossed her hands and looked away as if she had made up her mind.

"Hannah please, try to understand, there are dozens of fully trained bodyguards there, you can't come."

"It's not just your wife that is stuck there. It's also my dear friend. And any bodyguard that traps my friend Jenny, will have to pay for it." Hannah was super determined to help Rion.

Rion breathed deep, and finally gave in, "Okay, If you really want to come, then you can come." Hannah was satisfied. Rion continued "But remember, Jenny's life depends on this…"

"I know Rion, that's why I don't want to let you go alone."

"If god ever created an ideal friend, then that friend would be like you." Rion touched Hannah's cheek, admired her bravery and continued to say "You're right. I should start training at the gym as soon as possible. In fact, I will start training from now." Rion stood up from his bed with a mood of real determination, only to fall back down because of the pain he was feeling.

"First you get better," said Hannah nicely, "and then we will train."

"We will train too!" said Eddy, Harvey and Rion's mother as they burst back into the room.

"Mum! Harvey, Eddy! You were all listening?" Rion was shocked.

"Yep, we heard everything! Boy we are going to get some sweet, sweet revenge on that ugly old monster!" said Harvey with a cheesy grin.

"Uh huh, we will rescue your princess from the fire breathing dragon's castle Rion, don't you worry!" added Eddy.

"Hold on guys, you can't just spoil our plans, Jenny's life depends on it. Myself and Hannah will go, nobody else," outlined Rion.

"He's right, we have to keep the plan secret, so keep your voices down," said Rion's mother. "But Rion, it's important to include Harvey and Eddy in the plan. Let them come with you. They both want to help you, and the bigger your team is, the more chance you have of your plan succeeding," explained Rion's mother.

"And the bigger chance it'll get screwed up!" Rion muttered to himself.

"What did you say?" asked Rion's mother.

"Okay fine! If you all want to train and ruin the plan, then great. Let's all go... Harvey and Eddy can train with us too, Happy?" asked Rion reluctantly.

The Room fell into silence for a little while, but Rion's mother broke the silence, "You think about everybody, and you don't think about me?"

"Huh? What do you mean?" asked Rion.

"I want to be part of the plan too!" she said with fashionable confidence.

"You want to come to Jenny's house to help us rescue her?" Rion asked his mother.

"Yes, if you all go then I will feel left out. I want to train in the gym with you all too, that way I can lose some weight and look like I did all those years ago."

"It's okay Rion, let aunty come too, she can also help us," added Hannah.

"I have an idea! Why don't you invite the whole neighborhood? We can all go to rescue Jenny," said Rion sarcastically. "We can go around knocking on doors and ask everybody if they want to come and help out, how about that? And while we're at it, we can take George, India and Lucky with us too."

"That's a good idea!" said Hannah as she started thinking. Rion covered his face in disbelief. Then she said "No wait, we can't do that otherwise somebody will tell her father and he'll find out. Rion, just the four of us, okay, deal?"

"No, we can't all go there. This is not a holiday camp. I'm planning on rescuing my wife. Nobody will come with me, I will go alone," stated Rion.

The room fell silent again, but this time, Hannah broke it and said "You know, whenever I think in my heart, who is the person I think is closest to me in the whole world, I think of you." Rion looked up at Hannah reluctantly. "And today, you will leave me and go alone to fight the biggest fight of your life? I never thought you would do this."

"Yes but Hannah…"

"I don't want to hear anything," she interrupted. "Will you take me or not?" she asked adamantly.

"Okay I will take you, but I can't take…"

Rion's mother interrupted "And me, I thought you care about your mother, but today I realised, you don't."

Rion could see the emotional blackmailing going on around him, but it wasn't over. Harvey said "And what about us? You always said we are your best friends, and you won't let us help you in your battle?"

They all looked sadly towards the ground, they knew it would melt Rion's heart eventually. Rion's mother was looking through the side of her eyes to analyse Rion's facial expressions. Rion put his head into his hand, and started rubbing his forehead as if he was contemplating something. Rion's mother looked at Hannah and raised and dropped her eyebrows, as if to ask her what she thought Rion would say next. But Hannah shrugged her shoulders, as if to say *I don't know.*

Rion's mother, Eddy, Harvey, and Hannah all looked at Rion to see what his verdict would be. He looked up towards the heavens and took a huge deep breath to say "Okay, all four of us are a team, but one condition, we all have to train at the gym together, no slacking." The room erupted in commotion. They were all happy and celebrating by shouting and cheering.

Then they all put their hands together to do a team high Five and marked the beginning of the rescue mission.

Chapter Twenty-Two

Strength

After a few days, Rion had recovered enough to be discharged from hospital. That day, the local gym in the city of Boston, had five determined visitors. Rion, his mother, Eddy, Harvey and Hannah all walked into the gym like they had come on a mission. It was like a scene from an action comedy movie, where the team of five had been set a goal to accomplish. They all had one goal, to become as strong as possible as soon as possible, so that they could help Rion to bring Jenny back home.

Rion knew that he would need to prepare for this war, not just with his strength, but also with his mind. He knew that he needed to work hard and achieve a body which he did not have at that time. But he also needed to make plans, for the day that Jenny found a split second to phone him. Rion wanted to lose a little weight, and gain a lot of muscle. He wanted to become super strong, and also learn how to use this strength while fighting.

He would wake up early in the morning. Rion would do a cardio workout on the streets by running and running until he could run no more. He consumed protein shakes during every workout, along with his team. He organised personal training sessions for their group with the fitness trainer in the gym, a very motivating expert called Mike. Rion explained his goals to Mike, who made a personalized workout plan for him and for all the others.

Rion would work out according to Mike's instructions. He would work extra hard, and go beyond what Mike had taught him. Although everybody else was training hard, there was that extra sense of determination in Rion's workouts. Rion would push himself to the limit, and then push himself that extra bit more.

Rion's mother would run on the treadmill and lift a few weights, and then go to the Jacuzzi to relax. Hannah, Eddy and Harvey tried to last longer in the actual gym. But when everybody else had worked out enough, Rion would still be training hard.

After two weeks, he had lost weight, and his muscles had started to show. But Rion wasn't satisfied, he continued to train even harder. He would come up with ingenious ways to test his resilience. Rion would race with Hannah and Harvey who would be driving a car. He would challenge people much stronger than him at the gym to arm wrestles, such as Mike his personal trainer. The other more stronger athletes with the physique of macho wrestlers would beat Rion in seconds and laugh at him.

After one month of rigorous training, Rion challenged his personal trainer Mike to another arm wrestle. Mike had the physique of a wrestler. But this time, Rion could last a little longer. Harvey, and Hannah, were timing him on the watch, willing him to win. But then his hand was slammed down after just twenty seconds, and Rion lost. Mike however, did acknowledge his improvement.

Rion joined kickboxing classes to put into practice the art of fighting and push himself even further. His team also enjoyed the classes. Punching and kicking soon became second nature to them. Rion was growing in strength and muscle day by day. His philosophy was simple. He would do as much as he could until his body said he couldn't do any more, and then he used his mind to wake up, get ready and tell his body to do an extra ten percent.

After two months of working like a horse, Rion was beginning to look like a horse as well. He challenged the gym member who he arm wrestled two months earlier and lost to, to a rematch. This time, with all the training he had done, and all the hard work he had put in, Rion felt he had a chance. Harvey, Eddy and his mother were there to cheer him on, and Hannah was there to time him. Rion used all his muscle, he battled with all his strength. This time, the question was not how long he could last, because this time, Rion won! The opponent looked dejected, but Rion smiled and gave him a gentlemen's handshake to console him.

Rion didn't stop there. He continued his growth as a fighter, and kept on training every day. He knew that achieving the goal was hard enough, but maintaining that level was just as hard, and so he continued his rigorous schedule.

Rion entered the boxing ring. His personal trainer was the same, Rion learned the art of fighting from Mike. Skipping was a key part of training, as well as running and of course using a punching bag as a test of his stamina and strength. Mike was impressed, he said "I've been training you for three months now Rion, and I have to admit, I haven't worked with anyone with as much determination as you. I have a suggestion for you, why don't you go into professional boxing?"

Rion, who now looked like a boxer, with bulging muscles and a physique to match, said "I'm humbled that you said this sir, but I can't. The truth is that boxing is not the aim of my life. I didn't start training for that."

"Think about it Rion. You are very talented, with a little guidance you could be a great boxer, and there's a lot of money to be made in boxing."

"Thank you sir, but money isn't everything, and I have a different goal in my life."

"Okay if you insist, only you know what personal issues you have. Nevertheless if you change your mind, then let me know, I'm here to help."

"Sure sir, thank you very much. Without your guidance, I couldn't have achieved what I wanted." Rion took Mike's leave with a feeling of strength. He knew that boxing wasn't the aim of his life, and perhaps he had bigger fish to fry.

Rion knew that now, he had reached the point he was aiming for. At the end of three months, he achieved the goal he had set out to achieve. Rion was strong both physically and mentally, and he was educated in the field of fighting. Rion looked like a strong Lion which had accidentally come out of the jungle. However all his friends knew, that this strong lion had a heart of gold. His team was standing by his side. His mother, Hannah, Harvey and Eddy were all looking much fitter and stronger than before.

One evening, Rion was driving on his way home after training at the gym, when his phone rang. It was Jenny. Rion immediately stopped the car to speak to her. Cars behind him were sounding their horns. Rion said "Jenny how are you? Where are you? Is everything okay?"

"I love you. I will miss you."

"You will miss me, why? What happened?"

"My dad is taking me abroad Rion. They want me to have an abortion." Jenny started to cry.

"They can't touch my baby. Is the baby okay?"

"Yes, the baby is okay, and I'm fine too. My dad's gone out now to do a business deal. I managed to phone you somehow. Please rescue me from here Rion. Please."

"Don't worry Jenny. I will rescue you. Your husband is not so weak that he can't even rescue his wife and child. Tell me one thing, when is the best time for me to come to you? Shall I come now?"

"No don't come now, my dad could be back any moment, come on Friday."

"Okay, what time?"

"Two o clock in the afternoon. My dad will be out, he's going to have another business meeting, I heard him speaking on the phone."

"Okay, tell me how many bodyguards will there be on Friday?"

"Just one, my dad always takes his guards with him wherever he goes, but leaves one guard to keep a lookout for me. But don't worry."

"Why?"

"The guard will be out front, so you can come from the back, I'll meet you there."

"How can I go to the back of your house without the guard seeing me?" asked Rion.

"You'll have to come at night, and sleep in the farm... with the animals."

"Sleep in the farm! Jenny I think you misunderstood me. I'm not scared any more. Let me come from the front of your house, I'll beat the bodyguards to their grave," said Rion confidently.

"No, please don't do that. After last time, I have nightmares about what happened to you. Please come on Thursday night, sleep in the barn for me my husband, and the next morning, I will come to you myself."

"Okay, I'll come there on Thursday night. When you're ready, just come into the barn and we'll run away from there on Friday morning, okay?"

"Okay, Rion can I ask you something?"

"Yes..."

"Why do I feel like this is déjà vu?"

Rion laughed, "I guess because we ran away once before..."

"I feel so excited. It's like we're getting married again!"

"Okay Jenny! Now is there anything else I need to know?"

"Rion, please look after yourself, I can't live without you. Only god knows how I spent the last three months."

"Okay sweetheart, I will look after myself, get ready, I'm coming to get you on Friday."

Rion immediately called for an emergency conference meeting with his team at his house.

Eddy asked "Do you really want us to come? Won't it be like too many cooks in the kitchen?"

"Well I think you have a point, what do the rest of you think? Should I just go alone?" asked Rion.

"No," said Hannah. "We'll go together. I don't want anything to happen to you. If we're not needed that's okay, but we shouldn't stay home and then something goes wrong."

"In that case, listen carefully to the plan."

Rion's mother, Hannah, Eddy and Harvey were listening intently to Rion as he took out a map with a birds-eye view of Jenny's house. "So, this is the plan, we will all enter from this direction. We will climb over this fence, from here, and enter the back of the property from here... After spending the night in the barn, we'll sneak out as soon as we see Jenny. Harvey you have a good pair of binoculars right?"

"Yes, I'll bring them," said Harvey.

"Okay so Harvey will bring his binoculars and we'll all take it in turns to keep an eye out for Jenny when she appears from the back of the house. Please remember to wear dark coloured clothing, so that it's difficult for us to be spotted. Are there any questions?"

"Yes, what should I be doing?" asked Rion's mother.

"Mum do you have to come?"

"I want to come! This all seems so exciting!"

"You are just like Jenny," said Rion.

"I will pack some lovely food for all of us. We will get hungry waiting in the barn!" said Rion's mother enthusiastically.

"Mum, we're not going there for a picnic, we're going to rescue my wife and future child," reiterated Rion.

"I know, but your future child doesn't want his father to go hungry now does he?"

Rion gave up and said "Right, any more questions?"

Hannah raised her hand.

"Yes Hannah?"

"After we take Jenny from there, what should we do?"

"Bring her home, what else should we do?" said Rion.

"Well, isn't there the danger that Mr. Brown might send his men here? Instead why don't you take Jenny far away from here? How long will you keep worrying about Mr. Brown?" asked Hannah passionately.

"Yes Rion, I think Hannah's got a point," added Eddy.

"Okay, let me think about that. If I can figure something out, then I'll take her away from here forever okay? Any other questions about the plan?"

There were no more questions, so Rion wrapped up the meeting "Okay guys, Friday is an important day for all of us. Please remember to prepare properly, let's do this."

Chapter Twenty-Three

Mission

Early on Friday morning, at 2am, Rion and the team left home together. They parked a distance away from Jenny's house, and entered the Farm through the back route as planned one by one. They carefully made their way across the animal farm. Rion opened the cow shed and they all followed him in. Harvey and Eddy immediately noticed the unique smell radiating from the cows.

Rion was the first to admit "I know it smells a little foul, but it's all mother nature team."

"You're right but I never thought I would sleep next to mother nature," said Eddy.

After fifteen minutes of sitting in the shed, Rion's mother said "Let's have something to eat, all this hard work is making me hungry."

"Mum we only just got here!" said Rion.

"I know, but we have a long night ahead," so Rion's mother organised a picnic for the team in the most peculiar of locations.

"I never thought I would eat with mother nature either," said Eddy, as he saw a cow dung dropping live from a cow nearby!

After eating they all tried to sleep on the floor which was covered in hay, which surprisingly made it a little more comfortable. Soon enough, thanks to the food Rion's mother fed them, they all fell asleep like children.

The morning came soon enough, and Rion was the first to rise. He was watching the back of the house with binoculars for signs of Jenny. Hannah woke up next, and she observed Rion for a while, watching him look out for Jenny with such intensity. She asked, "Have you seen her?"

"No, I think her dad is still home," said Rion without moving his site from the binoculars.

"You know, Jenny is very lucky," said Hannah.

"Why do you say that?" asked Rion.

"Because you love her so much," said Hannah carefully. Rion smiled.

Slowly and gradually, the others began to wake, and Eddy said to Rion, "let me do the watching a while, you must be tired."

Rion looked at him and said "It's okay, let me carry on for a while. I'll let you know when I get tired."

"If you give the binoculars to Eddy, Jenny won't run away!" said Rion's mother. "Come and have breakfast, I've packed cereal for everybody."

"Where's the milk?" asked Harvey.

"There are cows all around us, I already got some fresh milk for everybody," she said. Harvey and Eddy made faces at that statement, as if it would be out of reluctance that they would drink the milk.

"Come on Rion, you will like it," added Hannah.

Rion agreed un-eagerly and handed the binoculars to Eddy, who kept a lookout for Jenny.

"This doesn't taste that bad!" said Rion, as he ate cereal and fresh milk.

"Off course, it will taste good, because it's fresh!" said Rion's Mother.

"It reminds me of India," said Rion reflectively.

"Why does it remind you of India?" asked Hannah.

"Because in India me and Jenny tasted fresh milk just like this in Selina's house, it was bliss."

"You mentioned Selina before as well... Who is she?" asked Hannah.

Before Rion could say anything, suddenly Eddy saw something through the binoculars "I think that's Jenny!"

Everybody gathered around Eddy while he was looking at Jenny through the binoculars, Rion asked "Is she coming?"

"No, I think she's talking to someone."

"Let me see," Rion took the binoculars from Eddy and saw who Jenny was talking to. "I think she's talking to Mr. Brown. I think Mr. Brown is coming... *Mr. Brown is coming! Quick, hide!*" Rion's mother, Hannah, Eddy and Harvey all started looking for places to hide in the shed. Then Rion looked through the binoculars again and said "I think Jenny stopped Mr. Brown... Jenny is coming now." Rion's mother came out from behind the hay stack. Hannah, Eddy and Harvey all came out of their hiding places, as Jenny walked closer and closer to the shed.

Jenny came in and saw everybody. She immediately hugged Rion and said "My dad is going to go out in one hour, then I'll come through the back door and wave at you. When I wave, you can come through my house and we can go out from the front."

"But what about the bodyguards?"

"My dad is taking everyone with him, we don't need to worry any more!"

Everybody was happy, Rion's mum started cheering. Rion said "Keep quiet mum!"

"You brought aunty, Hannah, Eddy and Harvey?" asked Jenny.

"Yes they all wanted to help me."

"Thank you all for helping us so much," Jenny was greatful.

"You are the light in my son's life, I will do anything to protect you," said Rion's mother.

"How is the baby Jenny?" asked Hannah.

"It's okay, but if my dad takes me abroad, then I don't know what will happen."

"Don't worry, we will protect you," said Harvey bravely.

"Thank you. I don't know what I'd do if you all didn't help." Jenny heard a voice calling, she said "I have to go back, my dad will be leaving soon. I'll see you guys in an hour."

Everyone said "bye," as she headed back to the house.

For the next hour, Rion kept the binoculars glued to his eyes and watched like a hawk to see when Jenny would appear.

An hour later, as planned, Jenny came from the back of the house and waved.

Rion saw her, and said "Let's go, she's waving at us!"

Rion and his team walked towards Jenny, who was standing outside her back door.

As Rion approached closer and closer to Jenny, he felt a sense of happiness and freedom like never before. Jenny was looking at Rion, and he was looking at her, when Jenny was within touching distance, Rion saw Mr. Brown come out. He was holding a gun in his hand, which was pointing at Jenny. Mr. Brown's bodyguards also came out. Rion's friends and mother stopped in their tracks behind Rion. Although Jenny was just a few metres ahead of him, Rion could do nothing, as she was being held at gunpoint by her own father.

"*Move back, now.*" shouted Mr. Brown aggressively. "*Eddy, come here,*" he said.

Rion looked at Eddy, and so did everyone else. Eddy, who was standing behind Rion, went and stood next to Mr. Brown. They both started laughing. "Even your friends aren't loyal to you Rion, how can you look after my daughter? Eddy told me everything about your stupid little plan, I knew every little detail. That's why I told Jenny that I'll be taking all my bodyguards with me when I go out today. I even pretended to leave with them." Everybody was shocked listening to this. Mr. Brown walked towards Rion and continued "Do you think I am so stupid that I will leave my daughter alone on purpose? That day when Jenny called you, I purposely left the house to allow her to call you, and see what you would say. When I heard that you don't only look stupid, but you're actually stupid enough to step foot into my kingdom again, I felt pity on you."

Rion completed Mr. Brown's sentence, "And you let us think that our plan is successful?"

"Exactly! And then I asked Eddy about the plan. Eddy, my loyal dog told me everything. In fact yesterday Eddy was with me all day from morning till night. He told me the whole plan. I just wanted to see your surprised faces when I burst your bubble and appear in front of you like your life long nemesis that never goes away. You all look so charming right now, the only thing missing is a photographer."

"Eddy, you traitor," shouted Hannah angrily.

"Rion gave you a chance and you still betrayed us?" said Harvey.

"I fed you breakfast this morning like a son, and you cheated Rion?" said Rion's mother.

"Thank you aunty, the breakfast was nice, but I wanted to have better breakfast with Mr. Brown, because he feeds me bundles of cash, not cow's milk." Eddy started cackling.

Mr. Brown said "Enough of the small talk, why don't you all tell me who wants to die first? Do you want to be shot first Rion, or shall I shoot one of your little friends first? Or how about your mother? Hmm?"

Rion said "You are a coward Eddy. If you really want to betray us, then you should shoot us. But you are just a big fat coward. You don't have the heart to shoot us yourself you loser."

"Don't tempt me Rion. You don't know how crazy I am. If I get angry I will kill you, do you understand?" said Eddy affirmatively.

"Really? You don't even have the ability to kill an insect," said Rion.

Mr. Brown said to Eddy, "Will you let this low life insult you like this, or will you show him what you're made of? Shoot him!"

"Look Rion, last time I'm telling you, shut up, or you'll get killed by me. I hate you. You always get the best grades in university. I always wanted to be successful like you. But when I saw this opportunity to ruin your life, I couldn't resist. Now, do you want to die quickly, or do you want a less painful death. I'll let you choose since you're my friend."

"You are not my friend you loser. You deserve to die a lonely death, like Mr. Brown will die one day. You want me to choose? I choose a more painful death, because first I'll punish you for being disloyal, then even if I get killed, I don't care."

"Well then get ready to die," said Eddy. He walked up to Rion, looked at him with hatred, and then he punched him in the face.

Rion's friends and mother began to move to help, but Mr. Brown shouted "Hey! You all stay exactly where you are. I want to see these two fight. If any of you move, I will shoot you."

Rion punched Eddy back. Eddy went to kick Rion and he fell to the floor. Rion kicked the bottom of Eddy's ankle to make him fall to the floor. Rion grabbed hold of Eddy's neck while he was struggling with him on the floor, and then Eddy kicked Rion away from him. Eddy then grabbed Rion's shirt and dragged him along the floor, before kicking him in the stomach. Rion was winded and couldn't breathe properly.

"Enough," said Eddy, he went to Mr. Brown, and took his gun and said "Let me shoot him now." Eddy took the gun, pointed it at Rion and said "Get ready to die."

Hannah took that moment to run and stand in between Eddy's gun and Rion. She said "No please don't kill him. All he wants is to care for Jenny, he loves Jenny, please don't punish him for that, I will do anything you say."

Rion said "Hannah, you don't need to beg him. I don't want you to beg a traitor. I don't want to live any more. I'm happy, I lived a good life. I had such wonderful friends, a wonderful wife, and you, you are the best friend anybody could hope for. We all need to die some day right? You don't need to beg anyone."

Rion stood up, and said to Eddy, "if you want to shoot me, then shoot me." Rion held the barrel of the gun and put it in the centre of his own head and said "Shoot me Eddy, you're right, I am too successful, I don't deserve that success. End my life Eddy, shoot me."

Mr. Brown shouted "Shoot him Eddy."

"Pull the trigger Eddy, shoot me," said Rion.

"Don't shoot, please don't shoot," cried Rion's mother, Jenny, Hannah and Harvey.

Amongst all this mayhem, Eddy was in a dilemma as to what to do.

Rion said "It's okay if you can't shoot me, then at least I can die peacefully knowing that my friend has conscience."

"Shoot him!" Mr. Brown ordered.

But Eddy couldn't do it.

Rion suddenly snatched the gun from Eddy and said "Let me give this gun to Mr. Brown, maybe he will be able to shoot me. Then quickly Rion pointed his gun at Mr. Brown and shouted "everybody put your guns down, or I will shoot your leader."

Mr. Brown said "Rion, don't be so foolish, you won't leave here alive." Rion went up to Mr. Brown and held the gun directly at his head. Rion put some bullets in the gun while he was stood behind Mr. Brown.

"All these bodyguards have guns Rion, they will kill you, don't be immature and throw your gun away," said Mr. Brown.

"All your bodyguards do have guns Mr. Brown, but none of those guns have any bullets."

All of Mr. Brown's bodyguards tested their guns, and there really were no bullets in the guns.

Rion shot the gun he was holding in the air and said "but this gun does have bullets, so all of you drop your guns and sit on the floor like good little children. Please."

All the bodyguards dropped their guns and sat on the floor. "Jenny, you go to my mum." Jenny ran to the safety of Rion's mother.

"I don't understand, how did you do this?" asked Mr. Brown angrily.

"Let me explain," said Eddy. "When you tabbed the phone in your house and discovered Jenny's plan, there was nothing we could do. So, I told Rion that you knew about our plan. I suggested that we should change the plan, and then Rion said…"

Rion completed the story "...I said to Eddy that we shouldn't change the plan. And yesterday night, I told Eddy to take out the bullets from all the bodyguards' guns. I knew Eddy wouldn't let me down, because after the first time when I knew he backstabbed me, I made him promise that he would betray you when you least expected it."

"Sorry Mr. Brown," said Eddy sarcastically, "But real friends are always real friends."

"But don't worry Mr. Brown, we won't hurt you, because unfortunately you are Jenny's father. And since you gave me one chance, I feel that I should also give you at least one chance."

Mr. Brown looked angry but a little part of him was greatful for Rion's intention not to harm him.

Rion continued "But you don't mind if we hit some of your bodyguards, do you?"

"Why do you want to hit my bodyguards?"

"You see Mr. Brown, my family and friends have been training very hard for the past three months at the gym to become stronger. I feel it will be a waste of their talent if they don't get to put what they learned into practice. If you could allow us to beat your bodyguards, then I will be extremely greatful."

Mr. Brown looked towards his bodyguards who were worried, he groaned "Okay, go on then."

Hannah, Eddy, Harvey and Rion's Mother all looked at the bodyguards like hungry dogs. They started beating them. Rion's mother used her slippers to hit them, while Hannah was using more of her legs. Harvey and Eddy were using their kickboxing skills to batter the bodyguards. Rion gave the gun to Eddy, who held it to Mr. Brown's head, while he hugged Jenny. "Are you okay?" said Rion, as he took Jenny's hand and started walking towards the car with her. His team finished off beating the bodyguards, and then they all left together.

When they sat in the car, Jenny said "Rion, I don't feel too well."

"What happened?"

"My tummy is really hurting."

"Where is it hurting?" asked Rion.

"Here," Jenny showed Rion her belly and there were bruises all over.

"What happened Jenny?" Rion was absolutely shocked to see her condition.

"Before I waved to you this morning, my dad beat me and said that if I don't call you then he will kill my baby. If it wasn't for the baby I wouldn't have called you from the shed Rion."

"Mr. Brown, I will show him," said Eddy as he opened the car door to go and beat him.

"Not now Eddy," said Rion. "We don't have time, we need to get Jenny to the hospital."

Eddy closed the door, Rion started the engine, and he drove as fast as he could to the hospital. Jenny was feeling terrible. Her own father had beaten her in the morning, and threatened her to kill her baby. Hannah and Rion's mother were trying to comfort Jenny and gave her water to drink. They needed to do their best because the hospital was still thirty minutes away. Jenny fell unconscious. Rion was driving as fast as he could. Jenny was falling cold, her skin was turning blue, and her heart beat was slowing. "Call the ambulance, see if there is one nearby, maybe they can get her their faster," said Rion.

Hannah called 911, and asked for an ambulance. The operator said "It will take twenty minutes for the ambulance to reach you."

"We don't have twenty minutes," explained Hannah.

The operator replied, "In that case I will let the hospital know, and the doctors will be alerted. When you reach the hospital, you don't need to find parking, just stop your car outside the main entrance, the doctors will come and get Jenny," explained the operator.

There were still fifteen minutes to go to the hospital. Hannah covered Jenny with a blanket and tried to speak to her, but she wasn't responding. Rion turned his hazard lights on, and sounded his horn to overtake traffic.

Finally, the hospital was in sight. Rion drove up to the front entrance of the hospital, and rushed out of the car. The doctors were waiting for Jenny and immediately put her on a stretcher and took her inside. The doctors gave Jenny medication and began treatment. Rion, his mother, Hannah, Eddy and Harvey all waited outside. Four hours passed, and then a doctor appeared from the treatment room. Everybody rushed to him to find out what happened to Jenny. The doctor said "Your wife has given birth to a baby boy. But..."

"But what doctor?" asked Rion purposefully.

"But the mother has lost a lot of blood because of the physical injuries she suffered. I asked her if she wanted to register a police complaint but she said she doesn't want any harm to come to her father."

"Never mind the police what will happen to Jenny doctor?" asked Rion to the point.

"She is alive now, but because her internal organs have suffered so much, on top of that the trauma of giving birth to a baby. I think that the chances of her surviving are low."

Rion felt as though his life had been taken out of him. His family members were also in shock. He entered Jenny's room like body with no soul. Rion sat on the bed next to Jenny, held her hand and started to cry.

Jenny turned her head and looked at Rion. She said "Don't worry. You said that everybody has to die one day. To tell the truth I'm very happy. I can die with you by my side, and also my beautiful baby." Rion looked at his angelic baby which was sleeping in Jenny's arms. Rion's tears just would not stop. Jenny continued "I want you to look after my baby. And I want you to make him the best in the world. Remember you said you want to make our child the best. You will, won't you?" Jenny was speaking slowly with very little energy. Rion nodded his head while continuing to cry. Jenny said "After I go, if possible please forgive my father. He is very hard on the outside, but his heart is very soft. I hope some day you can explain to him how much we love each other, and how much we love him."

"The doctor said there is still a chance you can survive," said Rion.

"I won't survive, I know. I've been hit too hard. Can I ask you for one favour?" Rion looked up at Jenny, she wiped his tears, and said "All my life I tried my best to explain to people that animals also have feelings, we shouldn't eat them. If possible, can you continue my work?"

"Yes, I will…" said Rion.

"See how much pain you are feeling now because I will leave you?"

Rion was listening to each and every word.

"Animals feel the same pain and suffering when they leave this world. When human blood drips, humans feel sad, but when animals lose blood, I don't know why humans forget their morals. Please look after George, Lucky and India, they are very close to my heart."

"I will look after them, we will look after them together. Nothing will happen to you Jenny, I can't live without you."

"Don't worry Rion, if you ever miss me, then you can see me any time. You can see me inside animals. I am inside the heart of every animal. I am in the animal's happiness, I am in the animal's sadness. I am in the animal's innocent eyes, and I am also in the pain that animals suffer when they are slaughtered. Please save animals, please save animals." As Jenny said this, she started to lose consciousness. Rion shouted "*Doctor.*"

But it was the end. Jenny had passed away. Hannah, Harvey, Eddy and Rion's mother came into the room as they heard Rion burst into tears, they consoled him, but now was a moment of sheer sadness, and no amount of consoling was enough. The love of his life had gone. The girl who he fell in love with in school, his first true love, was no longer responding. The love of Rion's life, Jenny, had died.

Chapter Twenty-Four

Diplomacy

It was the day of Jenny's funeral. Rion's family and friends were gathered at the ceremony, the weather was wet, and the mood was damp. Jenny's body was in the coffin, Rion was looking into her eyes and holding her hand one last time. She was about to be taken away forever.

Mr. Brown arrived. He walked up to the coffin, and looked at Jenny's body. He then looked at Rion with vengeance. Rion was drowned in the sorrow of his wife's death, he couldn't think about anything else. However, Mr. Brown's eyes were full of nothing but aggression. Nevertheless Mr. Brown controlled himself, even he knew this wasn't the time, or the place to say anything else. The priest offered some prayers for Jenny, everybody closed their eyes and prayed for her soul's peace. Then, her coffin was closed by the priest for the last time. Rion was watching for every split second that he could before the coffin was closed shut, and taken away to be buried.

Once Jenny's funeral ceremony was completed, Mr. Brown walked past Rion one last time, giving him an unforgiving look. Rion looked at Mr. Brown with hatred, had he not beaten Jenny, then she would still be alive. Rion clenched his fist, but Hannah saw this and put her hand over his hand. Mr. Brown smirked at Rion and left the ceremony. Rion and his friends were left to reflect on how life had taken away such an important part of their lives.

"I can't live without her," said Rion.

Hannah put her hand on Rion's shoulder and said, "I know you can't live without Jenny, but we can't live without you either."

Eddy reminded him, "Do you remember her last wish? She said if you ever miss her, then you can see her in animals."

"If you love Jenny, you should save the animals Rion, try to save the animals," added Harvey.

"You're right, from tomorrow, I will dedicate my life to saving animals. I couldn't save Jenny, but I will save the animals. But for today let me cry. If I hold these tears in, then I won't be able to live, the world will drown in my tears."

Rion spent the rest of the day alone, in his room, crying, remembering Jenny's magical memories. He remembered when he first saw her in school, the times they spent together at Burbage. He remembered the reunion many years later at Harvard University. He remembered the marriage, and the honeymoon. Then he remembered Jenny's last words before she died.

Rion looked at his baby, a sweet little boy, in a cradle near him. He looked at his eyes, they reminded him of Jenny.

Now, Rion had just one goal in life, he wanted to continue Jenny's fight for animal rights. He wanted the world to know that killing and eating animals is not something that should be morally acceptable in the modern age.

Rion started his journey the same place he began with Jenny. He stood in the Cambridge city Centre near Harvard University in America. He set up a stall and handed out leaflets to the public whilst allowing people to stroke his chicken Lucky, cow India and pig George.

Rion could see that people would treat the animals in the most kind and gentle way whilst they were in front of them. But once they were done petting the animals, people would head straight into the takeaway shops selling meat. Rion could see that people were kind, but they didn't understand the pain and suffering that animals had to go through. Rion also launched a YouTube channel about animal rights and began to upload new videos every week. Hannah, Harvey and Eddy even helped him with filming in different locations. But he didn't stop there. Rion began to send emails and letters to prominent business leaders of food chains, as well as powerful politicians. He wanted to discuss animal rights face to face with these leaders. He kept writing letters to different institutions, but the responses just did not stack up in return. Rion even wrote to the United Nations in the hope that perhaps his plea could be heard by somebody. Months and months passed like this without luck, but Rion was persistent and didn't give up.

On one particular day of his struggles, Rion walked into a branch of a fast food chain which also sold meat. "Hello, I'd like to speak to the manager if possible?" he said to the member of staff.

The assistant behind the counter replied, "Sure I'll call the manager but may I know the reason you wish to speak with him?"

Rion explained "I want to speak to the manager about changing the food items to only include vegetarian options. You see, I believe that animals also deserve the right to live and that's what I wanted to discuss with the manager."

"I'm sorry sir, but we cannot discuss that with you."

"I don't want to discuss with you, I want to discuss with your manager," said Rion.

"I'm afraid that won't be possible," said the assistant.

"I won't leave here without speaking with him," said Rion adamantly.

Rion was asked to leave the restaurant immediately. He didn't go, and so the staff called security to escort him out. Rion had many such experiences, which made him feel negatively towards the world. After writing hundreds of letters, and visiting several hundred restaurants, Rion saw that he was getting nowhere.

Every day was a new start for Rion. He was persistent, he would wake up, travel to different places, and hand out leaflets all day long. Rion travelled four and a half hours to the statue of liberty, where he believed that people may understand the issue of justice for animals in a more favourable way. He was getting some positive responses, specially from people who were already vegetarian. However he found that although people understood what he was trying to say, they didn't want to make any changes in their own lives.

On the surface Rion was out of the house and meeting people, and he was a lively, determined character. But inside, he was in a world of his own. His feelings were like an empty body which had the life sucked out of it. The only reason for his living was the yearning in his heart to do something for animal rights. Rion had the assistance of Hannah, Eddy and Harvey who would occasionally come along with him, but they too had other commitments, so most of the time, Rion would be battling alone. It occurred to him that perhaps he was speaking to the wrong people. Perhaps the public was powerless in controlling the destiny of animals. Although his YouTube Channel was a success, it was not going viral, like the video of him proposing to Jenny went viral before. *Perhaps people enjoyed watching a boy propose to a girl more than they did watching someone talk about animal rights*, he thought.

Rion was handing out leaflets one day, when he saw that the local state politician had come to town to visit. He saw that people crowded around him to hear what he had to say. Rion made his way to the crowd to see what was happening.

The politician was speaking on the stage "We are the servants of our great country. We represent you, the people. We will listen to you, because you are democracy. If there is something wrong in this city, if you have an issue, you can come to see me. If you have anything you want to discuss, whether you have problems with the way the police did their job, whether you have problems with water or even electricity. Whatever aspect of your lives you want to improve, you can visit me at my weekly surgery on Wednesdays at my office. I am the people's politician, and I want all of you to know that I am a public servant, and I will serve the public to the best of my ability. Just remember to vote for me in the upcoming elections. I am your politician, Jeremy Hughes, thank you." The public gave Mr. Hughes a round of applause.

Rion saw hope, he thought this was a different type of politician, somebody who fought for the people. Rion rushed towards Mr. Hughes, as he was getting into the car, and then he said "excuse me sir, sir," But there were too many people gathered around Mr. Hughes.

So Rion shouted a little harder and pushed his way further forward in the crowd, and shouted one more time "*Mr. Hughes!*"

So Mr. Hughes replied "Yes young man, how can I help you?"

"Sir I wanted to discuss something with you," said Rion politely.

"Oh sure, what did you want to discuss?"

"I wanted to talk to you about the animals sir," explained Rion.

"Oh you have some animals?" he asked.

"Yes sir, I have some animals, but actually it's not my…"

"You can come to my office on Wednesday morning at eleven okay, here's my card." Mr. Hughes gave Rion a business card for his Political party's office.

Rion was left with the card in his hand as Mr. Hughes was escorted away in his vehicle. Rion felt as though he didn't just have just a card in his hand, he had hope.

On Wednesday morning, Rion was at home, preparing to meet Mr. Hughes. Rion looked at Jenny's photo which was hanging on his wall, and said to it "I told you I would try my best to protect animals. You know, today I have a meeting with an important politician! He's a nice man, I'm sure he'll help us. I even wore a suit to impress him. Look, do you like it? Wish me good luck Jenny," he kissed her photo. Rion also kissed his little baby boy, and said "I love you my son, Orion." That was his name, Orion, Rion's first, and only son, with the one person who meant the world to him, Jenny.

Rion said "bye," to Lucky, George and India "I'm going for you guys, and the welfare of your entire species, wish me good luck." George snorted, India mooed, and Lucky flapped his wings. "Thank you," said Rion as he left home for perhaps the most important meeting in his life so far.

Rion waited outside Jeremy Hughes' office. There were lots of people there to see him. Everybody was seated patiently in a designated area, waiting to be called in to Mr. Hughes' office. Eventually his turn came, and Rion was called inside to see him.

"Please take a seat young man," said Mr. Hughes.

"Thank you," said Rion, as he sat down.

"What's your name?"

"Rion Sir, Rion Rai."

"Sounds like a Hollywood action hero!" said Mr. Hughes with a smile on his face. "You're not here to thrash me are you?" said Mr. Hughes jokingly.

"No sir!" said Rion.

"You look like a tough guy, your physique is just like a bodybuilder! You work out at the gym?"

"Sometimes sir," said Rion with a pleasant smile.

"Tell me, what brings you here today?"

"Sir actually my wife passed away three months ago."

"I'm sorry to hear that. How old was she?"

"Same as me, twenty two."

"At such a young age? Life can be so cruel," said Mr. Hughes genuinely.

"Yes sir, and before my wife died, she had a last wish. If you could help me to fulfill that last wish I would be greatful."

"Oh sure young man. Your wife has gone through so much pain and suffering at such a young age, she deserves to have her last wish fulfilled. How did she die?" asked Mr. Hughes.

"Sir there were complications during her pregnancy. Although our child was born fine, she died because she lost too much blood during her pregnancy."

"Oh, I'm deeply saddened to hear your story." Mr. Hughes was sympathetic, "what was her last wish?"

"Sir her last wish was that animals should have the same rights as humans."

"What what what? Animals should have the same rights as humans?" Mr. Hughes was surprised.

"Yes sir, her dream was that animals should not be killed to satisfy the tongues of human beings, and they should be allowed to live a normal life."

"Animals should have the same rights as human beings, right?" Clarified Mr. Hughes.

"Yes sir."

"You mean, animals should also be given the right to vote for political leaders?"

"No sir that's not what I'm saying, all I'm saying is…" Rion was speaking when Mr. Hughes interrupted him.

"All you're saying is you want the animals to have the same right to live as human beings, right?"

"Yes Sir."

"Mr. Rion Rai. Do you know how I became so powerful? I became powerful because 1.2 million people voted for me in the last elections in my constituency. And you want me to pass a law banning meat? In a state where 93% of the population are meat eaters, you want me to make people vegetarian, so that nobody votes for me again? Do you want me to get kicked out of power and beg on the streets?" asked Mr. Hughes

"Sir just because 93% of people kill and eat animals, it doesn't mean that it's right," argued Rion.

"Are you out of your mind? To fulfill the last wish of your dead wife, you want me to go against my citizens? I think you should go and see a psychotherapist Mr. Rai. No wonder your wife had complications during her pregnancy, because she was probably demented like you."

"Jeremy Hughes!" Shouted Rion as he stood up from his chair. He shouted affirmatively, *"The only reason you can sit here and tell me all this is because you are not an animal.* The only reason why in the twenty first century 93% of people still eat meat and think it is okay, is because of disgusting politicians like you. If animals had the ability to vote, then I am sure you would protect their rights. But unfortunately, they are simple, they are humble and they are innocent. Animals are like three-year-old children Mr. Hughes." Rion became more emotional. "If we give them love, they will give us love. When a human suffers, even if a child dies in the womb of mother, we feel pain. When a human being becomes paralyzed and stuck in a bed for life, we even protect that person's life. We humans always look out for each other. But when animals go through pain, we become like barbaric monsters. But you have the power to save animals sir. Please help Mr. Hughes, please do something," begged Rion with tears in his eyes.

"Get out," Said Mr. Hughes with extreme anger. "Get out from here and never come back again."

"Okay sir, I'll leave. But just remember, in this lifetime, you're a human, if you're an animal in your next life, then you'll know how they feel."

"Get out before I call security," shouted Mr. Hughes.

Rion lowered his head and left Mr. Hughes' office distressed and heart-broken. As he was leaving, he heard Mr. Hughes shouting for his assistant and venting his anger on him. *"Are these the types of demented people that I am sat here to listen to? Animals should be given the same rights as humans, is he kidding me?"*

Rion felt more alone than ever before as he came back home feeling like a failure.

"So, was the meeting successful?" asked Rion's mother. "Did the politician agree to help?"

"No," said Rion, he was dejected.

"But you said he is a nice man."

"Yes but he said there's nothing he can do," explained Rion with more energy this time.

"But I thought he would help because..."

Rion interrupted his mother by shouting angrily, *"He didn't help, how many times do you want me to tell you? He doesn't care about animals. He only cares about humans. Because humans can vote and animals can't. He only cares about humans because humans can stand up for themselves and animals can't."* Rion went to his bedroom, he sat on the bed. He sunk his head into his hands, which were firmly pulling on his hair. He looked in the mirror, and broke down into tears of depression. He wiped his tears, and started to smile, then he got angry again, and went into the room where his pets were. He shouted at the animals *"None of you deserve to live. Why were all of you born? You are all born so that you can all die and we humans can eat you."* Rion kicked George, and India, he said "You all deserve to be on my plate, so I can eat you. You all deserve to die." The pig and the cow both made noises to express their sorrow. Rion's mother stopped Rion and said "What have these animals done to you? Leave them alone."

"*Why don't you explain that to the world mum?*" Rion was angry. "*I kicked the animals and you're feeling so much pain. What about the billions of animals that get slaughtered every day? Why doesn't the world understand?*" shouted Rion with tears in his eyes.

"Don't give up son," suggested his mother. "You've started a battle which should have begun many years ago. There is no use giving up. Keep knocking on doors, don't give up."

"Do you know who I am mum?" asked Rion while crying in her lap. "I am the representative of these animals." Rion stood up from his mum's lap and wiped his tears, he became more determined. "I am the king of the animals. And now, the king of the animals will knock on the highest door, the door which belongs to the king of the humans."

Rion stood up purposefully and made a phone call, he said "Harvey, I need a favour, can you help me?"

"Sure, tell me Rion…"

The next day was a normal working day in the office of the United Nations headquarters in New York, perhaps one of the most iconic symbols of human unity. People working in the offices of the United Nations were getting on with their work as usual, until they saw a man appear from the horizon, walking down the centre of the road. An office worker said "Look, a man is coming."

"Don't worry, it's probably just another human rights activist," said his colleague.

But then they saw a man with hundreds of animals behind him. The office workers had seen nothing like this before.

It was Rion. As Rion got closer and closer, they saw his banner "Meet who you eat." The office workers were surprised at the ingenuity of this protest.

Harvey and Hannah joined Rion, and they were shouting slogans *"Animals deserve life, not death, meet who you eat. Animals are like innocent children, meet who you eat. Animals are more kind than humans, meet who you eat."* As the parade came closer, The United Nations employees could see Rion, Hannah, Eddy and Harvey with hundreds of animals marching in the centre of the road. There were several cows, sheep, pigs, chicken and even horses. The animals were being paraded by many of Rion, Harvey and Hannah's friends. Rion and the crew came closer and closer to the building until they were directly outside the United Nations.

A security guard came outside to escort Rion away from the front of the building. As the guard came closer to him, Rion punched the security guard to the floor. Another guard came, and as he was about to attack him, Rion kicked him away and used the security guard's own baton to smash him. More guards were alerted of the situation. Fifteen security guards were launching themselves to attack Rion at once, and destroy his chances of success. Rion was prepared, the guards came running towards him and just as they were about to strike, a senior officer came out from the building and shouted "Stop." The Officer came closer to Rion and asked him "What is the meaning of this? What do you want?"

"We are here to protest against the innocent killing of animals that takes place every day," said Rion with anger.

"Innocent killing of animals? I'm not aware of any animals being killed without reason?" said the officer genuinely.

"Sir, I'm talking about meat. People eat meat every day, and this is against the rights of these animals who are with me. These animals are my brothers and sister, and I am here to get an answer for them."

"Ah, I see. Well, why don't you come in and maybe we can discuss this matter inside peacefully?" said the officer politely.

"Sure sir, that is what I want too." Rion went in the United Nations Headquarters with the officer. The beaten guards looked on with jealousy.

After reaching the office, the official introduced himself "By the way I am Philip Howard. You didn't introduce yourself?"

"Sir I'm Rion Rai."

"Pleasure to meet you Mr. Rai, so tell me, what were you saying about animals?"

"Sir, I am here as a representative of all animals. I am not a human being. I believe I am just an animal who has the ability to speak English and vote for politicians," said Rion with clarity.

"Wow, that's powerful thinking," Mr. Howard was impressed.

"Sir, in a world where racism is wrong, how can killing animals and eating meat be right?"

"What does racism have to do with animals?" asked Mr. Howard.

"Racism is a form of discrimination between different types of people, and eating meat is a form of discrimination between different types of animals. We kill and eat animals depending on how we view their level of intelligence. We love dogs, but kill pigs, we love cats and we slaughter cows, if this isn't racism sir, then what is?"

Mr. Howard was listening carefully, it seemed as though Rion's words were connecting with him at some level.

Rion continued to explain "Can you imagine a world where everybody is a vegetarian and I come here and speak to you about giving me the right to kill and eat animals? Can you imagine how crazy I would look if I did that. But sir the unbelievable thing is that a vast majority of the world still kills and eats animals. I am here to explain why we should not kill and eat animals."

"Let me stop you there Mr. Rai. You do have a valid point. But there is a reason why you would look crazy if you wanted to eat meat when the whole world is vegetarian. The reason is very simple, the majority is always right. It is possible that one day the world might become vegetarian, but you cannot force the world to do what you want the world to do, now. Who are you to tell the world what they can and can't eat? I am a Christian, my religion says I can eat meat. Who are you to tell me what I can and cannot eat?"

Rion looked at the ground, smiled and said "You're right sir, I am nobody to tell you what you should do in your spare time. I am nobody to tell you what you should do in your life. But let me ask you something, who are you to decide which animal you can and can't eat? Just because you are a human being and you practice a religion it doesn't give you the right to kill other animals. Just because your religion says you are allowed to eat meat, it does not mean that you own the animal that is on your plate. And just suppose for a moment that my religion said that eating meat is wrong, does that make my religion right and your religion wrong? No sir. Because this matter is above religion, this matter is called humanity. There are religions in the world which permit cannibalism, eating humans, underage marriage, even rape, is that right?"

"How dare you point fingers at my religion?" said Mr. Howard.

"I'm not pointing fingers at your religion sir, I'm just saying that the issue of killing and eating animals should not be dragged into religion. If a religion gives us the right to kill animals if we need to, we shouldn't misinterpret that and kill animals by the truckload just because we can. Sir, I have a dream, today ninety percent of the world eats meat. I want to make a day when ninety percent of the world is vegetarian."

"Enough. You can leave. Anyway, I can't help somebody who has crazy dreams. I have no more time to discuss anything with you. You can go," said Mr. Howard with disgust.

Rion shouted, "**I live in a world where killing animals is the norm. Therefore, my dreams are not crazy, but your reality is.**" Rion looked at Mr. Howard one more time. He left the room with determination and went back outside.

Meanwhile Mr. Brown returned to his home, and found that all of his animals were missing from his farm. He shouted at his guards *"Where have all the animals gone?"*

"We don't know boss," said one guard.

"Well then find out you bloody idiot." Mr. Brown ordered his men to investigate where all the animals had gone.

Rion was stood outside the United Nations with Hannah, Eddy, Harvey and hundreds of animals from Mr. Brown's farm.

"What shall we do with these animals now Rion?" asked Harvey.

"They deserve freedom, set them free…" said Rion.

Harvey, Hannah and Eddy were shocked to hear this. They didn't know how on earth this would be possible.

"How can we free hundreds of animals?" asked Harvey. "We don't even know where to let them go."

Rion said, "I know a place." Eddy, Harvey and Hannah walked the animals to the nearest woodland, which was a few miles away. Along the way, they passed the sites of New York city. Many people looked at the most astonishing site of hundreds of animals being paraded by Rion, Hannah, Harvey and Eddy. People started recording Rion and uploading videos online. They passed the Statue of liberty and spent some time there educating people about their mission. It seemed the scale of their operation was attracting people.

Finally, they all reached the woodland in the evening, after spending the whole day walking and talking to onlookers. "Are you sure you don't want to return these animals to Mr. Brown?" asked Hannah.

"I'm sure. The time has come for this battle to change gears. These animals deserve freedom. Set the animals free." The mothers were reunited with their children. The families could be together again. Now the animals didn't have to live in cramped cages, they were free to roam the jungle. The chicken didn't need to fear anybody taking away their children and frying them as eggs. The cows no longer needed to give their milk to machines sucking on their breasts, rather the milk could be saved for their own children. The animals would not face a death on a factory line, rather their death could occur naturally in the wild. Rion gave freedom to animals for the first time in his life, and it felt more amazing than anything he had done before.

Mr. Brown's men were on the hunt for the animals, and they found out who was behind all this. The bodyguards went back to Mr. Brown and reported their findings to him.

Rion dropped Hannah, Harvey and Eddy to their home, and said, "Guys, without you, I could never have done all this. I really appreciate it, thank you."

"Don't be silly, that's what friends are for!" said Hannah with a smile.

"And we learned so much from you Rion, we never even thought about animals in the same way that you care about them," added Harvey.

"Your animal friends are so kind and caring, it's our honour that we are your friends," said Eddy.

"Thank you very much guys," said Rion one more time.

When Rion returned home, he went to the living room, where his mother was crying, she said to him, "they came, they took George, they took Lucky, they took India."

"Who came mum, who?" asked Rion quickly.

"Mr. Brown's men. They said if you want to see the animals alive then they have one condition."

"What is the condition?" asked Rion. Rion's mother kept crying, and didn't say anything. "Tell me mum, what is their condition?"

"They want you to go there... alone."

Rion's heart was pounding, his veins were bursting and his eyes were raging. This was a personal attack on his animals, and a personal attack on him.

Rion walked towards the door with the intention of going to Mr. Brown's home. His mother cried and tried to stop him "No, don't go, they will kill you. You can't go anywhere, stay here."

But Rion wouldn't listen, he asked her a question. "Mum. Are you the mother of a weak, insignificant person? Or are you the mother of a strong, meaningful warrior?"

"You are not weak or insignificant, but you can't go there, we can continue this fight later peacefully."

"Enough of the peaceful route mum, enough. Now, it's time to do what I was born to do. This is the purpose of my life. I have realised why I was born. I wasn't born to do some job in an office or run a business. I was born to protect animals. This is the day for which you gave birth to me. You should be proud." Rion's mother was crying. "Just tell me, am I a warrior, or not?"

"You are a warrior son," his mother said while crying.

"Then let me go. It's my duty to protect those innocent defenseless animals. They are not just animals mum, they are humans who can't speak English, they are my brothers and sisters. Don't make me a coward at such an important time, just give me your blessings, so that I can return victorious."

Rion's mother wiped her tears and said "You're right son. Go. Make your mother proud, so she can tell the world that Rion Rai is her son. May you be victorious son."

Rion was focused. The temperature in his body began to heat up. He left with fearless rage and utter determination. Rion drove to Mr. Brown's house, and parked in the drive. Bodyguards closed the front gate behind him. Rion stepped out of his car and walked into Mr. Brown's front door which was open. The bodyguards escorted Rion to the barn in the farm. Rion entered the barn and saw Mr. Brown, he said "I'm here, let the animals go."

Chapter Twenty-Five

The Moment of Truth

"Ah, Rion, just as I expected, the stupid emotional fool you are. Arrived you have, but leave you cannot."

"I am an emotional fool, Brown. But I'm not stupid. Emotional fools *choose* to use their heart more than their head. But clever fools only use their heads, because they do not have a heart. And yes, you are a clever fool."

Mr. Brown laughed and said "Maybe, but there's no denying, that you are also a fool. Nevertheless, I will give you one chance to choose your last wish before you leave this world."

"I have only one last wish Mr. Brown, let those animals go, they haven't done anything to you. I am your enemy, do what you want to me, but let these innocent animals go, please."

"Let the animals go? I will decide their fate in a moment, but first I want to ask you a question..." Rion was carefully listening. "You fell in love with my daughter, you even ran away with her, but after my men beat you into a pulp when you came to rescue her once, didn't you have the intelligence to realise that you are playing with fire? Why did you keep coming back, are you a mindless stupid fool?"

Mr. Brown was standing, looking at Rion as if he had won the battle and Rion was a loser. Then Rion spoke, "When Jenny was in my arms, about to die, do you know what she told me? She said *please forgive my father. Although my father is a very tough man on the outside, he has a very soft heart*. I lost my wife because of you Mr. Brown. I loved Jenny a lot. She was my life, and you took her from me. But I thought that maybe if you see the feelings Jenny has for these animals, if you saw the love that animals can give, then maybe you will also see how great your daughter was."

Mr. Brown was provoked to think differently by Rion's words for the first time in his life.

Rion continued "Do you know what I do when I miss Jenny Mr. Brown? I look at animals. Wherever I see animals, I see her love. Wherever I see animals I see her innocence. Wherever I see animals, I see Jenny, your daughter Mr. Brown. I understand that Jenny is incomplete without you. But what you have not understood is that Jenny is also incomplete without me. She is also incomplete without animals. Animals were her life. Let's end this enmity Mr. Brown. What is the point of turning our backs on each other? Instead, why don't we join hands and spread love in this world. Why don't we become powerful together and represent these innocent animals? Why don't we work together, and keep Jenny alive in the hearts of these animals? Look into their eyes Mr. Brown. You will see love, you will see innocence, you will see Jenny."

Mr. Brown looked into the eyes of George, Lucky and India, who were all there in front of the bodyguards. Mr. Brown was almost emotional. He felt something different, like he had never felt before.

Mr. Brown went up to Rion, he gathered the courage to look him in the eye and said "You know, until today I always looked at animals as commodities, as products we need to buy and sell. I never thought of them as living beings with feelings. I never thought that I would look at animals with the same feelings that you do."

"*That's because they are commodities*," shouted a voice from the darkness of the barn. A man appeared from the door, and spoke "Don't be fooled by this immature child Mr. Brown, surely you're above that?" It was Sebastian speaking.

"Sebastian, our fight is over, why are you still holding a grudge, let's move on," said Rion.

"A GRUDGE, is something I don't like to let go of. Because I have remembered this grudge for the past fourteen years. So you tell me, how can I move on from it so easily?"

"I will do whatever you want, just let the animals go," stated Rion.

"Anything hey? Well in that case, I would like you to admit that money is more powerful than love, and that you have lost your battle with me, then perhaps I will forgive you."

Mr. Brown asked Sebastian "Is there any need to do all this?"

"YES, Mr. Brown. This man ran away with your daughter. He ruined the respect and heritage of your family, because of his actions your daughter is dead, he deserves to be punished."

For the benefit of the animals, Rion swallowed his pride, and he said reluctantly, "Money is more powerful than love, I lose, you win, love has lost, money has won."

"Sebastian was ecstatic because Rion was at his mercy kissing. Sebastian grabbed Rion by his collar, and said "What did you think, hey? It would be so easy to earn money and become powerful in this world? You are weak Rion, weak! And your love is weak. You do not even deserve to be in Mr. Brown's presence, let alone marry his daughter. You are a loser."

Mr. Brown intervened, he said "But he regrets his actions. He said he's sorry, tell him you're sorry Rion, and if you had another chance then none of this would have happened."

"I am sorry," said Rion, "but if all of this happened again, I would do exactly the same thing. I would run away with Jenny and marry her, I don't regret one little bit of my actions."

"What did you say? You will still run away with my daughter if she was alive?" asked Mr. Brown while pulling his shirt collars.

"Yes, I loved her, and I will always love her."

Mr. Brown punched Rion in the face.

Rion continued to speak "I loved Jenny, and I will never regret loving her for one moment."

Mr. Brown kept beating Rion. Sebastian also joined in, he bashed his knee into Rion's stomach, and punched his face multiple times, making his nose bleed.

"I love Jenny, and I will always love her," said Rion defiantly. Mr. Brown and Sebastian were hearing these words and beating Rion more and more. They pushed him onto the ground, and ordered the bodyguards to gang up on him and beat him to death. They began kicking and punching him. Then they started using metal rods to attempt to break his bones. "Enough," said Sebastian. Rion was lying on the floor in pain, it looked as though he had no more energy left to defend himself. Mr. Brown reached for his gun and aimed it at Rion. Sebastian stopped him and said "No, not so easily, death is not the biggest punishment for him. His biggest punishment is to watch his animal friends die first."

Mr. Brown agreed and ordered his bodyguards to bring India the cow, George the pig and Lucky the chicken, so that they could all be killed in front of Rion. The bodyguards grabbed George, and hung hum upside down on the slaughter factory line. Then they also hung India and Lucky upside down, causing them severe pain. Rion was lying on the floor half unconscious. He could see what was happening, but not clearly. Sebastian picked up Rion's head and made him watch, he said "*LOOK, Rion look. Your best animal friends are all about to die. Won't you say goodbye to them?*"

Rion was severely injured, and couldn't concentrate on what was happening. Then Mr. Brown ordered the bodyguards to switch on the conveyor belt, so that George, Lucky and India's throats could be chopped off with the sharp industrial slaughter machine blades. The bodyguard was walking towards the green button to get the conveyor belt started. Rion suddenly realised what was going on, he saw that the bodyguard was about to push the button. Rion screamed and pushed Mr. Brown and Sebastian away from him. But the green button had been pushed and the conveyor belt was moving. The bodyguards all rushed towards Rion to attack him. Rion's whole body suddenly charged up with fury and revenge. His body defied the injuries he had and he started to fight. He punched and kicked one bodyguard out of the way at a time. He ripped a big plank of wood from the side fence and used it to smash the head of each bodyguard. Meanwhile the conveyor belt was moving and there were only a few metres left between the chopping saw and George, Lucky and India's throats. Rion was able to beat the competition of the bodyguards one by one. However, they were consuming precious seconds, which Rion did not have. He ran towards the button to stop the conveyor belt. Just as he was about to reach the conveyor belt, Mr. Brown stopped him, and then a couple of the bodyguards who hadn't already been knocked out came to assist Mr. Brown. Rion was being held back by just a few inches from the button to stop the conveyor belt. He could see George get closer and closer to the chopping saw. Rion was reaching for the button with all his force. He was being held back by ten people. Finally, George the pig entered the chopping saw, and his throat was being cut by the blade. Eventually his throat was cut in half, and his blood was pouring everywhere. George screamed in his last few moments with sheer pain, with no other way to express the suffering in his moments of death. Lucky the chicken entered the chopping saw next as Rion tried to punch away the bodyguards, Lucky's neck was also chopped in half, and he also screamed with agony before dying a painful death. Rion was crying and being pulled away from the stop button by many bodyguards. He finally witnessed India the cow enter the chopping saw. Rion had a flashback of all the happy memories with these animals. He remembered when Jenny introduced him to India at her second date with him at the animal right's protest. He remembered when they would sit next to his mother and watch TV with her. Whenever he would come home, they would come running to Rion for nothing more than affection. Those same animals, which were no less emotional than a dog or a cat were being killed for no reason in front of him. Rion saw India enter the chopping saw, and her throat was chopped in half. She made loud noises, as there was nothing else she could do except scream in agonising pain. India's blood was dripping everywhere, and that was the third execution Rion witnessed.

Rion dropped his head like a defeated soldier. But then rising from that defeat was exponential anger. A rage in his eyes which had never been seen before. His body was exploding with fury, which needed to be exhausted. Rion used all his might to swing the bodyguards away from him with a scream reverberating from his mouth which echoed throughout the farm. Rion picked up a metal pole from the floor, all the bodyguards, Mr. Brown and Sebastian were cautious. Rion walked towards the first bodyguard in front of him and swung the metal pole from behind his head at immense speed, smashing it into the bodyguard's head. He continued to smash the pole into the heads of each and every person that came in front of him. This was the extreme side to Rion that Mr. Brown and Sebastian had never witnessed or dreamt possible before. They were starting to get worried as Rion was successfully knocking out one bodyguard at a time. Rion continued to beat them all as they began to tumble like a house of cards. Rion knocked out the final bodyguard, when Mr. Brown and Sebastian were holding a gun to Rion's head at arm's length. Rion looked like a hungry lion at them, and nothing would stop him. He grabbed them both by the neck, and Sebastian and Mr. Brown both automatically let go of their guns. "You love treating animals like rubbish don't you?" He said with gritted teeth and every muscle in his face clenched ready to knock out Sebastian and Mr. Brown.

"Sorry Rion, sorry, please don't kill us. We'll do anything, just give us one chance," said Sebastian.

"Yes Rion, let us go, we promise we won't bother you again," said Mr. Brown.

Rion was angry, he screamed at the top of his voice and knocked both Sebastian and Mr. Brown unconscious with one huge blow to their heads. As they lay on the floor, he looked towards the dead bodies of his favourite animal friends, George, India and Lucky. He kneeled down and his tears fell on their corpses. Rion said "You were so kind, caring, you never hurt anybody. You just wanted love. And look what these bloody humans did to you. I hate humans. But don't worry, not all humans are bad. I am you're human brother. I will get justice for you. The people who did this to you, I will make them live like animals."

Rion stood up, and looked around at all the people that were on the floor from excruciating pain. Rion looked towards them with extreme anger. With tears rolling down his cheeks, he said "You humans think you're intelligent, don't you? You think you're better than animals don't you? Well now this human will take everything away from you, that made you think, you're civilized human beings." Rion commenced to rip and tear the clothes of each and every single person. He unclothed all the humans like a monster. Once all the humans were naked he said, "There, now you might be able to understand my animal friends better."

First of all, he grabbed Mr. Brown and Sebastian by the neck and pulled them along the floor. He slid them without any hesitation and threw them with enormous force, strength and speed into an animal cage. He locked them up. Then one by one, Rion grabbed the bodyguards he had knocked unconscious or severely injured and threw them into separate cages and locked them in there too. Soon enough each and every bodyguard was locked in a cage, and so too were Mr. Brown and Sebastian.

Mr. Brown gained consciousness, he shouted "You will be sorry Rion, you will not get away with what you have done."

"Yes," shouted Sebastian, "You will have to pay us compensation for the pain and suffering you have caused us in court."

Rion looked at Mr. Brown and Sebastian with ultimate rage, he walked up to their cage, he shook their cage with force and roared like a lion. "Compensation is paid to human beings, you aren't humans, you are animals."

From that day, it became Rion's aim to put all the people who contribute towards the death of animals in a cage in that farm.

Rion was walking along the street and he heard a man talking to his friends "Animals were made so that we can eat them." The man was laughing. Rion saw this, and turned into kidnapper mode. Ron waited. When the man finished eating, he followed him. Then the man entered a dark alleyway on his way home. Rion had set up a small explosive to knock the man unconscious. Nearby onlookers heard the explosion and came running to help the man, but Rion had a gun in his pocket and fired shots in the air to warn onlookers to back off. Then Rion picked up the man and put him in his car, and took him away to the farm. When the man woke, he was naked, in an animal cage.

"So you think animals were made so that we could eat them huh?" said Rion.

The man was scared. "Who are you, why am I here?"

"Does it look like I asked you to ask ME questions?"

"No, no, it doesn't," said the man in fear.

"Well then answer the question. Do you think animals were made so that we could eat them?"

"Yes," concluded the man, "but why, don't you think that?" he asked mustering up all his courage.

"No... I think humans were made for me to eat them." The man shut up with intense fear running through his body.

After the first kidnapping, when Rion turned on the TV, he saw that the news channels were all talking about one thing, the explosion, and the kidnapping. Rion realized that explosions and guns would get him caught by the police sooner or later, so he started kidnapping people with more subtle techniques. He planned and organized each kidnapping very carefully and gathered more and more people in the cages on what soon turned into the human farm.

One day Rion saw a girl holding a soft pig animal toy saying to her friend "Look, this animal is so cute!" Rion admired her for saying this, and wondered why all people weren't so empathetic. But then the girl's friend brought her a meat burger, and Rion could not understand how this girl, who seemed so beautiful and intelligent, could call a soft animal toy sweet, but then eat the real animal itself. Needless to say, the girl and her friend suffered the same fate. Before they knew it, they too were in a cage, stripped completely naked, with other captives, trapped on the human farm.

"Where am I?" asked one of the girls, while looking at Rion, who was looking at her a few inches away on the other side of the cage.

"You're on a farm, a human farm."

"Why did you kidnap me? Let us go or I will call the police," said the girl's friend.

"Can the police hear your voice from here?" said Rion in a sarcastic voice. "You're naked, in an animal farm, and you're threatening me with the police, are you stupid?" asked Rion.

"But why have you brought us here? What did we do wrong?"

"I know that ladies like to go first in everything, but if you don't mind I'd like to ask you something first, may I? Please?" said Rion so politely, that it was scary. The girls were shocked so Rion continued to speak. "When I was young, I thought girls are a symbol of kindness and love. I though no matter how bad the world becomes, women will always have kindness in their hearts, then why don't women care about animals?"

"We do, we love animals," said one of the girls.

"But you don't love all animals," shouted Rion. "Why do you discriminate? Why do you love dogs, and eat pigs? Why do you keep cats as pets, and eat Cows? Why do you eat chickens and eggs, when they too are women and children. Why do you love soft cuddly baby chicks, and then eat the mothers of those soft baby chicks, why?"

The girls realised what Rion was trying to say, and even in this strange situation, they could see what Rion was trying to do.

"Now all of you will live a life like animals, so you can realise the pain and suffering they go through." Rion turned around, and walked out of the farm, to let the captives dwell on their actions.

Rion also got revenge against the people who had rejected the idea of protecting animal rights in the past. He kidnapped Mr. Hughes the politician and even Mr. Howard from the United Nations. He kidnapped both men and women who were working in head offices of companies that dealt with the supply of meat. He kidnapped owners of slaughter houses, restaurant managers and even consumers of meat if he had the chance. These people were abducted through Rion's meticulous planning. He watched the times at which these people came to and went home from work. At the exact right moment, he would cover their faces from behind with a cloth containing either *chloroform* or *ether began*. Rion then took these people back to the farm, so that when they gained consciousness, they would already be locked up in a cage, completely naked. One by one, Rion collected these people like a lone soldier gathering rocks one at a time to build a mountain. With all these people he did one thing, he undressed them and made them live like animals.

After hearing Rion's story, Officer Williams was heart drenched. He was raging with anger at what animals have to go through, something he had never thought of before. He was wondering how on earth Rion was even alive until this point after having such an emotionally draining life. "Tomorrow is your day in court. If you admit your crimes you could get the death penalty," explained Mr. Williams. "Listen, if you deny your mental well-being and say that you lost your mind after the passing of your wife then maybe the courts will give you a lesser jail sentence."

"And what will happen to Jenny's dream? What will happen to the animals Mr. Williams?" asked Rion politely.

"Don't be emotional Rion, you don't know the…"

"I am emotional officer. I have nothing to lose. Worst come to worse, they will give me the death penalty. I don't want to live any more. I don't want to live in a world where people kill animals to eat them."

"You have to live on to fight Rion. You have to live to give those animals justice."

"Tomorrow is that fight Mr. Williams," said Rion with determination on his face. "Tomorrow is a trial of vegetarianism, and meat. Tomorrow is a trial of animals and humans, tomorrow is a trial of kindness, goodness, righteousness, and cruelty, ignorance and evil. It's late now, you should get some sleep, you've been working hard to search for me, your wife must be waiting, good night Mr. Williams." Rion smiled, stood up and walked into his prison cell." Mr. Williams was left with no other option than to make his way home, but in his heart, he was only thinking about tomorrow.

Chapter Twenty-Six

The Trial of Truth

Rion's trial was all set to take place in court. It was being covered by television, news and media crews from across the world. The American politicians wanted to make an example of Rion, and show all of humanity what happens to a criminal who attempts to tarnish democracy. And that's why the trial was going to be broadcast across the globe, live. The prominent politician Mr. Hughes who was also kidnapped by Rion was interviewed by a journalist "Sir, what do you think will be the likely outcome of today's trial of the deadly kidnapper Rion Rai?"

"Well what will happen is something I don't know. But I do know what should happen. He should be sentenced to death. That's the least her deserves for putting his hands on a respected politician like me."

Opinion polls across the country reverberated the same sentiments. People wanted Rion to be sentenced to death, so that justice could be served to the countless people who had been traumatized by his actions.

The media, press and live broadcast cameras were all set in position in the courtroom. Hannah, Harvey and Eddy were also seated in the crowded room. Mr. Hughes the politician and Mr. Howard from the United Nations, both of whom had been kidnapped were also sitting amongst the audience like hungry lions waiting for Rion to become dead meat. Mr. Brown was sitting with Sebastian anticipating Rion to be finally put in his place. Members of the public were also waiting for Rion to be severely punished. The court room was set. The cameras were running, and the world was watching. A parade of police officers brought Rion, who was wearing a prisoner's uniform, into the courtroom, handcuffed behind his back.

Then a voice commanded "Please stand for the honorable chief justice Rose. Everybody stood from their seats as the Judge entered the front of the courtroom. She had a fierce reputation of being a firm but fair judge. After the opening formalities, the hearing was finally in place to begin.

One after another, the witnesses gave accounts of how Rion tortured them. Many witnesses cried as they narrated their pain and suffering as explicitly as they could. The only glimmers of hope were when Rion's friends tried to explain the background of why Rion did what he did. Hannah, Eddy, Harvey and Rion's mother all testified. However, all their testimonies were neutralized by Mr. Brown, his bodyguards and Sebastian, who also gave their version of events.

Mr. Sanders, the police officer who interviewed Jenny and Rion when they returned from India, also explained how heartbreaking the story of Rion was when he lost the love of his life, Jenny.

However, the overbearing influence on this trial came from the witness accounts of those that had been kidnapped. They expressed the long lasting physical, psychological, and emotional pain caused by Rion's actions.

The final witness to be cross examined was the mother of the baby who Rion had eaten after bashing his head on the floor. The mother spoke whilst in tears, "Your honour, this kidnapper has dropped below the boundaries of humanity. He killed my baby boy when he was just a few minutes old. He didn't even think twice before putting my baby's dead body in his mouth and eating it as if it were some takeaway chicken wings. This man is an evil monster. He should be given the death penalty. Please give me justice your honour, please give me justice." The mother broke down into tears. She was helped back to her seat by her lawyer, who also represented all the other people that had been kidnapped.

After listening to all the witnesses, the judge looked at Rion sternly and said "Mr. Rion Rai, we have heard accounts from all but one of the witnesses. The final witness remaining to be heard from is you. We must give all parties a fair chance, that is what a democracy is. It is therefore the court's wish to hear your version of events. Please come and stand in the witness box."

Rion stood up slowly and walked steadily towards the witness box. Everybody was looking at Rion with hatred, hoping that such a disgusting kidnapper could be severely punished. People were watching the live broadcast of this trial in countries all over the world, including Australia, France, Russia, China and even India. Back in India, Selina, Johnny and her mother and father also tuned in to the live broadcast. Selina looked towards her father, she was worried. Her father put his hand on her head and said "Don't worry," as nothing more than a consoling sentiment could come from his mouth.

Back in London, Mr. McClymont, Rion's inspirational teacher from Burbage School was watching the trial. He remembered Rion, and couldn't understand why he would do something like that. Mr. Hill the head teacher was also watching at his home. He believed in his heart that perhaps Rion would've had a very big reason to commit such a crime, especially since he stood for values of love and peace when he was in school. But his mind was telling him that Rion deserved the death penalty.

Rion reached the witness box, he looked at the floor for a moment to compose himself. The whole world was going to listen to the words which came out of his mouth. He looked up at the judge and began to speak "Your honour, we live in a moral, civilized society. For thousands of years, we have fought for black and white people to be equal. We have finally reached that goal. For thousands of years, we civilized humans believed in witchcraft, and we killed innocent women who we suspected of being a witch. But then common sense prevailed, and we understood that there is no such thing as witches. But there is still one part of society that remains uncivilized your honour. There is one part of society that remains brain dead. Because even today, whether it's a five-star hotel or a small fast food restaurant, we still put dead animals on our plates every single day. In the USA it is illegal to kill dogs, and in China it's allowed. So does it make killing dogs right in China and wrong in the USA?" People across China were also watching the trial live, and many were trying to understand what Rion wanted to say. "Today no matter how backward a country is, racism is illegal in every part of the world. If discrimination between different types of people is wrong, then how can we be so discriminatory towards cows and love our dogs so much? How can we kill pigs and yet treat cats with love, is that also not a form of racism? A few years ago your honour, Martin Luther King had a dream. And today in front of you, I also have a dream. I have a dream that one day all animals could be loved equally. Not just dogs, cats and horses, but also chicken, cows and sheep. You are a judge, it's your duty to punish those who are guilty. I have killed an innocent child and kidnapped many people. I deserve the death penalty." Hannah, Harvey and Eddy were all shocked to hear this. Meanwhile in India Selina was emotional and felt like crying at the thought that Rion could be given the death penalty. People in the courtroom thought Rion's life was over, now that he had admitted his crime. Rion continued, "However, please also punish all of these people sat here today. They eat innocent children every single day. That woman, whose child I ate, where is she?" Rion looked for the woman in the audience, and then spotted her. He continued "She said that I ate her child like I was eating chicken wings. Yes your honour, I did. Because all these humans sat here today eat dead animals for only one reason, because animals are weak and can't defend themselves. Animals have brains like... sweet little children your honour. They don't deserve this, they deserve to be left alone. They deserve life. I am not a human being your honour, I am an animal who has the ability to speak English and vote for politicians." Mr. Hughes was looking at Rion, and knew exactly what he meant. "I am here as a representative of my animal brothers and sisters. Please allow animals to live your honour, please allow animals to live. Stop, killing, animals."

The judge looked as if she has been moved to a certain extent at least by the words she just heard from Rion's mouth. She asked "Would the claimant like to cross examine the witness".

The lawyer representing all the captives stood up to question Rion. "So Mr. Rai, because you are a vegetarian, and you want the world to be vegetarian with you, you took it upon yourself to kidnap 347 people, strip them naked, put them through hunger, thirst, sleep deprivation, de humanization, and then kill and eat a newborn child like a barbaric monster… Is this how to prove a point?"

"I had no other way," said Rion.

"No other way? You could have campaigned for change, marched in rallies, and written books," shouted the Lawyer.

"People have been doing that for thousands of years. If we continue like that god knows how many hundreds of years it'll take for society to change."

"Fine! It would have taken a few more years, but at least all these people wouldn't have gone through what they did because of you Mr. Rai. And baby Joseph would be with us today."

"Do you know why you're saying this?" The lawyer was interested in listening, Rion said "Because you're a human. If you were an animal, then you'd realize what a hundred more years looks like. When a human mother is about to give birth, you take her to the hospital, scan the womb to make sure if everything is okay. And if the baby dies because of a complication, all you humans cry. But what about when the same thing happens to animals? Humans feed chickens, those poor mothers are given many chemicals to make them lay more eggs, almost one egg every day. Chickens are made to grow so fat that they cannot bear their own body weight, and they live a life of suffocation. Meat is not a beautiful package we can pick up on supermarket shelves. Every second that goes by, every minute that we waste in talking, millions of animals are having their throats chopped off in slaughter houses around the world. And why do we not care? Because they are not our species. Animals are living, breathing creatures that feel pain, and we have turned them into commodities, just because they don't speak the same language as us. Every day millions, every month billions, and every year trillions of animals are slaughtered for you greedy, savage humans. This is not a small problem which happens in our dream fantasy, this is a humungous organised operation, carried out on enormous commercial scales across the planet. Animals don't deserve this, they deserve independence."

The Lawyer took a deep breath and asked "So you think it's wrong to kill animals?"

"Yes" replied Rion.

The lawyer tried a different approach, "Did you know that animals kill each other in the wild?"

"Yes I know. So is it okay if I kill you now?" asked Rion.

"*Off course not!*" shouted the lawyer with a disgusted look on his face.

"Why not?"

"Because I'm a human, there's a difference between animals and humans Mr. Rai in case you hadn't noticed."

"That's what I'm saying as well, there's a difference between animals and humans. Animals have an instinct, and they can't change it. They are programmed to kill. But we are humans. We have a moral decision making power. We have compassion, love, and we need to start loving all animals. So, we shouldn't kill animals just because they kill each other, if we did then there would be no difference between us and them."

"Mr. Rai what if I were to tell you that animals were made to be eaten? This is a lion," the lawyer showed him a picture of a lion with his mouth open. "This lion has long canine teeth to bite into its prey, and this is a cow, it has no canine teeth." The lawyer showed Rion a picture of a cow. "And unless you didn't know, let me tell you that cows are vegetarian. So, would it not make sense that perhaps the reason why human beings were given canine teeth by mother nature, was so that we could hunt for animals?"

Rion said "Your honour, humans were not given canine teeth to hunt for animals, they were given canine teeth to give them the option of hunting for animals. Our ancestors thousands of years ago had no knowledge of agriculture. They had times of extreme famine, when there was no choice but to kill and eat animals. If I was stuck on a desert island, with nothing to eat, maybe I too would kill an animal. But amongst all the world's creatures, only humans have such a supreme ability to make moral decisions. There are millions of healthy human beings who are vegetarian. If a lion lives on a vegetarian diet, it'll die, but if a human is vegetarian, then he can survive happily for life. And if mother nature wanted us to eat meat, then we would die without it. But more important that canine teeth, mother nature has given us a brain, and it would be good if people used it. Your honour I have six pets, and I would like to introduce them to the court."

"You may proceed Mr. Rai," said the Judge.

Six police officers walked into the courtroom. They each had a different pet with them. The first officer was walking a pig, the second was walking a calf, the third was holding a chicken, the fourth was holding a goldfish in a bowl, the fifth was walking a dog, and the sixth was holding a cage with a red cloth covering it.

Rion walked out of the witness box and up to his six pets. Rion kicked the pig, the pig made a sound to signal its displeasure at being kicked. Rion then kicked the calf, the calf also *mooed* in discontent. He then went on to kick the chicken, which ran away and flapped its wings while making a clucking sound. He then took the goldfish out of the water and let it flap around and suffocate for a while before putting it back in the bowl. He then kicked the dog which made a sound to express its sadness, and then the dog went into one corner. The audience was watching in awe, and so too were audiences across the globe.

Rion looked at the judge in anger and said, "They all feel pain your honour, they all feel pain. Just like me and you, they all feel pain. They all signaled their displeasure at being hurt. Just because we think that some animals are more cute than others, or some are more intelligent than others, does it give us the right to slaughter them in the millions every single day? All these animals, they are not more or less intelligent than each other. They all have different types of intelligence. Just like a doctor, or a footballer, they have different types of intelligence. Who are we to decide which type of intelligence lives, and which type dies?" The judge continued to listen intently just as everybody in the court room and around the world. "These animals are all like three year old children in a classroom. Just look at them, sweet, innocent, and in their own little world." All the animals looked intrigued! Rion continued "In the human world, do we kill people who are less intelligent? Do we slaughter those who look ugly? Do we end the life of those who are not cute? No your honour, none of these animals deserve to die. None of these animals deserve to die."

After just a couple of seconds of silence, the lawyer asked Rion "Yes you are right, perhaps, animals do deserve the right to live, so what do you recommend that we should eat, our knives and forks?"

"No" replied Rion. "You can eat my sixth pet."

"Sixth pet?" The lawyer asked with a perplexed look on his face.

Rion walked towards the cage with a red cloth over it, and said "Come on baby, that's it, slowly does it." He took out a potato and put it on the floor. Everybody in the courtroom looked with intrigue including the judge. Rion proceeded to kick the potato, it rolled along the floor. Selina and her family laughed at Rion's unique way of explaining things. Rion put his ears to the potato as if to hear a sound, but there was no sound, so he stood up and kicked the potato three times. He again lied on the floor putting his ear to the potato, but again there was no sound.

Rion said "This is what mother nature has given us to eat. Vegetables, fruit. Enough of the excuses, enough of slaughtering millions of animals. It's time to become truly brave human beings, and show the best quality that we humans have, kindness. If some day, a more intelligent species from space overtakes our planet, will we admit that we deserve to become meat for their consumption, or will we try to explain to them that all forms of life deserve to live? We have a chance to be kind to those beneath us, I say we grab this chance with both hands. Otherwise we won't even get a place in god's hell, let alone god's heart."

There was a mini round of applause for Rion from half the audience. The lawyer asked "If we leave all these animals, won't the world become overpopulated? And what about these vegetables, do they not feel any pain?"

Rion looked at the lawyer sternly and said "Overpopulation is a myth. There are plenty of animals which humans do not eat, those animals haven't overpopulated the world. The food chain looks after that problem by itself. In fact because of humans, these animals are kept in conditions to encourage them to give birth, so that they can keep up with our bloody demand. There is only *one* species which damages the earth because of it's overpopulation, and it's the human species. And, Mr. Lawyer, if you are so worried about the feelings of potatoes, perhaps you should convert to the Jain religion. Because in the Jain religion, they only eat fruit and vegetables which have fallen from above naturally, they don't proactively go out to kill vegetables either. But until that day, let's focus on these animals, shall we? I will fight for animals, because this is my generation. I will leave the fight for vegetables to you and your generation." The audience were laughing at the lawyer, who became slightly flustered.

The lawyer sat down, and Rion turned his attention to the judge. He said "Every revolution takes years of campaigning and hard work. Whether it's the campaign for fair treatment of prisoners, the campaign for the end of racism, or the campaign against the burning of witches, society has had to go through years of campaigning to realise that what it was doing was barbaric. But we are still barbaric today. It took thousands of years for people to realise that black or white, all human beings have the same right to life. How much longer will it take to realise that all animals have the same right to live as we do?" Rion looked towards the audience and news cameras and said "Why have you destroyed the lives of so many animals? As a representative of the animals let me ask you all, why have you enslaved my children? What wrong did they do to you? Every animal is equal, no animal deserves to go through this. God will never forgive you, there is justice in this world, and however many of you killers there are, you will all get justice. God will never forgive you." The mother of two girls who had been kidnapped listened to Rion's words and remembered that they were in fact her words when she was being interviewed by journalists.

Rion went on to say "I am not a human being, I am an animal, who has the ability to beg you all to leave my species alone. I am here to fight for the independence of the largest population of beings in the world, I'm here to fight for the independence of my animal brothers and sisters, from all of you human dictators. I hereby declare the beginning of the revolution for animal equality, right here right now. Martin Luther King had a dream for his community. I have a dream for my community. Give my brothers and sisters independence, they have had enough of being your slaves." Rion looked down in despair and tears were flowing from his eyes. The courtroom was silent for a moment, until the mother of the child that Rion killed began to clap, followed by a steady stream of applause from all people, which then turned into a standing ovation. People all across the world applauded Rion at their television sets. He had opened the eyes of billions of people around the world, and possibly saved the lives of trillions of animals.

The judge wiped a tear from her eyes emotionally. Eddy, Hannah and Harvey were applauding. Hannah had tears of happiness, and so too did Selina in India. The judge allowed the courtroom to naturally calm down and then concluded "It is clear from all the evidence gathered today along with Mr. Rai's own admission, that Mr. Rion Rai has committed an offence, for which he deserves to be punished. However, it is also clear, that in this great land of ours, the people of America have to some extent at least, forgiven Mr. Rai, as his motives were commendable. So, the court orders Mr. Rai to serve seven years imprisonment. After this time, Mr. Rai will be given the right to live a free and untarnished life as a regular citizen in this great country of ours, the United States of America. If the claimant wishes they may appeal the decision in the Supreme court. However, in my court the decision is final, Mr. Rai will serve seven years in jail and then be set free."

The judge looked at the woman whose baby was killed by Rion, the woman smiled and nodded her head to say "no, I don't want to appeal." The judge also smiled and said "Well in that case, Mr. Rai, you may commence your revolution in seven years' time. Until then, I'm gonna turn vegetarian."

Rion was escorted by police from the courtroom, everybody stood up, and gave Rion a round of applause, as he left handcuffed by the police.

Selina, Johnny and their parents celebrated. Mr. McClymont in London, was proud of Rion.

Mr. Hill said to himself "You've proved that love is more powerful than money Rion, you kept your promise, well done my boy, well done." Mr. Brown and Sebastian stood and watched as jealous bystanders while the whole courtroom erupted into cheers.

The media picked up on the events from this courtroom, and people around the world began to adopt new change. The percentage of meat eaters to vegetarians changed dramatically in favour of vegetarians. A revolution started to spread. Animal rights laws were being re-written around the world. No longer just dogs, cats and horses, but all animals including sheep, pigs, cows, chickens, fish, and even the feelings of insects were the topic of discussion throughout the world. This wasn't just a moment to think about this courtroom and the human race, rather it was a time to think about the whole world, and every race. Are animals a different species to humans? Or are they merely a slightly different type of human? These were the questions that were being asked by news teams around the world.

Although Rion's journey was tough, his legacy lived on, far outside the confines of the prison cell in which he was trapped. He was destined to be locked away for seven long years. However, on the other side of seven years, was hope. There was hope not just for Rion, but for every animal who would be impacted by this case. Every animal that would receive love from a human, and not slaughter. Every animal that lived, instead of died. Every animal, that finally got treated like a human. This was the beginning of the end for the barbaric acts of human kind that have gone on for millenniums. Rion, was one man, who finally explained to the human race, why it is more important to prove that you are human, than just assume you are good enough to be called a human. He explained why it is important to show our compassion and love, rather than just kill a living being, cook the living being and eat the dead body. Rion is one person, and that one person can be anybody. Rion can be me, he can be you. Rion is the lion that woke up when he saw injustice. Rion was the lion who wasn't just a hunter, but he had a good heart, he showed love and compassion towards those weaker than him. Rion is the lion within you. Don't let injustice happen in the world, wake up the lion within. Rion had the power to change the world. It was Rion's actions that changed the world forever... And your actions can change the world forever too.